ODDITY OF THE TON

Misfits of the Ton
Book Four

by

Emily Royal

ARE YOU SIGNED UP FOR DRAGONBLADE'S BLOG?

You'll get the latest news and information on exclusive giveaways, exclusive excerpts, coming releases, sales, free books, cover reveals and more.

Check out our complete list of authors, too!

No spam, no junk. That's a promise!

Sign Up Here

www.dragonbladepublishing.com

Dearest Reader;

Thank you for your support of a small press. At Dragonblade Publishing, we strive to bring you the highest quality Historical Romance from some of the best authors in the business. Without your support, there is no 'us', so we sincerely hope you adore these stories and find some new favorite authors along the way.

Happy Reading!

CEO, Dragonblade Publishing

Additional Dragonblade books by Author Emily Royal

Misfits of the Ton
Tomboy of the Ton (Book 1)
Ruined by the Ton (Book 2)
Thief of the Ton (Book 3)
Oddity of the Ton (Book 4)
The Taming of the Duke (Novella)

Headstrong Harts
What the Hart Wants (Book 1)
Queen of my Hart (Book 2)
Hidden Hart (Book 3)
The Prizefighter's Hart (Book 4)
All I Want for Christmas is My Hart (Novella)
Haunted Hart (Novella)

London Libertines
Henry's Bride (Book 1)
Hawthorne's Wife (Book 2)
Roderick's Widow (Book 3)
A Libertine's Christmas Miracle (Novella)

The Lyon's Den Series
A Lyon's Pride
Lyon of the Highlands
Lyon of the Ton

CHAPTER ONE

London, May 1815

H E WAS, WITHOUT doubt, the handsomest man she had ever
seen.

And the most terrifying.

The atmosphere shifted as he entered the ballroom—
tempering the incessant female chatter as the desperate debutantes and their even more desperate mamas caught sight of the
object of their desires, and engendering a reverential hush from
lesser gentlemen who recognized a superior rival.

And he *was* superior. To every other creature alive.

He need only crook his little finger to bring forth a rush of
devotees eager to worship his superiority in everything that
mattered—rank, fortune, and potency.

As he strode across the floor, the crowd parted with the fluidi-
ty of movement displayed by the most elegant members of
Society.

Unlike me—I'd trip and fall flat on my face.

Eleanor slipped her bracelet off her wrist, then twirled it
around her forefingers, seeking solace in the rhythmic motion
and the cool, smooth metal against her skin. Her heartbeat
steadied, and she allowed herself a smile as a riot of gaudy
feathered headdresses nodded in unison as the ladies' gazes
followed him. In the animal kingdom, he—the dominant male—
incited his rivals to lower their gazes in deference, and the females

to submit and offer themselves, like mares in season desperate to mate…

Heat flared in her cheeks, and she suppressed a little pulse of need. The mere thought of intimacy paralyzed her with fear. But she couldn't deny the magnificence of the notion of being claimed by him.

His gaze swept across the room, as if he were surveying his territory. Eleanor stiffened. Would he notice her? Dread and anticipation warred with each other, and, for a moment, she willed him to look. Then the anticipation of pleasure succumbed to terror and she shrank back, lowering her gaze to her bracelet, which she tilted until she could read the inscription inside.

To my darling daughter, on the occasion of your debut.

Papa had presented it to her three years ago. But now, on her fourth Season, the bracelet was, in Mother's eyes, a symbol of Eleanor's failure to secure a husband. But Eleanor cherished the bracelet because it had been given with love. A simple gold band, it lacked the ostentation of the necklace Mother had presented to Juliette on her come-out. But Eleanor's younger sister outshone her in every aspect—why shouldn't her jewelry do likewise?

"My pride and joy." A familiar, sharp female voice cut through the air. "We're confident she'll secure a husband before the Season is over. Eleanor's proven to be a disappointment, of course, but we can weather one spinster in the family when her sister's destined for a great match."

Eleanor glanced up to see her mother talking to Countess Fairchild. As if she sensed her watching, Mother glanced toward Eleanor and frowned. Eleanor slipped her bracelet on, concealing it beneath her sleeve, then resumed her attention on the man who'd entered five minutes before.

Montague FitzRoy, fifth Duke of Whitcombe.

Her stomach somersaulted, followed by a flash of shame, as if he were so far above her that it was a transgression to even *look* at him. There was a savagery about his features—a strong, furrowed brow beneath which sapphire eyes glittered darkly. Sharply defined cheekbones, as if carved from marble, and a strong, square jaw completed his features.

As for his mouth…

His lips were full and sensual—implying a softness that belied the rest of him. But an air of cruelty lay beneath the surface. Perhaps that softness gave rise to temptation—a promise of tenderness to entice a woman to offer herself to him, only to be devoured at the point of surrender.

The musicians began tuning their instruments, and Eleanor caught sight of her younger sister arm in arm with Colonel Reid. As the son of an earl, anyone might consider him a suitable dance partner. But he was a *younger* son, therefore, despite his obvious attraction to Juliette, he had no hope of securing her hand. Juliette was merely using him to elicit jealousy in the Duke of Dunton—a man whose title, if not his unsavory person, she'd set her cap at.

Eleanor glanced toward the object of her own desires. Whitcombe was staring at Juliette, and Eleanor's heart sank at the hunger in his gaze—the darkening of his eyes that signified interest in an attractive female.

And Eleanor's sister *was* attractive. With honey-blonde hair, clear cornflower-blue eyes, and a perfect rosebud mouth, Juliette was the prettiest girl in every room she entered—the epitome of female perfection, which, together with a respectable dowry, compensated for her lack of a title.

Whitcombe moved toward a group of young ladies, and they turned their hopeful gazes on him. He bowed toward one, and Eleanor recognized Lady Arabella Ponsford. The elegant creature nodded graciously, as if to convey humility, but her eyes glittered with spiteful triumph in contrast to her companions' frowns of resentment.

Lady Arabella was Whitcombe's perfect match—in all likelihood, they'd announce their engagement before the end of the Season.

But what if he were merely performing an act? What if, beneath the disdain and savagery, lay a tender soul, who yearned to be loved for himself, rather than his title?

What if, despite his having never looked at Eleanor twice, he secretly dreamed of holding her in his arms—as she secretly dreamed of him?

Stop being a lovesick fool!

She shook her head to dispel the childish dream.

Whitcombe existed at the peak of Society. Whereas she was nothing—a plain, awkward creature who could never begin to understand the *ton* and its absurd rituals, speeches, and customs, and who never knew what to say until it was too late to say it.

But nothing could stop her from dreaming.

Thwack!

A sharp sting exploded on her arm. She glanced up to see her mother standing before her, resplendent in deep purple silk, brandishing her fan.

"How many times must I tell you to sit *up?*"

Eleanor straightened her stance and rubbed her arm. "Sorry, Mother."

"I don't need you to be *sorry*. I need you to do as I bid. Have you danced?"

"No."

Her mother let out a sharp sigh. "Your sister's secured a partner for every dance. Colonel Reid danced with her twice."

"That must be a disappointment for *you*, Mother," Eleanor muttered.

"*What* did you say?"

Eleanor braced herself for an onslaught. "I—I…"

"Oh, never mind!" her mother huffed. "Why not take a turn about the room rather than hide in a corner? If you make an effort, there's bound to be some young man willing to overlook your flaws."

Eleanor glanced at the dance floor, where the couples moved in perfect formation to the music. How were they able to recall the steps—the intricate patterns of footwork? And how did they execute those steps without bumping into each other? Did they possess an innate sense—similar to starlings who flew together as one, moving back and forth, not a single bird dropping out of the sky?

More to the point—why hadn't *she* been born with such an instinct? As she cast her gaze over the elegantly attired people, perfectly at ease in their surroundings, all knowing exactly what to say and when to say it, Eleanor wondered, as she often did, whether she were a different species. Perhaps she was a changeling, left by faerie folk in place of the real child.

Her mother's voice tugged her back to the present.

"Did you not hear me, child?"

"I can't help it if I cannot dance," Eleanor said. "Last time I tried, I trod on Mr. Moss's toe. He called me a clumsy oaf."

"He can call you what he likes—he's heir to a baronetcy," came the reply. "You must dance if you are to have any hope of securing a husband—a hope that diminishes as each year passes. You cannot expect your father to sponsor a *fifth* Season. Why can't you make an effort for *my* sake? Your dowry should—"

"I don't expect Papa to pay for another Season," Eleanor said, "or a dowry. Papa said—Ouch!"

She let out a cry as her mother's fan came down on the back of her hand.

"Must you *always* defy me? And *look* at your hands! You've dirt under your fingernails again."

"It's paint, Mother."

"Paint, dirt—it's all the same. I don't know why you've not worn your gloves."

"Because you told me I'm always soiling them, and that soiled gloves are evidence of an undesirable lack of cleanliness," Eleanor replied.

"I said no such thing!"

"You did—last week you said those exact words when we dined with Lady Tilbury, after I splashed soup on my gloves."

"Oh, *did* I?"

Eleanor nodded. "And when Lavinia and her aunt came to visit, I spilled tea and you said it again. Don't you recall?"

She glanced up and met her mother's gaze. Green eyes laced with fury glared at her.

I've done it again.

How many times had Papa told her *not* to contradict her mother, even when Mother was in the wrong?

"I quite despair of you, Eleanor. If it were up to me, I'd…"

Eleanor was spared the knowledge of what Mother would do, *if it were up to her*, by the arrival of Countess Fairchild.

"Lady Howard, I came to…" She hesitated. "Forgive me, am I interrupting?"

"Nothing of importance, countess."

"Then might I tempt you with some refreshment? And your daughter…"

Eleanor flicked her gaze toward her mother, who, earlier that evening in the carriage, had delivered a lecture on the fit of her dress and her ungainly figure brought about by overindulgence.

"I-I'm not hungry, countess," she stammered. "Thank you."

Her stomach let out a low growl.

"Are you sure?" the countess asked.

"Eleanor intends to secure herself a dance partner," her mother said. "Don't you, darling?".

"Yes, Mother," Eleanor said flatly.

Her mother gave a satisfied nod, took the countess's arm, then headed for the side room where the buffet had been laid out.

Eleanor resumed her attention on the dancers, and her heart gave a little flutter as Whitcombe swept past.

Nobody could prevent her from admiring him—from relishing the way he moved to the music, as if it flowed through his veins, or how his lithe, athletic body formed such perfect outlines as he danced.

The human form—which exuded such vitality—was the most delectable subject to draw and paint. And Whitcombe was not merely a physical form—but a beating heart, rich, warm, blood, and sinew and muscle, binding the bones together. And a living, breathing soul, which, together with the physical form, had created the perfect human being.

Each time she observed him, she saw a little more—a crease around the eyes when he smiled, a ripple of muscles beneath his perfectly tailored jacket. And she committed every tiny detail to memory so that she might capture him in her sketches and portraits.

Why, then, could she never recall more than a few steps of a quadrille?

Her breath hitched as he approached, hand in hand with Arabella Ponsford.

Their eyes met, and Eleanor's stomach somersaulted. She held her breath as she lost herself in his sapphire gaze. For a moment, an invisible thread stretched across the air between them, and her heart began to soar, buoyed with hope.

Then his partner whispered in his ear. His gaze hardened and he curled his lip into a sneer.

Eleanor's heart plummeted. She turned away, biting her lip to stem the tears threatening to sting her eyes.

What a fool she was! The brief connection was nothing more than a fancy—which she should have grown out of the day she left the nursery.

Even if he were to want her, he could never give her the life she craved—a life where she could be herself, not Society's, nor Mother's, ideal of a young woman. Her dream was to live in peace, away from noise and people, where she could be free to paint. Not the soulless little landscapes that adorned the walls of the dullest parlors in London, but paintings that *meant* something—paintings that portrayed the subject as it ought to be portrayed, not as Society expected.

Marriage would destroy that dream. No husband wanted a wife unable to conform. Men wanted wives to provide them with cash the day they married, give them an heir within a year of uttering the vows, then associate themselves with the other matriarchs of Society to indulge in idle gossip, embroidery, and tea parties, while they sought pleasure in the arms of another.

That was the truth of marriage. And *that* was Eleanor's idea of hell—a prison inescapable except by death.

But a secret voice still whispered in the back of her mind that she could withstand any prison to be loved by *him*.

CHAPTER TWO

EVIL'S TOES—COULD LIFE get any worse?

Every bloody party was the same—a silt-filled pond in which he was the trout that all the preening misses and their overbearing mamas wished to hook, net, then gut before slapping him on a platter to pick at.

Monty steered his partner—a particularly voracious angler—across the dance floor, aware of the envious stares of the un-partnered ladies.

Desperation was such an *unappealing* quality in a woman. Monty preferred aloof, indifferent females—the thrill of the chase, and their feigned lack of interest that posed a challenge for the briefest of moments. But—once he claimed his quarry, they lost their appeal. Like a delectable entrée, their taste might be relished the first few times, until blandness set in. At which point he tossed them back into the water.

Sadly, women possessed different angling tastes to men. Once *he'd* been impaled on the hook, he'd be netted for life—stuck with the same dish day in, day out.

But not for some years, provided Mother didn't erode his resolve.

As if she heard his thoughts, Monty's mother came into view. Bedecked in a forest of black silk and lace, despite being at least ten years out of mourning, she watched over the company—a spider waiting to devour any unsuspecting creature who dared approach.

The dance took him closer to her, and she focused her gaze first on him, then his partner, the vain and shrewish Lady Arabella Ponsford. Her mouth creased into a smile of satisfaction, and she inclined her head in the manner of a monarch.

Heaven help me—I know that nod.

Mother approved of Lady Arabella.

Not unexpected, given her pedigree—Lady Arabella's late mother was the king's third cousin, and, to Mother, birth was everything.

Doubtless the whole room considered Lady Arabella his perfect match. But he wasn't ready to submit himself to matrimony. His late father was proof a man could sire a child in his fifties—though to mention *that* in Mother's presence earned him a tongue lashing, as if he were a wayward child.

"Sweet Lord!" his dance partner exclaimed. "What the devil is *she* wearing? A potato sack would look better. But I daresay, given her ample figure, her dress is the most expensive in the room, given the yards of silk it must have required."

She paused, expecting a response.

"Of course, Lady Arabella," he said.

One redeeming quality of ladies of the *ton* was that they talked, and never listened. Therefore, only a limited repertoire of responses was needed to survive their company. *Of course* and *indeed* often worked, particularly if accompanied by the woman's name—assuming he could recall her name. *I wholeheartedly agree* was a favored phrase for allaying a lady's suspicion that the man she talked at wasn't listening. And if the man were unfortunate enough to be married to the woman, he could limit his portfolio to *yes, dear*—a phrase Monty's father had placed great reliance on.

"I'm glad we're of one mind," Lady Arabella said. "That family should be applauded for elevating themselves from the gutter. The younger daughter is remarkably pretty, and could almost pass for a lady—I'm quite fond of her. But as to the elder—I've seen more attractive heifers. Just *look* at her!"

Like many young ladies desperate to ingratiate themselves with a man, Arabella sought to insult one of her own sex.

Perhaps he should share his opinion of Arabella herself—a grasping harpy whose outer beauty belied the ugliness within. But he had no wish to meet her gaze, lest she see the contempt he harbored. Instead, he stared out into the blurred faces of the onlookers, curling his lip in a sneer.

One day, Fate would ensure Lady Arabella paid for her cruelty.

The dance concluded, and he steered her toward her friends then retreated to the safety of the punch bowl, before any of them could catch his eye in the hope of securing a dance.

A hand clapped him on the back, and he turned to face the newcomer.

"Cranleigh!" he cried. "Some congenial company at last."

"You must be desperate if you refer to me as *congenial*, old chap," came the reply. "But I'm afraid I must abandon you. I'm expected on the dance floor."

"With whom?"

"Lady Arabella Ponsford. Exquisite creature—not the handsomest girl in the room, but her fortune renders her a little more attractive than she would be without it."

"She'd be handsomer still if she kept her mouth shut," Monty said.

Cranleigh barked out a laugh. "What man in his right mind listens to what a *woman* has to say?" He glanced across the room to Monty's mother, who stared at them, disapproval in her expression. "Of course, not all of us are still clinging to our mother's teat. Give my regards to the dowager. Now, if you'll excuse me, I must ingratiate myself with Lady Arabella."

"Take a detour to the buffet before you do," Monty said. "A harpy's voice can erode a man's senses before he notices. I'd recommend the strategic placement of cheese in your ears."

"You ought to make allowances for Lady Arabella, given that she's an orphan."

Monty snorted. "Don't pretend you have a conscience, Cranleigh. You consider her status an advantage because it'll make her one of the richest heiresses in England when she comes into her majority."

"Or on her marriage. I daresay her fortune is enough to compensate for being saddled with her for eternity."

"On your head be it," Monty said. "*Nothing's* enough to compensate being saddled with any woman for eternity."

"That's because you've not found the right woman."

"I won't find her *here*." Monty poured a glass of punch and swallowed it in a single gulp. Then he gestured across the room. "Look at them, Cranleigh. Do you want to know what these women remind me of?"

"No, but I'm sure you'll tell me."

"Hothouse orchids. Exquisite to look at, but they serve no purpose other than to be admired. When a man takes one on, he's burdened with a responsibility for life—to feed and water her while she strives to maintain her elegance. But when the bloom inevitably fades and the petals grow tired around the edges, the man must redouble his efforts while turning a blind eye to her fading beauty. And then, once the beauty has gone—do you know what the man's left with?"

"I cannot imagine."

"A bowl of dirt," Monty said, "and the realization that he wasted his better years seeking a perfection that never existed. Which is why I intend to wait until the last possible moment before marrying."

"And deny yourself the chance at happiness—not to mention an heir?"

"On the contrary," Monty replied. "By delaying marriage, I'm prolonging my happiness and merely deferring the production of an heir."

"Your mother will be disappointed."

"Mother is *always* disappointed," Monty said. "Therefore, I might as well act in a manner that furthers my happiness to the exclusion of all else. Go tend to your orchid, Cranleigh. I wish you joy of her."

"There's prettier orchids to be had," Cranleigh said. "Take that delectable specimen over there."

Monty looked where his friend indicated and recognized the young woman who'd been dancing with Colonel Reid. She approached Lady Arabella, and the two women exchanged the outwardly congenial smiles of good friends, tinged with the hardness of bitter rivals. Arabella's smile slipped. And well it might—the newcomer surpassed her in beauty as the sun outshone a dying match. Thick blonde curls shimmered in the candlelight as if her hair contained a piece of the sun. She glanced across the ballroom and met Monty's gaze. Brilliant blue eyes stared at him, and he looked away. Delectable she was to look at, but her expression conveyed a calculating nature.

Heaven help Colonel Reid. A master strategist he might be in a battle, but in courting *that* young woman, he was engaging in a war he had no hope of winning.

"Divine, isn't she?" Cranleigh whispered. "She surpasses Lady Arabella in looks, if not in breeding. But a man would be willing to put up with a little stain on his line of succession to have *that* pretty mouth around his—"

"Who is she?" Monty interrupted. The last thing he needed to hear was what Cranleigh wanted a woman to do with her mouth.

"Miss Juliette Howard."

"The silk merchant's daughter?" Monty glanced toward her again. "I've seen Mr. Howard at White's, though have yet to be introduced. He seems pleasant enough, though that wife of his is a little loud for my tastes. He's another man who'd benefit from stuffing cheese into his ears."

"It's *Sir Leonard* now," Cranleigh said. "A knighthood rather than a baronetcy, so it's unlikely to satisfy his wife."

"I doubt anything would satisfy her, save a titled husband for their daughter."

Monty caught sight of Mrs. Howard—*Lady* Howard, as she

was now—arm in arm with Countess Fairchild. Then he glanced toward Juliette Howard, then back to her mother.

A definite resemblance. Lady Howard's eyes, though green, were the same shape, and framed by a delicately featured face. She must have been captivating in her youth—no wonder Sir Leonard had been ensnared. But, like all elegant females, age had faded her brilliance to reveal something of her true nature. She couldn't completely disguise the sharp-nosed sourness, no matter how dazzlingly she smiled.

Miss Howard approached her mother, and they crossed the dance floor to sit beside another woman—an unremarkable-looking creature that Monty hadn't noticed before.

Miss Howard and her mother turned their attention to her, and she seemed to shrink, like a woodland creature trying to make itself smaller to elude a predator. She nodded and lowered her gaze in the manner of a servant.

Was she Miss Howard's governess? Though why she'd be invited to a party with the family made no sense. Perhaps she was a maiden aunt.

Ungainly and plain—whoever she was, she was Monty's opposite in every aspect, save one.

It was evident from her expression that she loathed being here as much as he.

"You should be dancing, not drinking, Montague," a voice said.

Mother always knew how to creep up on him, until it was too late for him to escape.

"Would you like a glass?" he asked.

"I'd like to see you settled," she said. "I'd like you to take up your responsibilities and provide the dukedom with an heir."

"I'll not achieve that by dancing," he replied, "and rutting in the middle of the dance floor is frowned upon."

"Don't be so tiresome!" she snapped. "You promised to accommodate me tonight."

"And I did, Mother. I danced—as I said I would."

"*One* dance!" she scoffed. "Lady Arabella would have welcomed a second—and Countess Fairchild has made it plain that her Irma is open to offers."

"I made no promise as to the *number* of dances, Mother. And I'll not make a promise that I cannot keep."

"Such as the marriage vows."

"I intend to honor my marriage vows," he replied. "But won't even consider making those vows until I'm convinced I *can* honor them."

"Heirs should be produced sooner rather than later to assure continuation of the direct line," she said. "You cannot remain a bachelor forever, Montague. I'm not getting any younger."

He let out a snort. "I know enough about the act of procreation to know that *you'll* have no part in it, Mother. Unless you wish to stand by my bedside and watch me perform, as a horse owner does when a stallion ruts a mare."

She closed her fan and slapped him across the hand. He winced at the sting and dropped his glass, which hit the floor with an explosion of shards and red liquid.

Almost at once, a nearby footman raised his hand, clicked his fingers, and pointed toward the floor. Another footman scuttled over and began clearing up the mess.

Devil's toes—were they all under constant scrutiny such that if a man so much as scratched his ear, someone, somewhere was taking note?

"That was *your* fault, Montague," his mother said, after the footman left, all remnants of his mishap obliterated.

"You hit me with your fan."

"I was provoked. *I* care about the dukedom, even if you don't. Why must you be so cruel as to deny the title an heir, and me a grandchild?"

Her voice wavered, and Monty caught the sorrow in her tone. He reached for her hand. "I'll give you a grandchild in my own time, Mother," he said. "Have no fear."

"But I *do* fear," she replied. "I fear that your taste for…" She wrinkled her nose, as if the very thought of his bedroom activities—and activities undertaken in all manner of interesting and imaginative locations—brought about nausea. "...for the more *indulgent* trappings of bachelor life is diverting you from your duty."

"I've years yet," he replied. "A man is capable of fathering a child later in life. After all, Father—"

"Speak no more of *that!*" she cried. "Is that what you intend to do—litter the countryside with natural children, while the estate is entailed elsewhere?"

"I've no intention of littering the countryside with bastards," Monty said.

"Such coarse language! I quite despair of you. Lady de Witt has remarked several times that I have the patience of Job when it comes to you. And Countess Ashford said—"

"I care not what those old crones have to say."

"You *should* care! Our position in Society is revered—and rightly so. But the plague of modern sensibilities is encroaching on our world. You can fool round as much as you wish with those doxies of yours—I know more than most that wives must turn a blind eye. But I fail to see why you cannot find yourself a respectable, well-bred girl to marry and accomplish your duty with."

Devil's toes—Mother's desperation for an heir must have reached new heights if she was signaling her approval of his indulging in extramarital affairs.

But that was something he'd never do. Once married, he'd keep faith with his wife. Having seen his mother turn increasingly bitter after Father sired a child with his mistress, Monty had no wish to cause such pain to any woman he married. Marriage—a *true* marriage, not just one accepted by Society—required sacrifices and compromises on both sides.

And until the allure of his mistress—or rather, *mistresses*—had faded, he wasn't ready to abandon the more pleasurable aspects of being a titled, wealthy man of the *ton*.

"I'll take a wife when I'm ready," he said. "I cannot understand why you insist on plaguing me."

"Because I'm in the right! Why must you torment your poor mother? Think of my heart?"

"I didn't realize you had one."

As soon as the words came out of his mouth, he regretted them. His mother plagued him, but he'd always prided himself in never stooping to his father's level of cruelty.

"If you had a heart, Montague, you wouldn't behave in such an unfeeling…"

He raised his hand. "Mother, I'm tired, and you've taken too much punch. I suggest we call a truce. You're in need of far more congenial company than I can give you, and I'm in need of air."

"So you wish to run away—into the arms of a doxy, I'll warrant."

"Perhaps."

"Mrs. Delacroix will break your heart."

Monty's breath hitched, and he stared at her. How the devil did she know he'd been spending much of the season parting Daniella's thighs?

Her stricken expression dissolved—proof, if he needed it, of her subterfuge—and a sly smile curled her lips. "Mr. Moss was seen entering her establishment last week—or so Lady de Witt told me."

"Many men enter Mrs. Delacroix's…*establishment*," Monty replied. "That's the point of her. And, as you so beautifully pointed out just now, I have no heart. Now, please excuse me." He inclined his head and turned toward the doors.

"You cannot leave!" his mother said. "How will *I* get home?"

"In the carriage," he replied. "I shall walk. I may be a disappointment to you, but I'm not such a bad son that I'd leave you with no means of getting home. I'll see you in the morning."

He strode across the dance floor, navigating his way around the couples. An uncomfortable sensation prickled the skin at the back of his neck—as if he were being watched.

His gaze fell on Lady Howard and her daughter. No—they were deep in conversation, admiring some trinket around the vain little debutante's throat. And the maiden aunt with them…

He caught his breath.

She was looking straight at him.

She lowered her gaze, and her body stiffened. She slipped what appeared to be a bracelet off her wrist and twirled it around her forefingers in a rhythmic, repetitive pattern, the candlelight reflecting off the plain gold band.

Had she been watching him?

Then Lady Howard spoke to her and she cringed, then nodded obediently.

No wonder he preferred the company of the *demimonde* to the savagery of Society ladies! And though Monty set little store by what his father told him, he'd taken one adage to heart.

Son, if you wish to understand what a woman will turn into after you marry her—you only need look at her mother.

Which was why, when he eventually married, the last woman in the world he'd choose would be a daughter of Lady Howard.

CHAPTER THREE

ELEANOR'S LOVER PRESENTED her with a rose. Then warm, strong arms circled her waist and drew her into an embrace. She leaned against his broad chest, relishing the faint heartbeat against her body.

"Eleanor—my darling!"

"Montague…"

"Beautiful creature," he murmured. "So unlike the others."

"Why do you pay court to them?"

"Because it's expected. But when the time comes, I'll declare our love to the world."

She tipped her face upward and met his gaze, relishing the softness that he revealed to no one.

Except her.

A smile curled his lips, then he lowered his head and kissed her mouth.

An unfathomable sensation bloomed in her center—a fluttering inside her stomach, followed by a warmth in her bones.

He lifted his hand and caressed her hair, and she closed her eyes, reveling in his touch.

He kissed her again, and she waited, in his arms, as scenes flashed before her mind—the two of them entwined in passion, declaring their love…

The scene faded. Frost crackled in the air, and his body grew cold and hard, icy contempt replacing the softness in his eyes.

"Just *look* at you!" His voice, sharp and high-pitched, bore a resemblance to Lady Arabella's nasal tones.

"My love?"

He threw back his head and laughed, his mouth a gaping black hole. "As if I could love *you*—a creature not fit to be seen!"

He pushed her away, then rose from the bed and strode toward the chamber door. He flung it open to reveal a crowd of onlookers, bedecked in bright silks and twinkling jewels.

"*Look* at her!"

They laughed at her ungainly form sprawled on the bed. A crowd of women—beautiful women who knew exactly what to say, and to do, women who were never in want of a partner at a ball, who would never face rejection.

"What would he want with someone like *you*?" A female form stepped forward. Tall, willowy, and exquisitely beautiful.

"Juliette…"

Laughter thickened the air, and giant wings flapped at Eleanor. She raised her hands to fend them off, but invisible chains held them in place. She opened her mouth to scream, but no sound came.

Then her world shattered in an explosion of light.

"Miss Eleanor!"

The wings retreated, and Eleanor opened her eyes.

She was lying on her bed. But, rather than a mocking crowd, a lone woman stood in the doorway.

"H-Harriet? Is that you?"

"Of course it is, miss." The maid approached the bed and regarded her with soft brown eyes. "Oh, Miss Eleanor, you look terribly pale. Didn't you sleep well?"

"Not really."

"And I've gone and woken you up early! Forgive me—I hadn't meant to disturb you, but it's such a fine day, and I know you like to draw when it's sunny outside. Shall I return in an hour, ready for breakfast?"

"No, thank you, Harriet," Eleanor said. The last thing she

wanted was to return to the world she'd just left, where her fears had come to fruition—where *he* mocked her as much as everyone else.

"I'll fetch you some tea."

"There's no need…" Eleanor began.

"There's *every* need, miss. A cup of tea, good and hot, will set you right."

Before Eleanor could protest, Harriet exited the bedchamber.

The last thing Eleanor wanted was to be waited on, but Harriet was always so kind, so eager to help, that she hadn't the heart to deny her. And if Mother believed Harriet to be anything less than what a lady's maid ought to be, she'd turn her out.

Harriet knew how to keep garments clean, how to fix Eleanor's hairstyle so it stayed in place for more than ten minutes, and how to keep the bedchamber in the manner that Mother expected it—neat and tidy. Harriet had an innate ability to know where everything needed to be.

In short, Eleanor didn't know how she'd survive the tedious little day-to-day rituals of a young lady of Society without Harriet.

She slipped out of bed and padded across the floor to the window overlooking the garden. Her gaze fell upon a rosebush, the soft pink blooms reminding her of a pair of lips. Then she gave a start, as the full extent of her dream crashed into her consciousness.

Heat warming her face, she retreated, as if she feared he would materialize in the garden to mock her from below.

Montague…

She'd called him Montague.

And he'd called her *my darling*—before humiliating her in front of everyone.

Perhaps it was best to be invisible. For as much as she yearned for him, she couldn't bear to look at him. Not the real thing—not yet. It pained her to look into anyone's eyes—not the physical pain when she scratched herself on a thorn bush, or stubbed her toe. Mother regularly admonished her for her clumsiness. It was a different pain—an unfathomable agony that burned in her soul, as if she were laid bare before the onlooker, exposing herself to ridicule and rejection. Or hanging from a precipice, doomed to fall.

Ridicule was something she weathered and had accustomed herself to. But rejection…

Rejection was something she could never survive.

At least while she admired him from a distance—from the safety of obscurity—she was spared the pain of admitting that, to him, she was nothing.

And she was spared the pain of the rest of the world knowing of her childish infatuation for a man who didn't even know she existed.

By the time Harriet returned with the tea, Eleanor had managed to don her undergarments without tearing anything, and was holding up her gown to the light.

"Here, let me." Harriet placed the teacup on the dressing table and plucked the gown from Eleanor's hands. Eleanor raised her arms while Harriet slipped the gown over her head. Then she stood, like an obedient child, while her maid fastened the ties, adjusted her lace tuck, and smoothed the dress into place, her soft, delicate hands caressing the fabric. Then she led Eleanor to the dressing table, sat her down, and proceeded to brush her hair.

Eleanor closed her eyes and let her body relax. This was her favorite part of the day, when the house was quiet, save for the distant sounds of activity as the servants set about their tasks, and she could relish Harriet's tender care—the smooth, repetitive motion of the brush running through her hair at just the right amount of pressure, unraveling the tangles that always seemed to amass overnight.

A gentle hand touched her shoulder, and she opened her eyes to see Harriet's warm, kind ones looking at her in the mirror.

"Drink your tea before it gets cold, miss. I made it how you like it."

Obediently, Eleanor lifted the teacup and inhaled the aroma

of cinnamon and honey. "Cook didn't see you with this, did she?"

"No, miss. I was careful not to get caught."

According to Mother, young ladies were only supposed to take milk or lemon with their tea, and Eleanor's eccentricities in taste reduced her already limited prospects for making a successful match.

As if a man would take heed of how a woman took her tea!

But perhaps they did—yet another custom everybody but her seemed to understand. Eleanor took milk with her tea in Mother's presence to avoid disapproval, but the taste and sensation—the way the liquid coated her throat—always brought about such nausea that she had to fight not to expel it. On one occasion, while taking tea with Mother at Countess Fairchild's, Eleanor had, under the pretense of admiring their hostess's aspidistra in the orangery, tipped her tea into a plant pot.

Houseplants were obliging in that respect. If only *she'd* been born a houseplant, she could sit quietly in a corner, accompanied only by her thoughts, with no expectations to mingle, make friends, or make herself look presentable to attract a suitor.

She let out a small sigh.

"Are you well, miss?"

Eleanor glanced at her maid's reflection. "I was wishing I were a houseplant, Harriet."

Rather than returning the ridicule or disapproval she'd earn from her family—even Papa, if he were in Mother's presence—Harriet merely smiled. "Is that because they aren't required to attend parties?"

Eleanor nodded.

"What about the poor plants that reside in a ballroom?" Harriet asked. "They're forced to endure a party. And, unlike you, they lack the means to leave the room."

"Then I wish I were a houseplant with legs."

Harriet let out a laugh. "How would you carry the pot with you, if you were to leave the room?"

"I'd find a way—*anything* to avoid a party."

"You didn't enjoy the ball last night?"

"No," Eleanor said. "But, nevertheless, I'll be required to relive the experience over the next few days while Mother and Juliette talk about how successful it was. Did you know Colonel Reid danced with Juliette twice? He asked a third time, but Mother forbade it."

The maid shook her head. "Poor colonel. He can't have appreciated the rejection."

"Poor colonel, indeed," Eleanor said. "Juliette has no intention of marrying him. She's set her sights above the younger son of an earl. But *he* thinks she's the most delightful creature in the world—I overheard him say as much."

Harriet finished brushing Eleanor's hair, then styled it into a plain chignon. "Did you dance last night, miss?"

Heat bloomed in Eleanor's cheeks, and understanding shone in her maid's eyes.

"Mother was furious," Eleanor said. "But what was I supposed to do—ask *them* to dance?"

She winced at the memory of the carriage ride home last night, when Mother told Papa how much of a burden Eleanor was, while Juliette looked on.

"There's plenty of other parties where you'll find partners, miss."

"No man would look twice at me when Juliette's around," Eleanor said. "Not that I'd want the attention of the whole room. But..."

She hesitated, unwilling to divulge her obsession—for obsession it was. Instead, she picked up her teacup and took a sip.

"Did someone catch your eye?" Harriet asked. "I'm sure there'd be some disposed to pay you attention."

Perhaps—but he wouldn't.

"Who's *he*?"

Oh, heavens! She'd spoken that aloud.

"Nobody of consequence," Eleanor said. "At least, I'm of no consequence to *him*."

"Then that's his loss, miss. What man wants a vain wife who'll plague him morning, noon, and night?"

Harriet lowered her voice, and a wicked gleam shone in her eyes. "What man could withstand your sister's temper?" Then she blushed. "Forgive me—I meant no disrespect."

"But you're right," Eleanor said. "Papa always says that if you want to look at a woman's true nature, you only need observe how she treats her servants—and her husband—behind closed doors. But from what I've seen, Lady Arabella is the worst culprit. She's reduced many young women to tears with her put-downs, not to mention how she treats the servants."

"The orphaned heiress?"

"How do you know that?"

"Gossip travels below stairs as well," Harriet said. "We know more about the upstairs folk than *they* do. Your friend Lady Marlow's maid once said Lady Arabella was taking advantage of everyone's sympathy over her orphaned state, to behave like a harpy."

Eleanor smiled at the mention of her friend. Dear Lavinia was returning from her honeymoon tomorrow. Which meant there'd soon be one person in London who didn't look down on her.

"Now," Harriet said crisply. "What will you do today? Some sketching before breakfast? Lady Howard won't be up for an hour, at least, so you'll not be disturbed."

"I could draw *you* again," Eleanor said.

"Don't bother yourself with the likes of me, miss. You've already drawn a beautiful likeness—I don't need another."

"I didn't get the shape of your nose right."

"It's the best likeness *I'm* ever likely to be given," Harriet said. "It's like looking in the mirror."

"Not quite," Eleanor said. "Your reflection isn't how you *really* look."

"Don't we see ourselves in the mirror?"

"Yes, but the other way around. The left side of your face isn't identical to the right. So when you look in the mirror, you don't see your true self." Eleanor gestured toward the mirror. "See the mole above your mouth? It's on the right side of your face. But the person you look at in the mirror—it's on *her* left."

Harriet lifted her hand to her lips. "Can you tell the difference?"

"Not at first," Eleanor said. "I have to study a face a few times. But once I've committed it to memory, it's like the face lives in my mind. Even if I close my eyes, I can see it. I-I can't explain it."

"It's a gift."

"Or a curse. Mother believes there's something wrong with me. Perhaps she's right."

"Now, don't go saying bad things about yourself, miss. You're just gifted—and you don't rattle on like other folk. That's what Mrs. Minks says."

Heavens—it was worse than Eleanor had imagined. So the housekeeper gossiped about her as well?

Soft in the head. That was what she'd overheard Mother say after her disastrous first Season. Papa had defended her—but only after Mother's soliloquy cataloguing all Eleanor's faults had culminated in a suggestion she be sent to an asylum, where she could no longer taint the family name and threaten Juliette's chances of success.

A gentle hand touched Eleanor's shoulder.

"Is anything the matter, miss?" Harriet asked. "I didn't mean to upset you. Mrs. Minks is fond of you—she told me so. She's seen your sketches."

Panic swelled in Eleanor's body. *Sweet Lord.* Had she seen…*him?*

"S-sketches?"

"She saw the sketches for your portrait of Miss Juliette. *Ever so good, despite what the mistress thinks*—that's what I overheard her saying to Mr. Minks." The maid colored. "You won't tell, will you? I'd get a thrashing if they knew I'd eavesdropped. But I couldn't help it, given how kind they were toward you."

"Of course I won't tell," Eleanor said. "You keep my oddities from the rest of the world. I'm sure if Mother knew half the things I told you, she'd send me away. She despairs of me quite enough, given my poor marriage prospects."

"Then she's mistaken, begging your pardon," the maid said. "You don't need a husband. You could earn a living with your portraits, as good as any man's." Then she shivered. "Forgive me, miss—I do rattle on! Mrs. Minks often chides me for notions that have no place in the world."

"What—notions that a woman can be valued in the world as much as any man?" Eleanor laughed. "Outrageous, indeed! And while it may be a disgustingly modern sensibility, I'd much rather earn a living doing something I love than being beholden to a man. Sadly, it's not what Mother or Papa want for me."

Which was only partly true. Papa would, most likely, support Eleanor's wish to earn her living as a painter if it were up to him. But he had little say on the matter. While it was true as a rule that a wife was subservient to her husband, Mother was the exception. She couldn't help it—she was a product of the Society in which she'd been raised, and of her own mother's expectations. And a woman in Society was expected only to do one thing.

Find a husband.

Eleanor rose and exited her bedchamber. Then she made her way to the small attic room at the back of the house where she kept her paints—a room she treasured, for it gave her respite from the world and its expectations.

Once inside, she slipped on the apron hanging on the back of the door, and approached the desk where her materials were arranged in a specific order—paintbrushes according to size, lumps of charcoal in order of texture, and a basket containing tubes of paint that Papa had procured from one of his business associates, in exchange for several bolts of silk. She sat at the desk and retrieved a key concealed underneath a jar containing dried grasses. Then she unlocked the top drawer and pulled out her sketchbook.

Her heart pulsed faintly against her chest as she placed the sketchbook on the desk and ran her hands across the smooth surface.

He was inside.

She opened the book and flicked through the pages. The earlier sketches lacked depth—as a child, she'd attempted to draw a subject literally. But the later sketches, when her pencil strokes had grown in boldness, began to convey the essence of the subject when her old governess had once made a throwaway remark about needing to see—*really* see—the subject before being able to capture that subject on the page.

Had Miss James realized that her casual remark affected Eleanor in the manner of a stone dropped into the center of a lake, sending ripples across the surface that magnified and reflected off each other until the entire lake boiled with life? From that moment, Eleanor had set about watching each subject she painted, committing every detail to memory until she only need glance at a person to imprint them on her mind.

She flicked through the pages, pausing at her favored sketches—a pencil drawing of dearest Lavinia, a series of charcoal studies of tree stumps—until, her heart racing, she reached the page she sought.

There you are.

The subject stared out from hooded eyes beneath strong, dark brows set in a frown—a face framed by thick waves of hair, with sharp cheekbones and a firm, square jaw. His throat was straight and strong, the tendons casting a shadow across the skin, leading toward a silk cravat, tied in a perfect knot, framed by a stiff collar.

He conveyed a savage strength, yet there was a softness around the mouth—full, rounded lips, slightly parted, as if about to declare something magnificent. Or perhaps he was on the brink of claiming his mate and kissing her into oblivion.

She traced the outline of his lips, taking care not to smudge the charcoal marks. What might it be like—to feel those lips against her skin?

Dare she meet his gaze?

Swallowing her apprehension, Eleanor let her gaze follow the contours of his face, until she reached the lines she'd drawn depicting the lower lashes. Then she looked into his eyes.

Though he was a mere drawing, the familiar fear rose within her—as if she bared her soul.

You cannot harm me—you're only a drawing.

Footsteps approached. Heat warming her cheeks, Eleanor closed the sketchbook and slipped it into the drawer. The door knocked and her father entered.

"Up early again, Ellie," he said. "Are you visiting the park today? Your mother and sister will want to take their usual walk to meet friends and discuss last night's party."

"I'd rather not, Papa."

He placed a hand on her arm. "*I'd* like it if you joined us."

"Us?"

"I thought, today, I'd indulge in the life of an idle gentleman, given that it's such a fine day. You'd be company for *me* if you came. You can show me the trees you've been sketching in the park."

Eleanor's breath caught, and she met his gaze. Did he know of her illicit dawn visits to the park, to indulge in the scenery unhindered by other people?

His eyes crinkled with a smile.

"Papa—do *you* mind that I didn't dance last night?"

"No, my precious child," he said. "You're not suited to the life of a debutante. But you needn't worry—we have Juliette for that. She can bear the burden of a brilliant match. You can concentrate on being happy."

"And if I don't make a brilliant match—or any match?"

"Then we'll blame the world of young men," he said. "Truth be told—I never expected you to find a suitable match."

Tears pricked her eyes, and she looked away.

"You don't ask why," he said.

"Is it because I'm inferior to other women? Or because I'm a…" She broke off, unable to say it.

Burden.

Oddity.

"No, my Eleanor," he said quietly. "You could *never* be a burden. You see the world with different eyes to the rest of us." He placed a fatherly kiss on the top of her head. "The reason I never expected you to find a match is that I doubt a young man exists in the world who could ever come close to deserving you."

At that moment, a metallic clang echoed downstairs, repeating six times, each louder than the last.

Papa offered his arm. "Charles is exhibiting his usual enthusiasm for the breakfast gong. Shall we? I swear I could smell kedgeree earlier."

Eleanor took his arm, and they exited the box room, making their way toward the breakfast room.

Perhaps there did exist a man out there who would value her as she was, and strive to make her happy. After all, Papa was such a man.

But her rational mind told her that such a man would be the very opposite of the one she craved.

CHAPTER FOUR

"BLESS ME, IF it isn't Whitcombe!" a voice cried. "Do join us."

Monty handed his greatcoat to a footman, then approached his friends—Sawbridge, Thorpe, and a recently married Marlow, who extended his hand. Monty took it, and Marlow shook it up and down.

"Good to see you, old chap! How are you?"

"You speak as if we've not seen each other for months," Monty said. "It must be a fortnight, at most." He gestured toward a passing footman. "My usual, please."

The footman bowed, scuttled off, then returned with a brandy almost before Monty had settled into an armchair.

"Marlow's a changed man," Sawbridge said. "That's what marriage does. He's been rattling on about the management of his *household*, don't you know!"

"All households must be managed," Monty said.

"By *women*, yes," Sawbridge replied. "I was about to ask him whether he'd lost his balls when you came in. What say you, Marlow—fancy dropping your breeches so we can ascertain the degree of your emasculation?"

"I doubt the other members of White's would approve," Monty said, glancing about the clubroom.

"You shouldn't be so critical of the marriage state, Sawbridge, until you've tried it," Thorpe said. "What say you, Whitcombe?"

"I've no intention of being shackled yet," Monty replied.

"It's a poor man who cannot find a life partner to make him happy," Marlow said. "I can't speak for Lady Thorpe, of course, but *my* wife, rather than weighing me down with leg irons, enjoys much more—ahem—*stimulating* pursuits, if you get my drift."

"You mean in the bedroom?" Sawbridge asked.

Marlow lowered his voice. "Not just the bedroom. We indulge in maneuvers in every location imaginable."

"Battles, more like," Sawbridge said before draining his glass.

"Perhaps," Marlow replied. "But you know what they say— the more intense the battle, the sweeter the surrender."

"All women surrender in the end," Monty said, then took a mouthful of brandy.

"But there's immense pleasure in the *man* surrendering."

The liquid burst into flames in Monty's throat, and he leaned forward, choking.

Thorpe slapped him between the shoulder blades. "I believe you've shocked our friend, Marlow!" he said, laughing. "Perhaps he's yet to experience the pleasure of yielding to a woman who knows what she wants and isn't afraid to take it. I think we should place an entry in the club's bet book. Who'll surrender first— Whitcombe or Sawbridge?"

"I won't indulge in puerile wagers," Monty growled.

"*You* needn't place a bet," Thorpe replied. "But I can. What say you, Marlow—ten guineas says Whitcombe falls first."

"No self-respecting gentleman would stoop to such a wager," Monty said.

"I don't know," Marlow replied. "Westbury placed a bet over a woman—he ended up marrying her."

"Westbury's wife was the subject of a wager?" Thorpe asked. "But they're one of the happiest couples in England—they have six children!"

"Westbury's a milksop," Sawbridge said. "He's served his balls on a platter for his wife to fricassee." He raised his glass and tapped the rim, and a footman scuttled over, decanter in hand.

"Watch your balls, Whitcombe."

"My balls are quite safe, I assure you," Monty said.

To his credit, the footman remained stoic, displaying only a slight slip of the hand, which shook a little more brandy than intended into Sawbridge's glass. Monty waited until the poor man retreated before proceeding, though doubtless he'd heard far worse in an establishment where discussion of the fairer sex was uninhibited by the need to observe social niceties.

"Men are like rocks," Monty said. "Impenetrable and firm."

"But *women* are like water," Thorpe said. "Water can erode a rock over the years—little by little, going unnoticed until it's too late." He leaned back and gave a self-satisfied smile. "Not that I mind. My Henrietta is particularly skilled at wearing down—"

"Spare me!" Monty said. "I'll *never* be ruled by a woman."

Sawbridge snorted, and the other two exchanged a smile.

"Care to share something, gentlemen?" Monty asked.

"The cleverest of women can erode a man without his noticing it," Thorpe said. "And your mother is nothing if not a clever woman. She's determined to see you provide her with an heir."

"She'll have a long wait before I submit myself to incarceration," Monty replied.

"What about Lady Arabella Ponsford?" Sawbridge asked. "You've danced with her a few times."

"Lady Arabella's a harpy," Monty said. "She finds fault in everything. When she marries, she'll spend the entirety of her wedding night criticizing the groom's performance."

"There's Juliette Howard. She's uncommonly pretty."

"The one Colonel Reid's been following around with his tongue hanging out?" Thorpe asked. "My Henrietta says she has a worse temper than Lady Arabella."

"Your wife's a gossip," Sawbridge said. "Is this what I can look forward to when I marry—a woman plaguing me with tattle morning, noon, and night?"

Thorpe smiled, satisfaction twinkling in his eyes. He didn't *look* like a henpecked husband. In fact, he looked replete, as if he indulged on the finest delicacies on a nightly basis.

Lucky bastard.

Monty gave a start. From where had *that* notion come?

"She has an older sister," Marlow said.

"Who?" Monty asked.

"Juliette Howard. Her sister Eleanor is two years older."

"I know of no sister," Monty said. "They were at the Fairchilds' ball last week—Sir Leonard, Lady Howard…" He pictured the exquisitely beautiful Juliette gliding across the dance floor on the arm of the unfortunate Colonel Reid, the purple-clad Lady Howard on the arm of the even more unfortunate Sir Leonard. And…

The dowdy-looking creature who spent the evening sitting in a corner…

"What does the sister look like?" Monty asked.

"She's as plain as Juliette is beautiful," Sawbridge said.

"She's not plain," Marlow said. "But she rarely wears bright colors. She prefers to blend into the background."

"A girl has no right attending a ball if she's not going to look her best," Sawbridge said. "Sir Leonard's known for procuring the finest silks. His daughter must be soft in the head if she won't wear them."

"Eleanor Howard is merely reserved," Marlow said, an edge to his voice.

"There's no place in Society for a reserved woman," Monty said. "Who wants a dullard who says nothing?"

"I recall Lady Fairchild saying the same about *you*, Whitcombe," Marlow replied. "My Lavinia heard her complaining that you sat next to her at dinner and said barely two words throughout the meal."

"I had nothing in particular to say to her."

"Perhaps Miss Howard has nothing in particular to say to anyone either," Marlow said. "She's disinclined to exchange the usual inane comments one's subjected to at social events, but I like her all the more for it. And she's my wife's particular friend."

"But I doubt she'll find a husband," Sawbridge replied. "No dowry would be enough to tempt a man to bore himself to death." He turned his gaze on Monty, a sly smile on his lips. "Perhaps she'll do for *you*, Whitcombe. By the time you get around to taking a wife, Miss Howard will still be in want of a husband—and a desperate woman would be willing to accommodate your every whim."

Monty let out a laugh "Heavens no! My wife must be presentable at least. I've no wish to be *pitied*."

Sawbridge let out a chuckle, but Marlow frowned. "You should stick to your doxies, Whitcombe, if you merely want an ornament for your arm and a willing body to rut—for a price, of course."

Monty flinched at the anger in his friend's tone. Marlow pulled out his pocket watch and flipped open the lid. "It's time I returned to my wife."

"Back to your gaol?" Sawbridge laughed.

"Not at all," Marlow replied. "I merely find myself in want of congenial company."

Thorpe set his glass aside. "It's time I left also."

The two men rose and inclined their heads in a bow. Then they exited the clubroom.

"Something we said?" Sawbridge asked.

Monty glanced after his friends. "Perhaps they're in love."

"I hope *I* never succumb," Sawbridge said as a footman appeared and tipped another measure of brandy into his glass. "Fill it to the brim this time," he added. "And don't forget my friend here."

"Not for me," Monty said, placing his hand over his glass. "Liquor—and love—are man's greatest enemies. I intend to be ruled by neither."

Sawbridge grunted and drained his glass—which was Monty's cue to leave. He had no wish to spend his afternoon with a drunkard. He'd rather be with Thorpe and Marlow—who looked decidedly content with their lives.

No, not content—*fulfilled.*

Perhaps there was some advantage to being in love, if it was with the right woman.

But the right woman for *him*? He was yet to encounter one who could even remotely satisfy him for more than a few minutes at a time.

CHAPTER FIVE

"M ORE TEA, ELEANOR?"

Eleanor nodded, and her friend poured tea into a cup, followed by a spoon of honey and a sprinkle of cinnamon.

There was something different about Lavinia today—a shift in her demeanor...

Then the pattern slid into place—the dilated pupils, the bloom on her cheeks. And if that were not enough—the attention she paid her midriff as her gaze settled on her belly a heartbeat longer than expected.

Lavinia had never looked more beautiful. Eleanor glanced toward her sketchbook as the familiar sensation swelled within her—the urge to draw. She only need lean a little to the right to reach her pencil...

"I've something to tell you, Elle," Lavinia said. "I wanted—Peregrine and I wanted—you to be among the first to know. I'm—"

"Congratulations," Eleanor said. "When do you expect the happy arrival?"

Lavinia's smile disappeared. "How did you know? Has Lady Betty been gossiping again?"

Eleanor's cheeks burned with shame. "I-I'm sorry, Lavinia—it's just, you looked more..." She gesticulated in the air, in an attempt to articulate her observation.

Why could she never think of the appropriate word to use?

"*Fulfilled*, I suppose," she said, "though that seems an inadequate description."

Lavinia's expression softened. "Forgive me, Elle. I sometimes forget you possess an extraordinary insight."

"Hardly," Eleanor replied. "I never know the right thing to say—or even *think*, most times."

"When it comes to important matters, you know *exactly* the right thing." Lavinia gestured around the parlor, toward the tea things that a maidservant had carefully placed on the table earlier, the teapot in exactly the appropriate place. "All this—elegant traditions orchestrated to maintain the situation exactly as it has been for hundreds of years—do you think anyone of worth cares about that?"

"Almost everyone I encounter does."

"Which says more about *them* than you, dearest," Lavinia said. "But I didn't invite you here to discuss Society. I wanted to ask if you'd be godmother to my child."

Godmother—a position that carried responsibility for another. Not to mention the need to stand up in church and make a declaration before a crowd of people.

"I-I couldn't," Eleanor said. "What would people *think*?"

"As if I care what people think!" Lavinia laughed.

"But Lord Marlow—surely he'd want someone appropriate?"

"And he does—which is why we've chosen *you*."

"Can I think about it?"

Lavinia opened her mouth, as if to protest. Then she nodded. "Of course, darling—it must be your choice. I love you dearly, and I couldn't wish for a better person with which to entrust my child's moral welfare. But I shan't press the matter."

She gestured toward Eleanor's sketchbook. "Have you brought more sketches for me to admire? You've been glancing toward your sketchbook from the moment I sat down. Or..." Recognition glimmered in Lavinia's eyes. "You wish to draw *me*?"

Eleanor nodded.

"Very well, I shall oblige. Would you like me to pose for

you?"

"No, just sit as you are," Eleanor replied. "I want to capture your happiness."

Her throat tightened as she uttered the word.

Happiness.

Lavinia had always surpassed Eleanor in desirability, looks, and the ability to function in Society. Her marriage had only widened the gulf between them. And with a child on the way, Lavinia was drifting into an entirely different world, in which Eleanor had no place.

Eleanor opened her sketchbook at a clean page. For a moment, she let the emotions wash over her—the fear of a blank page, and the thrill of stepping out on a fresh journey, to commit the soul of her subject to paper.

She lifted her gaze and studied her friend while her pencil moved about the page.

Lavinia was one of the few among Eleanor's acquaintance whom she could trust to look into her eyes. Their soft hazel color conveyed warmth, love, and sanctuary.

Lavinia nodded toward the sketchbook. "There's one thing I've always failed to understand about you, Elle."

Eleanor studied her friend's face, taking in the little creases around the eyes, evidence of a lack of sleep, but also crinkling into a smile to convey her contentment.

"Mmm?"

"How can you draw on a page when you're not looking at it?"

"Because I'm drawing *you*, not the page."

Lavinia laughed. "That's what I love about you—you're so literal!"

"I wish I wasn't," Eleanor said. "I often regret what I say as soon as I've spoken."

"Such as?"

"I asked Mother once if she were unhappy."

"Your mother looks discontented most of the time," Lavinia

said.

"But this time, she looked particularly sad. It turned out she'd been refused credit at a jeweler in Hatton Garden, when she tried to purchase her birthday present from Papa."

"She purchased her *own* birthday gift?"

"Not in the end. Papa was there when I said she was unhappy. When he heard what happened, he refused to give her the money, saying Mother had a necklace for each day of the year and had no need for more. Mother refused to speak to Papa for two days, and she confined me to the house for a week."

"I'm sorry," Lavinia said.

"Don't be. Papa told me afterward that he relished the respite and only wished it had lasted longer. As for me—I missed two dinner parties, including Lady Baldwin's soirée. I wish I could think of an opportunity to anger Mother again, so I might be excused from attending the Duchess of Westbury's party next week." She glanced up, hope surging within her. "I don't suppose *you're* going?"

"We've a prior engagement, I'm afraid. But the duchess is charming—totally unlike what you might expect. You have something in common, given that her father's a merchant. You might like her."

Eleanor resumed her attention on her work, making a few more strokes with her pencil. Then she held the sketchbook at arm's length.

"May I see?" Lavinia asked.

"Of course." Eleanor handed over the sketchbook.

Lavinia's eyes widened. "How do you manage to include such detail?" She turned a page. "What's this?"

Eleanor's stomach flipped. Had Lavinia seen the latest sketch of...*him*?

Her friend held up the sketchbook. "You're drawing tree stumps?"

Eleanor nodded, swallowing her relief. "They're fascinating," she said. "Look at the texture of the bark—it's uneven, yet it forms a pattern. And each tree is different."

"They look the same to me."

"That's because you're not looking close enough," Eleanor said. "The bark of a birch, for example, is different to that of an oak."

"Is it?"

"It's smoother—papery, almost, with pieces that curl and peel, like the skin of an onion. But the bark of an oak is thicker, with a deep, rough texture."

"I'll take your word for it." Lavinia laughed again, placing the sketchbook on her lap. "More tea? I can ring for some."

At that moment the door opened and Lavinia's husband appeared. Eleanor's gut twisted in apprehension, as it always did in the presence of a powerful man.

"Peregrine, darling," Lavinia said, "are you checking on my state of health, or have you come to prevent me from eating all Mrs. Brown's biscuits?"

"Both, my love." He took her hand and bowed to Eleanor. "Miss Howard, a pleasure. I take it you're well?"

"Yes, thank you, Lord Marlow," Eleanor said, rising.

"Please don't stand on *my* account, Miss Howard," he said. "May I join you?"

Eleanor resumed her seat, opened her mouth, then hesitated and swallowed her discomfort. It would do no good to respond truthfully. The truth was, after all, a concept that Society cared little for. What ought she say—something bland and benign, perhaps?

"I-I'd have no objection, sir."

He nodded and smiled.

Thank heavens! Her response had been acceptable, though it meant she had to endure his company.

"Excellent!" he said. "I'll ring for more tea." He tugged at the bellpull beside the fireplace then sat next to Lavinia. "I hear London's been enjoying very fine weather in our absence," he said.

Lavinia rolled her eyes. "Peregrine—for heaven's sake! Eleanor's not one for aimless remarks. If you've nothing of substance to say, then keep quiet."

"I find myself admonished," he said. Then he turned toward Eleanor. "My poor wife has suffered my company these past three weeks, and has been at her wits' end. She's been craving intelligent conversation, which, though rarely experienced among London Society, can, I believe, be found in your company. But I'm afraid I've disappointed her by inflicting social inanities upon you."

Eleanor stared at him. How was she expected to respond? Was he ridiculing her?

Then he leaned forward and gave a conspiratorial wink, and she struggled to contain a smile.

"Bravo!" he said. "I find myself forgiven, and will refrain from discussing the weather with you in future. Neither will I discuss the cut of a woman's gown—or the latest fashion for lace tucks."

Lavinia tapped him smartly with her fan. "That's enough, Peregrine. I wouldn't want Eleanor to think I married a fool."

"I fear I've already presented her with irrefutable evidence," he replied. "Do forgive me, Miss Howard." He gestured toward the sketchbook. "May I see?"

"Please do."

Lavinia opened the book at the latest sketch, and Lord Marlow gazed at it. His eyes widened, and a smile curled his lips.

"Beautiful," he said. "You've a rare talent, Miss Howard. This isn't just a likeness—you've captured Lavinia's soul. Look at those lines! The boldness with which you've drawn her features—the detail around the eyes…" He closed the sketchbook and handed it to Eleanor. "I can tell that you know the difference."

"The difference?"

"Between seeing and *looking*."

"Oh!" Eleanor cried, unable to contain her delight. "You understand!" Then, overcome with shame at her unladylike outburst, she shrank back.

"I do, Miss Howard. It's what separates the proficient from the masterful. Any fool can draw a passable likeness after a lesson or two on proportions—but to capture the soul of the subject requires a different quality altogether."

The door opened again, and a maid scuttled in carrying a tray with a teapot and a cup. After furnishing the company with fresh tea, she curtseyed and exited the room as quietly as she came.

Marlow drained his teacup in a single gulp. "I was in sore need of that. The brandy at White's isn't getting any better."

"Brandy, at this hour!" Lavinia said.

"I know, my dear, but it would have been uncivil to refuse. And"—he winked at Eleanor again—"I needed it as respite from social niceties."

"I'm sure gentlemen have more interesting conversations in their clubs than ladies endure in their parlors," Lavinia said. She glanced toward Eleanor. "Present company excepted, of course."

"You're right, my love," Marlow said. "I was subjected to yet another tale of Whitcombe and his determination *not* to seek a wife."

Eleanor's stomach tightened at the mention of...*him*. She curled her fingers around the handle of her teacup, willing her heartbeat to subside.

"We've placed ten guineas on which of the two—Sawbridge or Whitcombe—will marry first. Thorpe's for Whitcombe, but my money's on Sawbridge."

"How foolish!" Lavinia said. "That's ten guineas you'll never see again."

"I've every chance of success, Lavinia. Not even the brightest jewels of Society can tempt Whitcombe. Lady Irma Fairchild is too dull, Lady Arabella Ponsford too much of a harpy, and while Juliette Howard is the most beautiful, she has a reputation for breaking men's hearts, having led Reid on a merry dance before casting him aside."

Eleanor's teacup slipped from her grasp and fell to the floor, shattering on impact. Hot tea splashed onto her skirts, and she leaped from her seat with a shriek.

"Peregrine!" Lavinia admonished her husband. "Look what you've done—you've discomposed my friend."

"Oh, forgive me, Miss Howard," he said. "I often speak freely to my wife, but that's no justification for making a disparaging comment about your sister. In my defense, I often forget you're sisters—you are her opposite in every way imaginable."

Meaning that she's the most beautiful creature in the world—and I'm the least.

"That's enough!" Lavinia cried. "Did you come here to insult my friend?"

Tears stung Eleanor's eyes.

"I meant it as a compliment, Miss Howard," Marlow said. "Your *characters* couldn't be more different."

"Perhaps you should go, before you insult my friend further," Lavinia said.

He rose and offered Eleanor his hand. She took it, and he lifted her hand to his lips.

"Forgive me, Miss Howard," he said. "I'll do better next time."

He crouched down and collected the shards of porcelain at Eleanor's feet. Then he exited the parlor.

"Would you like a fresh cup?" Lavinia asked.

Eleanor shook her head.

"It wasn't what Peregrine said about *Juliette* that distressed you, was it?"

Eleanor glanced up to see her friend looking directly at her.

"It's because he mentioned the Duke of Whitcombe—isn't it?"

Eleanor opened her mouth to voice her denial. Then she nodded. If she couldn't confide in Lavinia, whom *could* she trust? Besides—Lavinia had already seen some of her sketches of him, and knew of her affection.

No—not affection.

Obsession. That was what anyone else would say if they knew.

But Lavinia was kinder than most—she understood. Or, at least, she didn't condemn.

"Whitcombe's not worth it, Eleanor dearest," Lavinia said. "He'd break your heart—that is, if he'd even notice you. And I don't mean to be cruel. He cares only for the superficial, and would be blind to your qualities. There's someone out there who'll appreciate and love you for who you are. And you'll find him. Look at Peregrine and me—I never believed we'd find happiness."

"*I* never doubted it," Eleanor said.

"And I don't doubt you'll find your true mate," Lavinia said. "But it won't be the Duke of Whitcombe. I doubt a heart beats inside that chest of his."

That very *broad* chest.

I'm convinced he has a heart.

"No, Eleanor. He doesn't. What you harbor is hope, not conviction."

Heavens! She'd spoken aloud.

"Forget about him, dearest," Lavinia said. "Your infatuation is making you miserable. Why not concentrate on your sketches of those tree trunks?"

Lavinia was right.

But Eleanor's hope could never completely be extinguished, even if she must keep it to herself.

CHAPTER SIX

As Monty descended the steps from Mrs. Delacroix's townhouse, streaks of soft blue light stretched across the sky, heralding the dawn. Daniella—or *Doris*, as he knew her name to be, but woe betide anyone who uttered it—had begged him to stay for breakfast, doubtless because she thought it would earn her an extra coin.

Why did everyone always *want* something? Men sought him out either as an ear to listen to their boasts of male prowess, or because they wished to associate themselves with a duke. Doxies wanted the gratification he gave in bed, as well as the trinkets he gave them. Single ladies of rank saw him as a title to bag at the altar, and their mamas saw him as a potential son-in-law to provide for them in their dotage when they'd driven their own husbands into the grave.

And his mother saw him only as a stud to maintain the Whitcombe bloodline.

Take, take, take...

Why was nobody willing to *give*? Did the world believe that, because of his rank and fortune, he was undeserving of a little consideration that came without a price attached?

Even this morning, as he pulled his breeches on after Daniella's ministrations, she'd initiated a discussion on the quality of silks to be had this Season. At first, she'd remarked on Sir Leonard Howard's ability to procure the most exotic shades. But soon her soliloquy turned to the price of Madame Chassineux's gowns and how, in a world where fashions changed at an alarming pace, a woman of her means could no longer maintain her wardrobe.

To extract himself from her twittering, he'd tipped a handful of coins into the jar she conveniently kept by her bedside, thereby concluding the conversation. He grinned to himself at the recollection of the smile of triumph on Daniella's lips. Did the foolish creature not realize he'd always intended to pay her for their night of continuous rutting? Her tales of woe only served to increase his contempt.

Bloody women—they're all the same.

Though perhaps they weren't, if the contented expressions in Thorpe and Marlow's eyes at White's last week were to be believed. Even that curmudgeonly old fossil Hardwick had been seen trotting along Rotten Row, a look of bliss in his eyes, his pretty young wife on his arm, unashamedly displaying her delicate state of health. And what had Hardwick said when Monty attempted to ridicule his slavish devotion?

"Whitcombe, my boy—you fail to understand the difference between a loving wife and a mistress. A loving wife wishes to please her husband for his own sake, and she takes her own pleasure from doing so."

Daniella, for all that she was talented, sought only her own gratification. Even when she'd kneeled at his feet last night, lips parted in anticipation of pleasuring his cock, she couldn't hide the greed from her eyes—the anticipation, not of pleasure, but of coin.

What it must be like to have a *wife* perform such a service— willingly, on her knees, reaching her peak purely from the prospect of servicing him? A woman who gladly spread herself for him to feast on…

Where could he hope to find such a creature? Not in Society's drawing rooms—nor at the Westburys' damned dinner party, which he'd promised Mother he'd attend tonight.

Perhaps the solution to marital bliss was to choose the very *worst* kind of woman for a wife.

He drew out his pocket watch. A quarter to seven. Mother would be up by now, waiting at the head of the breakfast table, ready to lecture him on the folly of whoring.

Then a stay of execution beckoned in the shape of the gates leading into Hyde Park. Beyond, a wide expanse of lawn, sloped gently down toward the water, covered with pockets of mist that lingered over the surface. He slipped through the gates and approached the gravel path alongside the lawn. Glistening dewdrops twinkled where the sun's rays penetrated the mist, and he caught a myriad of colors, as if the ground were dotted with diamonds. Soon, they would disappear. But, at that moment, they belonged to him.

And, at that moment, the park was his, and he could appreciate its natural beauty without interruption.

Then he caught sight of a blurred shape through the mist.

A deer, perhaps? It seemed the right size.

Were there deer in Hyde Park? It was a haven of countryside in the center of town—who knew what manner of wild creatures had made their way here over time to seek refuge?

He stepped forward, and the gravel crunched underfoot, but the creature gave no sign it heard.

Then the mist dispersed, and Monty realized his mistake.

The creature wasn't a deer. It was a woman, sitting on the grass, beside a thick tree stump, the hem of her skirts already stained with the dew.

A servant, perhaps, seeking a moment's respite before her employers demanded breakfast. Though if they saw the state of her dress, she'd be dismissed. Unless, of course, she belonged to one of the more liberal families, such as the Howards, whose fortune had been acquired through trade, rather than inherited.

But he couldn't envisage Lady Howard permitting a lack of decorum among her servants.

Feeling like an errant schoolboy, he slipped behind a nearby rhododendron to observe her unnoticed.

She had a book on her lap, and seemed to be writing, though

she continually looked up toward the tree stump, then back down to the page. Each time she looked up, she smiled—not the smile of gratification he'd seen on Daniella's lips half an hour ago, but a genuine smile of contentment.

She stopped writing, placed the journal on her lap, then pulled a bracelet off her wrist, twirling it between her hands—a gesture that seemed familiar...

Of course! The bland little governess from Lady Fairchild's ball.

No—not a governess—Sir Leonard Howard's eldest daughter.

What the bloody hell was she doing? Didn't she realize the risk to her reputation if she were caught grubbing about on the ground? Perhaps she lacked understanding.

Soft in the head—that was how Sawbridge described her, much to Marlow's obvious anger.

A splash echoed in the distance, followed by a volley of quacks. She stretched her arms, slipped the bracelet back on, then tilted her head upward as a beam of sunlight broke through the trees.

Then she turned her face toward the light, and Monty caught his breath.

Her eyes were the most extraordinary color—like an exotic ocean, a rich green, with shades of blue. Illuminated by the sunlight, they radiated intelligence and insight, with a peculiarly intense expression, as if she constantly strived to see beyond the superficial to discern the very essence of the subject she was observing. Then the sunlight faded as a cloud passed over, and she resumed her attention on her journal.

No—not a journal. A sketchbook. From his vantage point he could make out the image of a tree stump on the page.

A bird flew out from the bush, squawking in distress. Miss Howard leaped to her feet, clutching her sketchbook. She glanced in his direction, and his heart ached at the terror in her eyes.

Perhaps she *did* understand the risk to her reputation.

But though she—a young woman in the park, alone and unchaperoned—was the one at risk of vilification for breaking decorum, *he* was the interloper, having trespassed on her privacy.

Unwilling to disturb her peace, he retreated, and picked his way across the grass toward the park gates.

But rather than return to his townhouse and a judgmental mother, he found himself waiting beside the gates to see if his quarry would emerge.

Soon enough, he heard footsteps on the gravel—then they stopped.

What was she doing?

He peered around the gates. She stood in the center of the path, staring wide-eyed at the grass, where he'd left a trail of footprints.

Then she looked up and met his gaze. He stepped forward, and she gave a cry, dropping her sketchbook. He darted forward to pick it up, and she retreated, her body seeming to shrink under his scrutiny.

"You've nothing to fear," he said. "You've dropped your book."

Well done, Monty—nothing like stating the bloody obvious.

She remained, unmoving, her gaze fixed to the ground, and he found himself wanting to see her eyes again. Would they be as captivating at close quarters?

"Forgive my incivility," he said. "If I might introduce myself, my name is Montague—Montague FitzRoy."

If anything, that discomposed her further. Doubtless, if he'd added *fifth Duke of Whitcombe* to his introduction she'd have melted in a puddle of terror.

"Might I be so bold as to ask your name?"

For a moment, he thought she wouldn't answer. Then she tilted her head to one side and spoke in a barely discernible mumble.

"H-Harriet."

"Harriet?"

Why didn't she give her real name?

She looked up, as if she sensed he knew she'd lied, then her gaze returned to the ground.

"Well then…*Harriet*," he said, "might you grant me a wish, if I return your sketchbook?"

"I-I don't understand."

"Will you look at me?"

She stiffened, and for a moment, he thought she'd refuse. Then she lifted her gaze to his.

But rather than displaying the clear gaze that had captivated him earlier, her eyes were dark and narrowed, almost as if she were in pain. Unwilling to prolong her agony, he held out the sketchbook. She snatched it, bobbed a curtsey, then mumbled her thanks and fled.

Devil's toes—what extraordinary creatures women were! If they weren't throwing themselves at him, they were fleeing in terror.

If she couldn't even look at a man, imagine how she'd react at the prospect of the marriage bed.

She was, without doubt, the very *worst* kind of woman a man would want for a wife.

CHAPTER SEVEN

T HE GAZEBO WASN'T visible from the house, except from the topmost floor where the servants resided. And it had long since succumbed to the forces of nature. A rambling rose, left to grow wild, curled around the structure, such that Eleanor had to battle tendrils and thorns to enter. But her efforts were rewarded with a tiny haven away from the ornamental garden and manicured lawn, with not a single blade of grass out of place.

Though the air had grown cold, Eleanor had no wish to return indoors to endure the excited chatter about tonight's party—such as what color ribbon would enhance Juliette's eyes, or which necklace would best suit Mother's new gown to outshine Lady Stiles.

She tucked her feet beneath her body, settled back, and opened her sketchbook, tracing the outline of the tree stump she'd sketched that morning, just before she'd seen…

Her stomach fluttered, and she closed the book, her cheeks warming with shame as she recalled the encounter.

Why in the world did she say her name was Harriet—and, of all people to encounter, why did it have to be *him*?

She leaned back and closed her eyes, but couldn't dispel the image in her mind's eye of a savagely handsome face. But though she willed the image to soften and smile, it remained hard and unyielding.

He'd break your heart…

Lavinia was right—any attempt to cling to the hope that he might notice her would end in heartbreak.

"*There* you are," a voice said. "Mama's been calling."

Eleanor opened her eyes to see her sister's elegant form through the foliage.

"Aren't you coming out? I'm not crawling through the undergrowth."

"Hardly undergrowth, Juliette," Eleanor said. "It's a rosebush."

"There's no need to be uncivil. The carriage leaves in an hour."

"I won't need an hour to get ready."

"You would if you tried harder, Eleanor. You could be attractive if you made an effort."

Eleanor sighed. Her respite was over. She uncurled her legs and pushed her way through the rosebush. A thorn caught on her skirts, and she brushed it aside, pulling a loose thread in the muslin.

"You've torn your gown," Juliette said.

"I can see that."

"It'll need to be mended."

"I know that."

"I'm just *saying*," Juliette retorted. "What's wrong with you? You've been out of sorts all day."

"Nothing's wrong."

"I don't want you being your usual miserable self tonight. Mother worked hard to secure our invitation."

"Oh?"

"It's not just *any* party. It's the duke's grandmother's hundredth birthday. Can you imagine what it feels like to have lived for a hundred years?"

"Yes," Eleanor said. "I can."

Juliette frowned, then glanced at Eleanor's sketchbook. "Have you been drawing again? Show me."

Eleanor opened the sketchbook. Her sister stared at the page, and Eleanor caught a flicker of admiration in her expression.

"Would you like it?" she asked. Juliette didn't respond, and Eleanor tore the page out and handed it over. "I drew it this morning. I thought the shape was interesting."

Juliette sighed, then, before Eleanor could stop her, she crumpled the page in her fist.

"Why can't you draw something pretty? Nobody wants to see *that*. You should draw a flower, or a portrait—that's what people like."

"It's not what *I* like," Eleanor said.

"You'll never attract a suitor if you draw dead trees."

"It's not dead!" Eleanor cried. "It's—"

"Oh, spare me!" Juliette huffed, tossing the paper aside.

"I don't want a suitor," Eleanor said.

"You're only saying that because nobody would have you."

"Better that than leading a man to believe I'd accept his suit before tossing him aside for another."

Juliette's eyes flashed with fury. "*What* did you say?"

"That's why you've been encouraging Colonel Reid, isn't it—to make the Duke of Dunton jealous?"

Juliette's nostrils flared, and a pang of shame needled at Eleanor. Her arrow had hit home.

"Forgive me, Juliette. I didn't mean to offend," she said. "I—"

"Spare me!" Juliette huffed. "I only came to tell you to get ready. Mother wants us to look our best, and nonsense such as *that*"—she gestured toward the discarded drawing—"won't do you any favors."

She turned and walked away.

Once Juliette was out of sight, Eleanor retrieved the drawing.

"Sorry," she whispered, smoothing out the page and slipping it back inside her sketchbook. "*I* like you." Then she returned to the house and made her way to her bedchamber.

Once safely inside, she flicked through the book to the sketch she'd drawn that afternoon using her imagination.

It was *him*—not as she recalled him, but as she wished to see him. His features were sharp and masculine as ever, but with a few additional strokes of her pencil, Eleanor had softened his expression, depicting a gentle upward curve of his full, sensual lips, and small creases around the corners of his eyes, which twinkled with joy.

She traced the outline of his features with her fingertip. Then she closed the sketchbook, slipped it into a drawer, and rang the bell for her maid.

CHAPTER EIGHT

As Monty escorted his mother through the hallway, he caught sight of their hosts. The Duke and Duchess of Westbury stood by the drawing room entrance to greet their guests. Occasionally the duchess met her husband's gaze, and they smiled, as if sharing a delicious secret, and Monty could discern a sheen of excitement in her expression—the unmistakable look of a woman well pleasured—which matched the look of repletion in Westbury's eyes.

Lucky bastard.

The duchess, despite her origins, was a woman to be admired—accomplished, intelligent, and utterly devoted to her husband. She'd even taken Westbury's natural son into her embrace, treating him as her own. The boy had everything a young man could want, a life, love, doting parents—everything but the title. But perhaps the lack of title gave him more freedom than his younger half-brother. Standing beside the duchess, he was the image of his father, and Monty found himself envying the easy affection between him and his stepmother as she introduced him to each guest, pride and love in her eyes.

How might Monty's life had been had his own mother accepted his father's natural child into the family? But perhaps Mother was to be forgiven her bitterness. Westbury had fathered his natural child ten years *before* his marriage, rather than ten years *after*. Unlike Monty's father, Westbury was that rare beast—

a husband who kept faith with his wife. The man had it all—a prosperous estate, an adoring wife, and a brood of children.

Bloody lucky bastard.

Then Westbury glanced to his right and stiffened, as if he were a young lad caught transgressing, destined for a dressing-down from the family matriarch.

And what a matriarch!

Westbury's grandmother, tonight's guest of honor—dowager duchess, survivor of wars, riots, and at least two plagues of influenza—stood at the end of the line, her arachnid gaze sweeping over the guests while they bowed, curtseyed, and showed due deference. As each guest passed, she lifted a single eyebrow, then gave a slight nod, before turning her attention to the next disciple come to worship.

And now it was Monty's turn.

"Augusta, darling!" his mother cried. "How well you're looking."

"Did you expect otherwise?" the dowager replied, and Monty smiled inwardly at his mother's look of discomfort.

"I meant no offense, Augusta, I was merely making—"

"A bland social nicety, rather than a truthful observation. You should know by now, Matilda, I'd rather hear the truth from one of my dearest friends. The crow's-feet around my eyes are deepening with the passage of each year, and my bones creak every time I move. Yet this incorrigible boy"—she gestured toward Westbury—"sees fit to parade me about the place to applaud himself on having preserved my life to the point where the family received a personal letter of congratulation from that vain fop, the prince regent."

Westbury blushed.

"Grandmama Augusta," his wife said, "do you recall what we discussed earlier today about how few people in Society appreciate your unique style of frankness?"

"Of course I do, Jeanette!" the dowager huffed, though a spark of affection shone in her eyes. "But I deem it a privilege, now that I have lived a century, to be permitted to say precisely what I think without recourse."

"Oh, no!" The duchess laughed. "That simply *won't* do in a world where we're expected to be civil even to those we dislike."

"Then Society had better prepare itself for an onslaught from my tongue."

"Nothing the world isn't already used to, Grandmother," Westbury said. Then he addressed Monty's mother. "Duchess—it's a pleasure to see you. My grandmother has been looking forward to seeing you again."

Then the dowager turned her attention to Monty. His stomach fluttered with anticipation as she lowered her gaze to his feet, then lifted it, slowly, taking in every detail of his form—his attire, his countenance, and, most likely, his worth in the world.

Devil's toes! Mother possessed a stare that could wither a houseplant at fifty paces. But Westbury's grandmother had mastered the art with a glare that could fell an army from the opposite end of a battlefield.

"Is this *your* boy, Matilda?" she asked.

"Permit me to introduce myself," Monty said. "I'm—"

"Yes, yes—I know who you are!" she exclaimed. "You must be thirty at least, and still unmarried. Not even courting, I hear. Do you *ever* intend to take a wife?"

"Grandmama!" Westbury's wife exclaimed. "You cannot ask so frank a question."

"I'll ask what I like, Jeanette. He's a grown man, capable of defending himself."

Westbury's wife turned to Monty, laughter in her eyes. "I'm afraid you're in for a salvo of questions tonight regarding your marital status, Your Grace."

"Nothing I'm not used to on a daily basis at home, Duchess," Monty replied, "though I confess I'd hoped, for the sake of my poor ears, for a little respite tonight."

He offered his arm, and his mother took it as he steered her into the drawing room.

"*Must* you be so tiresome, Montague?" she said. "Not only did you insult me, you insulted our hosts. Augusta was within her rights to ask you anything she wished."

"I'm in no mood to discuss marriage tonight, Mother."

"Nor *any* night. Why can't you be more like Westbury? He takes his duties seriously, *and* he respects his grandmother."

"I do respect you, Mother," Monty said. "I'm merely in no mood to take a wife."

"Westbury may have married beneath him, but the girl has at least done her duty by giving him an heir. The more robust constitutions and wide hips found in the lower classes may be inelegant, but they do at least facilitate the production of healthy heirs."

"Should I inspect her teeth as well?"

"Don't be so insolent! Westbury's heir is a fine-looking young man—the image of his father. It's heartening to see the bloodline hasn't been tainted by his wife's stock."

"Ye gods, Mother, you make the duchess sound like she's a prize heifer!" Monty exclaimed. "And I'll have you know that the young man standing beside her is Westbury's *natural* son. But the duchess is kind enough to treat him as her own, rather than banish him into obscurity. She, unlike you, understands that a child should not be forced to pay for the sins of his—or her—father. It is for *that*, not the duchess's ability to breed heirs, that we must applaud her."

She paled, and then stumbled against him. Regretting his words, he steered her toward a footman holding a tray of champagne glasses. By the time she drained two glasses and was halfway down a third, she'd recovered her composure, if not her temper.

"I've told you before not to mention that brat," she said, her voice a harsh whisper.

"You mean Olivia?"

"I care *not* what the creature's name is—I only care that Rosecombe Park is being tainted by her presence."

"What rot!" Monty said. "She's tucked away in a cottage on the far reaches of the estate, to satisfy your sensibilities. You've never set eyes on her."

"Her very *existence* is an insult."

"There's nothing I can do about that, Mother," he replied. "I suggest you visit Father's gravestone and take it up with him, given that he's the one responsible. You can hardly punish his daughter merely for existing."

"How dare you refer to her as his daughter! I've a good mind to…"

But Monty was spared the knowledge of what Mother had a good mind to do by the announcement of dinner. He rose, took her arm, and led her into the dining room.

When he stopped at his place on the dinner table and read the place card next to his, his heart sank.

Lady Arabella Ponsford.

Devil's toes—that was *all* he needed.

He gritted his teeth and bestowed a warm smile upon his dinner companion as a liveried footman steered her toward her place.

"Lady Arabella, a pleasure."

She inclined her head in response, then stood beside her seat and glared at the footman. "Well?" she snapped. "Must I seat myself?"

The footman—who couldn't have seen more than fourteen summers—colored and drew back the chair. She gave a sharp sigh, then slapped his hand off the back of the seat.

"What must our hostess be *thinking*, employing such an incompetent creature! I've a good mind to suggest she has him dismissed."

"Perhaps he's only recently entered her employ," Monty said.

"He shouldn't be allowed above stairs until he's fit to be seen."

Was this what he must endure for the duration of the meal?

And it was. Despite the exquisiteness of the dishes, Monty's dinner partner found fault with everything. The fish was too cold, the wine too sour—the meat was too tough, and the dessert too sweet. So engrossed was Lady Arabella in her soliloquy on the inferiority of the meal that Monty was able to say little, provided he punctuated his responses with the occasional nod or appropriately timed murmur of agreement. And as long as he fixed his gaze on the food in front of him and not meet his companion's eyes, he could avoid being drawn into a full conversation.

Never before had the pattern on the dinner set, or the facets of the wineglass, provided such an object of interest.

"And the taste of it left a lot to be desired. What did you think, Your Grace?"

Bugger.

This question required more than a simple *yes* or *no.*

"In my opinion it was over-salted," she continued, removing the necessity of a response. "I abhor an excess of salt, don't you?"

"Yes, Mother."

"I beg your pardon?"

Shit.

"Yes, Lady Arabella."

She frowned, then nodded. "I'm glad we're of one mind. If we had no standards, where would the world be? Ruination, that's where."

"Our hostess might appreciate the benefit of your wisdom on standards," Monty couldn't resist saying.

"Well, at the very least she should treat her subordinates with a firmer hand, rather than let them take advantage. But *I'm* not one to criticize."

Monty's body convulsed with mirth, and he let out a snort, disguised it as a cough, then took a mouthful of wine.

"If I *were* to say anything, I'd advise her on the folly of letting her husband's"—she hesitated, wrinkling her nose—"*brat* run unfettered about the place as if he were part of the family."

"Westbury's natural son *is* part of the family," Monty replied.

"He's also sitting directly across the table."

The fear in Lady Arabella's eyes as she snapped her head up and looked around was almost worth having endured her company over dinner.

"If you were to criticize one course the most, which would it be, Lady Arabella?" Monty asked.

"The soup, of course. It was appallingly served."

"How so?"

"That footman splashed some on my napkin."

"An accident?"

"No. An *insult*."

"If the footman intended to insult you, he'd do more than spill soup on your napkin."

"Such as?"

Monty shrugged. "Perhaps your soup had a sharper taste than you might expect."

"I don't understand."

"Or…perhaps it was a little more yellow in color than every-one else's?"

A snort, followed by a volley of coughing, came from across the table. Sitting opposite, a few places down, was the woman from the park that morning—the eldest Miss Howard—flanked by her father and Westbury's eldest son. For less than a heartbeat, she looked directly at Monty, a flash of mirth in her green gaze. Then her eyes narrowed and she resumed her attention on her plate.

He'd not noticed her before. She seemed to blend in with her surroundings. Her gown, a light blue muslin, lacked adornment, save a thin lace trim about the neckline. And her hair, fashioned into a simple style, was dotted with what looked like daisies. She was the opposite of her sister—the exquisitely beautiful Juliette—who sat next to Westbury, at the far end of the table, wearing a gown of bright pink silk, a necklace of rubies and diamonds about her throat, her hair studded with pearls.

"Eleanor, what are you doing?" Lady Howard's voice cut

through the conversation. Miss Howard mumbled an apology, her features creased with distress. Then Sir Leonard leaned toward her and whispered something indiscernible, and she gave a quick, tight smile. The young footman Lady Arabella had complained about refilled Miss Howard's wineglass, and she nodded her thanks.

"Oh, *Lord*," Lady Arabella said. "I know we must make allowances for the lower classes, but even the most generous hostess should draw the line when it comes to inviting those who cannot understand proper decorum. Thanking paid subordinates, indeed! I fail to understand her lack of propriety when her sister is so charming. Of course, you know what's been said about her..."

But before she could tell him what gossip circulated around Miss Howard, Westbury stood and tapped his wineglass.

"Care to join me for a brandy, gentlemen, while the ladies seek respite from our company?"

The men murmured their assent.

"Lady Arabella, please excuse me," Monty said. "We must continue our conversation another time."

She nodded, then gestured toward the young footman. "I must have a word with our hostess about *him*."

"Leave it with me, Lady Arabella," Monty replied. "*I'll* deal with him."

Spiteful triumph glittered in her eyes. She offered her hand, and he held it close to his lips, not quite able to bring himself to kiss it. Then he rose and followed the gentlemen out. As he passed the footman, he stopped and leaned close.

"May I help you, Your Grace?" the boy asked, his voice wavering with apprehension.

"I wish to commend the excellence of your service," Monty said. Then he left the astonished young man standing while he exited the dining room. As he reached the doorway, he glanced back to see Miss Howard, her gaze flicking between him and the footman, a smile on her lips. Then she lowered he gaze once more.

CHAPTER NINE

"**Y**OU'LL BE ALL right," Eleanor's father whispered. "The duchess is a kind woman." Then he followed the men out, leaving her alone with the women.

"Well, ladies," their hostess said, "shall we retire to the drawing room while the men congratulate themselves on their prowess?"

Polite titters threaded through the company—the other ladies wishing to ingratiate themselves with the duchess, but only thinly disguising their disapproval. Clearly it wasn't done to say anything critical of the opposite sex. Across the table, Lady Arabella Ponsford smiled, but her eyes remained cold and hard, discontent in their expression. What that unpleasant harpy had to be so dissatisfied with, Eleanor couldn't fathom. Independently wealthy, titled, and with the statuesque figure that elicited the admiration of all who saw her, Lady Arabella was like Juliette in that she always seemed to know where to go and what to say to fit into the world and elicit praise from everyone in it.

And she'd been sat next to *him* at dinner.

But, rather than appreciate her good fortune, she'd complained her way through the entire meal, wrinkling her pretty little nose while she tasted the soup.

The soup…

A bubble of mirth threatened to burst at what Whitcombe had said. Most likely the footman hadn't relieved himself in Lady

Arabella's soup, but wouldn't it have been wonderful if he *had*?

And—*oh my*—Whitcombe had heard her laugh, and *looked* at her. Was he disgusted that she'd understood his meaning? Or perhaps he considered her unladylike laugh unfit for Polite Society.

Their hostess stood, and the ladies followed suit. Eleanor winced as her chair scraped along the floorboards, and Mother shot her a look of irritation. But the duchess appeared not to notice. Lady Arabella approached Juliette, and the two exited arm in arm.

Eleanor folded her napkin, placed it on the table, then approached the door where her hostess stood, waiting.

"Shall we, Miss Howard?" The duchess smiled and offered her arm.

Eleanor nodded her thanks and took it.

"Your sister seems good friends with Lady Arabella," the duchess said as they entered the drawing room, where footmen were already serving coffee to the ladies.

"Y-yes," Eleanor replied. "I believe they're best friends."

"And you?"

Eleanor shook her head. "I have no friends. At least, none here tonight."

"A situation I must remedy."

"Oh no!" Eleanor cried. Then she winced at her outburst as several pairs of eyes fixed their gazes on her. "I-I mean—Forgive me—I've no wish to…"

Her voice trailed away. Propriety dictated that she *not* complete her sentence.

I've no wish to pursue a friendship with anyone here.

The duchess arched an eyebrow, then glanced about the room. Her gaze fell on Juliette and Arabella whispering together in a corner. Then she nodded.

"Of course, my dear. To consider someone a friend, one must have something in common with them. Next time I include your family in an invitation, I'll make sure your particular friend—Miss de Grande, I believe?—is able to come. Or Lady Marlow, as she is now. My husband is well acquainted with Lord Marlow."

The duchess paused, as if anticipating a reply. But Eleanor couldn't think of anything to say, other than "oh."

The duchess smiled. "Quite so," she said. "I was merely making conversation. A rather odd phrase, isn't it—making *conversation*—when all one does is utter inane remarks with nothing of any real import to say? I find such a habit tiresome, do you not?"

"Oh, *yes*," Eleanor said. "I've always failed to understand the necessity of making a bland speech about the weather, who knows whom, who's a member of which ladies' club, or whether private parties are to be preferred over a public ball. Why say anything at all if there's nothing to say?"

The duchess laughed, then led Eleanor toward the coffee table. "Have some coffee." She nodded to a footman, who filled a cup and handed it to Eleanor.

"Thank you," Eleanor said. The footman smiled and gave a stiff bow.

"And...a piece of marzipan?" the duchess asked, gesturing toward the bright array of sweets.

"I don't know..." Eleanor glanced toward her mother, who only that evening had warned her about the damage sweet things could do to her figure.

"Just one won't do any harm," the duchess whispered. "Almonds are known to have restorative properties. I have it on good authority that marzipan does more good than harm. Please, I insist."

"Very well." Eleanor plucked a piece from the display. The surrounding pieces shifted, and one slipped from the arrangement and landed on the floor.

"Oh, forgive me!" she cried. The duchess raised her hand.

"There's naught to forgive, Miss Howard. I know of one member of my family who'll thank you for your consideration." She crouched down, picked up the piece, and brushed it with her fingers. Then she handed it to the footman. "Would you have this sent to Gargantuan, please, James, with Miss Howard's compliments?"

"Very good, Your Grace." The footman bowed, took the marzipan piece, and exited the room.

"Gargantuan?" Eleanor asked.

"My pug. He was the runt of the litter, so I deemed his name something of a consolation, and, as it transpired, it's an appropriate name, given his appetite."

"I love pugs," Eleanor said, "though I've not been permitted…"

She stopped herself mid-sentence. How many times had Mother told her not to speak of family matters in public?

The duchess appeared not to notice her faux pas. She placed a hand on Eleanor's arm and smiled. "A pity," she said. "My instinct tells me you'd be an ideal mistress for a pug."

Footsteps approached, and Eleanor heard a familiar voice.

"Oh, poor thing! *Such* a misfortune for you, always having these little mishaps."

Juliette stood before her, a consolatory smile on her lips. She turned to her companion. "I was just telling Arabella how you spilled an entire bowl of soup the other week—wasn't I, Arabella?"

"You were," Arabella said. "Most unfortunate for you—and your family."

"You can rest assured, Duchess," Juliette told their hostess, "that I've pledged to help Eleanor in any way that I can. That's a loving sister's duty, is it not?"

"Your sister needs no help, I can assure you," the duchess said, an undercurrent of ice in her voice. "She's delightful as she is."

Before Juliette could respond, the door opened, bringing with it the odor of brandy and cigar smoke and the murmur of male voices.

"Ah!" the duchess cried. "The gentlemen have decided to

grace us with their presence."

Eleanor glanced toward the door, her heart rate increasing with a mixture of dread and excitement at the prospect of seeing…*him*. She took an involuntary step backward, and collided with a body.

"Ouch! You trod on my toe!"

Eleanor turned to see her sister's face contorted with anger, before it smoothed into a smile once more.

"Poor Eleanor! What *shall* we do with you?"

"It's not my fault if you're in my way, Juliette."

"There's no need for incivility. You should have been looking where you were going, not staring at the men."

Eleanor's cheeks warmed with shame. "Keep your voice down!"

"Don't tell me you've set your cap at someone?" Juliette laughed. "I wonder who? Arabella—what do you think?"

"Perhaps it's Mr. Drayton," Arabella said. "You sat next to him at dinner. He'd do for you. Did you enjoy his company at dinner, despite his being the duke's…*natural* son?"

What did she mean by a *natural* son? Was it another term for firstborn, perhaps?

Eleanor returned the smile. "I enjoyed Mr. Drayton's company, yes."

"And, of course," Arabella said, "you're in no position to have any qualms about which side of the blanket he was born."

"Blanket?" Eleanor asked. "What do you mean, *which side of the blanket?*"

"Ahem."

Eleanor glanced up to see their host, the Duke of Westbury, staring directly at her, cold fury in his eyes. He took a step toward her, and her stomach tightened with fear. Then the duchess placed a hand on his arm. He shifted his gaze to his wife, and his expression softened. Seizing her opportunity, Eleanor fled across the drawing room and slipped through the doors out onto the terrace, willing the darkness outside to swallow her whole.

What the devil had she said—or done—to anger their host?

Why, despite her best efforts, and her promises to Mother, did she always end up making such a fool of herself?

CHAPTER TEN

A s Monty entered the drawing room, his senses were assaulted by the pitch of female voices. Ye gods—no wonder gentlemen sought solace in their clubs. Women might believe gentlemen's clubs existed to assert their mastery over the world. But, in reality, they were sanctuaries from nagging wives.

And nagging mothers.

He cast his gaze over the drawing room and caught sight of his own mother deep in conversation with Westbury's grand-mother, as if they plotted something.

Which didn't bode well.

The duchess gestured toward the coffee table, and, with murmurs of appreciation, the gentlemen milled about while footmen busied themselves pouring coffee and plucking sweets of eye-wateringly bright colors from the display in the center of the table.

The footman who'd earned Lady Arabella's disapproval was nowhere to be seen. Surely the duchess hadn't dismissed him for inadvertently offending Lady Arabella, who held everyone and everything in contempt?

Then a side door opened and the footman entered. He exchanged a few words with the duchess, who nodded and smiled, placing a hand on his arm. Across the room, Monty noticed Lady Arabella watching the exchange, her mouth creased with disgust as if she'd just ingested an unripe plum.

Sorry, Miss Harpy, you'll have to find another victim for your spite.

"*There* you are, Montague. At last."

Mother appeared at his elbow, together with the dowager duchess—who, though ancient in years, clearly possessed the ability to scuttle about the place as silently as a spider. And as quickly, despite the silver-topped cane she held in her claw-like hand.

"Duchess," he said, addressing the dowager. "And Mother—may I bring you some coffee and one of"—he gestured toward the pile of sweets—"whatever *they* are?"

"My coffee-drinking days are over," the dowager said. "But some of the young women here tonight might appreciate your gallantry."

"I agree, Augusta," Mother said. "Lady Arabella's without a cup. I'm sure she'd appreciate a little something."

"Quite so." The dowager raked her gaze over Monty, then arched her eyebrow in appreciation.

Sweet Lord—was he the *little something*?

"I've no wish to impose myself on Lady Arabella," he replied. "She appears to be having a private conversation with Miss Juliette Howard."

"Is not my son terribly ungallant, Augusta?" Mother said. "And after the lengths we've gone to secure his interests."

To secure your *interests, more like, Mother.*

But he daren't voice his response. The dowager carried the air of a woman who was not to be refused—or disobeyed—and Monty suspected that her cane was put to a great deal more use than merely supporting her as she walked.

"I'm sure the boy meant no offense, Matilda," she said. "Young men must be forgiven for their disrespect of their elders. But they always come around to our way of thinking eventually. They must enjoy their little rebellion before they don the mantle of duty." She fixed her gaze on Monty. "Dear boy, I'm sure you'll be a credit to your mother once you embrace your responsibilities. In fact, I have the very thing to bring together two young people who are so obviously well matched. What say you to a little dancing?"

He couldn't think of anything worse.

"Oh, yes!" his mother cried. "That would be a perfect end to a perfect evening. The two of you were partnered so well at dinner, I've no doubt you'll shine on the dance floor. Augusta, would your granddaughter play for us?"

Devil's toes—one dance with Lady Arabella at the Fairchilds' ball was enough to last a lifetime. After enduring her complaints throughout dinner, the last thing he wanted was to spend the rest of the *evening* with her, let alone the rest of his life.

The dowager approached her granddaughter-in-law. "Jeanette, darling—the young people are wild for dancing. Would you oblige?"

A ripple of enthusiasm threaded through the company, and Monty's heart sank as he spotted Lady Arabella staring at him, expectation in her eyes.

"Mother—have you been scheming again?" he asked.

"Of course not," she said, a little too forcefully. "Augusta's merely giving you a helping hand."

"Oh, *is* she?"

"She's taken pity on me, on account of your failing to do your duty."

"Not this again, Mother." He sighed. "I've already said—"

"Don't *I* have a say? I don't want to see the Whitcombe line expire while you refuse to entertain the prospect of Lady Arabella as your bride."

"Why not say that a little louder, Mother, and announce your desperation to the whole room?" he retorted. "If I want a bride, I'll take one on my own terms. I must *like* her, at the very least."

"And, in order to like her, you must first get to know her. Augusta has been most obliging in that quarter. Our hostess had originally placed you next to the vicar's wife until Augusta intervened on your behalf."

Sweet heaven—was there no escaping female wiles? If Mother had recruited the dowager to her campaign to shackle him to that harpy, then all hope was lost. He must surrender, or desert—the latter of which was infinitely more preferable.

"Will you not dance tonight to oblige me, Montague?"

"No," he said, ungraciously. "I won't."

"Don't you *want* a wife?"

"At the moment, all I want is solitude." Ignoring her protests, he strode across the room and headed for the terrace doors. Lady Arabella stepped into his path, her eyes shining with triumph.

Clearly she believed he was in a hurry to partner her, as opposed to being in a hurry to get *away* from her.

"Oh, Your Grace..." she began.

"Excuse me," he said, veering to one side.

She scowled, giving him a glimpse of what would be in store for him for the rest of his life were he to shackle himself to her.

Once outside, he closed the terrace doors behind him and drew in a deep breath, cleaning his lungs with the night air. Strains of music filtered through the doors, and he strode across the terrace and leaned on the balustrade, looking out into the garden bathed in moonlight.

Incivility had its benefits, not least the ability to extract one-self from disagreeable company. Doubtless Lady Arabella would describe him as *the very worst of brutes* to that sharp-nosed friend of hers.

Let them! They believed him to have a heart of ice—but they were wrong. Ice, like his interest in a woman, melted away with each encounter, until it was no more. His heart was fashioned from granite—a stone that, no matter how belligerently a woman tried to erode it, remained as cold and as fixed as it had ever been.

"Oh, Lady Arabella," he said. "How little you know of my heart!"

A sound—like a small cry—came from the end of the terrace, where the surrounding trees cast deep shadows.

"Who's there?" he called.

He discerned faint shapes in the darkness—a stoneware urn

bearing a plant with thick, sharp-edged leaves, a pair of statues guarding a gap in the balustrade where a staircase descended into the gardens, and a row of bushes lining the far wall.

He took a step forward, then froze. A faint rustling sound carried across the terrace—too deliberate to be attributed to the wind.

Had Mother sent someone to spy on him?

"Show yourself!" he demanded.

One of the bushes seemed to be quivering, though there was no wind. As his eyes grew accustomed to the dark, he thought he could discern a shadow within the bush. Was it a spy—or perhaps another man, seeking respite from the flesh market inside?

"You're at liberty to tarry here as much as I," he said. "If you're here to escape the company inside, then I applaud your good taste."

His words were met with silence.

"Of course, if you've no right to be here, then I'm within my rights to alert the Duke of Westbury to a trespasser. One of my fellow guests is a magistrate, I believe."

He smiled to himself. The threat of the authorities would flush out any coward.

Then he saw it—at the base of the bush. A shape, moving along the ground, about the size of a man's hand. A long nose, black eyes gleaming in the moonlight, stubby legs, and a body covered in spikes.

He approached the bush and the creature froze. The nose seemed to withdraw into the body, together with the legs, until all that remained was a ball of spikes.

He burst out laughing. What a fool he was to think someone was there! No wild animal would have ventured so close to the bush if that were true.

"I know how you feel, little fellow," he said. "My spikes may be invisible, but I wear them as you do, to ward off predators.

He pulled his gloves out of his pocket, slipped them on, then picked up the creature, wincing as one of the spikes penetrated the fabric.

"Let me take you to safety, *mon ami.*"

He descended the staircase and placed the hedgehog in a sheltered corner of the main garden. When he glanced back toward the terrace, he saw a shadow moving across the balustrade. Then he blinked and it was gone.

CHAPTER ELEVEN

AS SOON AS Whitcombe was out of sight, Eleanor emerged from her hiding place, dashed across the terrace, then slipped back into the drawing room.

What a fool she'd been! She should have declared herself as soon as he'd come outside, but she had been paralyzed with fear at the thought of being so close to him. The longer she waited, the worse it became, until she would have looked an utter fool had she made her presence known.

And then…

Then he uttered the words that sliced her heart in two.

"Oh, Lady Arabella. How little you know of my heart!"

She was a fool to believe him different to the rest of them—with their arrogant disdain of anything and anyone beneath them. And yet…

And yet, when he'd leaned on the balustrade and looked out over the garden, his profile illuminated in the moonlight, Eleanor could swear she caught a flicker of emotion in his expression—a softening about the eyes that, while slight, was discernible to someone who'd spent so long observing him in silence, and capturing every expression, every emotion, on the page with her pencil.

And then the care with which he'd lifted the little hedgehog and held it so tenderly…

Stop being such a fool!

Once more she'd let herself be ruled by hope—a hope that far exceeded the harsh reality that he was, and would always be, insurmountably far above her.

Eleanor crossed the drawing room floor—skirting around the dancers—to find solace beside a large aspidistra in a corner. She drew her chair closer to the plant so she'd be partially obscured by the foliage, then sat and closed her eyes.

The loss of one sense calmed the storm in her mind. The clash of colors at parties always overwhelmed her. In contrast, the moonlight outside muted the colors, bathing the landscape in a cool blue light. Of course, it wasn't done to spend the duration of a party standing outside, away from everyone else.

Sadly.

The dance concluded, followed by a ripple of applause, and Eleanor opened her eyes.

The duchess was approaching her, a glass of red liquid in her hand.

"You look in need of refreshment, Miss Howard," she said. "I took the liberty—I trust you don't mind?"

"Why would I mind, Your Grace?"

"Some might consider it an imposition to assume. You're at liberty to refuse."

Eleanor took the glass, and the duchess sat beside her.

"It's noisy tonight," she said. "I'm not partial to crowds. I *much* prefer someone of a quieter disposition."

"Do you?" Eleanor asked. "Mother is always telling me I should speak up more at parties—that a young woman needs to be entertaining if she is to succeed. But I can never think of anything to say that others would find interesting."

The duchess placed a hand on Eleanor's arm. "My dear, there will always be those who appreciate what *you* have to say. For example, I hear you have some understanding of art. I'd appreciate your opinion on a Stubbs we have in the morning room."

"A Stubbs—a *real* one?"

The duchess laughed. "I hope so, though I overheard Countess Fairchild telling Lady Blessingham it must be a forgery. I believe I offended her when I married too far above my station. But disparity of rank is no reason not to marry when you're in love."

Unless the man you love doesn't know you exist.

Eleanor sighed.

"Oh, forgive me," the duchess said. "I didn't mean to distress you."

"It's nothing," Eleanor said. "I—"

"Jeanette!" a voice cried. "Over here, child, and play for us. The young people wish to dance to 'Mr. Beveridge's Maggot.'"

"Coming, Grandmama." The duchess rose. "I'll leave you in peace, Miss Howard. But if you do wish to dance, my stepson would be happy to oblige. He tells me you were very kind to him at dinner."

"I prefer not to dance," Eleanor said. "I mean—I wish I *wanted* to dance, but the only time I did, I trod on my partner's toe."

"Perhaps your partner placed his toe in the wrong place."

"Jeanette!" the dowager cried.

"Please excuse me." The duchess returned to the pianoforte, while the couples accumulated in the center of the room.

Then the terrace doors opened, and...*he* appeared.

Eleanor's heart somersaulted in her chest as he swept his cold blue gaze about the room before settling on Lady Arabella Ponsford, who stood, head upright, exuding confidence as she made a show of fanning herself.

"Montague!" a sharp voice said. Whitcombe's mother approached him and took his elbow. She hissed something in his ear, and his eyes darkened until they were almost black. She seemed to be admonishing him while gesturing toward Lady Arabella. He shook his head and gave a sharp response.

The music started, and the couples began to dance. Disappointment soured Lady Arabella's expression, then Westbury approached her and offered his hand, and they joined the dance.

Whitcombe and his mother continued to argue until he let

out an exclamation.

Then he strode across the room, cutting through the dance. The couples dispersed with cries of protest, but Whitcombe ignored them and continued his path in quick, powerful strides. Fear rippled through Eleanor as she realized he was looking in her direction, and she glanced either side, but there was nobody close by.

Heavens—he was walking straight toward her!

He stopped less than two feet away, and she glanced up, her stomach flipping at the determined expression in his eyes.

For what felt like an eternity, she met his gaze, fighting the urge to flee, while the world around them seemed to fade into oblivion. Then she realized that the dancing had stopped, and the crowd had formed a semicircle around the two of them.

Lord help me! They're all staring at me. He's staring at me!

Her palms grew slick under his scrutiny, and a nugget of desire pulsed thickly inside her body.

What was happening?

Then he lowered himself to one knee.

"Miss Howard," he said, his voice filling the drawing room, "will you do me the honor of accepting my hand in marriage?"

CHAPTER TWELVE

Monty kneeled before Miss Howard, his mother's admonishments ringing in his ears.

Lady Arabella's the prettiest girl in the room—why do you refuse to dance with her?

If you tarry, Dunton will snap her up—or even that upstart Mr. Moss.

And the final comment that had pushed him over the precipice...

If you don't ask her to marry you, I'll ask on your behalf.

"Miss Howard," he said, "will you do me the honor of accepting my hand in marriage?"

A collective intake of breath rippled through the room, as if the whole company were about to faint with shock.

And well they might. What the bloody hell was he doing?

Serving Mother right, that was what, by proposing to the least handsome, least congenial—and most undesirable—creature in the room, in the hope Mother would cease plaguing him.

Miss Howard stared at him, fear and astonishment in her eyes. She was so still, he might have believed her a statue were it not for the faint pulse at the base of her throat. He let his gaze wander across her chest, taking in her neckline and the swell of her breasts...

Perhaps not *so* undesirable after all.

Then, before his eyes, Miss Howard seemed to withdraw into

herself—almost as if she wished to make herself invisible to predators. But the whispers threading through the company told him that every pair of eyes in the room was fixed on her—and him.

"Miss Howard," he said, and she flinched. "For many months, I've admired you from afar. You set yourself apart from others, and the more I observed you, the more I saw your perfection. In fact, from the moment I first set eyes on you, I singled you out as the woman with whom I wish to spend the rest of my life."

With luck, that would convince the company. Miss Howard would, of course, understand that every word he spoke was false.

Then the fear in her expression morphed into hope. Not the material desire he saw in other ladies—but a purer, almost innocent form of hope, harbored by a soul that had been trapped in darkness, alone and unloved, and was being offered a beacon of light, in order for them not to merely exist, but to *live*.

It was the kind of hope capable of breaking a man's heart and which, if unmet, led to the destruction of the one who harbored it.

His chest tightened with a previously unknown sensation—as if his granite heart were at risk of erosion after all.

Which was nonsense.

This was nonsense. He ought to retract before it was too late. With luck, his little show would have humiliated Mother into keeping quiet for the foreseeable future about his marital prospects.

But before he could open his mouth, Miss Howard rose, the joy in her eyes rendering her almost pretty.

"Your Grace," she said, a tremor in her voice, "I would be delighted to accept your hand. Thank you."

She took his proffered hand, and a spark of desire threaded through his body at the feel of her skin on his. She drew in a sharp breath, then withdrew her hand.

"Oh, how wonderful!" a female voice cried. Monty turned to see their hostess, the Duchess of Westbury, approaching them.

"Whitcombe, Miss Howard—may I be the first to congratulate you?"

He took Miss Howard's hand again, and this time there was no mistaking the spark of need. Then he rose to his feet and cast his gaze over the company—their hosts, the Duke and Duchess of Westbury smiling in congratulation, the expression of horror on Mother's ashen face…

…and the thinly veiled anger in Lady Arabella's eyes.

As for the Howard family, he suppressed the urge to laugh at Juliette's sour-faced jealousy, and Lady Howard's hungry triumph. But Sir Leonard showed an entirely different expression. Rather than delight at his daughter making a magnificent match—or relief at believing she'd been taken off his hands— Monty saw only suspicion and mistrust. He'd have to take care not to reveal his true intentions to the older man, lest he find himself at the business end of a pistol.

There was only one beast in the world more imposing than an overbearing mother.

An overprotective father.

Monty lifted Miss Howard's hand and brushed his lips against her skin, inhaling the sweet, soft scent of exotic flowers—lighter than the expensive scents favored by most debutantes, and, for that, all the more alluring.

"I'll trespass upon your time no longer, Miss Howard," he said. "With your father's permission, I shall call upon you tomorrow at… Shall we say ten o'clock?"

With luck, she'd agree, then he could thank her for complying with his ruse and they could part ways. He could return to his life of freedom, and Miss Howard could return to…whatever the devil it was that she did with herself.

She curled her fingers around his, in a gesture not of possession, but of trust. Then she glanced across the room toward her father.

"Papa?"

Monty felt his cheeks warm under Sir Leonard's scrutiny. At

length, Sir Leonard nodded.

"Of course," he said. "I trust you'll abide by your word, Whitcombe, and not be late. I shall, of course, require an interview with you after your audience with my daughter."

Though he smiled, Sir Leonard's voice carried an undercurrent of threat.

Monty approached Sir Leonard to shake hands, and the older man took his in a firm grip, holding it for a heartbeat longer than necessary.

Yes—there was no mistaking it. Sir Leonard had issued a threat. But, in a world filled with men who fawned over him, Monty found the man's hostility something to be admired rather than scoffed at, even if it didn't bode well for their meeting tomorrow.

CHAPTER THIRTEEN

EACH TIME ELEANOR heard a footstep outside, her heart threatened to burst in her chest. The slightest sound set her pulse racing—when a messenger arrived with a letter for Papa earlier, she'd almost fainted as her vision blurred and her hearing muffled, as if she were underwater.

She slipped off her bracelet and twirled it around her forefingers, focusing on the smooth, regular movement, and, at length, the world shifted back into focus.

"Sit up straight, Eleanor dearest," Mother said, "and stop fiddling with that thing. You *must* behave properly when the duke arrives."

Eleanor *dearest*? Had securing the hand of a duke rendered her worthy of Mother's affection at last?

Juliette sat beside Mother, a sour expression on her face. "Perhaps he made a mistake last night," she said. "I'll wager he won't come."

"That's enough, Juliette!" Mother snapped, swatting Eleanor's sister with her fan. "Your sister's triumph is cause for celebration. Of course he'll come. But we must ensure your sister does not disgrace herself. Her peculiarities, which we endure in silence at home, will be subject to much scrutiny now she's betrothed. You must help her, Juliette."

Why did Mother always speak as if Eleanor was either absent or lacking in understanding?

"I *am* in the room, Mother," Eleanor said. "I can speak for myself."

She flinched as Mother turned her gaze on her, but before any admonishment came, she heard a loud knock in the distance.

"He's here!" Mother cried.

Footsteps approached, then the parlor door opened to reveal a footman. Standing behind him was…

Eleanor's breath caught as she caught sight of him.

My fiancé.

She could hardly bring herself even to think the words. Standing in the doorway, filling it with his powerful frame, he looked even more majestic than he had last night, surrounded by his own kind. His jacket clung to his frame as if it were a second skin. His breeches, a rich cream color, seemed to caress the muscles of his thighs, and his boots gleamed in the morning light, polished to perfection, most likely, by his valet until he could see his face in them. His hair, a little longer than might be considered respectable, formed thick, dark waves that seemed to absorb the light. And his eyes, the color of a deep summer sky, looked first at Mother, then Juliette, until, finally, settling on her.

His nostrils flared and he parted his lips, flicking the tip of his tongue out to moisten them.

Sweet heaven! She drew in a sharp breath to suppress a cry of need.

The footman ushered him in. "His Grace, the Duke of Whitcombe."

Whitcombe bowed to Eleanor's mother. "Lady Howard, a pleasure," he said, though his tone implied it was anything but.

Eleanor's mother rose to her feet, and Juliette followed suit. "Your Grace." Mother dipped into a curtsey. "Welcome to our humble home. I cannot tell you what an honor it is."

He arched an eyebrow, and the corner of his mouth lifted a little—not a smile, but a sign of wry amusement.

"Eleanor!" Mother snapped. "Where are your manners?"

Her cheeks flaming, Eleanor rose, then curtseyed and almost

lost her balance.

The amusement in his eyes turned to disdain. What must he think of her?

"Forgive my daughter, Your Grace," Mother said. "She—"

He raised his hand, curtailing her apology. "There's nothing to forgive, Lady Howard. I came to see your daughter—not to critique her ability to curtsey."

"You're most kind, Your Grace," Mother said. "Is he not kind, Eleanor?"

Eleanor struggled to contain the tremors in her body, but managed a passable "Yes, Mother" in response. Her mother cast a sharp glance in her direction, while Juliette's mouth curled into a sly smile.

"May I beg an audience with your daughter?" he continued. "After all, that's why I'm here."

There was no mistaking the irritation in his tone. Mother curtseyed, deeper than before, then held out her hand. "Juliette, my dear, come with me." Then she fixed her gaze on Eleanor. "Remember what I told you."

"Yes, Mother."

Her mother held out her hand and stared expectantly at the duke. He hesitated for a heartbeat, took it, and withdrew almost immediately. Then Mother exited the parlor, Juliette in her wake.

For a moment, Whitcombe remained standing. Then he gestured to the two-seater sofa beside the window.

"May I sit?"

Shame threatened to engulf her. How could she leave him standing? No wonder Mother had felt the need to tell her to behave.

"O-of course," she replied. "Shall I ring the bell for tea?"

"There's something I wish to say first, Miss Howard."

He took a seat and gestured to the space beside him. She sat, and the breath caught in her throat at his closeness. Their legs touched, and she could feel his body heat through the fabric of her gown. Then he reached for her hand and took it. A fizz of need ignited in her center, and she curled her fingers around his.

"I must thank you, Miss Howard," he said.

She glanced up. "For what?"

"For being so obliging last night."

Obliging? Hardly the words of a man in love.

"I was in a bit of a fix, you see," he continued. "My mother can be relentless, and I saw no other way to silence her. Of course, I had no wish to inconvenience you, but I trust you'll understand my motives."

"Inconvenience me?" Eleanor shook her head. "I-I don't understand—why would an offer of marriage be an inconvenience?"

"Oh, heavens!" He let out a laugh and withdrew his hand. "Devil's toes! Surely you didn't believe my proposal to be *genuine?*"

Icy fingers curled around her insides, and she winced as she looked into his eyes. Rather than the love she'd hoped for, she saw mirth and disdain.

"Your Grace, I—" She broke off, her throat tightening.

"I have no intention of marrying," he said.

"Then why…"

"Why did I ask you? I chose the woman everyone least expected me to approach. Had I asked any other young woman in the room, she'd have believed me to be serious in my offer."

His earlier laughter filled her mind until her head pulsed with it. She squeezed her eyes shut in an attempt to fight the humiliation. But it threatened to overwhelm her.

He was right—they were all right.

"You chose for your own amusement—to *ridicule* me?"

Hot tears stung her eyes, and she looked away, unwilling to reveal her pain.

A warm hand took hers, only this time his touch was gentle.

He caressed the back of her hand with his thumb. Then a hand touched her cheek, gently coaxing her to turn her head toward him. She lifted her gaze to see him looking directly at her, the cold blue of his eyes having softened to the color of a warm ocean.

"Forgive me, Miss Howard," he said. "It wasn't my intention to lead you to believe I felt anything for you other than…"

He made a random gesture with his free hand, as if searching for the right word.

"Other than nothing?"

"I fear I have no heart," he said.

"At least, not for me."

To his credit, he colored. Then he took a stray tendril of her hair and brushed it behind her ear, running his fingertips along the skin of her neck.

"I would never have made such a public offer for you had I thought you so lacking in understanding as to have believed it."

She blinked, and a tear splashed onto her cheek. Could her humiliation get any worse?

He sighed, and she shivered as his warm breath caressed her face. His proximity threatened to overwhelm her.

"I'm failing spectacularly at this," he said. "But I can say that, in all honesty, I didn't intend to cause you pain, and I deeply regret that I have."

"I-I'm in no pain," she said, but his brow furrowed and he shook his head.

"I can see your pain, Miss Howard," he said. "But let me atone for my behavior. Ask me anything, and if it's within my power, I'll grant it."

Her heart almost tore in two at the expression in his eyes, and for the first time, she saw genuine kindness, and a selfless wish to ease her pain. But, if anything, that was worse.

She bit her lip to suppress a sob, and another tear rolled down her face.

"Don't be kind," she said. "That last thing I want is your *kindness*."

His frown deepened. "Why not?"

"Because after today you'll never speak to me again—and I could better withstand that if I believed you to be an unkind man."

He sighed. "I've behaved abominably," he said. "Perhaps I should send for your mother."

"No!" she cried. His eyes widened at her outburst, and she lowered her voice to a whisper. *"Please*—don't."

What would Mother say when she learned the truth? The very notion was unbearable.

"Then let us have tea," he said. "I wouldn't blame you for evicting me, but I'm unwilling to leave you alone while you're distressed. Perhaps we can discuss how I might make amends."

"Very well," Eleanor said. "I—I'll find someone and ask them to bring some tea."

She rose and slipped through the door. As soon as she closed it behind her, the tide of sorrow she'd kept at bay burst. Tears spilled onto her cheeks, and she let out a low cry.

What a fool she'd been—a witless fool—to think he'd fallen in love with her! How everyone would laugh when they discovered the truth. How disappointed Papa would be. As for Mother and Juliette—the merest thought of their reaction was too much to endure.

She glanced at the top of the staircase. How easy it would be to flee down the stairs and outside, never to return!

"Left your betrothed alone?" a female voice said. "Not very civil. Or did he flee as soon as you opened your mouth?"

Eleanor's sister stood before her.

"Leave me be, Juliette," Eleanor said.

"I ask out of concern for your welfare."

"You've only ever been concerned about yourself."

"I'm concerned for the *family*, Eleanor," Juliette retorted. "If you've made a fool of us, it damages our reputation. Papa will never be granted a baronetcy if you're the laughingstock of London!"

"In what way am I the laughingstock of London?"

"Don't be a simpleton!" Juliette cried. "Everyone knows Whitcombe would only have asked *you* to marry him for a jape.

I've seen you—mooning over him with your tongue hanging out like a lovesick puppy. But he despises you! I overheard him describe you to his mother last night as the ugliest girl in the room!"

"You lie!" Eleanor cried.

"Ask Bella if you don't believe me. Ask the duke's mother. I *told* Mama his offer of marriage was nothing but a joke, but she didn't believe me. I suppose I'll have to be the one to tell her the duke was just indulging in a little sport—or shall you?"

"Neither of you shall," a deep male voice said.

Eleanor turned and let out a cry. The Duke of Whitcombe stood in the hallway.

She'd been wrong—her humiliation *could* get worse, and it just had.

It was plain by his expression that he'd heard every word.

CHAPTER FOURTEEN

EVIL'S TOES—WAS THIS how women conversed with each other when they thought themselves unobserved?

No—the expression on Miss Howard's eyes was that of a woman enduring torture, not a conversation. Her cheeks were bright red, and her eyes, glistening with tears, widened as she caught sight of him. She opened her mouth as if to speak, but no sound came, and then swayed to one side, as if afflicted by a fainting fit.

The ugliest girl in the room.

Why would any young woman say that to another—let alone her sister?

Juliette dipped into a curtsey, and the contempt in her eyes evaporated. The elegant congeniality and frank desire that replaced it as she turned her gaze on him made her look like a different creature entirely to the one he'd caught tormenting her sister.

"Your Grace," she said, her voice soft and melodic. "I trust you're being treated with the respect you deserve."

Monty glanced toward Miss Howard, who clung to the staircase railing. Then something shifted in his soul—as if he'd been living his life in ignorance, or under the influence of a dream, from which he had begun to awaken...

As if, for the first time in his life, he possessed a conscience.

Eleanor Howard's sister might have indulged in a little torture—but *he* was the real culprit, in having shattered not only her hopes, but her belief in her own worth. True, he had no intention of marrying her, but had he needed to declare his true intent so cruelly? Only one party had stood to gain from his scheme—and that was him, at the expense of Miss Howard's peace of mind.

You really are the very worst of cads.

He brushed past Juliette, approached Miss Howard, and placed his hand over hers. As if he were training a filly, he coaxed her to uncurl her fingers from the banister, then he hooked his arm around hers and drew her toward him. At first she complied passively, then she curled her fingers around his arm and leaned against him. A barely noticeable act of trust, but he recognized it for what it was.

What the devil was happening to him? Sawbridge would, no doubt, taunt him for going soft.

"Miss Juliette," he said, "I wonder if you'd oblige me?"

Juliette's eyes sparkled with delight, and she gave a gracious smile.

"Your sister was about to send for some tea. Might you oblige instead?"

The smile slipped, and he caught a flash of the expression Lady Arabella had displayed last night—the expression that warned an unmarried man to run away as fast as he could.

"Well!" she exclaimed. "I hardly think that's proper."

"Please send for your sister's maid, also," he said. "We'll be in the parlor."

"It's not my place to—"

"*If* you would oblige me, Miss Juliette."

She stiffened at the hardened tone of his voice, and he caught a flicker of fear in her eyes.

Good. The ease with which her expression had morphed from spite, when aimed at her sister, to faux innocence and cordiality when directed at him reminded Monty of the bullies he'd encountered at Eton—especially MacDiarmid, who, at best, could be described as a "nasty piece of work" who rallied his disciples to support his vendettas against those he deemed weaker than himself, yet turned into a sniveling wreck when challenged. Monty had caught the little toad tormenting one of the new boys and given him six of the best as punishment.

There was much to be said for the old ways of teaching bullies a lesson.

"Please excuse me, Miss Juliette, while your sister and I return to the parlor," Monty said. Then he turned to Eleanor. "Darling, shall we?"

She blinked and glanced up at him, and he caressed her hand, taking care to run his fingertips over the third finger of her left hand.

"My mother's ring will look exquisite on this finger," he said. "The emerald is almost the same color as your eyes. In my eagerness to see you again, I quite forgot to bring it. But I shall have it with me when next we meet."

Confusion clouded her expression, but she let him steer her into the parlor, where guided her to an armchair by the fire.

"Are you cold, Miss Howard?"

She looked at him, but her eyes were unfocused. At that moment, the door opened and a maid entered, carrying a tray with tea things.

"Are you Miss Howard's maid?" Monty asked.

"No, Your Grace. That'll be Harriet."

Harriet…

The name she'd taken to herself when he saw her in the park.

"Fetch her," he said. "Miss Howard is ill."

"Very good, Your Grace." The maid bobbed a curtsey.

"Quickly now!" he barked, and the maid scuttled off.

Then he resumed his attention on Miss Howard. "Would you like some tea?"

She leaned back and closed her eyes, and Monty approached the table.

He inspected the tea things—two cups, a silver teapot with a fluted edge and an ivory handle, a sugar bowl, and a jug filled with milk.

What the devil was a man supposed to do with all that?

He picked up a cup and turned it over in his hand, running his thumb over the pattern on the porcelain. Then he glanced at the teapot.

"I suppose I should pour some of that in first."

Miss Howard gave no response.

He poured brown liquid into the cup. Wisps of steam rose from the surface, dissolving into the air. Then he reached for the milk jug and poured some in. Was that enough?

Heavens! What the bloody hell was he doing—a man of his station, serving tea?

The door opened and a young woman appeared. She bobbed a curtsey, then glanced across the room and let out a cry.

"Miss Eleanor!" She rushed toward Miss Howard and took her hand.

"I was just about to serve tea," Monty said.

The maid glanced at the teacup in his hand, and her eyes widened.

"How does Miss Howard take her tea?" he asked. "I've added some milk. Should I add sugar now?"

"She doesn't take milk," the maid replied. "She prefers honey and cinnamon."

"There's none of that here." He glanced at the tray. "At least, I don't *think* there is."

"Lady Howard doesn't permit it. But a little sugar, and no milk, should suffice."

"Oh," he said. "I've already put milk in."

"*I'll* see to it." The maid plucked the cup out of his hand and set it down, then she filled the second cup, dropped in a sugar lump, and stirred. Then she sat next to Miss Howard and took her hand.

"Miss Eleanor, it's me. Harriet. I've some sweet tea for you."

Miss Howard's eyes fluttered open.

"Perhaps she needs a doctor," Monty said.

"No!" the maid cried. Then she colored. "I mean—begging your pardon, Your Grace, but a doctor won't help. And you mustn't speak of this to anyone—not even the mistress."

"Lady Howard? Why ever not?"

The maid glanced at Miss Howard, distress distorting her features. "I-I can't tell you."

"Surely Miss Howard's mother will know what's best for her."

The maid shook her head.

"Does Miss Howard suffer from some sort of affliction?" he asked.

"Of course not!" the maid replied, a flare of anger in her tone. "Begging your pardon—she just gets a little overwhelmed, often when something's distressed her, or when there's too much going on around her. She'll be fine in a moment."

"Then why can't her mother know?"

"I-I shouldn't say."

"But you *shall*."

The maid flinched at his tone. "Miss Eleanor cannot help herself," she said. "I wonder what happened to upset her today— when *you* visited."

A servant had no right to take that tone with a duke. But he found himself admiring the love she evidently had for her mistress.

"I find myself admonished," he said.

"My duty is to Miss Eleanor," the maid said. Then she reached for the bracelet around Miss Howard's wrist, slipped it off, and placed it into her mistress's hands. Miss Howard blinked, then curled her fingers around the bracelet.

"The last time she had such a turn, Lady Howard demanded that a doctor be sent for—a very *particular* kind of doctor."

"A particular kind of doctor?"

The maid nodded. "The master, Sir Leonard—he's an easy-going man ordinarily, when it comes to her ladyship. But that day, he stood firm, and insisted Miss Eleanor remain here rather than be sent away."

"Sent away?" he asked. "You mean…"

The maid glanced at Miss Howard. "Please—don't speak of it in front of her." Tears glistened in Harriet's eyes. "She's the kindest young lady in the world, and she wouldn't hurt a fly. She's quieter than most, but that's for the good—and she may not seem to have feelings, but that's because she keeps them hidden. She feels a great deal more than she shows."

She met Monty's gaze, determination in her eyes. No servant had ever looked at him so directly before, except perhaps for his butler when he'd arrived home just after dawn, disheveled, reeking of the cologne of the women he'd been rutting all night.

"Miss Eleanor feels more than most, Your Grace."

Monty glanced at Miss Howard. "Yes," he said quietly, "I rather suspect she does."

Miss Howard seemed to react to his voice. Her eyes opened fully, and she lifted her head.

"Harriet?"

"I'm here, miss," the maid said. "Would you like some tea? I've made it good and sweet for you. It'll make you right in no time. Here—let me help you."

"No," Monty said. "Let me, if Miss Howard has no objection."

He placed his arm about her shoulders and helped her to sit upright while the maid held the teacup to her lips. She took a sip, and her expression uncurled—almost like the hedgehog that he'd set down in a secluded corner of Westbury's garden, where it had remained curled up for several heartbeats before gradually unfurling, then moving across the lawn and disappearing in the hedgerow.

Except he had no wish for Miss Howard to disappear.

"Y-Your Grace," Miss Howard said. "You're still here."

"I am."

"But I thought—"

"I'm going nowhere," he said softly. "You may leave us,

Harriet."

"But you don't know what she needs," the maid replied.

"Then tell me."

"Gentleness, Your Grace. She gets very little of that."

"I can give her that," he said.

"Make sure you do, Your Grace. Of all the young ladies in London, Miss Eleanor deserves to be loved."

Before he could answer, she exited the parlor.

Miss Howard stirred again.

"Would you like some more tea?" Monty asked.

Her eyes focused on him, their color growing in intensity.

"Miss Howard?"

She remained silent, and he picked up the teacup.

"Eleanor?"

She blinked, and her expression cleared. "Your Grace."

He guided the cup to her lips, and she lifted her hand and curled it around the porcelain. He brushed his fingers against hers, then caught his breath as a small fizz of desire rippled across his skin.

"You must call me Montague," he said, "at least for now."

She drained the teacup, then set it aside. "What would be the sense in my calling you Montague?"

"While we're betrothed, we—" he began, but she interrupted.

"But we're not betrothed." She let out a soft laugh, though sadness lingered in her eyes. "It's the shortest betrothal in history, but it's more than *I* could have hoped for. And nobody could take *that* from me—a few minutes at the end of a party where, for once, the world didn't pity me."

"There's been many shorter, I assure you," he said. "But there's no need to break our betrothal just yet. I don't wish to humiliate you."

"More than you already have?"

She spoke the words so softly that he could almost have believed he'd imagined it.

"We cannot marry, of course," he said, "but I'm not averse to our retaining our betrothal until the end of the Season—if you have no objection."

"For what purpose?"

"It might be beneficial to us both. My mother will stop plaguing me about marrying, and you may find your life much improved."

"*May I?*"

His conscience—the newly discovered entity—needled at him. There might be some merit in extending their false betrothal until the end of the Season—merit for *him*. It would keep Mother, and the tenacious Lady Arabella, off his back. But perhaps Miss Howard could benefit also.

"Your sister might treat you less cruelly," he suggested.

"You oughtn't speak of Juliette in such a manner," Miss Howard said. "I often behave a little…eccentrically. Juliette's merely concerned for how my behavior might reflect on the family."

"You mean how it might affect *her* prospects."

"Please don't speak of her so unjustly, Your Grace."

Ye gods—even after the behavior he'd witnessed on the part of Miss Howard's sister, she still rose to defend her! The maid was right. Miss Howard deserved to be loved—even if he wasn't the man to do the loving.

More's the pity.

Ignoring the voice in his head, he took her hand.

"Would you be averse to remaining engaged until the end of the Season?" he asked. "I'll behave properly, of course."

"Behave properly?"

Devil's toes—must he spell it out?

"I'll"—he hesitated—"remain faithful. It's the only way to convince my circle of the authenticity of the betrothal."

"You mean you'll not ask anyone else to marry you while we're betrothed?"

Bugger. He *would* have to spell it out.

"What I mean is I'll not lie with another woman until our

betrothal is at an end."

"Oh." She blushed and lowered her gaze. Her lack of understanding of the world and its euphemisms reminded him of a child. Yet he could see in her eyes a sharp intelligence.

She was the most contradictory woman. Plain and uninteresting from a distance, but up close, she intrigued him with her intense expression. She seemed shy to the point of agony, but the brief moments when she'd looked into his eyes, the directness of her gaze threatened to tear away the armor he'd secured around his soul.

"I have no right to ask," he said, "but I would like you to consider my request."

"No," she said, and his heart sank.

But he'd acted like an utter cad—what else could he have expected?

"You have no right to ask," she continued. "But I'll help you nonetheless."

He took her hands. "Miss Howard—you'll have no cause to regret it. And when our agreement comes to an end, I'll make sure you emerge with your reputation enhanced. The world will believe that *I* have wronged *you*."

"Very well."

He kissed her hands, and caught his breath at the tiny pulse of need.

"What can I do in return?" he asked.

She shook her head. "You needn't trouble yourself."

"Is there *nothing* you wish for?"

She opened her mouth as if to reply, then closed it again.

"Eleanor?" Improper it might be, but he relished the feel of her name on his lips. "There must be *something*, even if you don't believe I can give it to you."

"There are many things I wish for," she said, "but nobody can give them to me."

"Give me leave to try."

"Very well," she said. "For one thing, I'd like to fit in."

"To fit in?"

"I've never *belonged*, you see. I don't speak, or behave, like other women. I don't even *think* like them."

He suppressed a laugh. "From what I understand of Society ladies, Miss Howard, if you wish to think like them, then you need to cease thinking at all. And I'd advise against that."

She withered under his laughter and tried to withdraw her hand. But he held it firm.

"My intention wasn't to make fun of you, Miss Howard," he said. "You must never change the way you *think*. But I can advise you on how to navigate your way through Society."

Her eyes sparkled with hope, and for a moment, the barriers to his heart were in danger of being breached.

"Would you take the trouble to do that?" she asked. "For *me?*"

"It's no trouble," he said. "You only need convince the world that you're one of them."

"I've *tried*," she said. "I try so hard to behave and speak like others—but it never works."

"Then let me teach you," he said. "And a lesson is always best undertaken in a practical manner."

Her eyes flared with apprehension. "Practical?"

"I must teach you in the very environment in which you wish to survive," he said. "In public."

"In p-public?"

"Yes," he said. "Such as in the park. We'll have enough privacy to discuss the principles without being overheard, then you can put those principles into practice when we encounter others."

"You want to take *me* for a walk in the park?"

He would have laughed at the astonishment in her voice had he not recognized the tragedy. The poor creature clearly couldn't comprehend the notion of anyone wanting to spend time in her company.

"Yes," he said. "I can think of nothing more pleasurable."

And, at that moment, he genuinely couldn't.

She gave a shy smile, and he couldn't help a prick of pride at the notion that he'd played a part in her recovery.

"Is there anything else you require, Miss Howard?" he asked. "It seems, at the moment, that I have the most to gain from our arrangement."

She shook her head.

"Do you wish to marry eventually?" he asked. "To have a home—a family of your own?"

"A *home*, yes," she said. "And…" She colored.

He caressed her hand, as if to coax a further response from her. "And?"

"I want to be loved," she said. "But all young women want to be loved, don't they?"

"In my experience, young women want to be *married*, not loved," he said, "preferably to a wealthy man with a title—the grander the better."

She withdrew her hand. "That may be the case with the young women *you* pursue. But *I'm* different."

She spoke with an edge to her voice. Was this timid little thing admonishing him?

"Not so different, Miss Howard," he said. "Had any duke kneeled before any woman in Society last night, she'd have accepted his offer of marriage—as you did."

She drew in a sharp breath, and his newly found conscience needled him at the distress in her eyes.

"I didn't accept your hand because you're a duke," she said. "I accepted it because I was—" She broke off and shook her head.

"You were what?" he asked.

"Mistaken," she said, her tone flat. "I realize that now. After all, what man in his right mind would—"

"*Plenty* would, I assure you," he interrupted. "Not all men are heartless rakes. Granted, we rakes are in the majority, but I'm convinced I could find you a kinder man before the Season is out."

"How would you know whether he was kind or not? A woman only discovers a man's true character after she's reached the point of no return. Given the limited opportunities men and women have to get to know each other before committing themselves for life, what chance has *any* woman of entering into a union with the full knowledge of what her life will be like?"

What an enigma she was! She expressed herself eloquently on the arguments against entering into the marriage state, yet she'd accepted his proposal so readily under the mistaken belief that his offer was genuine.

For a woman so disinclined to trust others, what had given her cause to harbor such trust in him last night?

And what in the devil's name was making him want, so badly, to be deserving of her trust?

"In that, I can help," he said. "In the company of women, a man hides behind a façade of gallantry and restrained politeness. But among his own sex, he speaks more freely. If you permit me, I can point out the more congenial bachelors with whom you have a greater chance of finding happiness."

Her eyes widened in horror. "Are you offering to find me a husband?"

"I'm offering to give you an introduction," he replied. "With hundreds of young women parading around the ballrooms of London, trying to secure the notice of hundreds of young men, it's no wonder that the chances of finding the right partner are so slim. If I can steer you toward those I deem more suitable, I would be saving you the effort of having to wade through a cesspool in search of the few gems that exist."

She let out a giggle. "Cesspool? Are you equally ungallant in your description of ladies?"

"Ah," he said, "I liken ladies to a barrel of apples—shiny, polished skins, all tempting a man to take a bite. Only when he sinks his teeth in does he discover whether the core is rotten."

Her laughter died. "Your view of Society is as bleak as mine, Your Grace."

"Then perhaps we're not so dissimilar after all."

The door opened, and Monty glanced over his shoulder to

see Miss Howard's parents standing in the doorway.

He rose to his feet and bowed. "Sir Leonard, Lady Howard—forgive my being so forward with your daughter."

Sir Leonard shifted his gaze from Monty to his daughter, then back again, suspicion in his eyes. Lady Howard glanced toward the tea things, lingering on the empty cup.

"Your Grace, my daughter doesn't appear to have served you tea. Eleanor—where are your manners?"

"Your daughter's manners are impeccable, Lady Howard," Monty said. "I'm simply not in the mood for tea."

"Perhaps port is more to your taste," Sir Leonard said.

"At this hour?" Lady Howard exclaimed, wrinkling her nose.

"Or a brandy?" Sir Leonard continued, ignoring his wife. "I've a bottle in my study, and it would give us the opportunity to discuss what, perhaps, ought to have been discussed before the events of last night."

"Leonard!" Lady Howard said. "His Grace is our guest. I doubt he'd take kindly to—"

"To not being granted an audience with his prospective father-in-law?" Sir Leonard interrupted. "Quite so. Your Grace—shall we?"

There was no mistaking the edge of steel in the man's voice, the backbone with which he had, no doubt, forged a profitable business—a *very* profitable business, according to half of White's.

"Of course, sir," Monty said. "I trust you can forgive my transgression of last night, which arose from being caught in the moment."

"Of course you're forgiven, Your Grace!" Lady Howard cried. "Isn't he, Leonard?"

Sir Leonard rolled his eyes, and Monty found himself pitying the man. Miss Howard had been right. Only after marriage did a man learn the true nature of the object of his affections—at which point, it was too late, and he was yoked for life.

Miss Howard rose to her feet.

"Eleanor, your father doesn't want you to be party to the

conversation," Lady Howard said.

Miss Howard colored. "I know, Mother—I merely fancied taking in the air. That is, if you'll excuse me, Your Grace."

Monty took her hand and lifted it to his lips. "Until tomorrow, Miss Howard," he said. "Shall I call at noon?"

"Yes, do," Lady Howard said, before her daughter could respond. Ignoring her, Monty waited until Miss Howard lifted her gaze. They stared at each other for a heartbeat, then she lowered her eyes.

What might those eyes look like widened in surprise and pleasure in the throes of her climax while she screamed his name?

His body tightened at the notion, and she curled her fingers around his hand, sending a ripple of desire across his skin.

What the devil was happening to him? Had his promise not to rut another woman for the rest of the Season addled his mind? Celibacy was not a state that came naturally to him. Since his first awakening to carnal pleasure at the hands of a doxy, he'd taken his fill night after night, until he became a master of the pleasures of the flesh—both his pleasure, and that of the women he bedded. Why, then, had he promised to abstain?

To prove yourself worthy of her.

He bade his leave of Lady Howard and her daughter, then followed Sir Leonard into his study. Now the real ordeal of the day was about to begin. Monty had to convince a respectable, honorable, and, by all accounts, sharp-as-a-whip businessman that he was worthy of the man's daughter—something which he knew, as an undisputed certainty, that he could never be.

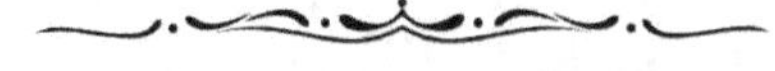

CHAPTER FIFTEEN

"**E**LEANOR, COME QUICK, he's here!"

Mother's voice echoed from downstairs, and Eleanor dropped her hairbrush.

Her maid picked it up. "Here, let me, Miss Eleanor," she said brightly. "You're all fingers and thumbs today!"

"Thank you, Harriet. I can't think what's come over me."

"*I* can, miss," the maid said as she brushed Eleanor's hair and secured it in a chignon. "There! You look quite lovely."

"I don't—"

"That's enough of *that*," Harriet said, placing a hand on Eleanor's shoulder. "You're always thinking bad of yourself—but the duke must have a reason for offering for you."

Yes—to deceive his mother.

"Where *are* you?" the voice cried again. "Tiresome child!"

"Coming, Mother!" Eleanor called out.

She exited her bedchamber and almost collided with her mother in the hallway.

"What is *that* you're wearing, child?"

Eleanor glanced at her dress—a gown of white muslin with a simple blue sash. "What's wrong with what I'm wearing?"

Her mother let out a sharp sigh. "I told Harriet to set out the pink dress—it's much more feminine than *that* dreadful thing."

"I like this dress," Eleanor said. "It's more comfortable in this heat, and—"

"Don't answer back! Lord save me, child, why must you always disappoint your poor mother? You want to look pretty for the duke, don't you?"

Before Eleanor could say that the last thing she wanted was to look pretty for anybody, there came a knock on the front door. Her mother took her wrist, ushered her into the morning room, and sat her down just as a footman appeared with Whitcombe.

Eleanor's heart fluttered, as it always did when she caught sight of him. Part of her had hoped he'd not turn up—but another part had yearned to see him again.

"Your Grace!" Mother cried. "How kind of you to—"

"Lady Howard." He inclined his head, a curl of amusement on his lips. "And Miss Howard."

His gaze lingered on Eleanor, and heat bloomed in her cheeks. What if he disliked her gown?

He reached into his pocket and pulled out a ring. "May I?"

Eleanor stared at the ring—it was enormous! The central emerald, surrounded by a cluster of diamonds, was huge. Clear-cut facets caught the light, reflecting it outward and shimmering deep inside with notes of blue and turquoise, as if the gem were a living entity.

Surely he wasn't entrusting her with *that*?

"Eleanor—where are your manners?" Her mother gave her a sharp nudge, and she glanced up to see Whitcombe looking directly at her, amusement in his eyes.

Was she nothing but an object of ridicule?

She lifted her hand and found it enveloped in a strong, firm grip. Then his fingers slid through hers, caressing the third finger of her left hand, before he slipped the ring on.

"A perfect fit!" Mother cried. "It's as if it were made for you, Eleanor."

Eleanor cringed. Why did Mother have to be so overly enthusiastic? What must he think of them?

But a smile gleamed in his eyes, and her heart fluttered with pleasure.

"Perhaps it was," he said.

"You must forgive my daughter, Your Grace," Mother continued. "She has a delightful day dress, which I'd hoped she would wear today—from Madame Chassineux. Do you know her?"

He inclined his head.

"But," Mother continued, "she chose not to wear it."

Irritation sparked in his eyes. "Your daughter's dress is delightful, Lady Howard," he said. "I've always wondered why young women feel the need to wear an overly bright dress merely to take a turn outside."

"A young woman must always look her best, Your Grace."

"Perhaps she already does."

What did he mean by that? Did he see little point in Eleanor dressing herself up in finery, given that she was too plain to carry it off with any success?

"Now, Lady Howard, you must excuse us," he said. "My driver is waiting."

He took Eleanor's arm and led her outside. An enormous barouche bearing the Whitcombe crest waited at the front steps, a liveried driver and two horses, their pelts shining in the morning sun, at the front. The horses moved restlessly, as if they anticipated the exercise, scraping their hooves on the road, and Eleanor caught the aroma of polished leather and the glint of brass, which reflected the sunlight as they tossed their heads.

"Whoa there!" the driver said. "Ready, Your Grace?"

Whitcombe helped Eleanor into the barouche, then he climbed in after her, and they set off.

HYDE PARK LOOKED different from a barouche—either due to the elevated position or because Eleanor no longer needed to continually check the ground for obstacles, lest she trip over her feet. But though she tried to lose herself in the beauty of her surroundings, her attention was continually drawn to the man beside her—his broad, masculine form, the faint aroma of wood and spices, and the warmth from his body. Her senses struggled to manage such an onslaught, and she found herself gripping the side of the barouche in an attempt to steady the tremors in her body.

A hand caught hers, and she startled.

"Are you well, Miss Howard? The motion of a carriage can bring about nausea to those unused to it."

"My father keeps a carriage, Your Grace," Eleanor said.

"Forgive me—I meant no offense," he said. "I spoke out of concern for your health. But, in turn, I must admonish *you*."

Her stomach tightened in apprehension. "What for?"

He stroked her fingers. "I recall asking you to call me Montague."

"B-but…"

"Might you indulge me?"

His tongue seemed to linger on the word *indulge*.

"M-Montague…" She cringed at the familiar address on her tongue, but she couldn't deny the secret thrill in the pit of her stomach at having his name on her lips.

"Hmmm," he murmured. "I shall have to be content with that. And now, I believe it's time for your first lesson. Modern languages."

"What language?"

"The most puerile language of them all. The language of Society—when one says nothing, but still manages to utter so many words."

"And when one speaks in riddles all the time," Eleanor said. "Will you teach me the riddles everyone speaks?"

"What riddles?"

"The other night, Lady Arabella said something to my sister about the Duke of Westbury's son being born in a—a blanket? I cannot work out her meaning."

His expression hardened. "Do you perchance mean being

born on the wrong side of the blanket?"

"That was it—yes! But the duke didn't seem to take the remark with favor. Do you know what Arabella meant by it?"

"It means the lad is Westbury's natural son." He sighed. "No wonder Westbury was angry. He's had men horsewhipped for referring to the boy's birth."

"Well, *I* see nothing wrong," Eleanor said. "Don't all men wish for a natural child?"

"A natural child is more trouble than it's worth, Miss Howard," he said, his voice stern. "My own father…" He shook his head. "Suffice it to say, my mother never forgave him."

"Now *you're* speaking in riddles," she said. "You're a natural child, aren't you? As am I."

"I'm no such thing! Do you think I'd be in possession of a title if I were?"

"I don't understand," Eleanor said.

"I'm saying…" he began, his voice laced with anger. Then he stopped and let out a cry. "Of course!" He laughed. "You assume *natural* to mean a child by birth, instead of, say, a ward."

First he was angry—now he was making fun of her. Could this day get any worse?

"Is there any other meaning?" she asked, blinking back tears.

His expression softened. "The expression refers to a child"—he lowered his voice—"born out of wedlock."

Her cheeks flamed, and she averted her gaze. No wonder Westbury had looked so furious—he must have thought she was insulting his son.

"I-I did not know," she said. "Is that why he's called Drayton, not Westbury?"

"Drayton is the family name," he said, "but the title is the Duchy of Westbury. Master Edward can take his father's surname, but not the title—in that, he's had to defer to his younger brother."

Eleanor shook her head. "You must think me terribly stupid not to know these things."

"The last word I'd use to describe you is stupid, Miss Howard," he said gently, taking her hand again. "The language of Society doesn't come as naturally to you as it does to most. Just as, say, the skills of the artist don't come naturally to most, yet you possess them to a greater degree."

"Me?"

"I hear you're an accomplished artist," he said. "The duchess told me as much the other night. And I saw it for myself that morning, when I encountered...*Harriet* in this very park at daybreak."

What must he think of her—using her maid's name and creeping about the park at dawn?

He smiled. "Your secret's safe with me. A young woman disposed to adventure in pursuit of accomplishment is to be admired."

"I don't draw for accomplishment."

He assaulted her with his sapphire gaze. "Then why *do* you draw, Miss Howard?"

Eleanor hesitated. Nobody had asked her that before.

"I suppose it's because I have to, Your Grace"—he squeezed her hand—"Montague."

"There!" he said. "Was that so difficult? Does someone compel you to paint?"

She shook her head. "The compulsion comes from within. Every time I see a blank page, I find myself driven by the urge to cover it with marks, to express what I see around me, and how I feel. It's...it's like I'm filled with water—filled to bursting, sometimes, and the only release I can find is to pour it out onto the page. As I move my hand about the page, creating shapes that are blurred, at first, then come into focus, the more detail I put in. Then, when the picture begins to form, it's like..." Unable to articulate the feeling, she made a random gesture in the air. "It's like I'm forming myself—becoming whole. And I cannot rest until the form is completed, until I've captured it fully on the page. Only then have I eased the ache from within..."

She paused to draw breath. What, in the name of heaven, had compelled her to make such a speech—to expose herself so fully—and to *him*, of all people? He must think her wits addled.

Or worse…

Unfit for the world. That was what she'd overheard Mother say to Papa one night after a particularly distressing party—the same party when she'd inadvertently trodden on Mr. Moss's toe during a dance, when the harsh voices, bright lights, cacophony of colors, and crowds of people had driven her into herself. One moment she was being crushed by all around her, her mind desperately attempting to withdraw to safety, and the next she was in Papa's arms in the carriage, Mother and Juliette's admonishments filling the air.

Eleanor cringed and lowered her gaze, waiting for the ridicule. But instead, a warm hand cupped her chin and gently tipped her face up.

She looked up, anticipating the discomfort of his gaze. But she saw no contempt, only wonder, and she was reminded of the moment when he took care of her after she'd been overcome by Juliette's taunts.

Finding she'd been holding her breath, she slid her gaze sideways and exhaled.

"There!" he said softly. "You can articulate yourself very well when speaking of something about which you're *passionate*."

She felt a pulse of longing as he uttered that last word, and tried to withdraw, but he moved closer. Their thighs touched.

"Forgive me," she said. "Mother's always telling me not to rattle on."

"Miss Howard, you can rattle on as much as you like, given that you have something *real* to say," he said. "What do you like to draw the most?"

"I draw anything in which I see beauty."

"Including a tree stump."

Was he ridiculing her?

"Most would overlook a tree stump," she said. "But that's

because they lack the ability to look—*really* look—at a subject. They're so caught up in what Society deems to be visually pleasing that they fail to look beneath the surface to observe the character within."

"And you find character in a tree stump?"

"Character is to be found in *everything* if one bothers to look. A tree stump might not conform to the niceties of Society, but I'll wager it has experienced more of life than most. Consider its history—it might have stood, towering over the park for decades, and though the tree is gone, the stump remains. It's only right that the artist gives it due consideration when drawing it, to reflect all that it has been, which can be seen in the texture of the bark, the deep cracks, within which all manner of tiny creatures have made their home…" She shook her head. "Oh dear, I'm speaking nonsense again."

"I applaud *your* nonsense, Miss Howard. It is much to be preferred over the nonsense one hears in drawing rooms. But I must ask whether you confine your talents to trees, or whether you employ them to draw likenesses of people?"

"I've drawn portraits," she said, "though they're not always appreciated."

"Why not?" he asked. "I find it difficult to believe you lack the talent, though I understand drawing true likenesses can be a challenge."

"I depict people as *I* see them, not as they wish to be seen."

"Which is entirely consistent with your character."

"You understand my character, Your Grace?"

"I'm beginning to, yes," he said. "Rather than converse in riddles to conform to Society, you speak—and depict—the absolute truth. Whether that gives offense is no reflection of your character, Miss Howard, but that of others."

"Oh!" she cried. "You understand."

He lifted his hand and, with light fingertips, traced a line along the side of her face. Then he plucked a stray tendril of her hair and tucked it behind her ear, caressing her earlobe. Her breath caught, and she closed her eyes, relishing the sensation.

I believe I do understand you, Eleanor, as you understand me.

She opened her eyes to see him looking directly at her, a flicker of need in his eyes.

Had he spoken aloud? Or had she merely dreamed it, as she had dreamed of him so many times before?

Then he lowered his hand, and her heart ached at the sense of loss.

"Would you permit me to see some of your portraits?" he asked.

Heavens! What would he think if he saw her portraits of him? There must be fifty, at least, each one revealing how she saw him—as a demigod. If he thought her soft in the head already, then one perusal of her sketchbook would confirm his suspicions.

"Forgive my forwardness, Miss Howard," he said. "It's not for me to ask such a thing. I merely wish to know you better."

Her heart leaped with hope. "Do you?"

"Of course. Any betrothed couple is expected to be well acquainted with each other. And we must convince the world that we are betrothed—at least until we part."

Eleanor swallowed her disappointment at the blunt reminder of the falsity of their circumstances.

"Yes, I suppose so," she mumbled.

"Excellent!" he said brightly. "And now, rather than continue with my inquisition, I should begin your first lesson in the language of the *dim-witted Society miss.*"

He winked, and she couldn't help smiling. Of course they'd part once their game was over. But, rather than wallow in self-pity over the inevitable ending, she should enjoy the time they had.

"Shall we begin with a few simple phrases, Miss Howard?"

She nodded.

"Good—very good. Now, you must repeat each phrase after me, then I'll explain its true meaning."

He glanced around the park, where people milled about—

couples strolling beside the Serpentine, children herded by their governesses, lone gentlemen riding along the path, their horses' tails swishing in the air to deflect the flies.

Eleanor's gaze settled on a small party ahead, Lady Arabella Ponsford together with Lady Irma Fairchild, and—*oh my*—they were accompanied by Mr. Moss.

"What is it, Miss Howard?" her companion asked, concern in his voice.

"Th-there's someone I know ahead."

"You mean the Ladies Arabella and Irma, and Mr. Moss? You've nothing to fear from *them*."

"I doubt that," she said. "I once trod on Mr. Moss's toe at a ball, and he's never let me forget—neither has Lady Arabella. She always gets the better of me."

"Then let us remedy that," he said. "Now, on first greeting an acquaintance, you ought to remark on the weather, or her state of health."

"Even if I have nothing of interest to say about either?"

"Precisely," he said. "Society language isn't intended to garner interest. It's merely the steps in a particularly dull dance to navigate oneself from one end of the ballroom to another. So, with Lady Arabella, you could begin your greeting by saying, 'I trust you are well.' Or, if you wish to elicit a response, you could ask her a question, such as 'And how are you on this fine day?'"

"Even if I care not one jot how she is?"

He let out a laugh. "The less we care about the person to whom we're speaking, the more we should enthuse over them."

"So, we should say the opposite of how we're feeling?" Eleanor asked. Then she glanced ahead at Lady Arabella arm in arm with Lady Irma.

"With that in mind," her companion said, "what might you say to greet Lady Arabella?"

Eleanor paused, watching the lady in question glide across the lawn, her pretty little nose stuck in the air as if the world around her elicited a particularly bad smell, and her dress a megriminducing riot of color.

Then the words came to her. "Good morning, Lady Arabella," she said. "How delightful to see you today."

"Excellent!" he said. "Though you might wish to place more emphasis on the 'delightful.' Perhaps you could remark on her dress."

"She looks like a peacock that's exploded."

He let out a laugh. "However marked her likeness is to disintegrated wildfowl, you must never speak the truth."

"Won't she know I'm being false?"

"Falsity is akin to social acceptance," he said. "All you need do is look her in the eye and speak firm. Come—we're nearing them. I insist you try."

Eleanor's heart gave a little jolt. "I don't know…"

"I have every faith in you," he said. "And, rest assured, I'm on your side in this particular battle."

"You are?"

He nodded. "I'll be here, as your faithful soldier, to catch you lest you fall. But you must win the battle. The trick is to be the one to fire the opening salvo."

He squeezed her fingers, and she drew strength from his firm grip.

Then he rapped on the side of the barouche, and they drew to a halt. Lady Arabella glanced up. Her dark eyes widened as she caught sight of Eleanor, and her lips parted in surprise. She really was one of the most beautiful creatures to walk upon the earth. Eleanor could never hope to get the better of her.

She glanced from Lady Arabella to Lady Irma, who wore an identical expression of surprise and disdain. Then she turned her gaze to Mr. Moss, who leered at her, eyes the color of ice glittering in the sunlight.

Whitcombe whispered in her ear, his warm breath tickling her neck.

"Courage…"

Lady Arabella opened her mouth to speak. It was now or

never.

"Lady Arabella!" Eleanor cried, with as much force as she could muster. "What an utter delight to see you—and your charming friends. Lady Irma—and Mr. Moss, of course."

Arabella's eyes narrowed with suspicion. And with good reason. Eleanor had scarcely spoken more than ten words to her in her entire life.

Then she inclined her head in greeting. "Miss Howard—likewise," she said.

"I trust you're well," Eleanor continued. "It pains me that I missed the opportunity to speak with you during the Westburys' ball. I was most concerned for your health."

"My health?"

"Yes," Eleanor said, suppressing the urge to laugh. "As the evening drew to a close, I fancied you were looking a little pale." She turned to her companion. "Did you not think so, Your Grace?"

"Lady Arabella always looks the picture of beauty," Whitcombe said, and Arabella threw Eleanor a look of spiteful triumph. "But," he continued, "I confess you looked out of spirits later in the evening. Some disappointment, perhaps?"

Arabella's mouth twisted into a scowl.

"Perhaps Lady Arabella was disappointed not to have *you* to accompany her, Mr. Moss," Eleanor said. "You're always so sprightly on your feet."

"I'm not flat-footed, to be sure," Mr. Moss replied. "Miss Howard, you're the last person I expected to see at large. I thought you were averse to company."

"I'm merely particular about the company I keep," Eleanor replied.

"But not averse to indulging in the hunt for a title."

Eleanor's courage wavered. She opened her mouth to respond, but the words refused to come.

"I trust you weren't impugning my fiancée's behavior," Whitcombe said, his voice a low growl.

"O-of course not," Mr. Moss said, his cheeks reddening. "I wish her every happiness—and you, of course."

Lady Arabella grimaced, rendering her face quite ugly. "Your Grace, I hadn't thought your antics of the other night to be sincere."

The remnants of Eleanor's courage deserted her. Arabella, and most likely the rest of Society, could never be convinced their engagement was real.

Then Eleanor's companion took her left hand and raised it. Lady Arabella's eyes widened as her gaze settled on the emerald ring.

"How kind of you to express such concern, Lady Arabella," he said. "I acted in haste out of the violence of my affections. But, as you can see, I am now treating Miss Howard with the respect she deserves, and I applaud you for showing her the same respect."

By now, Eleanor had recovered, and she smiled at her adversary. "We *both* applaud you, Lady Arabella, for your kindness," she said. "Rest assured, the degree of kindness that you have always bestowed upon me is not something I'll easily forget."

Eleanor could swear she heard a small snort from her companion.

Lady Arabella's expression clouded with confusion. "I-it was nothing," she said.

"And now, we must take our leave," Whitcombe said. "My objective in coming to the park today was not to display my ostentation to the world"—Eleanor suppressed a giggle as he glanced pointedly at Lady Arabella's dress—"but to enjoy the company of my fiancée. Drive on!"

The barouche lurched into motion, and Lady Arabella and her companions stepped back to make room.

"Don't look back," Whitcombe said, almost as if he'd read her mind. "They're not deserving of our attention. Now, shall we continue our lesson? What might you say if you were attending a dinner party and the meal was nauseating, but your hostess has asked whether you enjoyed it?"

"Such as Lady Fairchild's ball last month?" Eleanor asked.

He smiled. "Precisely. I swear, I almost lost a tooth on the steak."

"Yes, it was somewhat tough," Eleanor said. "I told her as much when she asked me, though I fear she took offense."

"Ha!" he said. "You said what the whole party was thinking. Bravo!"

Bravo, indeed! Her honest answer had earned her a tongue lashing from Mother.

"What might you say now?" he asked.

"I'd say, 'Very delicious, thank you, Lady Fairchild.'"

"Oh, you can do better than that," he said. "You must find a way to speak the truth to maintain your integrity, yet utter a socially acceptable response."

"Very well." She pondered for a moment, then nodded. "How about: 'Lady Fairchild, I have never tasted anything quite like this. Your cook is incomparable.'"

"Excellent!" he cried. "Are you attending Lady Francis's ball next week? We can test the principles you have learned on living specimens."

"And in the most hostile of environments," she said. "A Society party."

He let out a laugh, and her heart somersaulted at the beautiful expression in his eyes.

"I foresee a successful experiment," he said. "I'll make a lady of you yet."

His words, though intended to praise, doused Eleanor's confidence, serving only to remind her of her inferiority. To him, she was merely an experiment—an awkward creature whom he was teaching a few phrases to make her appear socially acceptable.

But to Eleanor—after he'd come to her rescue against her would-be tormentors—he was in danger of making her infatuation grow into something infinitely more dangerous...

Love.

CHAPTER SIXTEEN

AFTER RETURNING MISS Howard home, Monty stopped off at White's for luncheon—all that talk of steak had whetted his appetite, and the cook at White's, unlike the poisoner employed by Lady Fairchild, could, at least, cook a passable steak, by virtue of knowing the difference between *medium rare* and *charred to within an inch of its life*. Then, having waved off his barouche after he'd arrived at White's, he set off on foot to his townhouse.

As he neared his home, he spotted a carriage waiting at the front of his house.

Who the devil might that be? Neither he nor Mother were expecting visitors.

Had Sir Leonard come to discuss the finer points of the marriage settlement? Or perhaps he'd discovered Monty's ruse and had come to confront him over using his eldest daughter for his own nefarious purpose.

Which would be a pity, because despite Sir Leonard's low birth, Monty had found himself admiring the man.

There was considerably more to Sir Leonard than the persona he displayed in public. He was a combination of the two most formidable specimens of his sex: the businessman who made his fortune through hard work, insight, and a sharp eye for detail; and the father, stern and resolute in his determination to ensure the happiness of a most beloved daughter.

Sir Leonard put the rest of his sex to shame.

Including Monty himself.

He approached the carriage, then recognized the Whitcombe crest on the side. The carriage was his.

A liveried footman appeared, carrying a trunk, which he secured on the back of the carriage, then the driver strode into view.

"Thompson?" Monty called out. "What is all this? Surely you're not having to go out again? The horses will be tired, and—"

"There you are, at last!" a sharp voice cried.

Monty's mother stood at the top of the front steps, holding a valise, flanked by her maid and a footman.

"Mother? Are you going somewhere?"

"I'd have thought that was obvious, Montague," she huffed. "I'm returning to Rosecombe."

"We're not to go for weeks yet."

"*We* are not going. *I'm* going."

"Why?"

"Must I justify myself to you?" She held up her valise and gestured to her maid. "Well? What are you waiting for, Dora?"

"Pardon me, ma'am." The maid took the valise, bobbed a curtsey, then descended the steps, where the waiting footman helped her onto the back of the carriage. Monty's mother glided toward the carriage, then gave the footman a pointed look. The servant colored, then bowed and opened the carriage door.

"Is something the matter, Mother?" Monty asked.

"Don't be insolent. You know perfectly well there is."

"I accept it was remiss of me not to introduce Miss Howard to you before offering her my hand."

"No, Montague, it was remiss of you to offer for her at all," she replied. "I cannot believe you'd make such a spectacle of yourself—at the Westburys' party, of all places!"

"Is it the manner of my proposal that offends you, Mother, or my choice?"

"Both. But while I can forgive your unseemly behavior, I cannot understand why you'd cleave to a young woman rumored to be soft in the head."

Soft in the head—how dare she?

"Rumors!" Monty scoffed. "Since when must we be dictated by gossip?"

"Rumors are not without foundation, Montague. I ignored gossip to my cost once before—then I discovered the fruits of your father's infidelity. I shan't make the same mistake again."

"You can hardly compare Miss Howard to my sis—"

"Speak no more!" Mother cried. "Must you distress your poor mother so? That creature is *not* your sister! As for Miss Howard— Lady Fairchild has much to say about the girl's eccentricities. And Lady Francis called on me this morning to convey her sympathies."

Monty let out a snort. "Lady Francis is an empty-headed fool, with nothing but gowns and jewels on her mind."

"I will *not* be pitied!" she said. "If you must marry the girl, then so be it. But I shan't remain here to be ridiculed because of it." She reached into her reticule and drew out a handkerchief, dabbing it against her eyes. "Unless, of course," she added, "there's anything you might wish to say—or do—to ease your poor mother's heart."

He caught a glimmer of cunning in her expression before she dabbed her eyes again. Then she lowered her handkerchief— which, no doubt, was as dry now as it had been before—and looked at him expectantly.

Her show of fleeing to Rosecombe was a ruse. Perhaps she thought herself a gamester, attempting to persuade her opponent that she had the better hand.

Then he would do what any self-respecting player would— call her bluff.

He placed his hands on her shoulders and kissed her on the cheek. "Very well, Mother dearest," he said. "I shall bid you a safe journey."

Her eyes widened. "If you're resolved in this…"

"I am," he said.

"Then I wish you joy," she said, her tone conveying anything but. Then she nodded, and the footman helped her into the carriage.

Monty rapped the side of the carriage. "Drive on!"

The carriage set off, and he watched it roll away, the horses' hooves clip-clopping on the road. Then it turned a corner at the end of the street and disappeared.

CHAPTER SEVENTEEN

"SIT UP STRAIGHT, Eleanor!"

Eleanor jerked upright—a not inconsiderable feat, given that the carriage kept lurching sideways.

"No one can see me, Mother," she said.

"Why must you always answer back?" her mother retorted. "Leonard, tell her."

Eleanor's father raised an eyebrow, but said nothing.

"I was only stating a fact, Mother," Eleanor continued. "Can't I relax while we're not in public?"

"No. We must be wary at all times of being seen—especially now our family is connected to nobility."

"I'm not married yet," Eleanor said. "I—Ouch!"

Her mother rapped her across the arm with her fan. Eleanor drew her cloak around her and sat back.

"Eleanor, I *told* you not to slouch. I don't want the Fairchilds upstaging us because of your lack of decorum."

"Leave her be, Grace!" Papa said. He gestured to the carriage window, where raindrops battered the glass, forming rivulets that ran in jagged lines toward the sill. "The weather will ensure we're all on the same level tonight. We'll be soaked as soon as we step outside the carriage." He winked at Eleanor before resuming his attention on Mother. "Not to mention the horse dung underfoot from all the carriages. Knee deep we'll be, before we've even reached the front door."

"Not if our carriage arrives first."

Of that, there was little chance, given how long Juliette had spent fashioning her hair—an intricate array of ringlets and pearls that overshadowed the corsage of wild grasses Harriet had placed in Eleanor's hair.

The carriage drew to a halt, and Eleanor caught sight of a myriad of lights flickering in the evening air, and a crush of activity, that made her stomach churn.

So many people! Why did they take such joy from congregating in crowds?

Carriages lined the road, and footmen ran to and fro, carrying umbrellas and torches, as they escorted the guests toward the sanctuary of Lady Francis's front door.

If Lady Francis's house could be considered *sanctuary*.

Eleanor would have preferred to remain outside in the rainstorm. Outside, she could savor the fresh, clean water on her face, together with the unmistakable aroma of dust in rain—a veritable heaven compared to the chattering crowds with their sharp voices, shrill laughs, and bright colors that always tortured her senses.

"Oh, Mama!" Juliette cried. "The weather's ghastly—and we'll have to walk past all those carriages! Why didn't we leave earlier?"

"We would have done had your sister consented to wear the dress I'd chosen for her." Mother gave Eleanor a sharp glance. "I wanted you to look your best tonight—and you won't in that hideous thing."

"I like this gown," Eleanor said.

"Pink is *a la mode* this Season, not green. And you wore that dress at Lady Stiles's soiree last month. People will notice."

"Nobody will notice *me*," Eleanor said.

"*Everyone's* eyes will be on you tonight."

Eleanor suppressed a shudder.

"Which is why," Mother continued, "you must not let the family down. For Juliette's sake."

"For *Juliette?*"

"You mustn't take all the attention, Eleanor," Juliette said. "That would be selfish."

"Quite so," Mother added. "Juliette must not be without a partner tonight."

"The Duke of Dunton has asked to partner me for the first two dances," Juliette said.

"Excellent," Mother said. "But we mustn't grow complacent."

"You want to be courted by *Dunton*, do you?" Eleanor asked. "But he has a reputation for—"

"If you can secure a duke, why can't *I?*" Juliette said.

"Quite right, darling," Mother said. "You're the prettiest girl of the Season. Lady Fairchild says you're prettier even her Irma."

"What about Lady Arabella?" Juliette said. "Some say she's the prettiest."

"Ah, but she lacks your sweet disposition."

Eleanor met her father's gaze and bit her lips to stifle a giggle. Papa, unable to show similar restraint, let out a bark of laughter, which he disguised with a cough.

"Are you unwell, Leonard?" Mother asked.

"No, Grace, my love. The air's a little dry, that's all."

Mother glanced at the rain, which was forming a mist as it splashed off the pavement. She glanced at Papa and opened her mouth, but before she issued a reprimand, a face appeared at the window.

Montague.

Eleanor's stomach somersaulted. He was handsome enough in the middle of a ballroom, dressed in finery. But here—outside, his hair windswept and disheveled, with an undercurrent of primal savagery—he was breathtaking.

The door opened, and she was met with the full force of his gaze.

"Miss Howard, what a pleasure," he said. "Sir Leonard, Lady Howard—and Miss Juliette. Do you require assistance? This weather's not for the fainthearted."

"That's most kind, Your Grace," Mother said.

Whitcombe glanced over his shoulder. "My man!" he cried. "We're in need of assistance. You too, if you don't mind?"

Two footmen appeared. "Yes, Your Grace?" the first asked.

"Would you assist Sir Leonard and Lady Howard, and you"—Whitcombe turned to the second—"please attend to Miss Juliette."

Then his gaze returned to Eleanor. "I shall take Miss Howard."

A curl of desire licked through Eleanor's body at the possessive tone of his voice.

He barked orders to the footman as her parents and sister climbed out of the carriage. Then she found herself alone, with her betrothed, standing in the doorway. He reached out a hand, and she stared at it.

"Why the hesitation, Miss Howard? Were you not expecting me to attend you this evening?"

She continued to stare at his hand—his ungloved hand—and her body warmed at the anticipation of his touch.

Then he curled his fingers around her wrist. "Did you think I'd abandon you because our attachment is a sham?"

Must he remind her so brutally of their arrangement?

"In truth, I didn't know what to expect," she said, unable to disguise the bitterness in her voice. "I find myself unwilling to play the role of the happy guest merely for the sake of appearance."

"You wound me, Miss Howard, if you imply that you're incapable of enjoying my company."

"I'm sure you'd say the same about *my* company," she said, "and I understand that."

The mirth in his eyes died, and he lifted her hand to his lips. "How can you say such a thing, Miss Howard? I've been very much looking forward to spending the evening with you."

"Y-you *have?*"

"You think so little of yourself that you find it impossible that

I'd find your company agreeable?"

"Most people—"

"I'm not *most people*," he said. "And, before you lay an accusation of falsehood at my door, I give you my word that I shall never deceive you."

Eleanor's cheeks warmed under his scrutiny. How in heaven's name had he known precisely what she was thinking?

Then his expression softened. "You've every right to mistrust me, Miss Howard. But over the course of our…*arrangement*, I shall strive to earn your trust. Now, shall we?"

He helped her out of the carriage. She slipped on the bottom step and fell forward, but he caught her and held her close. Then he issued an order, and a footman ran toward them, holding an umbrella aloft.

"Take my arm, Miss Howard," he said. "It's treacherous underfoot."

Eleanor glanced at the road, slippery with the rain and laden with piles of horse dung, above which wisps of steam arose.

"The horses are insensitive to the guests' needs," Whitcombe said.

"Bravo to the horses," she replied. "*They* can act in any manner they choose without fear of admonishment."

"Nevertheless, I'd implore you to step carefully. Our equine friends seem to have been overly enthusiastic in depositing their—ahem—*gifts*."

She let out a giggle, while he picked a route toward the house. A cry of disgust rang out, followed by a sharp voice issuing a reprimand. A very familiar voice.

"I fear Lady Arabella Ponsford has suffered a calamity," Eleanor's escort said. "But, at least, it means we'll have early warning of her approach, even if we cannot see her."

"Early warning?"

"The odor of horse dung can be rather pungent indoors. I'll wager her shoes are smothered in the stuff."

"Perhaps I should step in a pile, if it'll ward off company,"

Eleanor said.

"*I* shall not be deterred," he replied. "I'd weather anything for the pleasure of *your* company."

"You promised not to flatter me, Your Grace," Eleanor said.

"What I promised was to be truthful," he said. "Now have a care—the ground is more treacherous near the steps."

Eleanor grasped her skirts and lifted them while she tiptoed over the piles of dung, taking care to ensure the hem was clear. Her companion helped her toward the steps, and when she glanced at him, she saw him staring at her ankles. Then she let her skirts fall, and he looked up and smiled.

"You're out of danger," he said, his voice hoarse, "from dung, at least."

Her blood warmed at the hunger in his eyes. Then he offered his arm and escorted her inside.

What had he meant, danger? A small voice whispered in her mind that it was a danger to be relished.

⋙✦⋘

AFTER THE INITIAL cloud of terror dissipated, Eleanor found herself enjoying a ball for the first time in her life. Whitcombe's presence wasn't as stifling as she'd expected, and she managed to conquer her body's instinct to flee from such a predatory male.

Then the musicians began tuning their instruments, indicating that the dancing was about to begin.

Couples lined up, forming sets of six, the ladies chatting gaily as if they'd been looking forward to the prospect of dancing all day.

Eleanor's partner led her toward the dance floor, and fear curled inside her stomach.

"Miss Howard, are you well?"

"Are you expecting me to…*dance*?"

"Is that not the principal reason for attending a ball?"

"Yes, b-but I…"

"Do you trust me?"

"I…" She hesitated, then he caught her chin in a firm, but gentle, grip.

"Look at me when you give me your answer…Eleanor."

He tilted her face, and she lifted her gaze. The bright sapphire of his eyes had darkened to the color of a midnight sky, and in their depths, she saw a flicker of desire.

He slid his fingers along her skin and stroked her cheek with his thumb. The air filled with the masculine scent of him, and she fought to contain the raw need curling through her body, but her legs crumpled beneath her.

Then, before she collapsed in a pile of undignified shame, he caught her in his arms and swept her onto the dance floor with the practiced movement of the expert seducer.

How many other women had he rendered helpless with a single touch?

Or was it just her—weak and unsophisticated as she was— unable to withstand such an assault on her senses?

She clung to him as he steered her toward two couples set apart from the rest. Her cheeks warmed with shame as she recognized the Duke and Duchess of Westbury, and the duke's eldest son. She didn't recognize the other woman.

Would Westbury rebuke her for having insulted his son's birth?

But, rather than frown, he smiled warmly.

"Miss Howard, how delightful to see you," he said. "You know my wife and son, of course."

"Thank you, Your Grace," Eleanor said. "And Mr. Drayton, I'm so pleased to see you again."

"As am I." The young man bowed, then gestured to his part- ner—a slender, sweet-faced woman in a pale blue gown. "Do you know Mrs. Trelawney?"

"I-I'm afraid not," Eleanor said, dipping into a curtsey. "A pleasure to meet you."

"Likewise, Miss Howard. I believe your father, Sir Leonard, conducts business with my husband—Mr. Ross Trelawney?"

"Oh, the wine merchant!" Eleanor said. "Papa speaks very highly of him, but I've never met him. Is he here tonight?"

"Alas, my husband is working tonight, of all things."

"So, poor Mrs. Trelawney must make do with *me*," Mr. Drayton added.

"If you're as accomplished a dance partner as you are a dinner companion, then Mrs. Trelawney is sure to elicit the envy of every woman in the room," Eleanor said.

"Ha!" Westbury said. "A pretty speech, Miss Howard. But I fear you've wounded poor Whitcombe. You're supposed to extol the virtues of *your* dance partner—not another's."

Oh, heavens, I've done it again! Why could she never think of the right thing to say?

"F-forgive me," Eleanor stammered. "I meant no offense."

"None was taken," Whitcombe said. "Westbury—don't be a tease. A man incapable of weathering the truth is no man at all. But I believe that, of all those dancing here tonight, we must pity Mr. Moss the most."

Eleanor turned and caught sight of Mr. Moss leading Lady Arabella Ponsford onto the dance floor.

Mrs. Trelawney let out a giggle, then suppressed it. "Whitcombe, for shame!" she cried. "Lady Arabella's an accomplished dancer."

"But perhaps less desirable with feet covered in horse dung," Westbury said. "I swear she's surrounded by a cloud of flies. But Moss always reeks of cologne, so is unlikely to notice the stench."

"Henry!" Westbury's wife admonished him. "If you continue, I'll insist *you* partner Lady Arabella for the next two dances as penance."

"Then I shall desist, to elude such a punishment." Westbury winked at Eleanor. "Ah!" he cried, as the musicians struck up a melody. "I've been saved by the music."

He led his wife toward the center of the dance floor, followed by his son and Mrs. Trelawney. Whitcombe steered Eleanor in their wake.

"I trust you'll not find the dancing unduly objectionable, Miss Howard," he said. "I've ensured we're among friends for *this* dance, at least."

"I don't understand."

"The Westburys are good company," he said, "and Mrs. Trelawney has the sweetest disposition. If I am to place you in that most hazardous of environments—the Society dance floor—then I must ensure you're surrounded by allies, rather than hostile forces."

"Hostile forces such as Mr. Moss and Lady Arabella?"

"Exactly!" he said. "Now, if you're unfamiliar with the steps, you'll pick them up soon enough. The pattern repeats itself, and you're in safe hands with me."

TRUE TO HIS word, Eleanor's partner steered her through the dance, issuing gentle instructions and soft praise throughout. Even when her ungainly body did not move as her mind intended, he guided her through the steps with his hands. And when the dance necessitated a change of partners, his replacements—Westbury, and then Westbury's son—displayed equal gallantry. Eleanor was almost ready to be persuaded to declare that she *liked* dancing.

When the dance concluded, Whitcombe steered her toward the edge of the room.

"Would you take a seat while I fetch you a drink?" he asked.

Eleanor glanced at the empty seats—each one surrounded by chattering misses and their enthusiastic mamas—and shuddered.

"Or perhaps you'd prefer to accompany me on my quest for refreshment?" he suggested. "If we're on foot, we can avoid the necessity of being engaged in conversation with others by simply walking away."

"I live in dread of finding somewhere quiet to sit, then being joined by someone who wishes to engage in conversation," she said. "I always feel obliged to say something back when people talk at me. I'd rather they left me alone, but I fear I'd offend them if I said as much."

"What would you do if Lady Arabella sat beside you?" he asked, mischief in his eyes.

"I wouldn't know *what* to say."

"Miss Howard, have you learned nothing from our tutorial in the park?"

"Very well," she said. "I'd say, 'Lady Arabella, what an unusual cologne you're wearing—most distinctive. I'm quite overcome.'"

"And to Mr. Moss?"

"I might ask him how he's able to hold a conversation with Lord Francis—and maintain his composure."

"Why Lord Francis?"

Eleanor lowered her voice. "Mr. Moss is indulging in liaisons with Lady Francis."

He glanced about the ballroom, then shook his head. "You must be mistaken. They're at opposite ends of the room."

"And have been all evening," she said. "*Diagonally* opposite ends of the room."

"Does that make a difference?"

"Of course," she replied. "A diagonal is longer than a straight edge. Therefore, by placing themselves at diagonally opposite ends, they maximize the distance between them. Now—why would a couple maintain the maximum distance apart for most of an evening?"

"Coincidence?"

"Perhaps if it happened occasionally, but I noticed it at Lady Fairchild's party—and again at the Westburys' ball, where…"

Her voice trailed away at the memory of *that* particular evening.

"They've never danced," she continued, "and they're never sat close to each other at the dinner table. I've only noticed two interactions between them all Season."

"Which are?"

"At Lady Fairchild's ball, they arrived at the same time, exchanged a glance, then moved rapidly away from each other—as if they were afraid of being seen in close proximity."

"And at the Westburys' ball?"

"Lady Francis paused to wipe a speck of dust from Mr. Moss's sleeve as she was walking past him."

"What's so unusual about that?" he asked. "Certain fabrics are notorious for attracting fluff. My valet is always brushing my jackets."

"Your valet, yes, but would you expect a guest at a ball—a *married lady*—to perform such a personal service?"

"What's so personal about brushing a man's jacket?"

"Think about it, Your Grace," Eleanor said, emboldened by her conviction. "Why should a woman care about a man's jacket? Most ladies might remark on a man's appearance, or utter some witticism at his valet's expense. But what woman would do something about it—and in such an absent-minded manner that implies a degree of familiarity? Can you think of an act more intimate?"

"As a matter of fact, I can, Miss Howard—a very intimate act indeed."

Eleanor's cheeks warmed at the low growl in his tone.

"You can hardly expect them to engage in—in…"

"*Intimate* acts?" he asked, a slow smile curling his lips.

"Not in the middle of a dance floor."

"No—I find a hallway infinitely preferable for such an act, where all manner of delicacies can be savored."

Eleanor swallowed, overcome with shame at the indecipherable urge deep within her body at the notion of *intimacy*. Once again she was reminded of how much more…*sophisticated* he was, and how he would, most likely, laugh at the prospect of finding her even remotely attractive.

"Yes, Miss Howard. I believe you're right," he said.

Sweet heaven! Had she spoken aloud?

Eleanor blinked back the moisture in her eyes. "I-I *am?*"

"About Lady Francis," he said. "One can often form conclusions based on what goes unnoticed rather than what is meant to be seen."

"There's merit in going unnoticed, Your Grace."

He drew her close. "Did I not ask you to call me Montague?"

"M-Montague," she breathed, savoring his name on her tongue.

"That's better," he said, his breath fanning her cheek. "I like hearing my name on your lips."

The hoarseness in his tone suggested some kind of impropriety, but what, exactly, she couldn't fathom.

"I find myself wondering if there's anything else that's caught your eye, but is invisible to others."

There it was again—the suggestion in his tone of something wicked.

"I suppose…" She hesitated, then glanced about her until she caught sight of their hostess. "There's the painting."

"What painting?"

"In the hallway—we passed it earlier."

"Ah," he said, the gravelly tone returning to his voice. "Are you inviting me into the hallway because you have something in particular to show me?"

His eyes darkened, and Eleanor was once again besieged by the notion that he was speaking in an entirely different language—a language she could never hope to understand.

"There's a painting in the hallway that I presume is meant to be a Stubbs," she said. "The painting of the horse."

"Stubbs is supposed to be a master, isn't he?"

"*Was,*" she said. "He died in the year 1806. I've always wanted to study one of his paintings. But I haven't had the opportunity."

"There's one at my country seat, I believe," he said.

"You *believe*?"

He shrugged. "I may be mistaken—there's a painting of a horse in the drawing room. Commissioned by my grandfather, if I recall, when he owned racehorses."

How could he not know whether a painting he owned was a *Stubbs*? But, perhaps, in having so much, he placed no value on what he owned.

A warm hand took hers. "My betrothed is disappointed in me."

"O-of course not," she said, averting her gaze, lest he employ his uncanny ability to read her thoughts.

"You'd be justified," he continued. "I've had no need to appreciate what I have. But no man appreciates what he has until he's in danger of losing it—or has lost it altogether. Would you like to view my Stubbs? Assuming it *is* a Stubbs—you can tell me whether it's genuine or not. In fact, I've been wondering whether to invite you to—"

He broke off, his expression hardening.

"Whitcombe!" a voice cried. "I thought it was you—why the devil are you not dancing? The ladies will be disappointed!"

Eleanor turned to see a tall man approaching. With thick blond locks, strong facial features, and an athletic frame that filled his perfectly tailored jacket to perfection, he might have been the handsomest man in the room were it not for Whitcombe.

"Sawbridge," Whitcombe said.

The man glanced at Eleanor, his eyes widening. He lowered his gaze to her feet, then followed a path along her body, as if devouring her form. Her cheeks warmed as his gaze settled briefly on her neckline. Then he met her gaze, and she looked away.

"Aren't you going to introduce us, old chap?" he asked.

Whitcombe tightened his grip on Eleanor's hand. "My dear—may I introduce you to the Duke of Sawbridge. Sawbridge—this is my fiancée—"

"Capital!" Sawbridge cried. "I'm anxious to know the woman who's tamed the most committed bachelor in England. You must possess considerable...*talents*, Miss Howard. Might you enlighten me as to what they are?"

"Well, I—" Eleanor began, but Whitcombe interrupted.

"There's nothing about Miss Howard that can interest you, Sawbridge. You should bestow your attentions on a worthier specimen."

Worthier? Must he insult her so publicly?

She tried to withdraw her hand, but he tightened his grip.

"There's no need to tell me more, dear boy," Sawbridge said. "I understand."

"Understand what?" Eleanor couldn't help asking, painfully aware of the bitterness in her voice.

Sawbridge leaned closer and lowered his voice. "Have you lifted your skirts yet?"

"Yes, I have."

He let out a roar of laughter. "Sampled the goods already, eh, Whitcombe?"

Goods? What did he mean? Why did everyone speak in a different language?

She was out of her depth among these people—a drowning woman, weighed down by lack of understanding, in a bottomless ocean.

Tears pricked at her eyes. "I-I don't understand," she said.

"Miss Howard was jesting with you, Sawbridge," Whitcombe said, drawing Eleanor close. "She's a virtuous woman—not the sort to lift her skirts."

"B-but I had to, to step over all that horse dung this evening," she said. "Or I'd have soiled my hem."

Whitcombe let out a sharp sigh and muttered something to himself.

"It seems the rumors are true." Sawbridge laughed. "You're safe from ridicule, Whitcombe. Want of understanding is a quality prized in a wife—there's no shame in being married to a woman who's weak in the head."

With a blur of movement, Whitcombe sprang forward and caught hold of Sawbridge around the throat.

"There's no need for—*Argh!*" Sawbridge broke off, and Eleanor shivered at the grim determination in Whitcombe's eyes as he tightened his grip.

"Say no more, Sawbridge, unless you wish to meet me at dawn," he said, his voice low and cold. "And believe me, I'm not so gentlemanly as to shoot wide when my opponent has insulted the finest woman in the room."

Sawbridge opened his mouth to speak, but no sound came.

"Miss Howard is worth *twenty* of you, Sawbridge. I insist you apologize—or suffer the consequences."

For a heartbeat, the two men stared at each other. Then, like a rival bear in the face of the dominant male, Sawbridge lowered his gaze in submission. But Whitcombe continued to hold him, his body vibrating with anger, like a gladiator.

Or a champion.

Eleanor touched his arm. "Let him go, Your Grace."

"Do you think he deserves it?" Whitcombe asked.

"We're in a crowded room. Someone might see."

"I care not if they do."

"He's not said anything I haven't heard before," she said. "Would you call out every person who says I lack understanding or calls me an oddity? If you do, you'll be meeting men—and women—at dawn for the remainder of the Season."

"Then I shall rise before dawn, each and every day, until I've dealt with them all."

He released Sawbridge, who clasped his throat.

"I believe you have something to say to my fiancée."

"I apologize unreservedly, Miss Howard, for any offense caused," Sawbridge said. Then he clicked his heels together and bowed his head before retreating.

Whitcombe lifted Eleanor's hand to his lips. "I also apologize on Sawbridge's behalf," he said. "And I should apologize on behalf of every creature who's looked at you and seen an oddity, as opposed to the truth."

"And what *is* the truth?" she asked.

A smile danced in his eyes, and their dark expression softened into tenderness.

"The truth, I'm beginning to realize, is that of all the company here tonight, I find yours the most agreeable."

She turned away, but he cupped her chin, and a thrill rippled through her body at his touch.

"No, Eleanor," he said, and her stomach flip-flopped at the way he curled his tongue round her name. "Don't look away from me in disbelief. I will never be untruthful where you're concerned."

The finest woman in the room…

That was what he'd said to Sawbridge not a minute before. Which meant…

No, you fool! He'll never love you back—the sooner you accept that, the better.

No matter how deeply she ached to be loved by him, or how vehemently he championed her—she needed to heed the voice of reason. When they parted ways at the end of the Season, he'd forget her within a sennight.

CHAPTER EIGHTEEN

MISS HOWARD SEEMED to transform before Monty's eyes—and it was all Sawbridge's fault. Beneath her uncongenial exterior lived a vibrant personality and a sharp mind, which had flourished during the dance, and again as they conversed afterward. But she retreated back into her shell after Sawbridge's talk of tossing up skirts. At first, Monty had thought her embarrassed at talk that was best indulged in the company of men—or harlots. But then he realized that the poor girl had no notion of Sawbridge's meaning.

Sawbridge was right in that she lacked understanding. But it wasn't due to slowness of the mind. In fact, it was her intelligence that hampered her—she interpreted what others said in a literal, logical fashion, and responded likewise.

A voice rose above the chatter in the ballroom—a footman declaring the arrival of more guests.

"Lord and Lady Marlow!"

A smile illuminated Miss Howard's eyes.

"Lavinia!"

"You know the Marlows?" Monty asked.

She nodded. "Lavinia—I mean, Lady Marlow—is my friend."

"We must call them over." He caught sight of Marlow's blond head among the crowd and raised his arm. "Marlow—over here!"

The crowd parted to reveal Marlow and his wife. Lady Marlow was pretty enough, but she always seemed a little out of place in Society. Which perhaps explained why she and Miss Howard were friends—misfits in a world that valued conformity and despised anyone who differed.

As they approached, Lady Marlow's eyes sparkled with delight as her gaze settled on Miss Howard. But, as she glanced at Monty, their expression hardened. She stared at him—too boldly, even for the wife of an earl apparent, to stare at a duke. Then she raked her gaze over his body, but with cold detachment rather than the heated desire he was used to—as if she were sizing him up.

Devil's toes! A stare like that was enough to castrate a man at fifty paces.

And yet Marlow—the witless fool—stared at his wife with slavish devotion.

"Your Grace." Lady Marlow dipped into the slightest of curtseys. Then she turned to Miss Howard and a smile transformed her features, like the sun bursting through a thundercloud. "Eleanor, I'm so glad you're here." She took Miss Howard's hands. "Have you been enjoying yourself?" She glanced at Monty. "I know how much you dislike balls when the company is not to your taste."

Marlow drew in a sharp breath at his wife's thinly veiled insult. Miss Howard colored but said nothing.

"Your friend *has* been enjoying herself, Lady Marlow," Monty said. "We've been dancing, have we not, Miss Howard?"

Lady Marlow's eyes widened. "Dancing? Not under duress, I hope."

Miss Howard's color deepened. "N-no," she said. "I didn't want to, at first, but His Grace was kind enough to show me the steps—and everyone else was so friendly."

"Everyone?" Lady Marlow shot Monty a look and raised her eyebrows.

Really! The woman sounded like an inquisitor. If she had her way, he'd doubtless be stretched out on a rack, answering her

questions under torture. Part of him admired her for champion-
ing Miss Howard, even though her barbs were directed at him.

"We danced in a set of six, with the Westburys, together with
Westbury's son and Mrs. Trelawney," Monty said.

"Oh—the wine merchant's wife!" Lady Marlow nodded.
"She's charming. As are the Westburys. That was lucky."

"It was *deliberate*—not luck," Monty said. "Westbury is a
friend, and he was happy to oblige me and my fiancée."

Lady Marlow's eyes widened. "Your *what*? Eleanor—is this
true?"

Miss Howard's eyes glistened with moisture.

"Forgive me, Lavinia, I thought you knew—it happened a
few days ago. I should have—"

"And *you* offered for her, Whitcombe?" Lady Marlow continued. "What nonsense is this?"

Monty drew Miss Howard toward him, his heart aching at
how violently her body trembled. "It's not nonsense, Lady
Marlow. Do you think your friend unworthy of a suitor?"

"Of course not, but *you*, of all men..." Lady Marlow shook
her head, then turned to her husband. "Did you know about this,
Peregrine?"

"No, my love, I'm not one to listen to gossip."

"Nonsense!" Lady Marlow scoffed. "You always have your
ear to the ground—and news as astonishing as this would have—"

"That's enough, Lavinia," Marlow said. His wife's eyes widened at the firmness in his voice. Then she let out a sigh.

"Forgive my outburst," she said. "Please accept my congratulations, Eleanor."

"Thank you," Miss Howard said. "I'm only sorry I didn't tell
you myself."

Lady Marlow glanced back at Monty, the challenge still in her
expression. Then she extended her hand.

"You've chosen well, Your Grace," she said. "I trust you'll
give me no cause for concern about whether my friend has done
the same."

Not particularly congenial—but preferable to having his balls sliced off.

"Now the pleasantries are over," Lord Marlow said, a hint of amusement in his voice, "we should find you somewhere to sit, my love—and perhaps something to drink?"

"Very well," Lady Marlow said. "Eleanor, would you accompany me?"

"Let me find you a quiet spot," Monty said. Taking Miss Howard's hand, he steered her toward a secluded corner where two young men were sitting—Lord Meredith's twin sons. They stared as he approached, amusement in their eyes as their gazes fell upon Miss Howard.

In fact, most of the company tonight, save the Westburys, had regarded Miss Howard with amusement. Rather than the bright colors and bejeweled headdresses favored by the other ladies tonight, she wore a dress of muted green tones, and a small posy in her hair fashioned from leaves and grasses. Eccentric by most standards, but she'd chosen well, for the ensemble emphasized the color of her eyes. Bright silks overwhelmed her complexion. But against the soft green tones of her dress, her skin seemed to glow, rendering her extraordinarily beautiful. Not a conventional beauty by any means, but all the more desirable for it.

And her beauty went unnoticed by the insolent young bucks who remained in their seats.

"Have you no manners?" Monty demanded.

The elder of the two opened his mouth to respond, but his brother nudged him, then stood. "Forgive us, Your Grace."

"It's not *my* forgiveness required," Monty said.

"Lady Marlow, Miss Howard, please take our seats," the younger said. The elder continued to stare, and Monty curled his hands into fists.

The elder stood and bowed. "Ladies, please," he said, gesturing to the seats. Then he strode onto the dance floor, his brother trotting in his wake.

"I've always said Phillip Meredith has no manners," Lady Marlow said. "Johnny is less troublesome, though he's too often under his brother's influence."

"They both need a good thrashing," Monty said as he steered Miss Howard to her seat. "My dear, would you like a glass of punch, or champagne?"

"I'd prefer water," she replied. "If it's not too much trouble."

He brought her hand to his lips and kissed it. "Nothing is too much trouble for you."

And at that moment—the urge to flatten the Meredith boys for showing her disrespect still burning in his veins—he meant every word.

⟫⟪

"WHAT HAS EFFECTED this transformation, Whitcombe?" Marlow asked while he filled two glasses with punch.

"What do you mean?"

Marlow gestured to the door through which the footman had gone to fetch Miss Howard's water. "Your gallantry."

"It's what any gentleman would do," Monty said.

"But you're not *any* gentleman. I've never known you to run an errand for a woman—usually, they're running after you."

"This one's different."

"She's certainly eccentric," Marlow said. "But my Lavinia adores her, therefore I'm obliged to like her."

"How can you be *obliged* to like someone?" Monty asked. "Surely you either like them, or you don't. The obligation is surely to give the *appearance* of liking them to appease someone you love."

"Are you saying that my wife is a harridan who must be appeased?" Marlow chuckled. "Perhaps you're right. I am in love—something *you'll* never understand."

"Because I'm incapable of love?"

"You once declared love to be an affliction that turned a levelheaded man into a numbskull"—Marlow leaned closer and lowered his voice—"which begs me to question your motives in offering for Miss Howard."

"I shall keep my motives to myself."

"As you wish, but it's obvious why you offered for her—at least, it is to me."

Monty glanced across the ballroom to the dark little corner where Miss Howard was engaged in conversation with Lady Marlow. They seemed to be having some sort of altercation.

"Your kindness is to be commended, Whitcombe," Marlow continued.

"Kindness?"

"Isn't that why you offered for Miss Howard? You're not in need of a fortune, and you never struck me as the sort of man who'd want an *attractive* wife. A pretty wife is more likely to stray, particularly once you lose interest in her, which a man of your appetites is bound to do. Therefore, I must conclude that you've chosen a woman who'll be grateful enough to turn a blind eye to your infidelity."

Monty stared at his friend in disbelief.

"I'm not saying you've acted purely out of self-interest," Marlow continued, "and for that I commend you—such charity is rare."

"*Charity?*"

"The dowry will compensate—her father's wealthy enough. Yes, on balance, I believe you'll not be sorry."

Monty could no longer contain his anger.

"What the bloody hell are you saying, Marlow?" he cried. A number of heads turned to stare at him, and he lowered his voice. "You think I've offered to Miss Howard out of *pity*? Don't you know how insulting that is?"

"I've no intention of insulting you, Whitcombe—I think it's a kind thing to—"

"I meant insulting to Miss Howard! You think her incapable

of attracting a genuine offer of marriage?"

Monty winced as his conscience pricked at his hypocrisy.

"Believe me, Marlow," he said. "What I feel for Miss Howard has nothing to do with *pity*."

Marlow's eyes widened. "I meant no offense. Forgive me—I hadn't realized."

"Realized what—that I'm not a heartless cad?" Monty asked.

"It's a reputation on which you've thrived before."

In that, Marlow was right. But that reputation was losing its appeal—at least where Miss Howard was concerned.

"Your water, Your Grace," a male voice said.

The footman appeared, brandishing a glass of water on a silver salver.

"Shall I take this to Miss Howard, sir?"

"I'll hand it to her myself."

Monty took the glass, then threaded his way through the crowd, which seemed to have swelled in numbers and noise. Before he reached his destination, the musicians struck up a lively tune, and a cheer rose as couples filled the dance floor, forming a cacophony of bright colors.

A reminder, if ever he needed it, of why he disliked parties. So much chatter, yet not a single one of them had anything of worth to say.

And those bright silks! Why had he never noticed before that such a cacophony of color could bring on a megrim?

Whereas Miss Howard, in her gown of muted green, looked the most natural creature in the world compared to the peacocks milling about.

She looked up and met his gaze, and he saw pain in her eyes.

"Your water—Eleanor," he said.

Her eyes widened at the familiarity, then she took the glass. Her hands shook, and water spilled onto her gown. He reached for her hand and steadied it, and she drew in a sharp breath as their fingers touched.

"Are you well?" he whispered.

"Quite well, thank you."

"No you're not, Elle," Lady Marlow said.

"Lavinia, I…" Miss Howard's voice died as Lord Marlow joined them.

"Your punch, darling," he said, handing a glass to Lady Marlow.

The music changed in tempo as the dance grew livelier, and a shriek of laughter rose up.

Miss Howard closed her eyes and drew in a sharp breath, and Monty took her hand.

"Miss Howard, might you oblige me?"

"W-with what?"

"I find all the noise rather tiresome. Shall we take a turn about the room?"

She glanced around her environment, at the colors milling about, the sparkling jewels and feathered headdresses.

"Or perhaps you might show me the painting you spoke of earlier—in the hallway. I'm anxious to resume our conversation about art."

"In the hallway?" Lady Marlow asked. "Is that proper?"

"For a gentleman and his betrothed to engage in a private conversation?" Monty said. "What could be more proper?"

"The presence of a chaperone, that's what," Lady Marlow said. She rose, then drew in a sharp breath and lifted her hand to her mouth.

"My love?" Lord Marlow asked. "Are you well?"

"Peregrine, don't fuss," she said. Then she swayed to one side.

Marlow caught her in his arms. "That settles it. You're to remain seated until you're feeling better."

Miss Howard watched the exchange, her brow furrowed in pain.

Propriety be damned.

Monty took her hand. "Miss Howard?"

She rose and let him lead her out of the ballroom. They

passed the dining room, where a number of guests were helping themselves to the buffet.

"Would you like something to eat, Miss Howard?" he asked.

She glanced at the people milling about, then shook her head.

"I'm not hungry either," Monty said. "Now—where's that painting?"

They moved along the hallway, and as soon as they were alone, her body relaxed.

About halfway along, he spotted the painting—an enormous picture of a stallion rearing up as if it were about to embark on a race on which its life depended. Or perhaps the animal had scented a mare in heat, given the hungry stare in its wide, dark eyes, their whites gleaming as if the beast were on the brink of madness. It was a look Monty had seen in countless men hellbent on seduction.

At the bottom of the painting was the inscription: *G. Stubbs 1796.*

"What do you think?" Miss Howard asked, her voice a soft whisper.

"It's very good."

"You don't see the flaws? It's certainly not a Stubbs."

"It's *signed* G. Stubbs."

"A forger's hardly likely to sign his *own* name if he's trying to pass his work off as a Stubbs, Your Grace," she said. "Besides—the signature's all wrong. He shortened his name in his signatures, but rarely used his initial. And he often wrote *pinxit* before the date."

"Pinxit? What the devil's that?"

"It's Latin," she said. "It means he painted it." She gestured toward the painting. "But Stubbs certainly did not paint this. It's a passable effort, but the proportions are wrong."

"It looks all right to me."

"The back legs are too long. Can you not see?"

Monty glanced at the rear end of the horse. Now she'd pointed it out, the legs *did* look a little long. But horses came in all different shapes and sizes, surely?

"Perhaps the horse had particularly long back legs," he said.

"Not if it's a thoroughbred," she replied. "Any horse breeder would have addressed an imbalance in shape. And look at the pelt. It's too flat. There's no indication of the muscles and tendons beneath the skin."

"Perhaps because they're beneath the skin."

"They'd still be visible." She held up her hand. "The bones in my hand are beneath the skin, but you can see they're there." She flexed her hand, then curled it into a fist. "See how the skin stretches over my knuckles? The change in coloration and shadows on the skin tell you that there's something beneath."

"And the same principle applies to horses?"

She smiled. "Precisely! What distinguished Stubbs from other painters is that he took great pains to study horses in terms of what lies beneath the skin. He knew the exact placement of every muscle and bone beneath the surface."

Heavens above! The wilting creature he'd pulled out of the ballroom had been transformed. Before him stood an intelligent young woman, talking animatedly about a subject with which she was familiar.

"How do you *know* all this?" he asked.

"I've been fascinated by Stubbs's work since I saw a copy of one of his sketches. But my interest only really started after Papa bought me a copy of *The Anatomy of the Horse.*" She glanced at Monty as if expecting him to know what she was on about. Then she smiled. "It's a book of Stubbs's sketches. Very precise sketches of bones and muscles."

"Of horses?"

She nodded. "The subject was an obsession for Stubbs. Did you know he used to dissect the animals to study their bodies? He'd strip away the body, piece by piece, so he could draw the muscles. Then he'd remove the muscles until the skeleton was left, and he'd draw the bones."

Monty suppressed a ripple of nausea. "Is that a subject a

young woman should be interested in?"

She colored. "You sound like my mother. I daresay I ought to restrict my interests to sewing cushions and donning myself in the latest fashions. But I happen to find Stubbs's work fascinating, even though the subject is a little gruesome. A resolve to study every facet of a subject—even that which is hidden—is a quality to admire. Wouldn't you rather commit yourself wholly to one subject than flit from interest to interest on a whim, never to become a true proficient?"

"But young ladies have many interests," Monty said. "I know of plenty who are accomplished at art and embroidery—as well as singing and playing the pianoforte."

"Are any of them *truly* skilled in their pursuits? Or do they only possess sufficient accomplishment to elicit polite applause at the end of a dinner party? I fail to see why we're obliged to applaud a young woman who's made only a cursory attempt at accomplishment."

"You wouldn't applaud out of politeness?" he asked.

"But *is* it politeness? It's deceitful to praise where that praise is unwarranted. Why should I applaud someone such as—let's say—Lady Arabella Ponsford, when she struggles to hold a note when she sings an air?"

"So as not to hurt her feelings?"

"I'd prefer honesty," she replied. "For example—were you honest with me when you said you didn't like the noise in the ballroom? Or that you wanted to see the painting?"

She glanced up, assaulting him with her green gaze. She was a woman who lacked an understanding of deceit—the little falsehoods uttered to make oneself appear favorable to others. And, consequently, she was not a woman it would be honorable to deceive, even if that deceit was for her benefit.

"Perhaps I wasn't completely honest," he said.

She frowned, then stepped back and lowered her gaze. He caught her hands and drew her close.

"My motives were honorable."

"Where's the honor in deceit?" she asked, her voice tight.

His conscience pricked at him. Though he believed he was doing her a favor, did she suffer from their arrangement because it required her to deceive others?

"Miss Howard, I can explain," he said, "but you must look at me."

"For what purpose?"

"So you can see the truth in what I say."

Slowly, she lifted her gaze until their eyes met, and his heart tightened at the pain in her expression.

"Do you trust me so little that it hurts to look at me, Eleanor?"

Her lips parted, and a rush of need coursed through his body at the prospect of savoring their sweet plumpness.

"I had no designs for myself when I asked you to accompany me into the hallway," he said. "I saw your distress, and recalled your dislike of crowds. But I had no wish to expose your own distress to your friends."

She blinked, and moisture gleamed in her eyes.

"Y-you mean…?" She trailed off, shaking her head in disbelief.

"I'm not known as a kind man," he said. "I've lived an indulgent life by virtue of my wealth and station, and have had neither cause nor desire to think of others. But, at that moment in the ballroom, I had not a care for myself, or for the other guests. At that moment, I thought only of you."

A tear spilled onto her cheek, and he lifted his hand to her face, wiping the tear with his thumb.

She closed her eyes and leaned into his touch, a soft whimper on her lips.

Overcome by her instinctive gesture of trust, he dipped his head and brushed his lips against her mouth.

Her eyes flew open, and his body tightened at the raw desire in their expression—a desire to match his own.

Gently, he flicked his tongue against the seam of her lips. With a sigh, she parted them, and he slipped inside, tenderly at first, as if approaching an untamed filly—then he stroked her mouth in a sweeping gesture, taking possession of the lush, uncharted lands. He moved slowly at first, so as not to frighten her, until she began to respond, flicking her tongue against his, seeking his tongue out when he withdrew it, and parting her lips further to invite him into her warm depths.

Sweet heaven! Unconstrained by convention, she was exploring her own needs—honestly and innocently. He could think of nothing more arousing.

He deepened the kiss, and, slowly, her body came to life. A spark of need ignited in his groin as he felt two hard little peaks nudging insistently against his chest.

Unable to stop himself, he wrapped his arms around her and caressed her body, moving his hands gently at first, before sweeping them across her back, taking possession of her. Then he dipped his hand lower until he reached her derriere and squeezed the soft, round flesh.

A small cry reverberated through her body, and she shifted her thighs apart. His senses were assaulted by the scent of lavender and spices, together with the sweetest, most delectable scent of all—the scent that all men craved.

The unmistakable scent of a woman ready to be fucked.

Devil's toes! What the bloody hell was he doing?

His conscience crashed through his ardor, dousing it as thoroughly as if he'd been thrown into an ice-cold lake. He broke the kiss and pulled back, holding her at arm's length.

Her eyes flew open, and, for a moment, his cock threatened to explode. Face flushed, eyes bright, she looked like a woman on the verge of her climax. Then the passion in her gaze turned to shame. Her hand flew to her mouth, and she let out a cry.

"Miss Howard—I must apologize," he said. "I have no idea what overcame me. Rest assured, I'll not take such liberties again."

If anything, his assurance seemed to increase her distress.

"Lady Marlow was right," he added. "I'm a cad of the worst

degree."

She shook her head. "No, Your Grace. You're kinder than you would have people know. I-I behaved abominably just then. I…"

He caught her hand. "*You* have nothing to reproach yourself over. If there's anything I can do to make it up to you, then you only need ask."

She glanced at the painting. "No, there's nothing."

"Except, perhaps, the painting," he said.

"The painting?" She frowned. "I doubt Lord Francis would sell it—and I wouldn't want it. If I wanted a Stubbs replica, I could paint it myself."

"Not *that* painting," he said. "Would you like to see *my* painting?"

"Your painting?"

Monty smiled to himself at the delight in her voice. "Yes," he said. "At my home."

"Wouldn't it be an imposition?"

"Of course not. It's only a day's carriage ride."

"Oh," she said, her eyes widening. "I-I thought you meant your house in London. So the painting's…"

"At Rosecombe—my country estate. Would you like to study a real Stubbs—that is, of course, if it *is* real?"

"Oh, yes!" Her exclamation, filled with childlike enthusiasm, touched his heart.

"And this time," he added, "I shall observe propriety and secure you a chaperone for your stay."

Her smile died, but she nodded. "Oh—of course. Yes—very well. I do need a chaperone, of course, but…"

"I was thinking of Lady Marlow," he said. "She's your particular friend, and I have no wish to impose on your mother, who no doubt wishes to remain in London to chaperone your sister."

He could almost taste the relief in her expression, and he offered his hand.

"Then it's settled?" he asked. "I shall speak to your father directly. After all, there's nothing unusual in a man taking his fiancée to see the house of which she'll soon be mistress."

She looked away, and he cursed himself inwardly.

But there was no denying that they'd entered into their arrangement knowing full well that it would soon come to an end.

No matter how much he wished that end would never come.

CHAPTER NINETEEN

"ELEANOR, ARE YOU *sure* you wish to go?"

Eleanor's father sat in his wing-backed chair beside the fireplace, holding a letter in his hand bearing the Whitcombe crest, while he stared at her over the top of his gold-rimmed spectacles.

"Of *course* she's sure, Leonard!" Eleanor's mother cried. "What a ridiculous thing to say."

"A fortnight's a long time."

"A *fortnight?*" Eleanor winced as her mother let out a shriek. "Well done, Eleanor! Imagine that, Juliette! You'll have suitors queueing at the door when you return."

"Grace, my love—"

"Oh, *Leonard!*" she interrupted. "I know it means missing the Granleighs' ball—and Lady Moss's dinner party, such a shame— but a stay at Rosecombe will do more to further Juliette's interests. You've no objection, do you, Juliette?"

"Of course not, Mama," Juliette said.

"No, I mean Eleanor alone has been invited," Papa said.

"She's *what?*" Mother cried. "That won't do! Eleanor, how *could* you?"

"Forgive me, Mother," Eleanor said, "I—"

"I *must* chaperone you. And it's unfair on Juliette to invite yourself but exclude her."

"Eleanor didn't invite herself," Papa said, an edge to his voice.

"The invitation came from the duke."

"It's most improper. Eleanor cannot go without a chaperone."

"And she won't. His Grace writes that Lady Marlow is to chaperone Eleanor. They'll be traveling in her carriage."

"Lady Marlow!" Mother scoffed.

"A viscountess is a fitting chaperone," Papa said.

"I'm sure you'd prefer that to a fortnight with *me* in the country, Mother," Eleanor said.

Papa shot her a warning look.

"That's not the point, child," Eleanor's mother retorted. If you knew an invitation was forthcoming, you ought to have ensured that the whole family was invited—don't you agree, Juliette?"

"Yes, Mama," Juliette said, sweetly, though she shot Eleanor a look of dislike.

"We're all invited to dine at Rosecombe at the end of Eleanor's stay," Papa said.

"Leonard, it's at least a day's ride."

"Grace, my love, do you wish to dine there, or don't you?"

Eleanor's mother huffed. "I suppose dinner at Rosecombe is better than nothing."

"And you were looking forward to Lady Granleigh's ball, weren't you?" Papa said.

Mother nodded. "I suppose I *was*. Her invitations are highly sought after—she's a friend of Lady Jersey, you know—and we weren't invited last year. I wouldn't want to be seen to snub her, not if there's a chance she might secure me a ticket at Almack's. Very well—Eleanor can go to Rosecombe on her own. I doubt Lady Granleigh would miss *her*."

Eleanor exchanged a glance with her father, and he winked.

"Have you already secured dance partners for Lady Granleigh's ball, Juliette?" Eleanor asked her sister.

"At least two. The Duke of Dunton and Mr. Moss. Colonel Reid asked me in Hyde Park yesterday, but, of course, I refused."

"Why?" Eleanor asked. "He seems amiable to me."

Juliette rolled her eyes. "Because I've refused his hand, of course. It's a waste of a dance card to fill it with a man in whom I have no interest. If he wishes to continue chasing me, then he's a fool."

"Perhaps he's still in love with you," Eleanor said.

"Your sister can do better," Mother said. "Reid might be the son of an earl, but he's only a *younger* son. Now, about your gown…"

Father stood—somewhat abruptly, but talk of gowns and frippery tended to result in him making a swift exit.

"Eleanor—would you accompany me to my study?"

"Of course, Papa." Eleanor rose and followed him out of the morning room.

Once inside the study, he settled behind his desk, while she took her usual seat opposite.

"I take it the invitation to Rosecombe was not a surprise."

She shook her head. "He invited me last night—he's offered to let me study a painting. A Stubbs."

"A Stubbs, eh? And it takes a fortnight to study one?"

"Is it too long to stay?"

"I'm only teasing, Eleanor love. You're to be mistress at Rosecombe, so there's no impropriety in your visiting. Though, of course, your mother and sister are disappointed."

Eleanor felt her cheeks warming under his scrutiny, and she lowered her gaze.

"Never mind," he said. "I'm sure they'll recover. But can I ask you something?"

She nodded.

"Do you *really* want to go? You're betrothed, so it's not unexpected—but it all seems to have happened so quickly. You're usually so careful when making decisions. This is the most important decision of your life—perhaps even your *last* decision."

"What do you mean, my last decision?"

"We live in a man's world, child," he said. "When a woman

marries, she surrenders her freedom of choice."

"Did Mother surrender her freedom of choice when she married *you*, Papa?"

He gave a smile of resignation. "That question is best left unanswered. But I'm hopeful that you'll fare better in your marriage than others have. Whitcombe may seem a rather cold sort of fellow, but he has one redeeming feature."

"Which is?"

"He always speaks highly of you."

"H-he does?"

Papa nodded. "He approached me last night and said you possessed the kind of intelligence that existed to further your mind rather than to give the appearance of accomplishment—and that set you apart from every other woman in the world. To hear such words from a man such as he—a man with no reason to utter a falsehood…"

He leaned forward and caught her hand, and she curled her fingers around his. "Perhaps you will be happy with him, my sweet girl. But I would caution you before you go to Rosecombe without your old Papa to watch over you."

Eleanor's heart swelled at the love in his voice. "What would you have me do, Papa?"

"Guard your heart, Eleanor," he said. "You're not like other young women. You don't take love lightly. When you do fall in love, I fear you'll fall in so deeply that you'll give yourself wholly to the one you love to the exclusion of all else, including your own heart." He stroked the back of her hand with his thumb. "I would not see my darling girl unhappily married to a man she loved, and who didn't love her in return."

He patted her hand with fatherly affection, then released her, and she exited the room. But rather than return to the morning room, she slipped upstairs and sought refuge in her bedchamber.

Poor Papa—if only he knew of her deception! And now she was faced with the prospect of his fears having come true.

Because she feared that she had fallen in love with a man who was incapable of loving her in return.

CHAPTER TWENTY

Rosecombe Park, Hertfordshire, August 1815

"STAND TO!"

An order rang out as Monty stepped outside. At once, the waiting servants stiffened and stood to attention, forming a line from the main steps.

He smiled to himself. Perhaps Jenkins thought himself an officer. Standing at the head of the line, body stiff and erect, a thick mustache adorning his face, the black-clad butler looked every bit the officious general. Standing beside him, the house-keeper rolled her eyes, then glanced at him with a look of sisterly affection.

"Is everything ready for our guests, Mrs. Adams?" Monty asked.

"Yes, Your Grace," she replied. "The guests' bedchambers have been cleaned and aired. Miss Howard is in the green room, like you asked. And there was enough ice for sorbet tonight."

"And dinner will be…?"

"At seven, on account of the dowager joining us. Tea will be ready as soon as your guests arrive."

"Where?"

"I thought the blue room in the west wing," the housekeeper said. "It catches the sun at this time of day, as you know."

Which Monty didn't, given how little time he spent in that

room. In fact, he spent little time on the estate, preferring to leave the management to Mr. Gregory, rather than have his steward endure an incompetent duke bumbling about the place with his ill-thought-out ideas. In fact, Monty spent most of his time at his country seat trying, and failing, to stave off boredom, staying still like an obedient child while his valet tended to him—tying his cravat in a knot that he'd had never learned to master himself—and wishing the day was drawing to a close before it even begun.

Until today.

Today he *did* have something to look forward to.

And there it was—in the form of a carriage, turning into the driveway, swaying gently to and fro as it moved closer, accompanied by the sounds of a whip cracking in the air and horses' hooves crunching on gravel.

The servants' chatter ceased as the carriage, the Marlow family crest emblazoned on the side, drew to a halt. Two footmen rushed toward the carriage and opened the door, then stood in attendance.

Marlow climbed out, followed by his wife. Monty waited, but there was no sign of anyone else.

Surely she'd not shied away from coming?

Then Lady Marlow stuck her head inside the carriage.

"Eleanor, we're here." She lowered her voice to an almost indiscernible whisper. "There's nothing to fear, dearest."

Marlow glanced toward Monty and gave an apologetic smile. Monty frowned at his friend, then strode toward the carriage.

"Miss Howard?"

A shape moved inside the carriage, then her face appeared in the doorway—pale skinned, the expression in her eyes reminiscent of a deer caught in a trap.

"I…" she began, then hesitated.

Monty offered his hand, but she merely stared at it. Then he caught sight of her maid climbing down from the back of the carriage.

Of course! What had the maid said the last time Miss Howard

seemed unwell—that she became overwhelmed when a lot was happening around her?

He glanced over his shoulder at the front façade of Rosecombe Hall. He'd known the building all his life, but this time, he viewed it through her eyes. Instead of his home, he saw an imposing structure three stories high, fashioned from cold gray stone, the central part topped with a dome, with two sections stretching either side, dotted with row upon row of windows, like multiple eyes looking outward. At the foot of the building, a row of servants in neat uniforms, their eyes on her—and at the end, a black-clad, dour-faced man whose spindly legs and imposing demeanor had the air of a predatory insect.

Devil's coach horse beetle—that was what Monty had called Jenkins as a boy. Harmless enough—benevolent, even—but he delivered a sharp bite when provoked. Metaphorically, of course—but Monty had felt the sting of the old man's tongue when he was caught stealing claret from the cellar. Jenkins was kind enough—but he was a stickler for tradition and decorum, and he didn't suffer fools gladly.

What would he make of Miss Howard and her eccentricities?

Monty turned back to her. "I'm so glad you've come," he said. "I hope you didn't find the journey too overwhelming—and I apologize if you did."

She stared at him, and his heart gave a little jolt at her clear emerald gaze.

"Apologize?"

"For insisting you travel all the way out here and be subjected to all this." He gestured toward the building. "But have no fear—it's less imposing inside, and you're free to come and go as you please. You must treat it as your own home."

She shook her head. "Oh, no—I couldn't possibly…"

"But it will be *your* home very soon, will it not, Miss Howard?" Marlow said. "I'm sure you'll take no time at all finding your way around. By this time tomorrow, you'll be wondering why you were so—"

He broke off as Lady Marlow gave him a sharp nudge, but it didn't take a great intellect to work out how he was going to finish.

…so frightened.

Monty helped her out of the carriage, then hooked her arm through his. His heart soared as she leaned against him.

"There!" he said softly. "Did I not promise to take care of you—Eleanor?"

She gave a shy smile at his use of her name, and he caught a faint blush on her cheeks.

Monty nodded toward the row of servants. "Ready to face the troops?"

She let out a giggle, and he steered her toward the row of men and women, who—given that news traveled faster below stairs than above—were doubtless eager to see the woman who was to become their new mistress.

Or the woman they *believed* would be their new mistress.

Each servant bowed and curtseyed as Monty passed them, until they reached the butler.

"This is Jenkins," Monty said. "He runs a tight battalion," he couldn't help adding.

Miss Howard giggled again, and extended her hand toward the butler. Then she withdrew and colored.

"I'm so sorry, Mr. Jenkins," she said. "I meant no offense."

"None taken, Miss Howard. And it's just Jenkins."

"Oh dear, yes," she replied, her color deepening. "I'm always forgetting that sort of thing. Papa doesn't mind, of course. Mother would be ashamed if she were here. But I always think it's polite to address someone as Mr., Mrs., or Miss, rather than just using their surname. A surname on its own has a certain abruptness to it. I mean—the other servants address you as Mr. Jenkins, do they not?"

Jenkins arched his eyebrows so high that they were in danger of disappearing off the top of his forehead. Miss Howard stiffened and shifted closer to Monty, as if seeking protection.

Then the butler's mouth cracked into a smile. "It's something I've never considered, miss," he said. "But it's part of the tradition that has existed for generations. Without tradition, mankind risks descending into savagery."

"I like rules," Miss Howard said. "There's comfort in knowing exactly what to do, and say, rather than having to work it out for oneself. But I cannot understand the sense in maintaining a tradition for the sake of it. Some rules can be unfair. For example, Harriet is expected to sit outside the carriage while I'm inside— even if it's raining, and—"

She broke off, and her hand flew to her mouth.

"Oh! I'm so sorry for rattling on. I never know when to speak and when to stay silent. I don't know what came over me."

"*I* do, miss," the butler said, and Monty gritted his teeth. Miss Howard may not behave as a Society lady ought, but she didn't deserve Jenkins's disapprobation.

"Wh-what's that?" she asked, her voice wavering.

"A sense of justice."

Then the butler winked—he actually *winked!*—before bowing and addressing Monty.

"Your Grace," he said, the pomposity in his tone returning, "perhaps you should escort your guests inside. There's a nip in the air. Lord Marlow, Lady Marlow—how pleasant to see you again."

"Thank you, Jenkins," Marlow said as he approached the butler, arm in arm with his wife.

Monty escorted Miss Howard inside. She flicked her gaze around the main hallway, then tilted her head back to look at the ceiling. "I hadn't expected it to be so huge!"

The little devil in his head let out a chuckle, and his manhood hardened at the thought of Miss Howard uttering those words in the bedchamber—her eyes and mouth wide open with wonder, before he led her on the path to her first climax.

Oh, to imagine the pleasure to be had at watching her writhing beneath him, surrendering her willing body before screaming his name as he buried himself inside her!

"Y-Your Grace?"

Her inquiry returned him to the present, and he patted her hand and smiled. "Tea?"

"I thought you'd never ask," Marlow said before Miss Howard could reply. "Does your cook still make that fruitcake? The one glazed in honey, with the toasted almonds on top?" He turned to his wife. "My love, you simply *must* try some. And you, of course, Miss Howard."

"I-I suppose so," Miss Howard said quietly.

"Or perhaps you wish to take your rest?" Monty suggested.

A flicker of hope ignited in her eyes, then she shook her head. "No, I ought to stay up."

"Why, because you think it's the rule?" Monty teased, then his conscience jabbed at him at the distress in her expression. He dipped his head, bringing his mouth tantalizingly close to her lips. "Some rules ought not to be adhered to."

Then he waved over the housekeeper.

"Mrs. Adams, have someone show Miss Howard to her chamber, then send for her maid."

"Very good, sir." The housekeeper offered her arm. "Come with me, my dear. A rest will do you good after being cooped up in that carriage. Traveling can be exhausting, even if you're sitting, I always find."

I always find? Monty couldn't recall the last time Mrs. Adams set foot outside the estate, let alone actually *traveled* anywhere. But her kind words had the desired effect, and Miss Howard smiled, then took the proffered arm.

"I *am* a little tired," she said.

"Of course you are, my dear! Come along and we'll make sure you're well rested in time for the evening. Dinner's at seven."

"I shouldn't need that long."

"You can join us when you've had your rest," Monty said. "Or, if you're eager to view the painting, I—or anyone else here—can take you to it."

"Thank you."

The housekeeper led Miss Howard across the hall. Monty watched them ascend the staircase, then they veered right at the turn and disappeared along the upper hallway.

Jenkins stood in the doorway, his gaze fixed on Miss Howard. But rather than the aloof disapproval that the butler bestowed on the majority of Rosecombe's female houseguests, Monty could swear he saw something akin to cordiality.

Or—dare he say it—*approval.*

Then Jenkins scuttled off to resume his duties, barking orders to every servant he passed, while Monty steered Lord and Lady Marlow toward the parlor for tea.

Perhaps it was a figment of Monty's imagination, swelled by wishful thinking, but he could swear that Jenkins—who'd been at Rosecombe for so many years that he was part of the fabric of the building, and who was notorious for disliking everybody, both upstairs and downstairs—had stumbled across a person whom he actually *liked.*

And that, if nothing else, set Miss Howard apart from every other creature in the world.

MONTY PULLED OUT his pocket watch and flipped it open.

Twenty past six. Enough time to return to the house before the dressing gong. Most likely, his valet would already be fussing around his dressing room, setting out an array of waistcoats and cravats for him to choose from. Didn't the man know he cared not which one he wore? There were more important things in life than whether his waistcoat matched his necktie.

Marlow and his wife were likely to be engaging in a more *energetic* pursuit—and certainly a more enjoyable one.

Unwilling to be forced to hear their cries of pleasure, Monty had slipped outside for air. Why the devil had Mrs. Adams put them in the red guest room? It was far too close to his own bedchamber, which meant that he'd be treated to their screams of ecstasy all night—that was, if Marlow had spoken the truth about his wife's talents in the bedchamber.

But a woman that feisty—and Lady Marlow was one of the feistiest women he'd met—was bound to provide excellent bed sport. No man wanted his bed partner to close her eyes and lie back, waiting for her ordeal to be over. No, he wanted a woman with a mind of her own who required a greater effort on his part before she eventually surrendered.

For, as all men knew, the chase, and the final conquest, were always better than what came after—a lifetime of being bound to the same woman forever.

Along the path back to the house, Monty spied a lone figure leaning against a fence, looking into the field beyond where a horse stood grazing at the far end, the roof of the stable building visible in the background.

Sketchbook in hand, her pencil sweeping across the page, it was Miss Howard.

As he approached, she startled and looked around.

"Oh, Your Grace! I didn't know you were outside."

"Nor I you," he said. "Weren't you supposed to be resting?"

"Yes, but I saw the horse as we came up the drive earlier today."

"And you felt compelled to draw him," he said. "Why didn't you say so?"

"Everyone was so keen on my taking a rest that I didn't want to cause offense," she said. "I did rest for a while. I didn't realize how tired I was until I reached my room—which is beautiful, by the way. I love the color particularly; it reminds me of..." She colored, then sighed. "I'm doing it again, aren't I? I always talk too much when I'm..."

"Nervous?" he prompted. "There's no reason to be. I meant it when I said to treat Rosecombe as your home." He gestured to the sketchbook. "May I?"

She nodded and held it out. He took it and studied the page. She had drawn a horse—more specifically, *his* horse. It was as if the animal stared out at him from the page. No item of detail was missing, from the heavy-lidded, thick-lashed eyes, to the velvety soft, slightly flared nostrils, to the white mark on the animal's forehead in the shape of a butterfly.

"It's Hercules!" he cried. "But how can you depict such detail from a distance? He's at the opposite end of the field, yet this portrait is accurate down to the last whisker! Do you possess an eyeglass, or inhuman eyesight?"

She let out a soft laugh, and his breeches tightened at her relaxed manner. She laughed so rarely that each occasion was to be savored—and his hungry body reacted with pleasure and need in equal amounts.

"He came over to say hello when I arrived," she said. "Just for a moment—then he lost interest and galloped over to the other side."

"He's a little restless at the moment," Monty replied. "One of the mares is in season—which is why he's been put out here."

Her cheeks flushed a delicate shade of pink. "Oh," she said, her mouth forming a delectable, round circle.

"But you were still able to sketch his likeness," Monty said.

"He was with me long enough for me to commit him to memory. But it's still not accurate." She turned the sketch upside down and stared at it for a moment, then nodded. "Yes, I see it— around the mouth, see?"

No, Monty didn't see—and nor did he see the point in turning a picture upside down.

"It's so I can see the drawing on the page, rather the drawing in my mind," she said.

Bugger—he must have said that aloud.

"When we look at something the right way up, our mind often replaces what's really there with what we wish, or expect, to see," she continued. "But invert the image, or look at its reflection in a mirror—we can see *beyond* what's in our mind, and the flaws become more apparent. More importantly, we see where the flaws are, and can remedy them."

She turned the sketch upright, then made a few pencil strokes around the horse's mouth.

"Yes, I think that's satisfactory."

"Satisfactory? It's exquisite," he said. "Hercules is *here* on the page. It's not merely a drawing—it's the essence of him."

Her blush deepened and she closed the sketchbook.

"Did you manage to see the Stubbs?" Monty asked. "I asked Mrs. Adams to tell the staff to direct you to it."

She looked away. "I-I didn't like to ask. Everyone seemed so busy, rushing about the house."

"You'll see it after dinner, when we retire to the drawing room," he said. "My mother knows more about the painting's history than I—she can tell you about it."

Her eyes widened. "Your mother's *here?*"

"She lives in the dower house, but she often dines in the main house when I'm at home. Tonight's no exception."

Miss Howard tried—and failed—to disguise the horror in her eyes, and she looked away.

"Do you ride?" he asked.

"Oh," she said, resuming her attention on him. "Not really. I tried it a few times, but I never saw the point. Mother and Juliette ride. They've been on a hunt—but it's not something I'd enjoy, thundering across the countryside in pursuit of a creature, only to see it being torn apart by dogs at the end."

Put like *that*, Monty also struggled to see the appeal.

"Let me introduce you to someone whom I think you'd like," he said, offering his arm.

"Who?" Her eyes widened and she glanced around, as if expecting an ambush.

"Lady Star."

"Are there more guests?" she asked, her voice tight. "I-I thought it was just Lavinia and Lord Marlow. Is it a large party tonight?"

"Lady Star is a *horse.*"

"Oh—you must think me an awful simpleton."

"On the contrary, I assure you," he said. "I'm at fault for having given my horses such ridiculous names. But the personification of animals is a common practice. My mother's named each of her dogs and speaks to them as if they are favored children. I daresay you've done the same for your pets?"

"I've never had a pet," she said.

"Oh, forgive me—if you're not fond of animals, there's no need to go to the stables. We can return to the house. It's almost time to dress for dinner, anyway."

"Oh no—I adore animals," she said. "At least—well—I find large animals a little intimidating, as you never know what they might do. But dogs—" She broke off and sighed. "It doesn't matter."

Clearly it did, but he prided himself in knowing a little more about her than he did at first—enough to know that, sometimes, it was best not to pursue her on matters. Sometimes it was best to let her say in her own time what was on her mind without forcing it out of her.

As they entered the stable yard, a groom appeared, carrying a bale of hay. He stopped and dipped his head. "Your Grace, sir. Are you wanting to ride?"

"No, Sam, I wish to introduce Miss Howard to Lady Star."

"Beggin' yer pardon, miss." The groom set the hay aside, then tipped his cap toward Miss Howard. "Lady Star's in the first stall."

"Not the far one?" Monty asked.

"No, sir. On account of Hercules…" The groom glanced at Miss Howard and blushed, which turned even the tips of his ears pink. "I-I had to move Artemis to the far stall."

"Very good, Sam." Monty steered Miss Howard toward the first stall, and its occupant approached the door.

"Hello, my beauty," he said, holding out his hand. The horse nudged his hand with its nose, and he let out a laugh. "Forgive me, I've nothing for you, but perhaps Sam does?"

"Of course, sir—there's some apple cores sent from the kitchen this morning." The groom scuttled off and returned with a bag. Monty reached inside and took one. The horse's lips quivered, and Miss Howard let out a giggle.

"Would you like to give her an apple core?" Monty asked.

"Oh…" She hesitated. "I-I don't know."

"Let me show you." Monty held the apple core in his hand, palm flat, and the horse took it. Then he rubbed the horse's nose, and the animal gave a low nicker of pleasure. "Now your turn."

She drew out an apple core.

"Keep your palm flat," he said. "That way she'll take the apple core and leave your hand behind." She hesitated, and he leaned toward her. "Trust me—Eleanor."

She met his gaze, and he smiled his encouragement. Then she held out her hand, and the horse deftly plucked the apple core from her palm.

"There's a good girl," she said softly, then reached out and stroked the horse's nose. Monty held his breath, and the animal grew still, as if it were doing likewise. Miss Howard continued to caress the horse's nose. Then, seemingly emboldened, she placed her hand on the animal's face. The horse blew out a soft breath from its nostrils and leaned against Miss Howard until their heads touched.

"She likes you, miss," the groom said. "She doesn't always take to strangers."

"Lady Star, meet Eleanor," Monty said. "Eleanor—meet Lady Star. Would you like to ride her during your stay?"

"I don't know…"

"She'll do for you, miss," the groom said. "She has the sweetest temperament—with the right rider."

"You don't want me to ride in a *hunt*, do you?" she asked.

"I was thinking of a tour of the estate—and perhaps a picnic at the end if the weather's nice enough," Monty replied. "There's plenty of fine spots just right for sketching. In fact, I know of a rather fine tree stump."

"The one by the lake, sir?" the groom asked. "That's a rare, fine spot for a picnic, miss, if you don't mind my saying."

"I don't mind at all," Miss Howard said. "In which case, I'd love to—if it's not too much trouble."

"Nothing's too much trouble," Monty said. "Besides, we've been planning this, haven't we, Sam?"

"Aye, that's right, sir," the groom said. "I'll make sure to pack a bag of apple cores for you, miss, for Lady Star."

"Oh, would you?" she cried. "That'd be so kind, Sam, thank you. Oh—I'm quite looking forward to it now. That is, if I'm able to keep my seat."

"You'll have no trouble with Lady Star," the groom said, patting the horse's nose. "The master will be there to help you— he's an excellent rider. And Lady Star here responds well to a gentle temperament such as yours."

"You're very kind, Sam."

The groom colored. "It's not kindness when I speak the truth, miss."

Monty smiled at the adoration in the groom's eyes. The shy, awkward young lad seemed utterly smitten with Miss Howard.

And she seemed utterly oblivious. Most young women would have taunted him, or demand he be punished for his familiarity. But Miss Howard spoke to him as if he were an equal.

"Thank you, Sam—you may continue with your duties," Monty said.

The groom tipped his cap again, then picked up the hay bale and disappeared into one of the stalls. Monty took Miss Howard's hand and hooked it around his arm, as if she belonged by his side, then steered her out of the courtyard.

"You've made quite an impression on young Sam, Miss Howard."

"Oh dear," she replied. "I suppose most of your guests know a great deal more about horses than I. Perhaps he was just being polite when he said I'd be able to ride her."

Monty stopped and drew her close. Her eyes widened as she tipped her face up to meet his gaze, and the desire that had been swirling deep within him came to the fore.

"He was not being polite," he whispered. "And neither am I when I say you're the most extraordinary woman I know."

She lowered her gaze. "Your Grace, I must insist—"

"No, Eleanor," he said, unable to conquer the hoarseness in his voice, and her gaze snapped back up, eyes widening to large emerald pools into which he yearned to dive. "Do not suggest that I'm anything but honest with you when I say that you are a jewel among women, and Rosecombe is all the better for having you here."

"Your Grace, I—"

"*Montague,*" he said, his voice a low growl in his throat. "You must call me Montague."

"Montague…"

His name on her lips was more than his resolve could withstand. Surrendering to his desires, he lowered his head and captured her lips. She let out a low cry of need and parted them, inviting him in. But before he could claim her, a familiar sound echoed through the air.

Curse that bloody gong!

He withdrew and sighed. "That's the dressing gong for dinner," he said.

"You have a gong for *dressing?*"

"I do. It acts as a warning."

"A warning of what?"

"That if I'm not in my dressing room in five minutes, I'll be in for a dressing-down from my valet."

She let out a laugh. "I can't imagine Harriet being cross with me. Not like…" Her voice trailed off, but she had no need to finish.

Devil's toes—no wonder she hid behind a thick shell, or always seemed to be searching for a quiet corner in which to melt into the shadows. She seemed to have been underappreciated and misunderstood by everybody, save for a few individuals who looked beyond her eccentric exterior to the pure soul within—such as her maid, Lady Marlow, and now Sam.

And, of course, Monty himself. The more he saw of that pure soul, the more he resolved to ensure she would be placed in safe hands when they came to part—even if those hands were not his.

CHAPTER TWENTY-ONE

THE SILENCE IN the drawing room thickened, until even the ticking of the clocks seemed to fade.

Not even the presence of the Stubbs over the fireplace could temper Eleanor's discomfort. And though she longed to inspect it, she found herself unable to articulate the words needed to present a proper request.

Not with that black-clad matriarch staring at her like a huge spider assessing her prey.

The butler had been bad enough—all spindly black legs and a hooked nose, reminding her of the long, thin beetles that often worked their way into the house at night, raising their hindquarters aggressively if disturbed. But at least he'd smiled at her. Eleanor doubted if the dowager Duchess of Whitcombe had smiled in the last ten years.

Or at all.

How might she word her request?

Your Grace, may I take a look at the painting?

That seemed benign enough—surely she'd not take umbrage at that. Though she ought to specify which painting.

Your Grace, may I take a look at the painting over the fireplace? His Grace tells me you know a great deal about it.

Was that how most people might open a discussion? A request intended not to offend, followed by comment intended to pacify her a little after the disastrous dinner.

But would the dowager think she was attempting to flatter her?

Oh dear! This was just the sort of occasion for which she needed Montague and his tutelage. He'd know precisely what to say.

Muffled laughter filtered through the hallway, and Eleanor exchanged a glance with Lavinia—her only ally in the dowager's lair.

"The gentlemen seem to be enjoying themselves," Lavinia said.

The dowager glanced pointedly toward Eleanor's hand—the same hand with which she'd picked up the wrong fork during the main course. "They are, yes."

"A-are *you* enjoying yourself, Your Grace?" Eleanor asked.

The dowager swiveled her head, subjecting Eleanor to the full force of her sharp blue eyes. They were the image of her son's, save for the tone—a glacial hue that sent a shiver through her blood, in sharp contrast to the heated gaze Whitcombe had tuned on her when they almost kissed at the stables.

"It's *Duchess*, Miss Howard."

"I-I beg pardon?" Eleanor stammered, and her coffee cup rattled against the saucer, no matter how tightly she gripped it. "I-I thought—"

"The first time you address a woman of my station, you say Your Grace, and thereafter you address me as Duchess. Didn't your mother teach you *anything*?"

"No, I had a governess."

If anything, Eleanor's response angered the woman further.

"I think Her Grace's question was rhetorical, Eleanor," Lavinia said, coming to her rescue. "But, Duchess, I'm afraid I must contradict you."

Sweet heaven! What was Lavinia trying to do—prod a viper?

"I beg pardon, Lady Marlow?"

"Miss Howard has yet to speak to you directly, Duchess. It's only right that she addressed you as Your Grace just then."

That, at least, was true. In fact, Eleanor hadn't spoken more than two words during dinner—to thank a footman, which had earned a glare of disapproval from the dowager.

The door opened, and the men strode in. Marlow crossed the floor to sit beside Lavinia, while Whitcombe approached Eleanor.

"Did you notice the Stubbs, Miss Howard?" he asked.

Eleanor glanced about, aware of four pairs of eyes trained on her.

He offered his hand. "Let me show you."

She took it, and he led her to the fireplace.

"What do you think?" he asked.

"It's definitely a Stubbs."

"Of *course* it's a Stubbs!" the dowager cried.

Oh dear—she'd caused offense again. Could she never think of the right thing to say?

"Miss Howard spotted a fake Stubbs in London, Mother," Whitcombe said, a hard edge to his voice. "She has an eye for these things."

"Oh, *does* she?"

To Eleanor's horror, the black-clad woman rose and glided across the carpet toward her. Had Eleanor felt herself snatched up by pincers, then dragged into a lair in the cellar, she wouldn't have been surprised.

"Y-yes—at Lady Francis's ball."

"Lady Francis, eh?" The dowager let out a snort. "I suppose I shouldn't be surprised—unless you're making mischief."

"Miss Howard doesn't make mischief, Mother," Whitcombe said.

"But she claims to be an authority on art."

"Oh, no, Your—I mean—*Duchess*," Eleanor said. "But I have a particular interest in George Stubbs." She turned to the painting, which depicted a horse standing proudly beside a groom, a rich myriad of browns and reds in the pelt, bringing the animal to life, such that Eleanor wouldn't have been surprised had the animal leaped out of the painting. Then she cast her gaze over the inscription at the bottom.

Geo. Stubbs pinxit 1762

"Pinxit!" Whitcombe said. "Just like you said that night."

"What night?" the dowager asked sharply. "Montague, explain."

"Miss Howard told me why she knew Lady Francis's painting was a fake."

"And will Miss Howard bestow her wisdom on *our* painting, and concede that it's genuine?"

Eleanor glanced at the painting once more, following the outline of the horse. Then her gaze settled on the animal's hind section, and she leaned closer. One of the back legs didn't look right—from the joint halfway up the leg, down to the hoof—and nor did the shadow it cast on the ground.

"It *seems* genuine," she said, then hesitated. Was now one of those times to suppress the truth?

"But?" the dowager demanded. "I sense there's a 'but' coming on."

"Mother!" Whitcombe sighed.

"No, Montague, I'm sure we're all eager to hear what Miss Howard has to say."

Eleanor shrank at the emphasis of her name—*Miss Howard*—delivered as an insult, as if the old woman objected to having a mere *miss* in her home. But, given that whatever she said would offend the woman further, she might as well speak the truth.

"There's something wrong with one of the back legs," Eleanor said. "It's as if"—she pointed to the hind leg—"this section was painted by another."

"What do you mean?" the dowager asked, a little less frost in her tone.

Eleanor ran her fingertip along the hind leg. "It's not discernible from a distance, but on close inspection, it's more obvious."

"Obvious?"

Eleanor pointed to the leg. "See the color? It's a good likeness to the rest of the horse, but the reds are a little too bright. And the way the light lands on the leg is all wrong—the tendons beneath the skin are far less prominent than those in the other hind leg, yet they're positioned the same. Then there's the hoof."

"What about the hoof?" Whitcombe asked, leaning forward to inspect the picture.

"The color is too cool," Eleanor said. "It's as if the artist mixed a little too much blue on his palette. Gray is a more complex color to mix—most artists think it easy, but because it's formed by mixing all colors together, the chances of getting the tone right are very small. And look at the base of the hoof—the shadow is cast in the wrong direction. And it's the wrong color. A shadow takes on the color of that on which it's cast. See where it hits the grass? It should be dark green there, not gray."

The party fell silent.

Oh dear—have I just insulted the whole room?

"Well!" the dowager cried.

Yes—she *had* insulted the room or, at least, the most imposing person in it.

"Mother," Whitcombe said, a warning in his voice. "There's no need to be angry. Miss Howard meant no offense."

"Oh, be quiet, Montague!" the dowager said. "I'm not angry—though I admit to feeling a little insulted, given how much the thing cost me."

"Y-Your Grace—I mean, Duchess," Eleanor said. "Forgive me. I meant no—"

"I'm sure *you* didn't, my dear," the dowager said. "That particular charge, I'll lay at the feet of Mr. Rivers."

"I don't understand."

"He's a painter," the dowager said. "The wretched man charged me a small fortune to restore the painting after it was damaged."

"Damaged—how?" Whitcombe asked.

This time it was the dowager's turn to blush, and she looked away. "That matters not. What matters is that the restoration was clearly *not* of the standard I paid for."

Whitcombe leaned toward the painting and inspected it. "It seems good enough to me."

The dowager let out a snort. "Perhaps if you spent more time looking about, and focusing on your duties here rather than your pleasures, you'd notice many more things around here."

"Mother, this is hardly the time…"

"No," the dowager said. "I suppose it's not." She glanced at Eleanor. "You've a sharp eye, my dear. You must take tea with me tomorrow, after breakfast."

"We cannot visit you tomorrow, Mother," Whitcombe said. "I've arranged a picnic."

"I wasn't asking *permission*, Montague," came the reply, and Eleanor winced inwardly at the sharpness in the dowager's voice—she was a woman used to barking orders and having them obeyed instantly and without question. "We can picnic once tea is finished."

We? Surely the dowager wasn't going.

"Mother, we're going for a ride tomorrow. And Artemis is in season."

"I can ride Persephone." The dowager set her mouth into a firm line. "That's settled. We can leave once Miss Howard and I have finished our tea. I've no objection to Miss Howard visiting me in her riding habit."

"I have no riding habit, Your Grace," Eleanor said.

"No?" Another eyebrow arched. "I suppose that can't be helped. I'll see you at nine."

Eleanor dipped into a curtsey. "Yes, Duchess."

"And now, I find I'm rather tired," the dowager said. "Montague—walk me to the dower house."

"Yes, Mother."

Had her stomach not been fluttering with terror at the notion of taking tea with the dowager, Eleanor would have laughed at Whitcombe's monotonic *Yes, Mother*, not unlike how she responded to her own mother when she knew she'd lost the battle, and wished to give an appropriate response that did not elicit further salvos.

The dowager barked an order to one of the footmen, then glided toward the door. Whitcombe moved closer to Eleanor and took her hand, and her breath caught as he slid his fingers between hers.

"Thank you," he whispered.

"For what?"

"For accepting Mother's invitation."

"That was a royal decree, not an invitation," Eleanor said. Then she let out a gasp. "Oh, forgive me! I didn't mean to say that—I only meant to *think* it."

"There's nothing wrong with saying what's on your mind, Miss Howard," he replied. "I find it refreshing."

"Montague," his mother called from across the room. "I'm ready."

He rolled his eyes then kissed Eleanor's hand again. "Please excuse me. I'll see you at breakfast."

"Montague! Now!"

"Coming, Mother."

He bowed and escorted the dowager out.

Alone with Lavinia and Lord Marlow, Eleanor felt her body lift, as if a great weight had now been removed.

But her respite would be short-lived with the prospect of an audience with the dowager in the morning. The woman might have remarked on Eleanor's powers of observation, but Eleanor doubted if anything got past *her* sharp eyes. Like a pig hunting for truffles, she'd root out every flaw, every eccentricity in Eleanor's character, stripping back her layers until she'd exposed the weak soul within.

It wasn't as if her engagement to Whitcombe was perma-nent—it was, after all, due to end as the Season drew to a close. But one audience with his superior, disapproving mother would extinguish even the faintest glimmer of hope that she harbored in her dreams. The tiny voice that whispered of her dream—that he might sweep away convention, defy his pledge to break off their engagement at the end of the season, and declare his love for her—would, by tomorrow morning, be killed stone dead.

CHAPTER TWENTY-TWO

THE PARLOR IN the dower house had the air of a mausoleum, with dark furnishings and mahogany-paneled walls that absorbed the light.

But the most imposing item in the room was the black-clad figure sitting across the table.

Tea was always an occasion to be feared—cups rattling against saucers, plates to balance on one's knee. Not to mention biscuits and cake to contend with. Biscuits always seemed to disintegrate as soon as Eleanor picked them up, often dropping into her tea and splashing her gown. Cake stuck in her throat, giving rise to a tickling sensation that necessitated all her efforts to prevent a coughing fit. All undertaken under Mother's disapproving stare.

But tea with the dowager presented horrors at an entirely new level, with more challenging obstacles to negotiate. A silver tea set gleamed in the sunlight, which she was bound to smear with her fingerprints, and two cups and saucers fashioned from a delicate porcelain decorated with roses and gold leaf. A matching cake stand dominated the center of the table, in two tiers, filled with brightly colored cakes, biscuits, and pieces of marzipan—colors bright enough to induce a megrim, or worse, stain the bone-white tablecloth when Eleanor inevitably dropped crumbs onto it.

That was, if she hadn't dropped one of those fragile-looking teacups first.

Two liveried footmen stood to attention beside the table—doubtless watching to see what transgressions she'd commit.

The dowager leaned forward. "Tea?"

Eleanor nodded. Her hostess then nodded at one of the footmen, who poured a measure of tea into a cup. Then he glanced at Eleanor and arched an eyebrow.

"I prefer not to have milk," Eleanor said. "Or sugar."

"Then what would you like in your tea, miss?"

Eleanor hesitated. Was this a test?

"Miss Howard?" The dowager leaned forward. "How do you take your tea at home?"

"With milk and sugar—but that's not how I prefer it."

"Why the devil do you take it so if you don't prefer it?"

Eleanor hesitated. What was the right way to respond without causing offense?

"Infuriating girl," the dowager muttered. "How do you prefer your tea? James can fetch whatever you need—can't you, James?"

"Yes, ma'am," the footman said.

"So? Spit it out, girl!"

"I prefer a spoon of honey, and a little cinnamon," Eleanor said.

"How very odd!" came the reply. "Can you satisfy my guest, James?"

"I think so, ma'am. I'll speak to the cook."

The footman bowed and disappeared, while the second footman poured the dowager's tea.

"So—you're betrothed to my son."

Eleanor nodded.

"Hmmm," the dowager muttered. The footman placed her teacup in front of her, and she stared at it.

Silence fell once more, swelling into a bubble of discomfort until the urge to lance it was more than Eleanor could bear.

"We're enjoying very fine weather."

She turned, slowly, toward the window and back again.

Eleanor tried another phrase. "This seems a pleasant room."

"Are you here to discuss the weather and my furnishings, child?"

"N-no—" Eleanor hesitated. "I-I'm sorry."

"Must you apologize *all* the time?" The dowager let out a huff. "Why do people always feel the need to apologize when they've committed no transgression?"

"Because they believe they *have* committed a transgression," Eleanor said. "Not necessarily in their eyes, but in the eyes of another whom they f—"

She broke off, her cheeks warming.

"Whom they fear? Was that what you were going to say?" the dowager demanded. "Why might you fear *me*?"

Because you have the demeanor of a spider and the manners of a tyrant.

The dowager arched an eyebrow, almost as if she'd read Eleanor's mind. And, with a glare that could tear down walls at fifty paces, in all likelihood, she could.

"Is it because you believe I disapprove of your marrying my son?"

"We're not married yet."

"What an extraordinary response! Is it because you ensnared him through nefarious means, and fear that he'll eventually see reason?"

"I didn't ensnare him, Duchess," Eleanor said. "A man such as the Duke of Whitcombe..." She shook her head. "I cannot begin to imagine how that might be done by even the most perfect debutante—let alone one such as I."

"Then how did you persuade him to offer for you in such a public manner?"

Despite her discomfort, Eleanor found herself having to suppress the little devil inside her mind that roared with laughter at the notion of her having the power of persuasion over anyone.

"You give me more credit than I deserve, Duchess, if you believe me capable of influencing your son."

"Yet you succeeded."

"I did nothing," Eleanor said. "Until he offered for me, I don't believe he even knew I existed."

"Yet you do exist, child—here and now, in *my* home, taking tea."

What right did this woman have to insult her?

"I'm here at your invitation, *Your Grace*," Eleanor said, smiling inwardly as the dowager flinched at her incorrect address. "And I'm engaged to your son at *his* invitation."

"You're a fool if you believe his motives to be honorable. My son's notorious for his want of feeling, his lack of any sense of duty toward his family or others. He's the very last man with whom a woman should entangle herself."

"You seem to have a low opinion of him."

"He's a *man*."

"Not all men are evil," Eleanor said. "Your son least of all."

"You say that because you don't know him."

"But I do," Eleanor said, untangling her hands and leaning forward. "Our acquaintance might be short, but he's shown me more kindness in the past few days than I've experienced in a lifetime from others supposedly closer to me. Beneath the imposing exterior is a man with the capacity to be *so* kind—but he's unwilling to show it to others."

The dowager leaned back, her eyes widening.

Eleanor glanced down, noticing that she'd been gripping the edge of the table, her knuckles whitening.

Sweet Lord! Most likely the dowager would have her sent back to London in disgrace. Eleanor held her breath, awaiting admonishment.

But it never came.

The door opened, and the footman returned with a dish of honey and a small jar containing a russet-colored powder.

"How do you take your tea, Miss Howard?" he asked.

Eleanor glanced at her hostess, who nodded. "Go on, Miss Howard."

"Half a teaspoon of cinnamon and a teaspoon of honey, please."

The footman obliged, and the aroma of spices filled the air as he stirred the cinnamon in.

"Thank you," Eleanor said. "You're very kind."

The dowager's eyes widened, and Eleanor silently cursed herself for committing yet another faux pas. She braced herself for an admonishment about how well-bred young ladies didn't thank the staff.

"Miss Howard, I believe you've shocked my footman."

Here it comes…

"Oh?" Eleanor glanced at the footman, who stared straight ahead.

"James isn't used to compliments. Most of my guests refrain from speaking to him with any degree of cordiality, lest they run the risk of him getting ideas."

"Such as a belief that members of Society treat their servants with consideration?" Eleanor couldn't help saying. "I doubt he'd ever be at risk of harboring such outrageous views."

"Should we ask him, Miss Howard?"

"I'd advise against it. Such a direct question would place him in a dilemma where he faces two choices, neither of which are acceptable."

"And they are?"

"To be truthful or tactful."

The dowager turned to the footman. "Which are you, James? Truthful or tactful?"

At that moment, the door burst open and several small fur-balls raced into the parlor, yapping excitedly.

A maidservant raced in after them. She stopped on seeing the dowager and dipped into a curtsey. "Begging your pardon, ma'am—the dogs escaped again."

"I can see that for myself," the dowager said.

One of the animals approached Eleanor and sniffed at the hem of her gown. Thankful for the opportunity to remove herself from the dowager's direct gaze, she leaned over to stroke the creature's head.

A pug—somewhat overindulged, given its portly frame.

"Careful, miss!" the maid cried. "She doesn't take to strangers. She's been known to bite."

But the little creature seemed far from dangerous. Eleanor stilled her hand, and the dog whined and nudged her fingers with its nose. She scratched behind the animal's ears, and it stretched out a hind leg, which began to twitch. Then, with another grunt, the dog rolled sideways and settled on Eleanor's foot, its body warmth seeping through to her skin.

"Aren't you a friendly lady?" Eleanor whispered.

"Unlike her mistress?"

Eleanor glanced up to see the dowager looking directly at her.

"Oh, Your Grace—I mean, *Duchess*—I meant no offense. I was merely saying—"

"That Ariadne is a more congenial hostess?" The dowager's mouth twitched into a smile. "I doubt Lady Fairchild would agree with you. Last time she visited, Ariadne bit her hand."

"What had she done?" Eleanor asked.

"Ariadne?"

"No. Lady Fairchild. An animal doesn't bite without reason. Most animals are quiet if left to their own devices, and only when threatened."

"Rather like unusual young ladies, then," the dowager said. "You said not one word during dinner last night."

"I had nothing in particular that I wished to say."

The pug at Eleanor's feet rolled onto its front, then nudged her with its nose again. She glanced down to see a pair of dark brown eyes staring at her from beneath a wrinkled brow, their soulful expression enough to melt the coldest heart. Eleanor reached down to pick the animal up, then hesitated.

"Go on," the dowager said. "She'll not rest until she has satisfaction."

Rather like her mistress, then. Though Eleanor wasn't about to voice *that* thought.

She scooped up the pug, and the little dog settled onto her lap, curling up with a contented sigh.

"Be gentle, miss!" the maid cried.

"I think we can trust Miss Howard if Ariadne does, Millicent," the dowager said. "Are you fond of pugs, Miss Howard?"

"I love all animals," Eleanor said. "They must make wonderful companions."

"Then, my dear, when Ariadne's litter comes, you shall have a puppy."

"Oh!" Eleanor cried, then she tempered her joy. "I'd *love* a puppy, but I'm afraid I cannot."

"Why ever not? Are you sensitive to animals? I had a cousin who sneezed every time he so much as *looked* at a dog."

"It's not that. It's just… My mother would never permit it."

"But you'll soon be mistress of your own home," the dowager said.

"I will?"

"Aren't you engaged to my son?"

"Oh—of course," Eleanor said.

How could she have been such a simpleton?

"In which case, the only one from whom you must seek permission for anything is my son. He'd have no objection, I assure you."

"Oh."

"Then that's settled, yes?

Eleanor nodded, then picked up her teacup, focusing on the pattern around the rim of the cup—anything to prevent her from having to meet the duchess's gaze.

The front door was knocked upon, and Eleanor startled, almost spilling her tea. The pug lifted its head and gave her a reproachful stare.

Then the parlor door opened and Whitcombe entered. Eleanor could have wept with relief at the sight of him, which marked the end of her ordeal.

"Miss Howard, Mother," he said. "Shall we set off?" He extended his hand to Eleanor.

The maid plucked the dog from Eleanor's lap, then Eleanor rose and took the proffered hand, drawing comfort from his presence. He pulled her close and dipped his head, and she felt his warm breath caress her neck.

"Did you survive?" he whispered.

She nodded, aware of the pair of cold sapphire eyes watching them.

She may have navigated her way through one ordeal and emerged alive, if not unscathed. But the dowager was not a woman to be trifled with—or readily deceived.

Chapter Twenty-Three

THERE WAS NOTHING pleasanter than spending a day outside, in the country, away from the expectations and demands that came with a dukedom.

Monty drew in a lungful of air, relishing the sweet scent of summer blossom and the sounds of the countryside—the whisper of the wind in the trees, the distant lowing of cows, and the gentle ripple of water. Near the edge of the lake, Marlow and his wife strolled side by side, she leaning on his arm while he held a parasol above them both.

Was there ever a couple so much in love? Last night, Marlow couldn't have been more attentive to his wife. But while a few weeks ago Monty might have sneered at Marlow's gallantry, last night his heart had swelled at the notion of two people caring so deeply for each other that the happiness of their loved one ranked above their own.

It was certainly not a state his mother had enjoyed. Her marriage with Father had been the grandest match of their Season—a perfect union by Society's standards. But Father's philandering had turned Mother into a resentful wife, an aloof parent, and now a bitter widow.

As Monty looked across the landscape, his gaze settled on Miss Howard sitting on a blanket, her sketchbook on her knees while she worked away, occasionally glancing up at her subject— the horse chestnut tree stump.

Eccentric, unfathomable—even awkward—she may be, but she was a woman who could never be deemed bitter, aloof, or resentful. She would never fit into the world's ideal of a Society marriage. She would either rise above it or...

Or she would be crushed beneath it.

Miss Howard's prospects for a match might increase once their arrangement was concluded, but she needed to be matched with the right man, if not one who appreciated her for what she was—but at least a man who would not confine her or stifle her personality.

"Montague."

Monty glanced across to where his mother sat beneath a canopy, a footman beside her holding a parasol—though, unlike Lord Marlow, he was doing it out of a sense of duty, rather than love.

"Are you hungry, Mother?" he asked, reaching for a plate of sandwiches.

She shook her head, then gestured toward Miss Howard. "What in the name of the Almighty do you think you're doing, Montague?"

"Having a picnic."

The stoic expression on the footman's face almost disintegrated into a smile.

"You know perfectly well what I'm asking, boy."

Boy? Was he a child to be admonished, then sent to bed with no supper?

"Enlighten me, please, Mother," he said.

"I'm asking why you're trying to deceive me?"

"Deceive you?"

"Me—and perhaps the whole of Society. Do you take me for a simpleton?"

"What do you mean?" Monty asked.

"That your engagement is a sham!"

This time the footman lost his composure. He drew in a sharp breath and stared at Monty open-mouthed.

"Mother, I don't think—"

"Tell me I'm wrong, Montague," she said. "Look me in the eye and say that you honestly intend to marry Miss Howard."

The footman tensed.

"Mother…"

"You owe me the truth, if nothing else," she said. Then she gestured toward Miss Howard. "And you owe it to *her*."

Monty sighed and dropped the plate of sandwiches back into the basket.

"No," he said quietly. "I don't intend to marry her."

The footman frowned, disapproval in his eyes.

"You must send Miss Howard home at once," Mother said.

"Why, because she's not grand enough for you?" he snapped.

"No, Montague," she replied coldly. "It's because keeping her here is stooping to a depth of cruelty I'd have thought beyond you. Your father might have taken pleasure in toying with a perfectly pleasant young woman—but I thought better of *you*."

"It's not like that, Mother," he said. "Miss Howard is aware of the circumstances of our engagement, and she agreed to them."

"Agreed, perhaps, but *willingly*? Was she party to the decision, or did you merely tell her?"

"I told her, but—"

"*When* did you tell her, Montague? The night of your proposal? Miss Howard told me that you hadn't spoken a word to her until that evening—and that she believed you weren't even aware of her existence until then."

Devil's toes—put like that, it made him sound like the very worst of cads.

"I told her the following morning," he said, his cheeks warming with shame.

"I thought I'd raised you better than that, Montague."

"You didn't raise me at all, Mother."

"Must you answer back all the time?" she cried. "Miss Howard is a charming creature, though she'd make a hopeless mistress of Rosecombe."

"Why's that?" Monty asked. "All a duchess need do is give birth to dukes and do what she's told."

"You underestimate what I did for your father if you think that. A duchess is at the pinnacle of Society. She must instill awe and respect in everyone she encounters. She must run a household steeped in responsibility and tradition, with none to help her, and maintain a position of superiority among the tenants and staff. And, not only that, she must turn a blind eye to her husband's roving one."

There it is.

"Mother, why must you always hark back to my sister?"

To his credit, the footman tried his best to remain stoic, but he couldn't disguise the sharp intake of breath at Monty's reference to the *disgrace that should not be named.*

"Must you be so cruel?" she cried. "I've told you not to mention that brat." She gestured toward Miss Howard, who continued with her sketch, oblivious—blissfully so—of the fact that she was being discussed. "I'm thinking of *her*, Montague. How do you think she'll cope when you inevitably cast her aside in favor of another and spawn a litter of bastards?"

"One child out of wedlock is hardly a *litter*," Monty said. "Isn't it time you let it go?"

"While that brat lives here, I'll not rest."

"Olivia has as much right to live here as you, Mother," Monty said. "It's not as if you've set eyes on her—she's never been to the house. If you wish to blame anyone for her existence, then blame Father—or, perhaps, ask yourself why he felt the need to look elsewhere."

"*I* didn't betray Beverly."

"There's more forms of betrayal than taking a mistress," Monty replied.

"Such as tricking a young woman into a false engagement?"

"Miss Howard is perfectly aware—"

"On the surface, yes," she interrupted. "But that young woman is unlike any other I've known. Most girls are like babbling brooks—all noise and chatter, making such a fuss about every-thing, yet when you look beneath the surface, there's no depth at all. Miss Howard is like the lake at the base of a waterfall—surrounded by noise, itself quiet and accepting, with still, dark waters that appear characterless at first, but when you delve in, you discover a depth previously unheard of."

Monty shook his head. "You talk in riddles, Mother. You've made your disapproval of her very clear, and now you speak in her defense."

"I caught a glimpse of the depths beneath her surface," she said. "Last night, she revealed something of her mind. This morning, she revealed something of her heart."

"Her heart?"

She nodded. "At first I thought her an awkward little thing, trying—and failing—to engage in conversation. Until I touched on a subject about which she was passionate. Then her true nature came to the fore. I cannot recall the last time someone spoke to me as she did, in defense of something she cared about."

"Which was?"

She shook her head. "It matters not. I believe she said more than she intended. It would be unfair to divulge what she said."

Monty stared at his mother. He'd rarely heard her speak with such softness. Perhaps she possessed a heart after all—which had been crushed over the years by the burden of being a duchess.

And perhaps she was right. Even if he'd intended to marry Miss Howard, she could never shoulder that burden.

But a part of him wanted to prove his mother wrong about Miss Howard—as he himself had been proven wrong.

CHAPTER TWENTY-FOUR

"Y OU SEEM A natural in the saddle, Eleanor dearest." Lavinia steered her mount alongside Eleanor's.

"I think that's due to the choice of mount rather than any prowess on my part," Eleanor said, leaning forward to pat Lady Star's flank, "but I wish these saddles were more comfortable."

"They take some getting used to," Lavinia said. "I prefer riding astride, but Peregrine looks at me as if I'm some wild creature whenever I suggest it." She smiled. "I daresay Whitcombe wouldn't have minded. He's far less imposing than I thought at first, and was most attentive in helping you with your mount. I hope you'll forgive me for warning you against him before."

"You only had my best interests at heart, Lavinia."

"That I did. I'll even venture to say that his mother seems to be warming toward you. Not enough to be considered *cordial*, but from what I've heard of her, *not* talking down to a young woman in public is her greatest compliment."

Eleanor giggled. "I was terrified of her at first, but she wasn't as bad as I feared. She even offered to give me a pug when I took tea with her."

"Excellent! Did you agree?"

Eleanor was spared the necessity of replying by a hail from Whitcombe, who, with Marlow, had drawn his mount to a halt beside a whitewashed, red-roofed building.

"This is the school," he said. "What do you think?"

The building seemed sound, and the surrounding garden tidy, if not particularly cheerful. But the front gate hung at an ungainly angle, as if one of the hinges had broken, and there was a crack in one of the ground-floor windowpanes.

"It looks in need of repair," Lavinia said. "Has it been occupied long?"

"Six months, maybe less."

"And you expect your tenants to reside in a building with a cracked window and a roof that undoubtedly leaks?"

"It doesn't leak, Lady Marlow," Whitcombe replied. Then he met Eleanor's gaze. "I had it repaired before the school opened."

Was it her imagination, or did she see a plea for approval in his eyes?

"It doesn't look like a school," Eleanor said, "but a school isn't about the building, is it? It's about the children, and those willing to teach them."

Her heart leaped as his mouth curved into a smile. "Quite so—Eleanor."

After they'd returned from the picnic yesterday, he'd asked Eleanor whether she'd be disposed to attend the school on the estate to teach the children about drawing. An odd request—quite out of the blue—but it had been delivered with such honesty and enthusiasm that she hadn't the heart to refuse, even though the prospect of a room full of strangers, albeit children, struck fear into her soul.

The eagerness in his eyes, which shone a brilliant blue in the morning sunlight, reminded her of an enthusiastic child, anxious for an adult's approval of a scheme dear to their heart.

"No, Montague," she said, and his eyes sparkled with joy at her use of his name. "I don't mind at all."

She lifted one leg over the pommel of the saddle, then slid to the ground. For a moment, her legs, still stiff from yesterday's ride, crumpled beneath her, then a pair of strong arms wrapped around her waist and held her against a solid wall of muscle. For a delicious moment, she inhaled the woody, spicy scent of him. Then he dipped his head and pressed his lips in her hair.

"I say, Whitcombe, old chap," Marlow said, amusement in his voice. "There's a time and a place."

"Aye, there is." Whitcombe's voice, a low growl, reverberated throughout Eleanor's body, igniting a slow pulse of heat deep within her center that threatened to swell. And...*sweet heaven*, the very male body pressed against her was hard and ready—though for what, she couldn't fathom.

At length, he released her. "You can leave us to it now, Marlow," Whitcombe said. "Lady Marlow."

Lavinia narrowed her eyes and glanced toward Eleanor.

"Your friend is safe with me, Lady Marlow. I can hardly dishonor her in a schoolroom filled with children. If you pass here on your return, we can all ride back together."

He spoke in the tone of a duke who expected to be obeyed, but Lavinia continued to stare at him.

"I'll be all right, Lavinia," Eleanor said.

"In which case, let's introduce you to the children." Whitcombe tethered their mounts to the gate, then steered Eleanor into the building.

Hoofbeats clattered on the road outside, fading into the distance as Marlow and Lavinia rode on, leaving them alone in a dark, narrow hallway. Voices came from behind a door—tiny, high-pitched voices, chanting in unison.

"*Two twos are four, three twos are six, four twos are eight...*"

He knocked on the door, and the voices stopped.

"Come in!" cried a female voice. Whitcombe pushed open the door and ushered Eleanor inside.

An array of chairs and desks of different shapes and sizes filled the room, seven of which were occupied. At the front, standing beside a large desk with a pile of books, stood a woman in a plain muslin gown and a pinafore. She looked about Eleanor's age, with delicate features, blonde hair fashioned into a neat braid, and wide, dark brown eyes.

"Oh—Your Grace!" She let out a cry then gestured to the children, who scrambled to their feet. Eleanor winced as they scraped back their chairs in their eagerness to stand to attention—apart from one child who sat apart from the rest, near the door. A little slower than the rest, he stood, then turned and carefully lifted his chair to set it back.

"How are you today, Olivia?" Whitcombe asked.

Olivia? A familiar address for a schoolteacher. Eleanor looked at the woman with renewed interest and—to her shame—envy. Was she one of his lovers? He'd had lovers in London—doubtless he'd broken several hearts in the country, also.

"I'm well, Your Grace."

Whitcombe steered Eleanor toward her. "I've brought someone I particularly wish you to meet, Olivia," he said. "This is Miss Howard." Then he turned toward Eleanor. "Eleanor, this is Miss FitzRoy."

FitzRoy...

Why was that name familiar?

The woman dipped into a curtsey. Eleanor did likewise.

"Pleased to meet you, Miss FitzRoy," Eleanor said. "Were you expecting us?"

"Oh." The woman glanced toward Whitcombe, her eyes widening. "No, my..." She hesitated. "I mean, His Grace didn't mention it."

"I thought Miss Howard could help you with the children's drawing," Whitcombe said.

"So *that's* why all that paper arrived this morning! I wondered if there'd been a mistake, and I didn't want to tell the children in case I was obliged to return it. They'll be so pleased." Her eyes sparkled with joy, and her mouth curled into a smile.

Then Eleanor saw it—the plumpness of Miss FitzRoy's lips, and the way her face creased around the mouth when she smiled. Her eyes were brown, not blue, but their shape was identical to Whitcombe's, right down to the arch of her eyebrows.

Montague FitzRoy...

"Miss FitzRoy, are you the duke's…" Eleanor's voice trailed away as she glanced toward Whitcombe.

The woman's eyes widened, alarm in their expression.

Oh dear. She'd said the wrong thing—*again.*

"F-forgive me," Eleanor said. "The resemblance…"

"Few are able to spot it."

"I meant no offense." Eleanor extended her hand. "Please accept my apologies. I hope I won't disrupt your lessons."

Miss FitzRoy stared at Eleanor's hand for a moment, then reached out and took it. Thin, calloused fingers slid across Eleanor's smooth palm.

Whitcombe watched with a shimmer of pride in his eyes.

It was pride in another, not himself. How could Eleanor have once thought him aloof and intimidating? As each day passed, he revealed another layer of himself: gallant suitor, ardent champion, tender fiancé—albeit a fake one—and now, the adoring brother.

Which raised the question…

"Why don't you live at the main house, Miss FitzRoy?" Eleanor asked. "You're a member of the family, after all."

The previous alarm in Miss FitzRoy's eyes turned to distress.

"Oh, forgive me!" Eleanor cried. "I meant no offense—have I said something wrong?"

Whitcombe let out a sigh. "No," he said. "You've merely voiced what social convention forbids the rest of us to say."

"Then I shouldn't have said it," Eleanor said.

"No—Eleanor," he replied. This time it was Miss FitzRoy's turn to look astonished at the familiar address. "A great deal that has not been said *ought* to be said. Olivia is my father's daughter— but not my mother's."

Miss FitzRoy blushed, then Eleanor caught his meaning and let out a cry of shame. "Oh, what was I *thinking?*"

"The same as the rest of us," Whitcombe said. "Olivia doesn't mind, do you, Olivia?"

The young woman shook her head. "Of course not."

Doubtless she didn't, given that she would have grown up surrounded by stigma and whispered words. The matriarch in the dower house might disapprove of Eleanor—but Eleanor couldn't begin to imagine what the dowager thought of Miss FitzRoy, a girl Society considered to have committed a heinous crime merely by being born.

"Shall we begin by introducing the children to Miss Howard?" Whitcombe suggested.

"Yes, of course," Miss FitzRoy said. "Children, this is Miss Howard. What do we say?"

"Good morning, Miss Howard," several voices said in unison. The boy at the back stood in silence, shuffling from foot to foot, casting only an occasional glance upward, as if wanting to satisfy his curiosity, but unwilling to be caught looking.

A feeling Eleanor was not unfamiliar with.

"Perhaps, children, you could tell Miss Howard your names?" Miss FitzRoy gestured to each child in turn, and they recited their names: William, Betsy, and Fanny—who, with their matching mops of unruly red hair, were clearly siblings—in the front row, then Peter, Lottie, and James in the row behind.

Miss FitzRoy gestured to the boy at the back.

"This is Joe," she said. "He's quieter than the others—but that means you listen better than the rest, don't you, Joe?"

The boy gave a curt nod, fixing his gaze on his shoes.

"You may sit now, children," Miss FitzRoy said.

"Might I make a request before they sit?" Eleanor asked.

"Please do."

Eleanor addressed the children. "Shall we see how quietly you can sit? Imagine there are pirates—or dragons—outside, and if they hear the chairs moving about, they'll come in."

"Children, can you do as Miss Howard says?" Miss FitzRoy asked.

"Oh, yes!" William, the boy in the front row, cried. And Eleanor placed her finger on her lips.

"Hush!" she whispered. "You must be quiet. Now—if you all

do as I say, I'll draw a picture of a ship, which I'll give to whoever is the quietest pupil today."

This was met by a volley of whispers, which were silenced when Miss FitzRoy raised her hand. Then the children took their seats, taking care not to scrape their chairs. But Eleanor's attention was focused on the boy at the back, who continued to cast shy glances in her direction, curiosity in his intense blue eyes.

"Perhaps I should leave you to it," Whitcombe said.

"Don't you want to spend time with your sister?" Eleanor asked. "I'm sure she'd prefer you remain here."

Miss FitzRoy gave a shy smile as she opened a drawer and drew out several sheaves of paper.

"Very well," he said. "But you must let me make myself useful. Here—I'll hand these out."

The children stared, transfixed, as their duke and landlord moved among the desks, handing out pieces of paper.

Who was this man who had, at first, seemed like an other-worldly creature insurmountably far above her—but now was assisting in a classroom of his tenants' children?

"What shall we draw today, children?" Eleanor glanced about the classroom and spotted a cracked vase on the windowsill, filled with dried grasses. "Aha!" She picked up the vase and placed it on the front desk beside the pile of books. Then she glanced toward Whitcombe. "Your Grace—may I borrow your hat and gloves?"

He handed them over, and Eleanor added them to the ar-rangement.

"Must we draw *all* of that, Miss Howard?" the red-headed boy in the front row asked.

"No, William," she replied. "Draw as much, or as little, as you want. But first, you must look at your subject before you begin drawing."

"What do you mean—*look?*" William asked.

"Let me show you."

Eleanor glanced toward Whitcombe and his sister, who smiled and nodded encouragement. Then the lesson began.

THE LESSON WAS less traumatic than Eleanor had feared. Miss FitzRoy managed the lively children with a kind, but firm hand, leaving Eleanor to demonstrate some simple sketching techniques—while aware of the silent, imposing man watching her from the corner. By the time she'd finished her demonstration, and the children began drawing, she was almost ready to admit that she was actually enjoying spending time in a room occupied by more than two people.

She settled herself at the front desk and began to sketch a ship—the prize for the quietest pupil.

Whitcombe approached. "That was well done. I've learned a great deal about drawing this morning."

"I'm no teacher," Eleanor replied. "Not like Miss FitzRoy."

"If I may be permitted to disagree," Miss FitzRoy said, "you've been able to instill your passion for drawing into seven young minds. I doubt any of them—save, perhaps, young Joe— would have taken notice of anything *I* said on the subject."

Eleanor glanced at the silent little boy at the back, hunched over his desk, concentrating on his work.

"Joe seems an extraordinary child," she said.

"He's Farmer Swift's youngest," Miss FitzRoy said, "but he's terribly shy, and rarely talks—his mother warned me that he doesn't speak at all to strangers. He cried so much the first time he came here. Sometimes I wonder if he's listening to anything I say, but he can read any book I give him, though he won't read aloud in class."

"Why does he sit on his own?" Eleanor asked.

"It's where he's happiest. I tried to sit the children together at first, but Joe was terribly distressed. At first I thought he didn't want to come to school at all. It took me a week to work out that he was only happy in that particular seat. He won't tell me *why* he prefers it, but I think it's because he likes to be set apart from the others. He doesn't like it if you're too close to him."

"And he doesn't like loud noises, either," Eleanor said.

Miss FitzRoy raised her brows, astonishment in her eyes. "How do you know *that*?"

"He looked almost in pain when the others scraped their chairs back," Eleanor said. "The noise set me on edge also—it almost made my teeth hurt. I've always detested loud noises."

She set her sketch aside, picked up the sheaf of papers, and circulated around the classroom. The children in the front row had all attempted to draw the vase, with William's attempt the closest likeness—by virtue, perhaps, of his being the eldest.

"Very good, William," she said. "Perhaps you could add some of the grasses to your vase—it seems a shame for it to be empty, doesn't it? And Betsy, you've done well to include the grasses, though some of them look as if they're floating in midair—you need to make sure the stems are drawn right up to the mouth of the vase."

After handing out a second piece of paper to Fanny, who insisted that she'd finished her drawing and wanted to start another, Eleanor moved to the second row, commenting on each child's artwork.

When she reached the back of the classroom, she approached the solitary little boy, taking care not to encroach on his space. She glanced at his handiwork and drew in a sharp breath.

The boy couldn't have been older than ten, yet he'd drawn a perfect likeness of the items on the desk, right down to the individual grasses and the crack in the vase, with its jagged edges that stretched halfway across the belly, then split into two.

"That's wonderful, Joe," Eleanor said, keeping her voice soft. "May I come closer, to take a proper look?"

The boy nodded, his attention fixed on his drawing. Eleanor approached, taking care to remain in the boy's eyeline. There was nothing worse than someone hovering in the background, out of sight. Eleanor had never liked the feeling of being watched—her mother had a habit of watching her, which elicited a sensation of discomfort, as if she could feel the disapproving and judgmental gaze burning into her skin.

She picked up a chair, placed it close to Joe's desk, and sat.

"Do you like drawing, Joe?"

The boy flicked his gaze up, narrowed his eyes, then looked down once more.

"Shall we play a game?" Eleanor suggested. "How about I ask questions and you *draw* your answers?"

She placed a second piece of paper on Joe's desk, then drew a smiling face at the top. "When I'm not in the mood for conversation, this is my way of saying that I like something. See? The smiling face means that drawing makes me happy. How about you, Joe?"

The boy reached over and scribbled something on the paper. Eleanor's heart lifted with joy—he'd drawn a smiling face and, beside it, the outline of a pencil.

"So you *do* like drawing," she said. "Do you draw at home?"

The boy shook his head. Then he drew a rectangle, followed by a diagonal line striking through it.

"Perhaps you could write your name, or just the letter J, at the bottom of your drawing of the vase—then we'll know who the artist is," Eleanor suggested. "Did you know that Stubbs, an artist who painted beautiful pictures of horses, wrote his name at the bottom of each of his paintings?"

The boy leaned over his drawing and wrote at the bottom.

"May I see?" Eleanor leaned over and smiled at the inscription.

Joseph Swift pinxit 25th August 1815.

An extraordinary child indeed.

Then he pointed to his name and held his pencil out to Eleanor.

"You want me to write *my* name?"

He nodded, and she scribbled her name at the bottom of her piece of paper.

Eleanor.

"Hello, Joe," she whispered. "I'd like to shake your hand— which is how we make new friends. But only if you want me to. Or is there another way you say hello to a new friend?"

He parted his lips, and for a moment, Eleanor held her breath. Would he speak? Then he closed his mouth and lifted his hand, curling it into a fist, save for his forefinger, which he extended toward Eleanor. She mirrored the gesture, holding her fingertip a hand's width from his.

Joe blinked and stared at her hand, then tipped his head sideways as if contemplating something. Then he moved his hand closer until their fingertips touched.

Eleanor's heart swelled at the gesture—the little boy's gift of trust.

"I never expected to make a new friend when I came here today," she said. "Miss FitzRoy tells me you live at a farm. Are there animals on your farm?"

The boy nodded, and his lips curled into a smile.

"Perhaps, while you're at home, you could draw me a picture of your favorite animal to show me when I next visit."

The smile disappeared.

She'd said the wrong thing again! Perhaps the poor child had no encouragement at home. Or was he forbidden from drawing?

Something she could relate to. Were it not for Papa, she wouldn't have been permitted to paint and draw as she preferred.

Footsteps approached, and Miss FitzRoy appeared at Eleanor's side. "That's a beautiful drawing, Joe. Do you think your mama would like it?"

The boy nodded.

"Are you sure?" Eleanor whispered.

"Oh yes," Miss FitzRoy said. "Joe's parents dote on him. They know he'd never be able to run the farm, poor little soul, so they want him to learn his letters. But he's good with the animals, aren't you, Joe? Your mama told me how clever you are at counting the eggs in the hen coop."

Eleanor glanced at the piece of paper on which the boy had drawn the rectangle with the line through it.

Of course!

He didn't draw at home because his family couldn't *afford* the paper.

"Would you like some paper to take home with you, Joe, if your mama permits it?" Eleanor asked.

The smile returned, and this time, the boy looked up and met her gaze. His eyes, a dark brown, held a curiously intense expression. With a smile, Eleanor placed several sheets of paper on Joe's desk, then returned to the front of the classroom with Miss FitzRoy.

"Now, children, I'd like you to hold up your pictures so we can all see them. Then, perhaps, our special guest"—she gestured toward Whitcombe—"can choose his favorite."

His eyes widened, and Eleanor stifled a giggle at the distress in his expression—a man with the world at his feet and the burden of a dukedom on his shoulders, terrified at having to test his skills in diplomacy by singling out one child over the rest without offending the others.

But, as the children held up their artwork, he was saved the trouble. The little girl in the front row let out a cry.

"Look at Joe's picture! His is the best, isn't it?"

Joe lowered his gaze, unsmiling, and seemed to cringe under the weight of all the attention.

"That settles it," Whitcombe said, relief in his voice.

A bell tolled in the distance three times.

"Gracious me, is that the time?" Miss FitzRoy said. "Children, tidy your desks—it's time to go. I'll see you Sunday after church."

The children leaped to their feet with the sound of scraping chairs, and Joe's eyes narrowed.

"What do we say to Miss Howard?" Miss FitzRoy asked.

Joe remained silent, but the other children said, "Thank you," in unison, then skipped out of the classroom, chattering loudly, leaving Joe standing beside his desk.

"Would you like to do some more drawing while we wait for your mama, Joe?" Miss FitzRoy asked.

Before the boy could resume his seat, a thin woman with graying hair peeking out from beneath her bonnet entered the classroom. She let out a cry as she caught sight of Whitcombe.

"Oh! Your Grace, I—"

"It's all right, Mrs. Swift," Miss FitzRoy said. "The duke brought a guest to help the children with their drawing. Joe—can you show your mama what you've been doing?"

The woman approached Joe, and Eleanor noticed how she walked around the classroom to approach him from the front, rather than from behind. "May I see, Joe, love?" she asked.

The boy pushed his drawing across the desk. His mother picked it up, her eyes shining with pride.

"Well done, love," she said quietly, her voice wavering with emotion. "Shall I put it on the kitchen wall, so we can all see it?"

Joe nodded.

She held out her hand. "Shall we go home now? There's a nice bit of stew waiting."

"Off you go, then, Joe," Miss FitzRoy said. "Thank you for working so hard."

The boy glanced toward Eleanor.

"Come along, love," his mother said.

Joe hesitated, then darted toward Eleanor. He collided with her and wrapped his arms around her waist.

"Joe!" his mother said. "I do beg your pardon, miss!"

"It's quite all right," Eleanor said, embracing the boy. "It's what friends do, isn't it, Joe?"

"This lady isn't a sheep, Joe."

"A *sheep*?" Eleanor asked.

"Begging yer pardon, miss! Joe likes to hug the animals. He started last year, and poor old Shep—my Jacob's collie—had such a fright when Joe tried to embrace him. He's taken to hugging the sheep to say goodnight to them—only his *favorite* sheep, mind, not the whole flock, or we'd be there all night, wouldn't we, Joe?

Forgive him—he means no harm."

"There's nothing to forgive," Eleanor said. "You must be proud to have a son who's so kind and bright."

The woman's eyes glistened, and she nodded. "That I am," she said. "He tries his best around the farm, but he's always preferred to be alone with his books. Now, come along, Joe—we mustn't be taking up any more of this good lady's time."

She dipped a curtsey toward Eleanor, a deeper one to Whitcombe, then took the little boy's hand and led him out of the classroom.

"I think we can say that was a success," Miss FitzRoy said. "You did well with Joe, Miss Howard."

"I saw in him a kindred spirit," Eleanor said, staring out of the window, her gaze following the boy as he walked by his mother's side, one hand holding hers, the other clutching his precious pieces of paper.

"And you can add, to your many qualities, the distinction of being one of Joe's favorite sheep," Whitcombe said.

His eyes twinkled with mirth, and Eleanor's heart skittered in her chest.

"Will you be bringing Miss Howard again, Mont—I mean, Your Grace?" Miss FitzRoy asked.

"If she wishes," he replied. "We can come again after church on Sunday."

"Would you like that, Miss Howard?" Miss FitzRoy asked.

Eleanor nodded. "Yes—but on one condition."

Miss FitzRoy's smile faded. "Which is?"

"That you call me Eleanor—if I may be permitted to call you Olivia?"

"Of course!" Olivia replied. "That's very kind."

"In which case," Whitcombe said, "I must place an obligation on you also—*Eleanor.*"

A little pulse of longing threaded through Eleanor's body at the way his tongue curled around the syllables of her name.

"A-an obligation?"

"Aye," he whispered. "You've failed to act in accordance with my wishes, despite my continued request. But, with Olivia as witness, I insist that you promise, from now on, to call me Montague."

Heavens! No woman could fail to fall utterly, irrevocably in love with him.

And, as Eleanor met his gaze—two sapphire pools into which she would willingly drown—she realized she had done just that.

CHAPTER TWENTY-FIVE

"**I** TRUST YOU didn't disgrace yourself during your stay, Eleanor."

Monty glanced across the table at the straight-backed, brightly clad form of Lady Howard. Since the arrival of the rest of the Howard family, the atmosphere at Rosecombe—which, during the past week, had taken on a relaxed air—had returned to the coldness of propriety and perfect decorum that he'd been brought up to adhere to, and to impose on others.

"O-of course not, Mother."

Eleanor flushed bright red. She pushed her dessert aside, untouched, despite having declared two nights ago that apple pie was her favorite.

She'd hardly touched any of the courses set before her tonight—not since she'd spilled her soup, leaving a bright green stain on the tablecloth, resulting in a haltering apology, prompted by Lady Howard's orders, and a smile of triumph from her younger sister, who was resplendent in a gown of vivid pink, her hair styled in an intricate array of curls.

In fact, from the moment the Howard family descended on Rosecombe, Miss Howard had become, once more, the unresponsive creature who sat at the edge of the ballroom, shrinking back to blend into her surroundings.

Like an animal seeking to conceal itself from predators.

Gone was the laughing young woman with the intelligent

expression who had melted Monty's heart when she'd taken his bastard sister into her embrace. Since he'd taken Miss Howard to the school—on a whim at first to irk his mother—Monty had also taken her to the Swifts' farm. His heart had melted when Joe shyly approached her, slipped his hand in hers, then led her outside to meet his favorite sheep.

And she'd taken Olivia into her heart, paying no regard to his sister's illegitimacy. He found himself wondering, as Eleanor had asked so bluntly, why Olivia didn't reside in the great house, rather than hidden away on the edge of the estate.

He glanced across the dining table, where his mother was staring at Lady Howard. Mother met his gaze, arched a perfectly plucked eyebrow, and curled her lip into a sneer. Oblivious of Mother's disapproval, Lady Howard began enthusing about the dinner set. Last night, Eleanor had declared it to be the ugliest she'd ever seen. But tonight, as soon as Mother alluded to the set's worth, Lady Howard declared it the finest in all England, with her daughter Juliette agreeing and stating that she simply *must* have one like it for her future home.

Her future home. *Ye gods*—what unfortunate soul had Juliette Howard sunk her talons into?

Sir Leonard, on the other hand, seemed uninterested in his wife's exaggerated enthusiasm, and more concerned for his eldest daughter. Monty even saw the man rolling his eyes when his wife complimented Mother on the quality of the beef, the intricacy of the crystal wineglasses, and even the smoothness of the wax candles.

"What have you done during your stay, child?" Lady Howard asked Eleanor.

"W-walking, and riding, Mother."

Even the tremor in Eleanor's voice had returned.

"The grounds here are delightful. Have you attended a hunt?" Lady Howard leaned toward Monty's mother, as if enjoying a confidence with a bosom friend. "I've tried so hard to persuade Eleanor to join a hunt, for it really is quite the thing, is it not? I quite gave up on her, but perhaps she responded to your influence, Duchess."

Mother glanced at Lady Howard and bestowed upon her a smile of cold politeness.

"I flatter myself when I say that my Juliette was *born* to be a duchess, but it's gratifying to know that Eleanor, through a little effort on her part, is showing some capability in that area."

"By chasing an animal to its death over the countryside?" a voice asked.

The party fell silent. Lady Marlow, who had spoken, cut a forkful of apple pie and lifted it to her mouth. Then she swallowed and glanced around the table.

Marlow addressed the party. "You must forgive my wife. She's a little out of sorts today, aren't you, my dear?"

"Well!" Lady Howard cried. "I've never heard the like. I'm of a mind to—"

"Of *course* we forgive Lady Marlow," Monty's mother interjected. "You're only speaking your mind, aren't you, my dear? Over the past fortnight, I've come to appreciate the value of a woman who speaks her mind, rather than one who says what she believes she must say to flatter another."

Oblivious to the insult, Lady Howard nodded, shifting her feathered headdress in the air. "I quite agree, Duchess. Don't you, Juliette?"

Monty's mother pushed her plate aside with half her dessert remaining. "Take it away, James."

A footman approached and picked it up.

"Thank you," she said. "I've lost my appetite. This dinner set is hideous enough to turn even the strongest constitution off a meal. Do you not think so, Miss Howard?"

Eleanor glanced up and colored. "I-I believe so."

Monty stared at his mother as the corners of her mouth creased into a smile. Who the devil *was* this woman who put a chill in the atmosphere of every room she entered—but now looked at him with something akin to mirth in her eyes, after she had done the unthinkable in publicly *thanking* the staff?

The rest of the diners set their cutlery down, and the footman circulated around the room, removing their plates.

"I must compliment you, Duchess, on the elegance of your meal," Lady Howard said. "I always find that the quality of the meal reflects on the quality of the hostess, does it not? Only last week, when the Fairchilds came to dinner, Lady Fairchild told me that I was the best—"

Monty scraped his chair back and rose to his feet. "Marlow, Sir Leonard, would you join me for a brandy? Ladies—please excuse us."

Before Lady Howard could resume her speech extolling the virtues of her skills as a hostess, the gentlemen rose and followed Monty out of the dining room.

"Would you excuse me for a minute, Whitcombe?" Sir Leonard asked.

"Of course—James, please attend Sir Leonard, then show him to the library."

"Very good, sir." The footman bowed, then escorted Sir Leonard along the hallway.

Monty led Marlow into the library, poured two glasses of brandy, then raised his glass.

"To the good riddance of unwelcome guests."

"I trust you're not referring to Sir Leonard," Marlow said. "He's good company when not in the presence of ladies."

"You mean when he's found his balls?" Monty gestured toward the door. "Perhaps he deposited them in the privy before dinner and has gone to fetch them."

"Poor fellow," Marlow said. "Do you suppose he entered the marriage state with his eyes open?"

"Does any man enter the marriage state fully aware of what he's getting himself into?"

"*I* did," Marlow said.

"Your sickeningly happy state is the exception, Marlow. Marriage, for most men, is an afternoon sojourn to church, a day or two of dutiful rutting, followed by a lifetime of regret." Monty waved his glass in an aimless gesture. "I find I'm beginning to understand regret myself, and I have no intention of suffering it more than necessary."

"Regret?" Marlow raised his eyebrows. "Surely you cannot regret attaching yourself to Miss Howard. She's not the sort of woman *you'd* be expected to wed—but you needn't concern yourself with the opinions of others." He sipped his brandy. "This is a very good bottle."

"Enjoy it while it lasts—there's no more '86 in my cellar."

"There's many worse that you could have chosen."

"Like the '87?" Monty nodded. "A terrible year."

"No, you dolt—I mean worse than Miss Howard."

Monty sighed. "I haven't chosen her. Our engagement is a sham. I won't be marrying her."

"A *what*?" Marlow spluttered and wiped his mouth. "After berating me for saying it was kind of you to marry Miss Howard, you now tell me that you have no intention of marrying her at all? Bloody hell, Whitcombe, I thought you were a cad, but I didn't think even *you* could stoop to tricking a respectable young woman—and one less capable than most of weathering heartbreak."

"Miss Howard is aware," Monty said. "She entered into the agreement with her eyes open."

Marlow shook his head. "No matter what you've said to assuage your conscience, I doubt Miss Howard fully understands."

"You do her a disservice," Monty said.

"No, my friend, it's *you* who does her a disservice. Does Lavinia know?"

"I don't think so."

"You're probably right," Marlow said, "given that you're still in possession of your balls. Lavinia would cut them off and feed them to our farmer's prize porker if she knew. She loves Miss Howard—which is more than I can say for that damned family of hers."

"Ahem."

Monty glanced up at the sound of the footman clearing his throat.

Shit.

Standing beside the footman, his intelligent green gaze flicking from Monty to Marlow and back again, was Sir Leonard Howard.

How much had he heard? His expression was impassive—though, on recollection, Monty hadn't seen any other expression on his face. Perhaps that was how he'd succeeded in business—not just for the sharp intelligence evident in his eyes, but for his ability to conceal his emotions. Doubtless he could have earned himself a fortune at the gaming tables. But, instead, he'd chosen to work for his living, earning a knighthood in the process.

Which was ironic, given that the men and women of the *ton* were more likely to look upon with favor a man bestowed with luck on the gaming tables than one who soiled his hands with work.

"S-Sir Leonard—may I offer you a brandy?" Monty found himself stuttering, overcome with the knowledge that he was in the company of a better man.

Sir Leonard eyed the decanter, his expression unchanged save for a slight tightening of the corner of his mouth.

"It's an '86," Monty added.

Sir Leonard's eyes narrowed a fraction, as if he were questioning whether Monty intended to impress him merely by virtue of owning a superior cognac.

"I never acquired a taste for brandy," he said.

"Then perhaps—" Monty began, but Sir Leonard interrupted.

"Perhaps we should rejoin the ladies."

Marlow let out a laugh, a tremor in his voice. "Don't you want a few minutes' respite?"

Sir Leonard's eyes darkened, and he set his mouth into a hard line. "I've not seen my daughter for a fortnight, Lord Marlow," he said. Then he flicked his gaze over Monty, and his frown deepened. "I'm anxious to reassure myself that she has been treated well here."

There was no mistaking the tone of Sir Leonard's voice, which made it abundantly clear that he'd already formed a conclusion to the contrary.

Monty drained his glass, then gestured to the door. "Shall we?" he said. "I've no wish to keep you from Eleanor a moment longer than necessary."

Sir Leonard raised an eyebrow at the familiar address, then nodded, and the three men exited the library.

As they approached the drawing room, Lady Howard's voice could be heard cutting through the air. Sir Leonard let out a sigh, and though Monty longed to express his sympathies, he had no wish to subject himself to more of the man's disdain. He found himself wanting Sir Leonard's approval. But, unlike his wife, the shrewd man was impervious to flattery.

Monty led them into the drawing room.

Good—Jenkins had followed his instructions to the letter. Fewer candles than usual gave the room a homelier appearance, with a softer light unable to reach the furthest corners of the room.

One of which Miss Howard had placed herself in—coincidentally, or perhaps *not*, on the opposite side of the room to her mother and sister—while she toyed with her bracelet. Lady Marlow sat close to the fireplace, engaged in conversation with Monty's mother.

"Bloody hell, Whitcombe, what's all this?" Marlow asked. "Do you expect your guests to stumble about in the dark?"

"Some of my guests prefer a softer light," Monty said, "and a darker room always seems to mute the conversation. Loud chatter is to be abhorred at the best of times—more so after a lengthy meal."

Sir Leonard glanced across the room at his daughter, and back at Monty.

"Leonard! Over here."

Sir Leonard flinched at his wife's voice. Then, with a sigh of resignation, he sauntered over in her direction.

"You simply must tell the duchess about your newest consignment of silks." Lady Howard leaned toward Monty's mother. "They're the most *exquisite* colors," she said. "Everyone in London is *wild* for them. Sir Leonard is very discerning when it comes to his clientele, but he'll make an exception for your modiste."

Monty's mother turned her head, slowly, until she faced Lady Howard, her eyes glittering with warning.

Did the woman ever cease talking? Her voice was enough to induce a megrim in the strongest of constitutions.

Monty approached Miss Howard. "Are you well—Eleanor?"

She nodded, not meeting his gaze, and continued twirling her bracelet.

"It's no trouble, I assure you, Duchess!" Lady Howard cried, and Eleanor visibly shook.

"Mother," Monty said, "might you oblige us with a little music?"

"Of course, dear boy." The dowager rose and crossed the floor to the pianoforte.

Dear boy?

If Mother kept up such cordiality, he'd be obliged to inquire whether she'd taken a bump to the head.

She lowered herself onto the piano stool and began to play a gentle tune. The room seemed to sigh with relief as the air filled with soft music against the backdrop of the crackling of the fire. Not even Lady Howard would dare talk over the performance of a duchess.

Monty sat beside Eleanor and reached for her. She hesitated, then placed her hand over his.

What greater pleasure was there to be had, here in his home—and in the company of a remarkable young woman— away from the harsh chatter of Society?

What a pity their arrangement was soon to come to an end!

The evening drew to a close, and James escorted the dowager to her carriage, while the remainder of the guests dispersed to their various chambers.

Lady Marlow beckoned to Miss Howard. "Come along, Eleanor—we've an early start in the morning."

"I'll escort Miss Howard to her chamber, Lady Marlow," Monty said.

She narrowed her eyes. "I don't think that's entirely—"

"It's all right, Lavinia," Miss Howard said.

"Very well," Lady Marlow said, "but mind you treat my friend with respect."

What a harridan she was! Did she think that as soon as her back was turned, Monty would toss up Miss Howard's skirts and fuck her against the wall?

Saints alive!

He drew in a sharp breath as his cock stiffened against his breeches at the delicious notion of Miss Howard's eyes wide with surprise, and dark with need, as he pounded inside her, pinning her to the wall while she writhed in pleasure and screamed his name.

She tipped her face up, her soulful eyes breaching the armor that encased his heart.

He took her hand. "I find myself somewhat melancholy to-night," he said.

"How so?"

"My house will be empty once more tomorrow."

"You'll still have your mother, and"—she lowered her voice—"Olivia is only a short walk away."

Yes—his half-sister was merely a walk away, though he found himself cursing the rules of propriety that kept her from the main house.

But didn't *he* rule over Rosecombe? In which case, he should be able to decide for himself what must be, and not be dictated by tradition merely because it was how others before him had behaved. Olivia deserved her place in his family as much as…

No—do not tread that path.

"Tomorrow you will be leaving us, Miss Howard," he said.

You fool! Can you not think of anything better to say?

"Yes," she replied. "Will you return to London also?"

"I'll follow in a few days. Rest assured, I intend to carry out my duty. I shan't abandon you once our arrangement is concluded."

"Won't you?"

"I'll not break our engagement until I'm satisfied that your future is set."

Her eyes widened. "Do you intend to find me a *husband?*"

"Did I not promise to assist you in that quarter?"

"Yes—but perhaps I don't want one anymore," she said. "I've no wish to marry if I cannot find a man to accept me for who—and what—I am, and who'll give me the freedom to pursue my dreams, no matter what. But perhaps such a man does not exist."

She was right. No man who walked the earth came close to deserving her.

"I should thank you, Your Grace," she said.

"Montague, please."

She hesitated, as if negotiating a dilemma, then nodded. "Montague. You've helped me see the world with different eyes—and shown me that there's a whole world outside the little circle in which I've been confined all my life. Though the prospect is terrifying, I'm convinced I can make a life for myself—without being a burden to others."

He squeezed her hand and lifted it to his lips. "Eleanor, you could never be a burden. Whatever you decide to do—and whomever you choose to spend your life with—you will always brighten the world around you."

She tried to withdraw her hand, but he held firm.

"No—Eleanor," he whispered. "Let me speak frankly. I might have taught you a few inane phrases to navigate yourself around a shallow Society—but I'm the one who's benefited the most from our arrangement."

"Because of your mother?"

He shook his head. "I might have set out intending to silence my mother—but I have benefited so much from your companionship. You've shown me how to look at the world with different eyes—with *your* eyes. And for that, I shall be eternally grateful."

He lowered his head and brushed his lips against hers. "Goodnight—Eleanor. I promise that if there's anything I can give you, you only need ask."

She curled her fingers around his, then opened her mouth, as if to speak. But she colored and withdrew, and his heart ached at the yearning in her expression.

He caught her hand. "Eleanor—tell me what you desire."

"I-I don't…"

"You do, my love—I can see it in your eyes. Tell me."

She drew in a deep breath, as if summoning courage.

"I-I want to be loved," she said, her voice barely a whisper.

"You *are* loved, Eleanor. You have friends who care—"

"No!" She let out a low cry. "I-I mean, loved *properly*. J-just once. So I know what it's like."

She met his gaze, and his heart ached at the tears in her eyes. The pain in their expression told him of the risk she had taken in making such an honest plea—a plea from the heart.

But he couldn't do that to her—no matter how greatly he desired it.

"Oh, Eleanor," he said, his voice hoarse. "You know not what you ask."

"I-I'm sorry. I shouldn't have presumed…"

"Sweet Lord, you presume right!" he cried. "But I cannot ruin you, Eleanor—and ruin you I would."

"Do you think I care?" she asked. "I'm never likely to marry. I thought I might, once, but not now. Not after…" She shook her head. "Would you deny me this one request? It means so little to you—but to me…" She shuddered as she caught her breath. "It would mean *so much.*"

Her voice, an agonized whisper, spoke to his soul. He drew her to him, burying his head in her hair and inhaling her sweet scent.

"Oh, Eleanor—you're so wrong," he said. "How can it mean so little to me when I've thought of nothing else this past fortnight? My body and soul are in agony for the want of you. But if you yield to me now, we will cross the threshold beyond which we can never return—beyond which I'll be unable to resist the urge to bury myself inside you until you scream my name."

She tensed, and for a moment, he thought she'd bolt, like a spooked filly. But, slowly and carefully, she curled her fingers around his hand and lifted it to her lips. Desire fizzed through him as she flicked her tongue across the back of his hand.

Sweet Lord—what might she look like, kneeled before him, ready to worship his body, her eyes lifted to his?

"Please…"

That single word, spoken through her soft lips, was enough to breach his defenses. He swept her into his arms and strode along the hallway to her chamber.

CHAPTER TWENTY-SIX

FEAR AND EXCITEMENT threaded throughout Eleanor's body as she clung to the man who had lifted her off her feet as if she weighed no more than a bird. She had now embarked on a path from which she could never return.

What previously unknown sensations would he awaken in her body?

What if he found her inadequate? He must have bedded all manner of women. All the women she'd seen on his arm—from sophisticated, hungry widows, to bright, beautiful courtesans—would know exactly how to pleasure a man such as he. Oh, how she'd envied those women! What pleasure had he given them—and received in return?

And now, she, herself, was on the brink of that pleasure.

But she knew nothing of such things. Compared to those women, she was a mere child—an ignorant creature unable to hold a conversation in a drawing room, let alone attract such a virile, powerful man.

He stopped outside her chamber door, and Eleanor cringed, anticipating the moment when he'd set her on her feet with a laugh, then saunter back to his chamber, leaving her alone.

But he did not. He dipped his head, and his warm breath caressed her cheek.

"Eleanor…" His voice, low and husky, reverberated through her bones. "Inside this chamber, I will give of myself…" He brushed his lips against hers. "Inside this chamber, I shall honor the gift of your trust, if you'll bestow it upon me…"

Then he peppered her face with kisses, moving across her skin until he reached her neck, where he nuzzled her ear.

"Inside this chamber," he said, his voice a low growl, "I will show you what it is to be loved—thoroughly, completely…and *very* scandalously."

He nipped her earlobe, and the notion of his claiming ownership in such a primal fashion sent a lick of pleasure through her.

Then he steered her into her chamber, closing the door behind them to shut out the world.

"Before we proceed," he said, "I ask you to trust me—Eleanor."

Her name on his lips, spoken so tenderly, threatened to unleash the tears that swelled within her.

"You have my word, Eleanor—I shan't do anything that you don't wish me to, or anything that you won't take pleasure in. But I can do nothing without your trust." He took her hand. "Your trust is a precious gift—and it's not my right to demand it. It's a privilege that I pray with all my soul you'll gift me, if you deem me worthy."

Oh, heavens!

It was all too much. The surge of sensations threatened to overwhelm her, and she closed her eyes to retreat from the world.

"No, my Eleanor," he said, his voice laced with urgency. "Do not close your eyes—not to *me*."

But though she willed her courage to rise, it faltered at the notion of him looking into her eyes…into her soul.

"Eleanor…"

His soft whisper crawled into her mind, enveloping it in a tender embrace.

"You must look at me tonight," he whispered. "Only then will I know you've given me your consent—and your trust."

She clung to him as he moved forward and placed her on the

bed. Then she drew in a sharp breath and opened her eyes.

Heavens! This was happening—*really* happening…

He caressed her cheek, and she met his gaze, steeling herself to withstand the intensity of his sapphire eyes.

"That's it, my darling," he whispered. Then he claimed her lips. She parted them, and he slipped his tongue inside, sweeping across her mouth in slow, tender caresses.

He lowered his hand, running delicate fingertips along her neck, across her throat, until he reached her neckline. Then he dipped his hand inside her gown. The first flush of shame disappeared as quickly as it came, replaced by a tiny pulse of pleasure that swelled inside her body as he curled his fingers to cup her breast.

"Do you take pleasure when I touch you, Eleanor?"

"Yes," she whispered.

"Good…very good…" He caressed the skin of her breast, moving his fingertips in ever-tightening circles until he reached the peak at the center—the little nub of flesh that had grown hard at his touch. Then he flicked it with his thumb, and she drew in a sharp breath at the fizz of pleasure. He claimed her mouth, silencing the cry in the throat.

"Mmm…" he murmured, his body vibrating against hers. "Are you taking pleasure from my attentions, Miss Howard?"

"It's lovely, Your Grace."

He withdrew his hand. "Must you disappoint me already?"

"D-disappoint?"

"I told you to call me Montague." He caught her chin and tipped it up. "May I undress you, Eleanor?"

Heat flooded her cheeks at so bold a request.

"I-I…" She hesitated, and he placed another kiss on her lips.

"You've no idea how much I relish the notion of tossing your skirts up and claiming you this very moment," he said. "But I promised to make love to you—not rut you. When we make love, I want there to be nothing between us. To be naked, in the arms of another—it's supposed to be the most glorious experience, and I want to share it with you."

"*Supposed* to be? D-don't you know?"

"No, my Eleanor," he said. "In *that*, if nothing else, tonight will be *my* first time."

If nothing else...

Once again, she was reminded of all the women he must have bedded—that she was merely the latest in a long line of conquests.

"Eyes on me, Eleanor," he said, his voice sharp. "Now—may I undress you?"

"Yes," she whispered.

Deftly, he removed her gown, unlacing her stays until only chemise and stockings remained. She held her breath as he lifted her chemise over her head. Then he sat before her, hunger glittering in his eyes.

His gaze wandered over her naked body, until she could almost feel his touch. Then he smiled.

"A man is said to feast with his eyes before he tastes the dish placed before him."

"T-tastes?"

He flicked out his tongue and ran it along his bottom lip until it glistened. Then he dipped his head and captured her breast in his mouth. The swirling sensations of pleasure tightened into a hard knot, and she let out a low mewl.

"Ooh," she whispered. "M-Montague, what—Oh!"

A sharp cry escaped her lips as he sucked hard, drawing her nipple into his mouth. *Sweet heaven*—how was it that such sensations could be had from such a simple act?

"So responsive," he murmured, his hot breath rippling across her skin. Then he drew back, his gaze ravenous as he stared at her breast. "So perfect," he whispered. "So pink."

The ache in her center swelled at his gentle praise, and she squeezed her thighs together to ease it. He lowered his gaze to her thighs and ran a fingertip along the top of her stockings. Then he drew back, his eyes darkening as he stared at her naked form.

Unable to conquer her shame at her nudity, she lifted her hands to cover her breasts, but he caught her wrists.

"No—Eleanor," he said, his voice thick and hoarse. "Remain where you are so that I may enjoy looking at you while I undress. Uncurl your hands and touch your thighs."

Her body moved in an instinctive desire to obey, and she placed her hands at the top of her thighs. Then he covered her hands with his and guided them toward her center, until the tips of her fingers touched the source of the ache, where the flesh was slick and hot. He slid his hand along her, and his fingertips brushed against her center, as if by accident—but the flare of triumph in his eyes spoke of his intent…

Wicked, *pleasurable* intent.

Then he withdrew his hands. "You must remain still, my love, though you may yearn to touch yourself."

His words ignited the very yearning he spoke of.

Sweet heaven! He was a master at seduction—and she a novice who could never hope to match him.

A knowing smile curved his lips while he peeled off his jacket, followed by his waistcoat and his necktie, with slow, deliberate movements, as if to prolong her agony.

The ache in her center pulsed again, and she shifted her hand to ease it.

"No," he chided. "You must be still. Pleasure must not come too soon—the longer the wait, the sweeter the release."

She held her breath while he removed the rest of his clothes, and her cheeks warmed at the sight of his firm, powerful—and very *naked*—body shimmering in the light of the fire. Shadows played across the planes of his muscles—muscles that nestled in pairs, covered with a light dusting of dark hair that grew thicker lower down, toward…

A delicious pulse of fear threaded through her as she caught sight of his manhood jutting out from a thick nest of curls, shifting faintly as if it carried his lifeblood.

Sweet Lord! It was so—so…

So *big*.

She shrank back, but he caught her hand.

"There's nothing to fear, Eleanor," he said. "Touch me."

"T-touch you?"

"Yes…" he breathed.

She reached forward and placed her hands on his chest.

"Oh, yes," he said, his voice a low growl. "That's good."

Emboldened by his praise, she began to caress his skin, running her hands along the contours of his chest, relishing the soft, downy hair under her fingertips. Then she slid her hand lower, where the hair grew coarser and his skin hotter, until her hand was inches away from the proud, jutting essence of him. She stilled her hand, staring at it.

"Don't be afraid," he said. "With this, I shall worship you."

She lowered her hand and wrapped her fingers around him. He caught his breath and stilled while she moved her fingers along the shaft—firm steel encased in soft, silken skin.

Then she squeezed, gently, and his body jerked.

"Oh, woman, you unman me!" He clamped his hand over hers. "No more, I beg you."

"D-did you not like it?"

"I liked it very much—but I fear that if you continue, I shall spend."

"Spend?"

"Aye, my love—and no man can call himself a gentleman if he cannot abide by the unbreakable rule of lovemaking."

"What unbreakable rule?"

"Ladies first," he said. "And now—I believe it's *your* turn."

He placed his hands on her shoulders and pushed her back on the bed until she lay before him. Her thighs parted, and a flare of need pulsed in his eyes.

"My Eleanor is overdressed."

He placed a kiss at the top of her thigh, then peeled off the stocking, following a line of kisses along her leg until he reached her toes. Then he repeated the gesture with the other stocking and paused at the top of her thighs to inhale deeply.

"Ah—the sweet, *sweet* scent of woman. There's nothing in the world to compare—my delicious, clever darling."

He crawled along the bed, covering her body with his, and nudged her thighs apart with his knee.

"At last," he said. "You're ready."

She shifted her legs, and he slid between her thighs, moving slickly against her flesh, while a thick wall of pleasure pulsed deep inside her body, swelling with each heartbeat.

Dear Lord—no…

The myriad of sensations threatened to overwhelm her, and she closed her eyes, retreating into her mind, fighting the desire raging through her body.

Then he stilled.

"Eleanor," he said, "I shall go no further until you can look at me—until I look into your eyes and see no pain."

"Montague, I—"

"Only when you trust me completely will I take you."

She opened her eyes. Two sapphire pools stared back at her, filled with desire. Then he smiled and began to move against her, and the tide of pleasure swelled at the delicious friction. The pleasure began to crest, and a wave of panic rippled through her. She drew in a sharp breath and lowered her gaze.

Almost immediately he stopped. She glanced up to see him looking at her, raw agony in his eyes. His jaw bulged as if he gritted his teeth, and his whole body trembled with restraint at the spike of pleasure. Then he moved again, and she closed her eyes once more.

He stilled once more, his arms trembling as he held his body above her.

Then she understood.

He was waiting for her—to be certain of her trust, despite his own needs.

Did he show the same consideration to every woman he made love to?

"No," he said.

Sweet Lord! She'd voiced her fears aloud.

"I've never shown such consideration—because this is the first time I have truly made love."

His words shattered her fears, and she lifted her gaze to his, no longer afraid to bare her soul—and, for a moment, they simply stared at each other.

Then he thrust forward, and she felt a tight pinch between her thighs.

"Hush," he whispered. "There's my brave soul."

At length, she relaxed, letting her body accommodate him.

"Good girl."

Pleasure swelled within her at his gentle praise, spoken in a deep growl. Then he began to move, gently at first, shifting in and out, until the pleasure coiled in her insides, thickening and swelling.

"This body was made to be mine," he said, "made to be pleasured…"

He increased the pace, and she parted her legs further to draw him deeper in.

"Oh, you wondrous creature!" He plunged inside her, and she arched her back, meeting him thrust for thrust. "Oh, that's it!" he cried, his movements becoming more frenzied. Then he threw his head back, the tendons in his neck protruding with the strain. Mouth open, he continued to thrust, and a primal growl shuddered through his body.

Then his breathing grew more ragged. Eleanor thrust her hips up, and her body disintegrated as pure pleasure burst inside her.

"Montague!"

She threw back her head and screamed as a great wave washed back and forth, pulling her to pieces.

He plunged into her again, roaring out her name as he filled her completely. Then he drew her to him and fell forward, his voice growing hoarse while he continued to thrust, weakly, until his groans of need quietened into the satisfied little grunts of a primal beast who, having claimed his mate, was now replete with pleasure.

Then he sighed, and her heart almost cracked at the expression in his eyes, which glistened with moisture.

"Did I hurt you?" he whispered.

"A little, at first," she said. "There's an ache—but it's a delicious ache."

He began to withdraw, and she lifted her legs and wrapped them around him.

"Please," she whispered. "Stay inside me a little longer."

"I'll stay all night if you wish it, Eleanor."

"Thank you."

He smiled and shifted onto his side, still inside her. Then she nestled against his chest, relishing the warmth of his body, and drifted into a doze.

CHAPTER TWENTY-SEVEN

WHEN ELEANOR OPENED her eyes, a soft orange glow flickered in her chamber. The fire was not yet out—it must still be the middle of the night.

She opened her eyes and let out a cry.

She was lying on the bed, as naked as the day she was born. And standing over her…

Standing over her, equally naked, a hungry expression in his eyes, was Montague FitzRoy, fifth Duke of Whitcombe.

"Oh!" She sat up, her cheeks warming with shame. *Heavens!* Her thighs were wide apart—and he'd been looking at her— down *there.*

His eyes glittered with relish. "You're beautiful when you sleep, Eleanor."

She looked away. "I thought you promised never to flatter me."

He sat beside her, and the bed shifted under his weight.

"It's not flattery," he said. "I've seen the barrier you erect around yourself—to hide from the rest of the world." His mouth curled into a smile. "On occasion, you have lowered that barrier and gifted me with a glimpse of the woman inside. But tonight…" He gestured toward her body. "Tonight was the first time you removed the barrier completely. And it remained gone while you slept. Tonight is the first time I really *saw* you."

"And I you," she said.

He shook his head. "I have no cause to conceal myself as you do."

She caught his hand. "We may be opposites in the eyes of the world—but we are also alike. You would have the world believe that you care little for others." She lifted his hand to her lips. "But you *do* care. I saw it in the way you helped those children—in how kind you were to give books to Joe, even though you said they were nothing and you'd have cast them aside had he not taken them. And I saw it in how you treated Olivia as your sister despite how she's viewed by the world." She smiled up at him. "I even saw it in the way in which you ensured that the drawing room tonight would not be well lit so that I might not be overwhelmed by the noise and lights with my family here. You even asked your mother to play the pianoforte to ensure the conversation was kept to a minimum."

"It's not much to boast of, Eleanor."

"I disagree," she said. "It means the world to *me*. What is a grand gesture, intended to draw in the admiration of the world, compared to the small, almost insignificant gestures that go unnoticed by most, but make a world of difference to one person? It's the very fact that those gestures are unnoticed that makes them honest, and pure. For they were not done with your own gratification in mind—but for the comfort and pleasure of others."

"You're too kind," he said.

"And..." She hesitated, lest he be offended by her request. But they were soon to part—where was the harm in asking?

"Is there something you desire?" he asked.

"I wondered if I might be permitted something to remember you by."

He captured her mouth in a swift kiss, then brushed his knuckles against her breast, grinning as her nipple beaded. "I've already given you that. But the night is young—I can do so again."

"N-no—I meant..." She inhaled, summoning her courage.

"May I sketch you—I mean, from life this time?"

He cocked his head to one side. "You've sketched me before, from memory? May I see?"

"If you grant my request."

"Then, my Eleanor," he said, stretching his long, lithe body along the bed, "your wish is my command."

THE PLEASURE OF sketching him from memory was nothing compared to the pleasure of having the living, breathing man before her, his perfect naked form at her command, to draw as she liked, to follow the contours of his body—the muscles, the sinews, right down to the detail around his knuckles.

She cast her gaze over his body, settling on the very essence of him that had given her such exquisite pleasure earlier that night—thick and beautiful, nestling among the dark curls. She ran her pencil over the page, curling around its form, depicting every wrinkle in the skin, from root to tip, and her body tightened with the memory of him inside her…

"I believe the artist is *blushing*," he rumbled.

She initialed the sketch. "It's done."

"May I see?"

She handed over the sketchbook, and he flicked through it. He had posed for two full sketches, several studies of his hands, his feet, and his manhood, and a line drawing as a portrait.

"You called me a flatterer, Eleanor—but you are just as guilty of that particular crime. You've made me too perfect."

"It's how *I* see you."

He sighed. "If only I could draw you as well. Could you draw yourself?"

"It would be somewhat vain, wouldn't it?" she said.

"But for me?" he asked. "As a keepsake?"

She could hardly refuse. "You want a portrait?"

"A full sketch. I want to remember that beautiful body."

She rose and studied herself in the mirror—her unremarkable body with its soft curves and overly large breasts that Mother had said were too vulgar for Society, but that Montague had worshiped with relish, making her feel beautiful.

"Look at yourself," he whispered, placing his hands on her shoulders. "Look at yourself through *my* eyes—not the eyes of those who fail to understand you."

She continued to stare, imagining the woman in the mirror was desirable. Then, with a nod, she sat and began sketching.

Minutes later, she'd completed a line drawing of a naked woman. Then she initialed it, tore it from the page, and handed it to him.

"I'll treasure it," he said. "And have no fear—I'll keep it concealed in my chamber. I'll not ruin your reputation by letting it fall into the wrong hands. My chamber is my haven, in which I shut out the rest of the world."

"Is that why you made love to me here, instead of your chamber?" she asked.

He let out a soft chuckle. "I had a more practical reason for bringing you here. I asked Mrs. Adams to set your chamber apart from the other guests—I thought you'd prefer the quiet. Had we made love in *my* chamber, the rest of the guests would have heard you screaming my name."

"Oh."

"In fact," he said, shifting closer, "I'm minded to hear my name on your lips again. I find I'm ready for you again."

It was folly to make love a second time. The taste of pleasure at his hands was like an opiate—the first rush of ecstasy, followed by an ever-increasing need for more, until she grew dependent and was driven mad for need of it.

And then, when the opiate was taken from her forever…

But she would accept the pain of withdrawal to have him inside her again—just once more. And the pleasure would be tenfold now she understood the joy of sharing her body with a man she loved.

"Very well," she said. "Let us make the most of tonight."

The second time, pleasure came quickly. He mounted her swiftly, slipping inside her with ease, then, with a few sharp thrusts, brought her to climax. After they crested the wave, he pulled her to him and held her in his arms, their bodies sticky with sweat, while their breathing steadied.

As she drifted into sleep once more, he caressed her hair in an absent-minded gesture.

"I love you, Eleanor."

She caught her breath. Had he spoken? Or had she heard an echo of a dream, fulfilling a wish that could never come true? She waited several heartbeats. Then, with a soft sigh, she drifted into sleep once more.

The next time she woke, her maid was bustling about the room, drawing the curtains and chivying her to prepare for the journey home. Her clothes were neatly folded in a pile on a chair, and beneath them, her sketchbook. There was no sign that Montague had even been there.

CHAPTER TWENTY-EIGHT

MONTY RAISED HIS hand in farewell and watched the carriages disappear as they turned a corner at the bottom of the drive.

He was due to follow them to London, but he would have to endure three days alone at Rosecombe.

Three days without *her*.

That morning, before dawn, he'd slipped out of Eleanor's chamber and returned to his chamber. He'd almost been caught by a kitchen maid as she shuffled along the hallway, coal scuttle in hand, to light the fire in the breakfast room. Servants should have more to fear from an encounter with their master above stairs, but he was the one who'd hidden behind a curtain, his heart racing, while the girl scurried past.

"I trust you've ended your engagement, Montague."

He winced at the disapproval in his mother's tone.

"No, Mother. Not yet. We've agreed to end it after I return to London."

"Why prolong it?" she asked. "It's time you found a proper bride."

"Proper?"

"One more suited to you."

"You mean one more suited to *you*, Mother," he said, unable to temper his irritation. "It's a pity you can't find a perfect little debutante and marry her yourself."

"Don't be petulant, it doesn't suit you," she said. "I had no objection to Miss Howard as an individual."

Monty snorted. "Who are you trying to fool?"

"I admit I didn't think much of her at first, but she's intelligent—at least for a young woman. Had she a title, I might have grown to like her, in time."

"You're an insufferable snob, Mother," he said. "I saw the look of horror in your eyes when I offered for her—have you never wondered why I did?"

"Ye gods!" she cried. "Does Miss Howard know you entered into a false engagement with her merely to irk me?" She shook her head. "I don't know whether she or I should be the most insulted. At first I thought Miss Howard deserved my pity for what you're doing—elevating her hopes before abandoning her. But in abandoning her, I believe you'll be doing her a great service."

"Why? Because marriage to me is a punishment?"

"For Miss Howard, perhaps," she replied. "A girl of her class most likely harbors an expectation of marrying for love. But those of our rank do *not* marry for love."

He glanced at her and saw sadness in her eyes—a sadness born of a loveless marriage to a faithless duke who believed that his title gave him free rein to behave as he liked, and rut whom he liked, no matter how many hearts he broke.

Monty had no wish to follow in his father's footsteps—a man who'd broken his vows and his wife's heart, leaving behind a bitter widow who, instead of directing her resentment at the man responsible for her misery, had pushed her hatred toward the man's natural child.

Olivia. How his life might have been different had his half-sister been in his life from the beginning! He could have indulged and protected her, and accompanied her to her first London Season. And no older brother would have been prouder.

"Perhaps Lady Arabella Ponsford—"

"*No*, Mother," he interrupted. "I've no intention of inflicting that harpy on Rosecombe, or on myself."

"But propriety demands—"

"What part of 'no' don't you understand?" he cried. "Over the years, you've said, and done, enough for the sake of propriety—and it's made you bitter and miserable. Well, propriety be damned! When I've concluded my business with Miss Howard, I'll return to Rosecombe and take up the responsibility that I have thus far neglected."

"I'm delighted to hear that, Montague."

"I doubt it," he said, "for I refer to my responsibility to my sister."

"I told you never to mention that."

"Stop right there!" he roared. "Like it or not, *I'm* head of this family, of which Olivia is a member, not only by virtue of being a direct descendant of the fourth duke, but *because I say so.*"

She stared at him, curling her hands into fists, and for a moment he thought she might strike him. Then she nodded.

"Perhaps my son has finally grown into a man," she said. "Go to London, Montague. Do your duty to Miss Howard and let her down gently. Then come home and do your duty to your title."

Before he could respond, she returned inside, tap-tapping her cane on the gravel drive.

Yes—he would do his duty to Miss Howard then part ways with her. But he would always carry a piece of her in his heart.

CHAPTER TWENTY-NINE

O F ALL THE delights of London, he'd miss Hyde Park the most. As summer drew to a close, the park became a riot of color—the leaves of the trees, ranging from green, to orange, to vibrant red, illuminated by the sunlight until they looked as if they were on fire.

He checked himself. Since when had he become so damned poetic?

Since Eleanor.

He glanced at the woman on his arm, but she was too preoccupied with the view across the Serpentine to notice. Her face was in profile, wisps of hair dancing about her face in the breeze; her eyes shone in the sunlight, their vivid green reflecting the leaves that were yet to succumb to the onset of autumn. A soft smile curled her lips—lips he now knew tasted of honey and cinnamon, the sweetness of innocence with a spicy undertone of uniqueness.

Would he ever taste lips as sweet?

In fact, would his life ever be the same, or would it forever be divided into two?

The time before, and the time after, Eleanor.

The *Time After Eleanor* would begin tomorrow, when he would parade about this very park with Daniella and Cerise on his arms, before he left for the country to spare Miss Howard too much humiliation.

They approached the water's edge, where a man in regimentals stood, reading a booklet. He turned as they approached, and Monty recognized Colonel Reid. The man's eyes widened as his gaze fell on Eleanor. Then he looked to one side, toward the rest of Eleanor's family ahead on the path, where Juliette Howard was walking arm in arm with the Duke of Dunton.

Juliette was a fool, casting Reid aside for that lecherous old fossil! And she was an even greater fool if she believed she had a chance of becoming Dunton's duchess. Dunton used his title not only to open doors to the best clubs in London, but also to open the thighs of every debutante desperate to wed a title—only to cast them aside.

Many young women had entered into hasty marriages with men below their station shortly after having been seen on Dunton's arm. Or they disappeared from Society altogether.

How many firstborn children had arrived after just such a hasty marriage, with features that bore an inexplicable resemblance to that lecher—an eternal mark of its mother's ruination?

Dunton often boasted of his conquests when in his cups at White's. He seemed to take pride in the number of maidenheads he'd claimed—fifty at the last count, if his boasts were to be believed.

Which is what I did five nights ago.

What made Monty any different to Dunton?

Eleanor had consented—nay, she had *asked*—in the full knowledge that they would part company. Dunton's conquests were sordid fumblings. What Monty had shared with Eleanor was far more—it was a union of souls.

Colonel Reid dipped his head in a bow and clicked his heels together. "Miss Howard, a pleasure," he said. "And Whitcombe, of course."

The colonel's features were open and honest. His mouth lifted into a smile, and his eyes—a soft, warm chocolate brown—sparkled in the sunlight. The poor man hadn't stood a chance with Juliette. Reid might be capable in battle, but in Society, he lacked the predator's instinct. Any fool would have known that Juliette had encouraged his suit merely to further her cause of attracting Dunton's attention.

Reid colored under Monty's scrutiny.

"Colonel Reid," Eleanor said, stepping forward. "How delightful to see you. It's a fine day for a walk in the park, is it not?"

Monty smiled to himself. He'd taught her well. She could now break an awkward silence with aplomb. If nothing else, he'd given her the ability to survive a social encounter, even if she'd never completely enjoy it.

"That it is, Miss Howard," the colonel replied. "It's the perfect balance of the season and sunshine."

What the devil was he on about?

"Oh yes!" Miss Howard cried, evidently able to translate. "The summer is drawing to a close, and yet nature is bestowing upon us brighter colors than we could ever hope to see in a hothouse. Just look at that horse chestnut—have you ever seen anything so magnificent?"

"The sunlight makes it look as if it's glowing from the inside," Reid said.

She nodded, her eyes sparkling with joy.

Curse the man! He was voicing precisely what Monty himself had been thinking.

"I've often wondered what it might be like to paint that tree."

"You're an artist?" Eleanor looked at Reid with renewed interest.

"I dabble, nothing more. When a man has a profession, he has little time to indulge in pleasures that are deemed, by his family, to be mere frivolities."

Had Monty imagined it, or did the colonel cast a look of disdain in his direction? Perhaps he considered a gentleman less worthy of existence than a man with an occupation.

"I assure you, *I'm* also kept very busy, colonel," he said.

Reid merely inclined his head.

"I'm sorry to hear you've no time to paint, colonel," Eleanor said. "A man shouldn't occupy himself with work all the time—otherwise, there's little point in existing." Then she colored. "Forgive me. I'm being too forward. Sometimes I let my enthusiasm run unchecked."

"No, Miss Howard, you're right," Reid said. "There's no shame in having a passion for art. Mankind is nothing without art or music."

"Is that why you spend much of your time shooting the French?" Monty asked.

It was a petulant comment, which he regretted almost as soon as he'd said it.

"I daresay, Whitcombe, you understand soldiering as much as I understand…whatever it is a duke occupies himself with."

There was no mistaking the bitter edge to the colonel's voice. Juliette had done a thorough job in breaking the man's heart. Monty would almost have pitied Reid, had the colonel not vented his frustration on him—as if Monty and his kind were responsible for all the miseries of the world.

Eleanor glanced at Monty, then back to Reid, a faint blush on her cheeks.

"I understand little of soldiering," she said. "Is it very frightening?"

"No, Miss Howard." The colonel smiled. "There's order, an honor, in soldiering," he said. "I trust my men with my life, and in turn, they place their trust in me. And while those with limited understanding view our occupation as one of violence, we are merely striving to ensure the freedom Society takes for granted."

"Such as freedom to enjoy art?"

"Precisely! And while I'm unable to partake in the arts in the manner in which I have always wanted, I can, at least, savor the efforts of others." He held up the booklet, and Monty read the front page.

THE

EXHIBITION

OF THE

ROYAL ACADEMY,
M.DCCCXV.
THE FORTY-SEVENTH

"Oh, the Academy Exhibition!" Eleanor cried. "Colonel, have you seen it? I've always wanted to go. Is it as wonderful as I've always imagined it to be?"

Reid smiled again. "It's remarkable—though, knowing you so little, Miss Howard, I'm unsure whether it would meet *your* expectations."

"Are there any pieces you particularly like?" she asked. "I overheard Lady Fairchild mentioning a portrait of the Marchioness of Stafford, painted by Sir Thomas Lawrence. Have you seen it?"

"Yes. Sir Thomas has several pieces exhibited this year, including portraits of the Bishops of London and Norwich. Do you like portraits, Miss Howard? I hear there's a rather scandalous painting by a young artist by the name of Etty." He lowered his voice to a whisper. "A *nude*—would you believe it?"

She cast a glance at Monty, her eyes flaring with need. "I-I enjoy looking at some portraits, but I confess to having little interest in viewing a portrait of someone, unless I know or care about them."

"And you care little for bishops or marchionesses?"

"Do *you* care for them, colonel?"

"Only insofar as they present a challenge for the artist. I can appreciate the effort and natural ability that has gone into producing a painting, even if I wouldn't choose to have it on my wall."

"Was there anything that you *would* hang on your wall, colonel?" she asked.

He smiled, and Monty caught a flicker of love in his eyes.

"Aye," he said. "I'm fond of paintings of ordinary folk going about their daily business—natural, honest depictions of honest, hardworking people."

"Is there such a painting?" Monty asked.

The colonel glanced at him and widened his eyes, as if he'd forgotten Monty's presence.

"There is. A painting by William Collins, depicting young boys at Cromer."

"What would boys be doing at Cromer?" Monty asked.

"Catching shrimp, I imagine," Eleanor said. "That is—if they're working. Am I right, colonel?"

"You are, Miss Howard," Reid said, smiling. "I find myself ashamed."

"Of what?" she asked.

"Of all the times I came to visit—to take tea with your family. Not once did I speak to you. To think of the conversations we might have enjoyed about art! In fact, I hardly noticed you, perhaps because…"

His voice trailed off, and he glanced across the park to where Juliette was leaning on Dunton's arm, her laughter filtering through the air.

Reid had only been guilty of the same crime as any other man—he'd overlooked the plain elder sister in favor of the beautiful younger one. There was no denying that Juliette Howard was a beautiful creature. But Eleanor's beauty shone from within, because it was ingrained in her heart, and in her soul. Few were privileged enough to glimpse her beauty—and now, it seemed as if Reid had joined their ranks.

"Perhaps some things are best left unsaid," Reid said. "But whatever happened in the past shouldn't preclude me from inviting you to accompany me to the exhibition, Miss Howard. That is, if Whitcombe has no objection. Or"—he turned his gaze to Monty—"*he* could accompany us, if you prefer."

"Oh." Eleanor blushed and met Monty's gaze. This time tomorrow—as per their agreement—their engagement would be over. But he could leave Eleanor in good hands.

"I'll be otherwise occupied, Reid," Monty said. "But I've no objection to Miss Howard accompanying you. She would testify to my ignorance in relation to the arts—I was even fooled into believing a fake Stubbs was genuine."

"You mean the one that graces Lady Francis's hallway?" Reid laughed. "The horse is out of proportion."

"Isn't it just?" Eleanor giggled. "I wondered whether to tell her, but decided against it."

"You're quite right," Reid said. "A lady would rather be deceived into purchasing a fake painting than be proven wrong by a lady of greater intelligence."

Could the man be any more obvious?

"Do you attempt to flatter me, colonel?" Eleanor asked.

"It's not flattery when I speak the truth, Miss Howard."

Devil's toes! Was she to fall for that ruse? It was what Monty himself had said to her often enough. But his words had come from the heart.

Maybe Reid's words were genuine, too. As Monty cast his gaze over his rival, he couldn't help but notice the sensitivity around the mouth, the kindness in the man's eyes—so totally unlike the hard-edged, rakish expression that glared back at Monty each time he looked in a mirror.

Reid was not the sort of man to break a young woman's heart.

"You simply *must* see the Collins painting, Miss Howard," Reid said. "Perhaps I might call on you next week? I have no engagements on Monday."

"You seem particularly keen for me to see the painting," she replied. "Is Mr. Collins an acquaintance?"

"Before I enlisted in the army, William and I studied together," Reid said. "We were to enter the Royal Academy, but my father wanted me to distinguish myself in the militia." He let out a sigh. "Father, of course, was right. I have found—and still find—soldiering a worthy occupation. I often wonder how I'd have fared had I pursued my love of art. But I lacked William's talent. I could never dream of having any of my meagre little drawings hanging on the academy's hallowed walls. But what about you,

Miss Howard? If you're a painter, you might see one of your works exhibited one day."

"I'm a *woman*, colonel," she said. "Such opportunities are denied me."

"That's where you're wrong. Here…" Reid flicked through the booklet, then stopped, his finger on the page. "See? Exhibit 111, by Miss Geddes."

She peered at the page. "*A study*—I wonder what it's a study of?"

"We'll have to see when we visit, won't we? And there are plenty more works by women. Your sex shouldn't prevent you from doing anything you want."

She smiled, her eyes shining with hope.

"Eleanor!" a voice hailed, and her demeanor changed.

"Forgive me, Colonel Reid—my mother's calling," she said. "We're due to take tea with Lady Francis."

"In which case, you have my sympathies," Reid said, offering his hand and giving her a wink.

She took it, and he brought her hand to his lips.

"Until Monday, Miss Howard." Then he lifted his chin at Monty. "Whitcombe."

"Reid."

Monty steered Miss Howard toward the path where her family stood waiting. As he caught sight of her father's stern gaze, then looked over his shoulder at Colonel Reid, who was watching them intently, his concerns for Miss Howard lessened.

Tomorrow she might suffer humiliation, but she would emerge triumphant and, in all likelihood, would end up in better hands than his—as the wife of Colonel Reid.

CHAPTER THIRTY

"**A**REN'T YOU GOING to drink your tea, Eleanor?"

Eleanor glanced up. "I'm sorry?"

Her mother nodded toward the cup in Eleanor's hand. "Your tea. Either drink it or put the cup down. I can see that cup toppling over, and you don't want to spill tea on your gown again, do you?"

Eleanor placed her cup on the table.

"So you're *not* going to drink it."

"No, Mother."

"Then why did you take it?"

Because you would have hounded me until I did.

Eleanor's mother let out a sharp sigh and stirred her tea, rattling the spoon against the cup as it went around and around…

Around and around…

Clink-clink-clink…

Eleanor gritted her teeth. But though she longed to ask her mother to stop, or to excuse herself and return to her chamber, she was not in the mood to weather the inevitable outburst of indignation.

Not today, of all days.

She sighed and glanced out of the window. It was past ten. Montague would already have done the deed.

How long would the news take to spread?

At least she'd be spared her sister's taunts. Juliette had disappeared earlier that morning to take a walk. She'd looked a little out of sorts during breakfast—paler than usual, her eyes red-rimmed as if she'd been crying—but when Eleanor inquired after her health, she'd been sharply told to mind her own business.

The stirring continued—*clink-clink-clink*—the rhythm growing in intensity until it resembled footsteps…

Then the door burst open, and Juliette rushed in. Face flushed, eyes bright, at least she seemed to have regained some of her color. But what had distressed her?

No—not distressed. Her expression was one of excitement—and triumph.

Juliette glanced about the room. Then her gaze settled on Eleanor. The corner of her mouth lifted into a smile, before she smoothed her expression—but she couldn't disguise the satisfaction in her eyes.

She knows.

"What is it, Juliette?" their mother asked. "You look unwell."

"I'm all right, Mother," Juliette said. "But I fear for poor Eleanor." She let out a deep sigh. "Oh, Eleanor, I'm *so* sorry! It pains me to be the one to tell you—truly it does."

Since when did someone say *truly it does* or *I swear it* other than to convince someone to believe their lies?

"What's happened?" Mother asked.

"The Duke of Whitcombe was seen coming out of a woman's house."

"And? Perhaps he was visiting her husband—or he had some business there."

"He most certainly had *business*," Juliette continued. "It was Mrs. Delacroix's house."

"That harlot!" Mother scoffed.

"He was seen with her on his arm—everyone knows she was his mistress." Juliette's eyes widened, almost with relish. "There was another doxy on his other arm. Cerise, or so I was told."

"Who told you?" Mother asked.

"Mr. Moss told us."

"Us?" Eleanor asked, nausea curling in her stomach.

"Irma was with me when Mr. Moss told us. *Everybody's* talking about it." Juliette glanced at Eleanor. "My poor sister."

Mother rose to her feet. "This is outrageous! And so unjust—what a disgrace!"

A sense of loss curled in Eleanor's gut. Though she had anticipated the manner by which her engagement was to end, she hadn't expected the pain, the dark ache spreading through her body. Yet, despite the pain, she clung to a glimmer of hope—the indignation of Mother's voice as she defended her. Was it indignation born of a mother's love?

"Mother..." Eleanor began, but Lady Howard raised her hand.

"Enough!" she cried. "Say nothing, lest my disappointment in you increases. How *could* you?"

"How could I *what*, Mother?"

"I knew it was too good to be true. What could you have done to drive Whitcombe into the arms of harlots?"

"*Two* harlots," Juliette said.

"We must rise above this," Mother continued, "which means we don't indulge in gossip. Perhaps Mr. Moss was mistaken."

"I doubt it," Juliette said. "Everyone's talking about it! They were seen in Hyde Park—Whitcombe was parading his doxies along Rotten Row. Mr. Moss told us—*and* Lady Francis."

"We must act swiftly," Mother said. "Our family is innocent in all this. Yes—we can salvage our reputation if we make it known that we've been wronged. We must act as if none of this has happened. That means you too, Eleanor."

"M-me?"

"Yes, you." Mother's eyes narrowed. "You don't appear surprised—or discomposed. Did you expect this to happen?"

"I suppose I did."

"You *suppose*!" Mother scoffed. "Well, one thing we can be thankful for is your lack of concern. You must use it on Saturday."

"Saturday?"

"Our dinner party. It's our opportunity to salvage the family's reputation. Everybody will be there—the Fairchilds, Mr. Moss, Lady Francis, the Duke of Dunton..."

Sweet Lord, no! The very worst people in all Society—coming to dine and gloat at Eleanor's expense.

"M-Mother, I can't—"

"Yes you *can*, child. You owe it to the family. You owe it to your sister. *You* may not be able to hold on to a suitor, but you cannot be so selfish as to wish the same fate on Juliette. Dunton's shown a marked interest in her, hasn't he? If we cannot have two duchesses in the family, I'll be content with one."

"You really *don't* look that upset, Eleanor," Juliette said.

Eleanor rose, fisting her hands to control the tremors in her body. "What do you expect?" she cried. "Do you want me to scream? Or suffer a fainting fit and collapse at your feet to feed your gratification?"

"Eleanor, that's enough!" Mother cried. "Just because *you've* failed, it doesn't give you the right to upset the rest of us. I—"

The door burst open, and Eleanor's father appeared.

"What the devil's going on?" he said. "You can be heard in the street outside!" He glanced at Eleanor, and his eyes widened. "What's happened, daughter?"

"She's lost her fiancé, Leonard," Mother said.

"What do you mean, *lost?*"

"He's been seen with a harlot."

"*Two* harlots," Juliette added. "Her engagement is no more."

Papa's eyes narrowed. "Are you sure?"

"Yes," Juliette said before Eleanor could respond. "Mr. Moss said—"

"I was speaking to your sister," Father said, his voice sharp. Then he let out a sigh. "Damned tiresome business." He held out his hand. "Eleanor—come with me."

"Leonard," Mother protested, "you can have nothing to say to Eleanor that I needn't be party to."

"Grace, for *once*, will you refrain from talking and let me have my way?"

"What do you mean, *have your way?*" she replied. "Surely *I* have the right—"

"That's enough!" he roared. "Haven't I enough to deal with, without you nipping at me like a terrier?"

Mother and Juliette's eyes widened simultaneously, as if they were marionettes being manipulated by the same puppeteer.

"Eleanor, stop dawdling and come with me."

Her cheeks flaming, Eleanor followed her father to his study, where he closed the door, took his seat behind the desk, and gestured to the chair opposite.

She sat, while he placed his elbows on the desk and steepled his fingers together, in the manner of a vicar about to deliver a sermon about fire, brimstone, and eternal damnation.

But the sermon never came. He observed her in silence, and the air filled with the gentle ticking of the clock over the fireplace, the steady sound of his breathing—and her own heartbeat pulsing faintly in her ears.

When she was a child, Father's study was a place to be revered. Rarely was she—or even Mother—permitted to enter. It was, to him, a sanctuary from female company. It was the essence of him, a strange mix of untidiness and order—books stacked on shelves according to color, the gold leaf on the spines forming a regular pattern, a sheaf of papers high enough to be in danger of toppling over...

It even smelled of him—brandy, cigar smoke, and cinnamon.

He reached for the squat-bellied decanter in front of him, removed the stopper, and splashed a quantity of brown liquid into two beveled glasses. Then he pushed one toward her and nodded.

She stared at it. Mother said brandy was a drink exclusive to men—that for a woman to indulge in the stuff was the first step to ruination.

He pushed the glass a little closer. "Go on. I won't tell your mother."

She leaned forward, tipped the glass up, and took a sip. The liquid burst on her tongue with an explosion of heat. Not unpleasant, but she caught her breath at the intensity.

"Different to wine, isn't it?" he said. "Good for nasty shocks—manly due to its effect on your senses detracting from your troubles. Though"—he leaned closer—"you don't look particularly troubled. Or perhaps your sister is mistaken and your engagement isn't over?"

She took another sip. "No, Papa, it's definitely over."

"If your sister speaks the truth, the duke was seen this morning with a woman on each arm. You parted on good terms when he joined us in the park yesterday—hardly the behavior of a couple breaking an engagement. Or did you meet afterward?"

"No—that was the last time I saw him."

He drained his glass, then Eleanor startled as he slammed it on the desk.

"Damn him!" he cried. "What the devil's he playing at? I should call him out."

"Papa, there's no need…"

"But he's acted like a cad!" He poured another brandy and took a gulp. "To think—he sat in the same chair you're in and spun me a tall tale to convince me to consent to your engagement. I knew of his reputation as a rake, of course—but I still fell for his lies."

He sighed, drained the glass, and poured a third.

"I can't recall a time when I was more disappointed—nay, disgusted."

Eleanor leaned forward. "Please, Papa, he's not as bad as you think."

"What nonsense! Surely you're not condoning your fiancé cavorting with *harlots?*"

She suppressed a shudder. "It's not like that, Papa. I-I know what it looks like—and I'm sorry if you're disappointed in me."

Of all the trials she might have faced—humiliation at Montague's hand, even if it were planned, her mother's ever-constant irritation, her sister's spiteful triumph—the one assault she could not weather was her father's disappointment.

She closed her eyes, willing the tears to subside. Then she felt a warm hand over hers.

"Oh, my sweet girl," he said. "I could never be disappointed in *you*. In truth, I'm not disappointed in him, either—for he's exactly what I first believed him to be." He shook his head and sighed, and Eleanor's heart gave a little jolt at the tiredness in his eyes. "No, I'm disappointed in *myself*, for having been taken in. He led me to believe he's an honorable man who would never break a promise."

Eleanor blinked, and a tear splashed onto his hand. She placed her other hand over his and wiped it away.

"Montague is an honorable man, Papa," she said. "He has not broken faith with me."

"Then what *has* he done?"

She sighed. The truth would emerge sooner or later. Better it come from her lips than any other's.

"It was all a pretense," she said. "We never intended to marry."

"You *what?*" he cried.

"W-we made an arrangement, to pretend to be engaged."

"Whatever for, child?"

"H-he said it would help me in Society," she said. "And he *has* helped me, Papa. I can more easily speak to strangers. It's down to his tutelage that I could speak to Colonel Reid during our walk and secure our invitation to the Academy Exhibition."

"And what was in it for Whitcombe?" he asked. "I doubt he did it out of kindness."

"I…" Though she longed to speak the truth, shame prevented her.

"Foolish girl," he muttered, as if to himself. "Let me hazard a guess. Hounded by young women hunting a title, he chose to deter them by entering into a false arrangement with another.

Doubtless he chose you because he thought so little of you that he expected you to meekly comply with no thought for your own self-respect. The bastard! I've every right to—"

"No, Papa!" she interrupted, tears spilling onto her cheeks. "It wasn't like that! Perhaps at first—but we struck a bargain. I had as much to gain from it as he—don't you see that?"

"All I see is a foolish girl who was tricked into a masquerade by a cad who thought of nothing but his own self-gratification." He let out a bitter laugh. "He'll have done himself no favors. Society doesn't look kindly on a man—whatever his rank—who breaks off with his fiancée by making a public show of himself with harlots. And as to his being hunted—he's only bought himself a reprieve. Next Season, the scavengers will be out in greater force. Curse him! I was beginning to like the man."

He opened a drawer in the desk and pulled out a sheaf of papers.

"I could sue him for breach of contract."

"No, Papa—I couldn't let you do that to him. And you have every reason to continue liking him. Despite what you may think, we're still friends."

"A man and a woman can never be friends," he replied. "Not when there's love involved."

She caught her breath at the intensity of his gaze, then she looked away. But it was too late—he'd already delved into her soul.

"You love him."

It was not a question.

Eleanor flicked her gaze up to find him still staring at her.

What was the point in denial? She reached for her glass and took another mouthful.

Papa was wrong. The effect of the brandy did nothing to detract her from her troubles.

"Sometimes love is not enough," she said quietly.

"Oh, child! Love is *everything*. I've learned over the years that it's titles—and fortunes—that are not enough when it comes to finding a partner in life." He set the papers aside. "I must do something. If you object to my shooting him at dawn, I could toss him into the Thames."

She fought to suppress a giggle at the notion of her diminutive parent throwing the large, powerful duke into the river.

"There's my girl," Papa said. "Stoic to the last. That's one thing I've never fathomed about you ever since you were old enough to talk—you often weathered adversities with little reaction, but, at other times, the slightest provocation sent you into a fit of temper."

"I shan't lose my temper today," Eleanor said. "But I'd rather not attend Mother's dinner party on Saturday."

"Because you believe everyone will be laughing at you?" Papa shook his head. "A respectable woman wronged will always garner sympathy. And, though I hate to admit it, your engagement to a duke will have given you a degree of respectability and admiration. Saturday's dinner may be awkward—the guests are bound to be curious. But if you weather it with aplomb, you'll emerge triumphant. I can make things easier for you by tampering with the guestlist—to give you an ally for the evening, at least. Is there anyone you would wish to see invited?"

"Only Lavinia, but she's in the country. I don't think her husband would take kindly to her traveling to London merely for a dinner."

Papa's mouth curled into a smile. "What about Colonel Reid? You seemed to be getting on well with him."

"I don't know…"

"You share an interest in art, so you'd have plenty to talk about—and you are attending the exhibition with him on Monday, so you must find his company agreeable."

"But Juliette—"

"Your sister's a fool for rejecting that respectable young man," he said. "If his presence makes *her* feel uncomfortable, then she only has herself to blame."

What reason did she have to object to Colonel Reid's invitation? Loyalty to Montague? He himself had spoken of her future—a future without him. And with Colonel Reid, at least she wouldn't be forced to trust her repertoire of vacuous Society phrases—they could have a real conversation rather than exchange meaningless remarks.

But if Papa was right, and a man and a woman could never be friends—did that mean sitting next to the colonel might give rise to an expectation?

What if I never want to marry?

"Then you say no each time a man asks, my dear, rather than cry out your acceptance before he's even finished his request."

She glanced up at her father, her cheeks flaming. *Heavens!* She'd spoken aloud.

"The colonel would do very well for you," Papa said. "He would, at least, be more amenable to your being a little…" He made a random gesture in the air.

"Odd?" she offered, and he colored.

"I was going to say *different from other young women,* which, at least, sounds more favorable than *eccentric.* And he'd be more willing than a titled man to grant you freedom to paint. A soldier, after all, understands the need for occupation, and I daresay he'd not object to a wife who wished for an occupation of her own. You were never suited to the life of idle luxury, my dear."

"I do like Colonel Reid," she replied. "But I hardly know him. He barely noticed me when he was courting Juliette."

"Don't punish him for that, Eleanor—men are often swayed by what they first see. It's only later that they understand the true nature of beauty. I daresay both you and Colonel Reid have learned a sharp lesson these past weeks."

"And if I cannot find a man to make me happy—or give me the freedom to do what I want, and be myself—what do I do then?"

"And what do you *want,* Eleanor?" he asked.

"To live in freedom, where I am not subject to the judgment of others. I-I could paint to earn my keep. I'm not like Juliette—I have no need for fine gowns or jewels—so I'm sure I could live within my means. My fortune could secure me an annuity."

"It wouldn't be an easy life, Eleanor. Could you bear living on your own?"

"How could I not, when I crave peace and quiet?" she replied. "If I never attended a dinner party or ball again, I'd be the happiest creature alive! And I'd have enough money to hire a maid to take care of me, so you needn't worry on that count."

"Is that what you want, child?"

"It's what I've always wanted—but nobody would listen!"

"And Whitcombe?"

"He was someone I grew attracted to," she said. "A dream—terrifying, yet beautiful. I'll always hold him in the highest regard. But if I cannot…" She hesitated as her chest tightened. "If I c-cannot find happiness in marriage, then I wish to find happiness in occupation."

She drained her glass and waited. Papa remained silent for a moment, then he leaned forward and covered his face with his hands.

"My poor child," he whispered. "Where did I go so wrong?"

Her heart tightened with sorrow. Was she such a failure in his eyes?

Then he lowered his hands and reached for her, taking both her hands in his.

"I've been such a fool," he said, "guided by the ambition of others. Your mother and I always wanted the best for you and your sister—a comfortable life so that you need not toil, and respectable marriages where you'd enjoy the trappings that wealth and a title can give you."

He stroked her hands, running the pad of his thumb across her skin. "But my unique little Eleanor was made for greater things. Fool that I was, I failed to champion your uniqueness—I was too weak to go against your mother's wishes. After all, your mother was the daughter of an earl—she understood Society far better than I ever could."

He lifted her hands to his lips. "Perhaps we can only reach true happiness through taking the more difficult path." He nodded, setting his mouth into a firm line. "If independence is what you crave, Eleanor, then I'll not stand in your way."

"You won't?"

"No, child. First thing Monday, I'll speak to Mr. Stockton and have him make the arrangements to give you control over your fortune. But on one condition. Give Colonel Reid a chance on Saturday. I believe you could be as happy with him—certainly more than—" He broke off and patted her hand. "I'll not speak of *that* particular gentleman anymore."

Then he released her hands and glanced at the clock. "Gracious! Is that the time? I've much to do—be off with you, tiresome child."

His words belied the affection in his voice, and she rose to her feet.

"Yes, Papa," she said. "Thank you."

"Do not thank me, dear one," he replied. "I'm only doing what I should have done years ago. Now—why don't you spend the rest of the day painting?"

"What about Mother and Juliette?"

"Leave them to me. You have my word that neither of them will dictate your life anymore."

He picked up the sheaf of papers—the marriage contract he'd agreed on with Montague—and for a moment, Eleanor's resolve wavered. Then she bowed her head and exited the study, her future looking a little brighter than it had yesterday—when she'd parted from Montague for the last time.

CHAPTER THIRTY-ONE

L IKE MANY SOCIAL occasions, the anticipation of tonight's dinner had been considerably more traumatic than the occasion itself.

Papa was right—rather than sneer at Eleanor for having been abandoned by her fiancé, the company viewed her with sympathy as the innocent party, and interest as a woman who had secured the attention of a duke in the first place. Even Mr. Moss addressed her with cordiality, and though she suppressed a shudder as he bowed over her hand and kissed it, his gallantry was preferable to his taunts about her clumsiness. Even when she dropped her fork, the company didn't punish her for it—other than Mother, who shot her a look of exasperation.

And Juliette…

Eleanor's sister seemed preoccupied. She'd hardly swallowed a morsel tonight, despite the lamb cutlets being her favorite, and seemed disinclined to touch the pineapple that Mother had gone to such pains to procure.

"Miss Howard, are you well?"

Eleanor turned to her dinner companion. "Perfectly so, thank you, colonel."

"I'm glad to hear it," he said. "Almost as glad as I was to receive your father's invitation. What good fortune I had no prior engagements tonight."

Juliette frowned from across the table. Then she closed her

eyes as if in pain and pushed her plate aside.

"Your sister seems unwell," Colonel Reid said. "I trust my presence hasn't discomposed her."

"You're too kind," Eleanor replied, "given that—" She broke off, her cheeks warming.

"Given that she denied my courtship? I believe she did me a favor. I could never have made her happy. Dunton will give her everything she wants. I take it they're courting?"

"I believe so," Eleanor said, "though I've yet to hear an announcement. He was invited tonight, but he's not come."

"I'm happy for her. Your sister was born to be a duchess, whereas…"

This time, it was his turn to blush.

"Forgive me. I didn't mean to cause you pain."

"And you haven't, I assure you," Eleanor said. "When one suffers disappointment, there's little merit in yearning for what might have been. Some battles are not meant to be fought—instead, one must surrender the ground to another, and seek victory elsewhere."

"As a soldier, I would disagree," he said. "But as a man, I see the merit in your argument." He raised his wineglass. "In which case, shall we drink a toast to future victories?"

They touched glasses before taking a sip.

"Gentlemen!" Papa announced. "Care to join me for a brandy?"

"I must away," Colonel Reid said. "But I shall claim you for the first dance when I return."

"Then you're either a brave soldier or a fool," Eleanor said. "I have a reputation for tripping over and crushing toes."

"Then I'll be thankful for the sturdiness of my regimental boots in shielding my feet while engaging with hostilities on the dance floor."

Eleanor let out a giggle. Then she startled at a clatter from across the table. Juliette stared at her, clutching her wineglass, her knuckles whitening.

The gentlemen trooped out, then Mother rose. "Ladies, would you follow me to the drawing room?" With a murmur of assent, the ladies stood and followed her out. Juliette rose and teetered to one side, before placing her hand on the table and righting herself. Eleanor waited until the dining room was empty, save for the servants clearing the plates, before she approached her sister.

"Juliette, what's wrong?" she asked, touching her sister's arm.

Juliette slapped her hand away. "Nothing!" she snapped. "Do you have to make such a show of yourself?"

"I don't understand. I—"

Juliette scoffed. "It's all 'me, me, me' with you, isn't it? First you parade about the place with a duke on your arm, basking in everybody's attention, then tonight, you lap up their sympathy. And now…" She pitched forward, then drew in a deep breath. "Now, you're all over the colonel like a twopenny whore!"

"I'm not a—"

"Yes, you are!" Juliette cried. "How else could an unremarkable little thing like *you* trick a duke into offering for you? But you failed, didn't you? A duke's a difficult prize to snare. He'll promise the world to get what he wants—then abandon you when he's taken it."

"Juliette, you're unwell. Let me take you to your chamber. I could bring you some hot cocoa like I used to when we were children?"

"I don't want cocoa!"

The despair in Juliette's voice stabbed at Eleanor's heart.

Something was wrong—*very* wrong.

"Juliette—it pains me to see you distressed. Can you not tell me what ails you? Perhaps I can help."

"Nobody can help me," Juliette snarled, "least of all *you*! Do you think I don't know what you're doing? Taunting me with the colonel?"

"The man you rejected in favor of the Duke of Dunton?" Eleanor shook her head. "In what way am I taunting you?"

Juliette winced, then her expression hardened. "Don't take me for a fool, Eleanor! You have everything you want, whereas I..."

Tears glistened on Juliette's cheeks, and she raised her hands to wipe them. Her heart aching for her sister's pain, Eleanor approached her, arms outstretched. This time, Juliette made no move to resist.

"Dearest Juliette, I'm far from having what I want, believe me," Eleanor said. "But you've much to look forward to. Despite our differences, you're my sister, and I want you to be happy. Can't we return to how we were when we were younger? Sisters should unite against adversity, not foster adversity between themselves."

For a moment, Juliette looked as if she might burst into tears, and Eleanor glimpsed a deep yearning in her eyes.

Then the moment was gone. Juliette pulled herself free and curled her lip into a sneer.

"You must be drunk to think such sentimental nonsense, let alone *say* it."

Swallowing the stab of pain in her heart, Eleanor retreated.

"Why, Juliette?" she asked. "What is it about me that you hate so much? I can't believe you take pleasure in hurting the feelings of others."

"Feelings!" Juliette huffed. "You *have* no feelings. You sit about the place with that perpetually glum expression on your face, never taking interest in anything *I* enjoy—always placing me in a position where I have to excuse your eccentricities to my friends. You don't know what it's like to *feel*."

"You're wrong," Eleanor said. "Just because I hide my feelings, doesn't mean I don't have any."

"Perhaps I should put that to the test."

"What do you mean?"

A sly smile slid across Juliette's mouth. A spark of fervor glittered in her eyes, and Eleanor's gut twisted in apprehension. Then it was gone, as Juliette closed her eyes again, her forehead creasing in pain.

"Perhaps I'll take my rest," she said. "Please give my excuses to Mama. Tell her I'll join the party in a little while."

She offered her hand, and Eleanor took it.

"Shall I send someone with some hot chocolate or water?" Eleanor asked.

Juliette shook her head.

"Or perhaps a doctor? I'm sure Dr. McIver wouldn't object to—"

"No!" Juliette pushed Eleanor back. "Why must you be so persistent?"

Eleanor raised her hands in appeasement. "Forgive me, Juliette," she said. "I'll say no more."

With that, she exited the dining room.

⤙⤙⤙⤚⤚⤚

BY THE TIME the men rejoined the ladies, Juliette had still not returned.

Which was, perhaps, for the best—not only for her own sake, given that she'd looked decidedly ill, but also for Eleanor's. To see her sister so unhappy had given rise to a turmoil of emotions—a yearning to comfort her, tempered by fear of Juliette's dislike.

How strange that one could care for someone, yet not bear to be in their company!

"Miss Howard, I am deeply hurt," a voice said.

Eleanor turned to see Colonel Reid staring directly at her. She held his gaze for a moment, then looked away. She might feel easy in his presence, but there was only one man whose gaze she completely trusted.

And he was not here tonight—nor was she likely to look into his eyes again.

"F-forgive me, colonel. I'm afraid I was preoccupied."

"Evidently. I've asked three times for your opinion on whether Stubbs or Gainsborough was the better painter."

"I cannot make an informed comparison," she said. "I've yet to study a Gainsborough in detail. But I consider Stubbs's work more appealing."

"Gainsborough was a favorite of the king and queen—and he was a founding member of the academy, whereas Stubbs—"

"Was only an associate of the academy, I know." His eyes widened, and she laughed. "Just because I'm a woman, it doesn't mean I don't read. And Stubbs is something of an obsession."

"I find his work a little gruesome."

"His sketches in *The Anatomy of the Horse* are exquisitely detailed, but, of course, they were drawn from life, after stripping away the flesh." She leaned closer, impelled by a wicked urge to shock, and lowered her voice. "Did you know he dissected human cadavers also?"

Colonel Reid paled. "Ye gods…"

"Not merely for gratification," she continued. "He put his work to use in a medical journal, but I've not had the opportunity to read it."

"I'm glad to hear it," he said. "While art should be encouraged, everything has its limits. I have seen death up close, Miss Howard. It is not something to be celebrated."

The general murmur of voices—which always rendered it an ordeal to take part in a conversation—quietened, and Eleanor glanced up.

Mother stood in the center of the drawing room.

"It's time for a little dancing," she said, fixing her gaze on Eleanor's companion. "Colonel Reid, could we prevail upon you to lead the first dance?"

"I'm engaged to your daughter for the first dance, Lady Howard," he said, "if she'll oblige me."

"Of course she will, won't you, Eleanor?"

"I-I don't dance very well," Eleanor said.

"Nonsense! You're an excellent dancer," Mother said.

"Yes," a new voice said, in a sneering tone. "Perfect in every way, isn't she?"

Juliette stood in the doorway, her face flushed, body swaying from side to side, clutching a book in her arms, as if her life depended on it.

"Daughter!" Eleanor's mother cried. "Whatever's the matter? You look quite ill."

"Nothing's the matter with *me*, Mama," Juliette said, her words slurred. "It's *Eleanor* you should concern yourself with."

"Juliette, compose yourself," Mother said. "Our guests have no wish to see you in such a state."

"Perhaps not—but I'm sure they'd love to know what my *perfect sister* does when they're not watching."

She unfolded her arms and held up the book.

No—not a book. Eleanor's sketchbook.

"Where did you get that?" Eleanor said. "Did you go into my study?"

"It's a good thing I did," Juliette replied, "or your sordid goings-on would have gone undiscovered."

A cold hand clutched Eleanor's stomach in a viselike grip as she recalled Juliette's warning.

Perhaps I should put that to the test.

"Juliette, that's enough," Eleanor's father said, rising to his feet. "You make me quite ashamed. James, please return Miss Juliette to her chamber then send for Dr. McIver." He addressed the rest of the party. "Do forgive my younger daughter—she appears to be having some sort of fit."

"I'm having nothing of the sort," Juliette replied, holding up the sketchbook. "*I'm* not the one to be ashamed of. See this?"

She flicked through the pages, then held the sketchbook aloft.

For a heartbeat, silence filled the air. Then a ripple threaded through the room as one guest after another drew in a sharp breath, their incredulity giving way to understanding.

On the page, for all to see, was Montague, lying naked on a crumpled bed, instantly recognizable by his physique—the planes of muscles lovingly depicted, his partially erect manhood jutting from the nest of curls, with not a single item of detail left to the imagination…

…and the smile of repletion on his full lips—the intensity in his eyes that had magnified at the point of his climax.

There would be no doubt in the mind of any observer that here was a man who'd engaged in a session of eager, vigorous lovemaking, who stared hungrily out of the page at the woman he'd just claimed.

"Wh-what is the meaning of…?" Eleanor's mother stammered, for once, at a loss for words.

"Isn't it obvious?" Juliette said. She turned the page, and the party gave a collective gasp as she revealed a study—a very *intricate* study of the part of him that had given Eleanor so much pleasure.

"Bloody hell!" Mr. Moss cried. Lady Fairchild lifted her hands to her mouth in a gesture of outrage that would have been far more credible had her eyes not first flared with lust.

"That's *obscene!*" she said. "Lady Howard—I demand to know what's going on."

"I think the drawing speaks for itself, Lady Fairchild," Mr. Moss said with a grin. "It's remarkably well executed."

"It's not a laughing matter!" Mother said. "Eleanor, what have you *done?*"

"Calm yourself, Grace," Papa said. "I'm sure there's a perfectly reasonable explanation."

"An explanation, yes—but I doubt it's reasonable. I always knew she had an overactive imagination—but *this*? What kind of a mind dreams up such things? I *told* you we should have had her seen. I knew almost from the moment she was born there was something amiss."

"Mother—" Eleanor began, but she was cut off.

"Hold your tongue! You've no right to speak. How *dare* you disgrace our family!"

"I'm sure it's just a silly prank," Papa said. "Isn't that right, child?"

Eleanor opened her mouth to reply. Then she glanced around the room. Multiple pairs of eyes stared at her. She glanced from one to the other—the cold mirth in Mr. Moss's eyes, the haughty disdain in Lady Fairchild's… Then she shifted her gaze to Colonel Reid, and her heart faltered at the anger in his expression.

"Colonel…"

"I should have known better," he said flatly. "Is this how you and your sister plotted to humiliate me a second time?"

"Surely you don't think—"

"I don't think what? That you'll spread your legs like any harlot to get what you want?" He glanced at Juliette, then let out a sharp laugh. "Of course! I should have guessed."

Juliette paled and lowered the sketchbook. Then she swayed to one side. A footman caught her before she collapsed, and the sketchbook fluttered to the floor.

Eleanor's mother stooped to pick it up, but Eleanor darted across the room and snatched it out of her hands.

"That's mine!" she cried. "And it's private!"

"Not anymore it's not." Mr. Moss chuckled.

"You're hardly one to take the moral high ground!" Papa scoffed. "It's Society's worst-kept secret what you get up to with your paramour."

"I'm afraid I don't know what—"

"Heath, please!" Lady Fairchild interrupted, and Eleanor could have wept with relief as she felt the party's attention shift away from her, the release from the burden of their gazes almost making her lightheaded.

But not all of them looked away. Colonel Reid still stared at her. With her gut twisting at the disgust in his eyes, she turned and fled.

SHORTLY AFTER ELEANOR entered her chamber, clutching her precious sketchbook to her breast, Harriet appeared at the door.

"Oh, miss!" she cried. "I came to see if you're all right." She glanced at the sketchbook and blushed.

"So you've heard," Eleanor said.

"James is tending to Miss Juliette. He said you might need some assistance."

"Are the staff gossiping?"

Harriet's blush deepened.

"I see," Eleanor said. "And do *you* think I'm a harlot?"

"Of course not!" Harriet replied. "I only heard that you'd drawn some very…*revealing* portraits of the duke."

Eleanor shook her head. "What was I *thinking*?"

"You mean what was Miss Juliette thinking, showing them to everyone? What was she doing in your private study? *She's* the one to blame."

Eleanor sighed. "No, it's *my* fault. I should have known someone might find the pictures. Oh, Harriet, what shall I do?"

"You must tell him, miss."

"Who?" Eleanor asked.

"The duke. He'll know what to do."

For a moment, Eleanor envisaged Montague coming to her aid, sweeping her off her feet to sanctuary. Then another image darkened her mind—a marriage of necessity, followed by a lifetime of resentment and the loss of her freedom. Or worse…

A life as his mistress—tucked away in an obscure little corner of his estate in disgrace, to be vilified and looked down on by his mother, desperate for his visits when he remembered that she existed, and her children…

Her children banished like Olivia, to never fit in—too far above the villagers to be deemed one of them, yet too much of a disgrace to be included in the family.

No—a life of obscurity was better than that.

Anything was better than that.

"I cannot burden him with this," she said. "Besides, he made it clear that we couldn't be together."

"Surely that's changed now?"

"I don't want his pity, Harriet," Eleanor said, "or to be rescued out of obligation. I want to be *me*, Eleanor—not some disgraced creature forever under obligation to those who took pity on her. No—I must leave."

"To go where?"

"I care not, but I must go tonight, and you must help me pack my things. I cannot face them after what's happened—I cannot face *anyone*. I'm on my own."

Harriet placed a slim hand on Eleanor's arm. "No, miss," she said. "You're *not* alone. You have me. If you must go, let me come with you."

The maid reached inside the chest of drawers beside the door and began to pull out the contents, folding them and placing them on the bed.

Dear Harriet! Her steady, practical approach was just what Eleanor needed, together with an occupation to divert her attention from whatever must be going on in the drawing room right now. Taking comfort in the repetitive act of folding petticoats and stockings, she began to pack her trunk.

Before they finished, the door was knocked upon softly, and Eleanor froze.

"Daughter—I know you're in there."

The door opened, and her father entered the chamber.

"What has my girl been up to?" he asked.

"Papa, I'm sorry—I'd never have done those drawings had I known…"

He shook his head. "It's not just the drawings," he said, "but what they signify. Did you…"

He gestured to the space between them, as if unwilling to voice his fears.

Blinking back tears, she nodded slowly.

"I thought as much."

"You did?"

"The morning we left Rosecombe, when you said your good-byes, the two of you seemed..." He hesitated. "The only word I can think of is *united*. I noticed it again in Hyde Park. But then—when your engagement ended—I thought perhaps I was mistaken." He lifted his hand to his forehead and narrowed his eyes, as if battling a headache.

"Are you very angry, Papa?" Eleanor asked.

"What would be the sense in anger? Besides—I leave that sort of thing to your mother."

"Sweet Lord—*Mother*!" she cried. "And the guests! What will they—"

He raised his hand. "I've taken care of it. The guests have gone, and we'll be hearing no more about it."

"You can't be sure of that, Papa—you know how people love to gossip. Lady Fairchild—"

"Lady Fairchild has her own secrets, which I'll wager she'll do anything to retain, given her friendship with Lady Jersey." He gave a wry smile. "For once, I see the benefit in women obsessing over their ability to procure a ticket at Almack's."

"I don't understand."

"Suffice it to say, Eleanor dearest, both Lady Fairchild and Mr. Moss value their reputations more than they value the satisfaction of spreading gossip. And what can they spread? That they were shown a series of anatomical drawings? There are plenty to be viewed at the Academy Exhibition, where the artists are lauded for their skill rather than vilified."

"You mean you resorted to..."

"Blackmail is an ugly word, Eleanor, and should never pass your lips. I merely suggested that our guests look to their own proven sins before casting aspersions about the alleged sins of others."

"And M-Mother?"

"She's taken to her bed with a fit of nerves," he said. "Doubt-less she'll recover, as will your sister. But as to you, Eleanor..." He glanced at the pile of clothes on the bed. "What do you think you're doing?"

"I'm leaving."

"You can't leave—what will people think?"

"You can't believe I care what people think!" she cried. "You said yourself, the other day, that you'd let me go—you'd find a house for me. Or was that a ruse to get me to attend the party tonight to secure Colonel Reid's attention?"

Then her gut twisted with horror.

"No, Papa—you're not going to force me to marry *Colonel Reid?*"

He shook his head. "Certainly not. He's disappointed me tonight."

"More than I?"

He drew her into an embrace, and she inhaled the comforting, familiar scent of cinnamon and cigars.

"You could never disappoint me, Eleanor," he said. "And you needn't worry—Colonel Reid won't say a thing. I think he regrets his words. He asked me to apologize to you on his behalf. He even asked if he could call on you tomorrow." She opened her mouth to protest, but he raised his hand. "It's all right—I refused."

"I don't want to see him," she said. "I don't want to see anyone, Papa. I just want to go."

"Eleanor, you don't run from your troubles."

"I'm not running! You said I could go—you *promised!*"

He let out a sigh. "That I did, my dear one—and the last thing I want is to be yet another person who has betrayed your trust." He released her and placed a chaste kiss on her forehead. "Very well—if that's what you truly wish for, I'll visit Stockton in the morning to make the arrangements."

"On a Sunday?"

"As soon as we return from church—for which you may be excused. I think it's best if you remain in your chamber until I've made the arrangements. I'm sure the Almighty will understand." He glanced toward Eleanor's maid. "Will you take care of my daughter, Harriet?"

"Oh yes, sir—I've already said I'll go with her."

He smiled. "Then I can rest assured that my daughter is in safer hands than her family ever provided."

"And you don't mind?" Eleanor asked.

"Of *course* I mind," he said. "I'll miss having my Eleanor about the place with her thoughtful quietness and sharp insight. But you're no longer a child. I may be your father, but a parent's role is not to cage their children forever—his role is to free her from her cage and give her wings so she can fly to her destiny."

She reached for his hand. "Thank you."

He smiled, then patted her hand. "I envy you. You're setting out in the world just as I did when I was a young man, carving out a life for myself and committing to an occupation that I loved. My only wish is that you don't make the same mistakes that I once did."

For a brief moment, his eyes glistened with moisture. Then he blinked and it was gone. She dipped her head and kissed the back of his hand, where paper-thin skin stretched over the tendons and knuckles. And, for a moment, she caught a glimpse of what he once was—a young man with a zest for life and a determination to work hard, who had entered into marriage and thereby sacrificed his freedom.

And, in letting her go, Papa was ensuring that *she* never need make such a sacrifice. She had caught a glimpse of bliss, in the arms of a man—but now was the time to return to the real world and shape her own future.

CHAPTER THIRTY-TWO

ONTY CLIMBED OUT of the carriage, then walked past the row of servants who, at a sharp word from Jenkins, bowed and curtseyed in unison. The butler creaked into a bow, his body bearing a greater resemblance to a devil's coach horse beetle than it had when…

…when *she* had visited.

With Eleanor beside him, he'd struggled to suppress the urge to giggle at the butler's absurdities—but faced with Jenkins's impassive expression, the urge to laugh receded.

"Welcome home, Your Grace."

"Thank you, Jenkins." Monty brushed past the butler and entered the hallway.

The main house, which he'd always thought overly large, now seemed cavernous, desolate, and empty. As if a chasm existed that had not been there before. A chasm in the shape of…

"Your Grace!"

Monty startled at the butler's voice. "What is it?"

"I've been asking what time you'll be wanting dinner?"

"Do I look like I care?" Monty snapped.

Save a slight widening of the eyes, Jenkins showed no reaction.

Monty softened his voice. "Forgive me—I'm rather tired."

This time, the butler's eyebrows shot up almost through his hairline, and Monty suppressed a laugh at the fact that incivility was met with stoicism, but an apology for said incivility was met with surprise.

But there was nobody to share his observation with—nobody to appreciate the irony.

"I'll take dinner whenever the dowager wishes it."

"Her Grace is not joining you tonight."

Well *that*, if nothing else, was something to be thankful for.

Monty shed his coat and hat and tossed them to a nearby footman while he pulled off his gloves.

"Would you like tea, sir?"

"No. I'll take an early supper then retire. I'll dine at seven."

"Very good." Jenkins bowed, then gestured to the rest of the servants, who moved back like a receding tide before disappearing to go about their lives. Monty found himself envying them and their days filled with occupation, giving them little time to sit idly and wonder what might have been.

Devil's toes—since when had he grown so melancholy?

He climbed the main staircase, moving absent-mindedly forward until he reached his bedchamber. It was a room he rarely entered during the day—a functional room in which he slept and did little else. Each day he rose from the bed and entered his dressing room, where his valet stood waiting to tend to his every whim. And each night, he reversed the process, standing meekly while his valet peeled off his clothes, then slipped into his bed, falling asleep as soon as he lay down, with no thought for the men and women who strove to ensure that the room was kept tidy, the sheets clean, and the fire made.

But today the room served a different purpose. He crossed the floor, slipped his hand beneath the mattress, pulled out a piece of paper, and unfolded it.

There she was, in her naked glory, staring boldly out of the page, a smile of satisfaction on her lips—a smile for *him*, and him only.

His body tightened at the memory of the pleasures they'd shared. He shifted his legs as his manhood swelled, then he traced the outline of her form with his fingertips, lingering on her breasts, before lowering his gaze to the juncture of her thighs, where paradise awaited…

"Your Grace—sir!"

Monty turned to see his valet standing in the doorway. He folded the drawing and hid it behind his back, his cheeks warming as if he were a schoolboy caught fisting himself.

"What do you want?" he growled.

"Nothing, sir—I was just unpacking your trunk."

"Then get on with it."

"Very good, sir." The valet turned to go, but Monty held up his hand.

"No, wait. Have Mr. Gregory meet me in my study. As soon as possible."

"Very good, sir."

As soon as Wilkins was safely out of the way, Monty slipped the drawing back underneath the mattress. Then he set off for his study.

He might never see her again, but she would live on in Rosecombe. To honor her—and to honor what was right—significant changes needed to be made.

The first of those was to set up proper funding for the school—hire a schoolteacher to assist Olivia. And the second…

He would publicly recognize Olivia as his sister so that she'd never have cause to feel shame for her birth. Olivia was a Whitcombe. Anyone who objected to that could go to hell.

Perhaps it was a shame, after all, that Mother wouldn't be joining him for dinner tonight. Nothing would give him greater pleasure than to see the look on her face when he told her.

Nothing except the notion that Eleanor—his Eleanor—might be proud of him if she knew what he was doing in her honor.

But Eleanor—who might, even now, be enjoying Colonel Reid's courtship—would never know.

CHAPTER THIRTY-THREE

Sandcombe, Lincolnshire, September 1815

"THERE IT IS, Mrs. Riley. Shore Cottage."

Eleanor continued to stare at the sea as the carriage rolled to a halt. It seemed to stretch to the end of the world, glistening in the afternoon light, the blue color intensifying toward the horizon. No wonder some people believed the world ended where the sea met the sky. Such a vast expanse must have seemed unsurmountable in the years before ships circumnavigated the earth.

To think—Papa had often crossed the horizon in one of his ships, traveling to another world, returning home with the silks and spices that had made his fortune. It was only befitting that she begin this next phase of her life on the threshold of the path to other worlds.

She brushed a stray tendril of hair from her eyes, then leaned out of the carriage, inhaling a lungful of sea air, with its salty, almost metallic aroma. The cries of gulls filled the air, and she lifted her gaze to see their slim shapes silhouetted against the sky.

"Mrs. Riley!"

A hand rapped on the window opposite, and she turned to see the coachman staring at her.

"Mrs. Riley, begging your pardon, we've arrived."

Harriet's face appeared next to the coachman's. "We're here, ma'am."

Ma'am...

Her new name would take some getting used to. But the widowed Mrs. Riley, recently out of mourning, would attract considerably less attention than the ruined Miss Howard. Widows were respected by virtue of having performed their marital duty, and were ignored by virtue of the assumption that, having already survived marriage, they no longer posed a threat to the husband-hunting single girls of the world.

How often had she heard a woman described as a *respectable widow*, yet no woman had ever been referred to as a *respectable spinster*.

Respected and ignored. What could be more blissful in a world filled with people and noise?

The carriage door opened, and she climbed out, taking the coachman's hand. She was only too glad to leave the coach. The ride from the inn—a rambling, red-bricked building with a thatched roof, and a sign depicting a red-faced man in a sailor's uniform dancing a jig—might have been less than a mile, but the wheels, and the road, were in need of repair. It was a wonder the coach hadn't disintegrated when the wheels hit that last rut.

"Careful, ma'am," the coachman said. "The steps are slippery, on account of the rain."

"Rain? But it's a beautiful day."

"It was right dreadful first thing. Sandcombe's like that, ma'am—a downpour worthy of the Great Flood one moment, then clear blue sky the next. I daresay ye'll get used to it. Have ye traveled here before?"

"When I was a child, but I recall very little apart from the sandy beaches."

"Aye, ye're right there. Sandcombe has the finest beaches in England. And ye're in luck—the path from Shore cottage leads straight to the beach."

He turned to his companions, two lads with identical dark brown eyes and mops of dirty blond hair peeking out from beneath their caps.

"Johnny, Tom—get to it. Those trunks won't move themselves."

"Aye, Mr. Legge." The boys lifted the first of Eleanor's trunks from the carriage and carried it across the road. Eleanor followed them with her gaze until she caught sight of their destination—a two-story cottage with a red-tiled roof. The front door and window frames had been painted a pale green, and a rambling rosebush grew around the front door with the last blooms of a fading summer—red blooms against glossy red leaves. The cottage was enclosed by a fence and fronted by a neatly clipped lawn, bordered with shrubs dotted with white and purple flowers.

"It's beautiful!" she cried.

"My Molly's da's been tending to the garden while it's lain empty."

"Would he like to continue?" Eleanor asked. "I'm afraid I know little about tending to gardens, and am likely to do more harm than good."

"He'd be glad of the work, thank ye. And Tom and Johnny here would be able to help with any odd jobs ye have going, won't ye, lads?"

The boys, on their return journey to fetch the second trunk, tipped their caps in unison.

"Are they your sons, Mr. Legge?" Eleanor asked.

"Bless ye, no, ma'am! They be Mr. Ham's boys—the innkeeper at the Merry Sailor. Mrs. Ham does a fine fish pie at the Sailor, if ye're wanting supper tonight. The main rooms can get a little rowdy, but she keeps a parlor for lady guests. I can bring the carriage for ye, if ye like?"

"Thank you, no," Eleanor said. Her body would never forgive her if she set foot in that carriage again. "I prefer to walk— perhaps I could dine there tomorrow?"

"Mrs. Ham would like that. We're always interested in newcomers to Sandcombe. Are ye intending to stay here long—if ye don't mind me asking?"

"I hope to settle here," Eleanor replied.

"Did ye always want to live here?"

"Forgive me, ma'am," Harriet interrupted. "We should get you settled inside. Would you excuse us, Mr. Legge? My mistress has had a long journey, and she's very tired."

"Oh, begging yer pardon, ma'am!" The coachman tipped his cap. "My Molly's always telling me how I rattle on. She says I'm worse than any woman. I'll tell Mrs. Ham to set aside a slice of her fish pie for ye tomorrow. She'll see ye right."

"Thank you, Mr. Legge," Eleanor said.

The coachman climbed back onto the carriage and barked an order at the young boys, who scrambled onto the back. With a flick of the reins and several cries of "steady there!" the carriage turned, lurched sideways as the wheel hit another rut, then, swaying from side to side, rattled along the road until it turned a corner and disappeared.

"Well, Harriet," Eleanor said, "shall we explore our new home?"

Eleanor's maid offered her hand, then, arm in arm, they followed the gravel path to the front door and entered the cottage.

The furnishings lacked the ostentation of Papa's townhouse, but the uncluttered simplicity was a balm to Eleanor's soul—the clean lines and pale yellow walls of the main parlor lacked any adornment, save the candle sconces. A smaller parlor at the back overlooked the sea, and the walls had been painted blue, as if to bring a little of the sea indoors. It would do very well for a studio. The kitchen was functional and tidy, with a solid wooden table, a polished iron range, and a dresser filled with white pottery plates and bowls decorated with a pattern of dark blue flowers. Upstairs the bedrooms had been furnished with the same light touch, with delicate floral furnishings and windows that filled the rooms with a natural light.

"What do you think, Harriet?" Eleanor asked. "Shall we make do here?"

"We'll make do very well, miss," the maid said. "You deserve to be happy. Perhaps, now, you can."

Eleanor looked into Harriet's eyes—her maid, companion, and friend. Then she glanced around her new home—a haven where she could, at last, be truly herself, without judgment.

Then the walls she'd erected around herself disintegrated, and she collapsed into her maid's arms and burst into tears.

CHAPTER THIRTY-FOUR

Rosecombe Park, Hertfordshire, December 1815

CHILDREN'S LAUGHTER FILLED the great hall, echoing off the walls and spiraling toward the ceiling. The very bones of the building seemed to vibrate with life. Most likely because Rosecombe had never experienced such a cacophony of unbridled, childish merriment.

At least not in Monty's lifetime.

And the scent of spices and citrus—an aroma that always evoked the spirit of Christmas—was almost enough to lift the spirits.

Almost.

He glanced toward the fireplace, where the children had gathered around Jenkins, sitting cross-legged on the carpet under the watchful gaze of Olivia and a young girl from the village who now ran the school. The children stared, wide-eyed, at the butler while he related tales of folklore and faeries. One child sat apart from the rest, a notebook in his hand.

Who would have known that old fossil Jenkins, of whom Monty had been terrified as a boy, possessed a talent for entertaining children?

Jenkins finished his story, and was met with a chorus of "oohs" and "aahs."

"What do we say, children?" Olivia asked.

"Thank you, Mr. Jenkins!" the children chorused.

"And now—before you get your treats, can anybody tell me what's special about today?"

Several hands shot up.

"Yes, Lottie?"

"It's Christmas!" the little girl cried.

"Not yet," Olivia replied, laughing, "though our host has treats for you all. Anybody else?"

The quiet little boy on his own shifted forward, his body tense, and Olivia kneeled beside him.

"Do *you* know what's special about today, Joe?"

He scribbled in his notebook and showed her the page.

"Excellent, Joe—well done!" she said. "That's right—it's St. Nicholas's Day. The duke has treats for you all. Isn't that kind of him?"

A ripple of enthusiasm threaded through the children at the prospect of sweets, and Monty's heart sank at the prospect of two dozen children enlivened by a dose of sugar.

Time for a brandy to numb the senses.

He approached the sideboard, unstoppered the decanter, and poured a measure of dark brown liquid into a glass.

"I take it you're unused to children's parties, brother?"

Olivia had followed him.

Monty tilted the decanter toward her and raised his eyebrows in question.

"Offering brandy to a woman, before dinner?" She smiled. "I'll stick to tea. I need my wits now my class has trebled in size."

"That's why we've employed Miss Akroyd," Monty said. "Now you're a member of the family, there's no need for you to teach anymore."

"I still have a duty to the children—especially Joe."

Monty glanced toward the children. The little boy was now scribbling again, absorbed in his work while the others laughed and chatted together.

"Must I change who I am to suit you?" Olivia asked.

Monty shook his head. "No, Olivia. I want you to be happy here as my sister—but the last thing I want is to have you change yourself to suit the expectations of others."

She laughed. "Who are you—and what have you done with the Duke of Whitcombe?"

"I don't follow you."

"You don't sound at all like the soulless aristocrat I always believed you to be. Where have you been hiding that kind soul? Or have you experienced an epiphany?"

An epiphany…

Yes, he'd been struck by a revelation that the world would be a better place were individuals to embrace their individuality rather than conform.

"Perhaps I *will* have a brandy," she said.

He poured a measure and handed it to her. They clinked glasses, and she took a sip.

"I suppose there's no point in my asking where she is now," Olivia said. "It was too much to hope she'd be here when I arrived. Will she ever return?"

He drained his glass and poured another measure. Why did the mention of his mother always bring about a thirst for brandy and the oblivion it gave?

"I didn't mean to upset you," Olivia said.

"I'm not upset," he replied, "merely frustrated that Mother refuses to acknowledge you. It's not your fault that—"

"I didn't mean the dowager, Montague. I meant *her*."

Monty had no need to ask who Olivia meant by *her*.

"Though you were opposites in terms of countenance and rank, you seemed well suited," she said. "Like the sharp sauce that was served at dinner last night. The beef, which you told me was the finest cut, was nevertheless bland in its refinement. Yet the sauce complemented it perfectly, rendering it palatable—and even enjoyable."

"Are you likening me to a fillet steak in need of enhancement to render my company bearable?"

"No," she said quietly. "But you lack completion."

At that moment he felt a hand tug his sleeve. He glanced down to Joe standing before him.

"Joe, sweetheart, what is it?" Olivia asked.

The boy flicked through the notebook until he came to a page with a drawing on it, and he held it up. On the page was a portrait of a sheep's head, portrayed with extraordinary accuracy and attention to detail, such that the sheep's eyes seemed to be alive and staring at Monty from the page.

"Joe drew that last month, didn't you, Joe?" Olivia said.

The boy nodded, then offered the notebook to Monty.

"Is this a gift for me?" Monty asked. "Why, thank you, little master. I'm much—"

"N-no."

At first, Monty thought he'd imagined it. Surely the boy hadn't *spoken*?

"E-Eleanor," the boy added, craning his neck to meet Monty's gaze. "It's for Eleanor."

"Miss Howard isn't here, Joseph," Monty said.

"It's Molly. My favorite sheep. W-will you give it to her?"

"I'm sorry, Joseph. I don't know if I'll see her again."

The boy closed the notebook and tucked it under his arm.

"I'm sad."

"Perhaps Miss FitzRoy and I can find you something good to eat," Monty said. "Would you like some of Cook's spiced biscuits?"

The boy shook his head. "I don't want biscuits. I want Eleanor. I miss her."

His words, delivered matter-of-factly, pricked at Monty's heart more than any speech articulated with emotion or tears.

He crouched beside the boy and took his hands. "Shall I let you in on a secret, Joseph?"

The boy met his gaze for a moment, then looked away.

"I miss her also," Monty said. "I didn't realize how much until I returned here without her. She was able to look beyond that which I portray to the world around me, to see the true man behind my façade."

The boy nodded—and Monty smiled at the notion of such a young mind understanding his words.

"Eleanor sees people without looking at them," the boy said. "I hate being looked at, but I don't want to be invisible—a-and Eleanor saw me."

Monty stared at the boy who, behind the silent, withdrawn exterior, hid a wise soul with remarkable insight. Then the boy colored and lowered his gaze. Monty touched his shoulder, but he flinched and jerked free.

Miss Akroyd approached. "Joe, would you like a custard tart? I've set one aside for you."

A maid circulated among the children, carrying a tray laden with a huge pile of tarts, diminishing rapidly as several pairs of hands eagerly reached for them. With a nod, Joe slipped his hand into Miss Akroyd's, and they returned to the fireplace, where Jenkins sat with Lottie on his lap.

"I've never seen my butler with such an informal attitude," Monty said.

"Lottie's his granddaughter," Olivia said.

"Really? How did I not know that?"

"Because it's the servants' responsibility to know everything about their masters, not the other way round," she replied. "Eleanor knew, of course. She spotted the resemblance after she visited the school the second time."

He smiled. "As young Joseph says—she saw people without looking at them. I never thought the boy capable of such an observation—or such a speech."

"Joe speaks so rarely that it's wise to heed what he says," Olivia said. "He sees much and says little. Such people are to be treasured."

"Aren't they just," he said, almost to himself.

Devil's toes—what have I done?

The enormity of what he'd lost—nay, what he'd had in his

grasp but let slip through his fingers—crept toward him like a thick black tide, relentless in its determination to obliterate his prospects for a happy and fulfilling life.

He shook another measure of brandy into his glass and drained it.

I've made the grandfather of all mistakes, haven't I?

"Yes, brother. I rather think you have."

He turned to Olivia. "Did I say that aloud?"

She nodded. "Even if you hadn't, your expression told me all I needed to know." She gestured about the room. "Christmas is a time for loved ones. Why don't you invite her back?"

"What's done is done," he said. "Besides—she wouldn't come."

"That's a coward's response—an excuse to avoid doing that which is difficult or awkward. You love her, don't you?"

"Should you be asking such a direct question, Olivia?"

"Where's the sense in frittering away words on niceties when directness is the only way to achieve one's objective?"

"Heavens, Olivia, you sound just like..." He caught himself.

"Like Eleanor? You can speak her name, you know. You miss her, after all." She held up her hand in anticipation of his protest. "You said it yourself to Joe, and not even *you* would be callous enough to lie to a child." Then her expression softened. "Did she reject you?"

"It was a mutual parting," he said, "though I'd long lost sight of why I intended to break off our engagement."

"You *intended* to break it off? I don't understand."

"Neither do I. Nevertheless, it's what we'd embarked on. And though it was only a few months ago—it feels like a lifetime."

"*Eleanor* agreed to it?" Olivia shook her head. "I can imagine *you* entering into such an arrangement—but I'd thought better of Eleanor. Did she not think of what else might be affected by such an act—her family, the sanctity of marriage itself? I find myself disappointed."

"You've every right to be disappointed," he said, "but in me—

not the finest woman I have ever known. She entered into our engagement believing it to be genuine."

Olivia paled. "You mean…" Her voice trailed off as if she couldn't bear to contemplate his meaning.

"After I explained my motives, Eleanor agreed to maintain the façade. In return, I offered to teach her a few social graces."

"How very gracious of you," she said.

He flinched at the sharp sting in her voice.

"I was content with the arrangement at first," he said. "As was she, until…"

"Until you realized you'd fallen in love." She shook her head. "You fool! Do you mean to say that you ended your engagement simply because that's what you set out to do? Why would any man in possession of his wits undertake such a scheme?"

"I did it to stop my mother from plaguing me."

"You *what?*"

"She kept insisting I find a bride, foisting a host of dull heiresses onto me—perfect ornaments for my arm, but who'd plague me into my grave if I married them. So I chose the very antithesis of what Mother wanted."

"You mean the woman you deemed the least elegant, least beautiful, and least suitable?"

He caught a blur of movement out of the corner of his eye, before she delivered a stinging slap to his cheek.

"You swine!" she cried. "I suppose that's why you chose to recognize me publicly as your sister—not out of any sense of obligation, or fondness, but to torture your mother by tainting the shades of Rosecombe with your father's bastard!"

"No!" he said through gritted teeth, painfully aware of a bright pair of brown eyes watching him. "I asked you here because I care for you. You're my family, and I want you here!"

"And Eleanor?"

"Yes!" he bellowed, unable to stem his emotion. "Yes—of course I want her! I *love* her—how could I not? Does it give you satisfaction to know that?"

"Then go and win her back."

"It's not that simple. She'll never accept me. I ended our engagement very publicly. I made sure I was seen with a doxy—*two* doxies."

Olivia's eyes widened, and she curled her hand into a fist.

"It was a ruse," he said, eyeing her knuckles, his cheek still smarting. "I cannot bear to touch another woman. I left Eleanor in the care of another—a man more deserving of her."

"You think her love for you was so shallow that she'd transfer it to another?"

Heavens! What an outspoken creature she was! Perhaps that was due to her upbringing—raised by straight-talking villagers with little time to school her into a simpering Society miss.

No other woman had granted him such honesty and made him look at himself with clear eyes unfettered by the self-importance brought about by his savagely handsome looks, his fortune, or his title.

None except Eleanor.

Why did every train of thought—or, come to that, every waking moment—begin and end with her?

Then the door opened, and Monty's heart sank at the announcement.

"Her Grace, the dowager Duchess of Whitcombe!"

Shit. That's all I need.

The last time he'd seen his mother, they'd parted on bad terms—he fueled by his anger at her cruelty toward Olivia, and she filled with indignation at the disgrace he brought to the family name by elevating a *grubby little bastard* to the status of a lady.

Olivia stiffened, and Monty took her hand—the same hand that had struck him moments before. But now, they faced a common enemy.

"Mother, what brings you here?" Monty asked.

She swept past the footman, her black silk gown rustling. "Do I now require an invitation to enter my home, Montague?"

The room fell silent as the children, with their innate sense of danger, turned to face the newcomer. One of the younger ones began to sniffle and was quickly silenced by Miss Akroyd.

Olivia, who seemed to recover first, slipped her hand from Monty's and clapped.

"Stand up please, children!" she said in a singsong voice.

After they scrambled to their feet, Olivia turned to Monty's mother.

"Children, this is tonight's guest of honor—the dowager Duchess of Whitcombe. We mustn't forget our manners, must we?" She dipped into a curtsey. "Good afternoon, Your Grace," she said. "Happy St. Nicholas's Day." She gestured to the children.

"Good afternoon, Your Grace!" they chorused. "Happy St. Nicholas's Day!" Then they bowed and curtseyed.

For a moment, Monty feared Mother would turn her back and stride out of the room—or worse, issue a comment about allowing peasants onto the hallowed grounds of Rosecombe. Instead, she merely inclined her head. She cast her gaze about the room until it landed on Jenkins, who'd leaped to his feet, little Lottie clinging to his breeches. Though he stared straight ahead in the manner of the staid butler, he'd placed his hand on his granddaughter's head—a tender gesture of comfort that pricked at Monty's heart.

"Don't let me disturb the children's party, Miss…?" Mother asked the young woman.

"Miss Akroyd, Your Grace."

"Farmer Akroyd's girl?"

"Aye, Your Grace. I teach at the school."

"Very good," Mother said. "Do your charges give you trouble?"

"No, ma'am. They're ever so keen to learn. I cannot thank you enough for all you've done for the school."

Mother arched an eyebrow then glanced toward Monty. "I daresay it's my son who deserves the credit—but your appreciation is welcome. Please"—she gestured toward the children—

"don't stop the merriment on my account."

She crossed the floor toward Monty, her gaze fixed on Olivia.

Olivia curtseyed again. "Thank you, Your Grace."

"What for?" Mother asked.

"For permitting the children to remain here."

Mother stared at her—the girl whose very existence pained her—and Monty braced himself for another onslaught of hysterics. Then she inclined her head.

"You're welcome, my dear," she said stiffly. "My son is head of the family, and while I have every right to my opinion, I must bow to his judgment in all things."

"Whether you agree or not?"

"Yes, Miss"—she hesitated, as if steeling herself—"Miss Fitz-Roy."

Evidently as surprised as Monty himself, Olivia drew in a sharp breath, her eyes widening at Mother's address.

"Your Grace, I—" she began, but Mother raised her hand.

"I can never look upon you with a mother's affection, young lady—you'll always serve as a reminder of my late husband's betrayal. But this is the season of goodwill and forgiveness. If you can forgive my bitter words the last time we met, then I'm willing to acknowledge you as a FitzRoy. I cannot promise more than that, for I'd be at risk of breaking my promise. It's better to make no promise at all than to break faith with another." She met Monty's gaze, her expression hardening, and he felt his cheeks warming under her scrutiny.

"Thank you for your kindness and honesty," Olivia said, dipping into a curtsey once more. "I think Miss Akroyd is in need of assistance. The children always get a little boisterous when they've eaten too much sugar."

She retreated toward the children, leaving Monty alone with his mother.

"That was well done," he said.

"You left me no choice if I was to avoid banishment from my home of thirty years. But the closer I draw to my final appointment with the Almighty, the more I understand the futility of regret."

"That which you regret was not of *your* doing, Mother."

"Unlike *you*, Montague. I daresay you have much to regret. I'm a woman who has lived her life and is merely waiting for it to draw to a close. But *you* are a man with the power to do, and take, what you wish, without reprobation."

She nodded toward the decanter. "Aren't you going to offer me a brandy, at least?"

He reached for a glass and poured a measure before handing it to her. She lifted her glass and took a sip.

"I happened to pass Mrs. Swift on my return from the village yesterday," she said. "She asked me to pay her respects to Miss Howard when I saw her next."

"Oh?" Monty took a mouthful of brandy in an attempt to feign nonchalance.

"Even the staff ask about her," she huffed. "Jenkins had the temerity to note that Miss Howard was the politest young lady he'd ever had occasion to meet, and that he'd have no objection to her being mistress of Rosecombe."

"Whatever induced Jenkins to say such a thing?"

"Because I asked him."

"Mother!" Monty cried. "Aren't you the very last person to believe Miss Howard worthy of me—and of Rosecombe?"

"My dear boy," she said, "you're asking the wrong question."

"Then what is the *right* question?"

"Whether you—and Rosecombe—are worthy of *her*."

Her words served as a wind to dispel the fog of denial shrouding his mind. Of *course* Eleanor was worthy of Rosecombe. He had realized that weeks ago when he'd fallen in love with her. He'd pushed it to the recesses of his mind while he continued with their ridiculous charade. But as he'd grown to know her better, her character had emerged. Not the shy, foolish creature scared of looking others in the eye—but the extraordinary woman with a heart as big as any ocean, and a mind intelligent and independent enough to enable her to carve out her own path in life, if only the world would let her.

And he had pushed her into the arms of another.

"Why not invite Miss Howard to Rosecombe again, Montague?" Mother asked.

"And if she refuses to come?"

"Then at least you won't suffer the regret of not having asked."

Mother was right. There was no harm in trying. Even though the thought of Eleanor in the arms of another was more torture than he could bear, he would weather it for the chance, however slim, that she might be waiting for him.

CHAPTER THIRTY-FIVE

Sandcombe, Lincolnshire, December 1815

"M RS. RILEY."

Eleanor slipped on her gloves as she continued along the gravel path leading out of the churchyard.

"Mrs. Riley!" the voice called out again.

"Miss Howard!" Harriet hissed, and Eleanor turned to see the vicar approaching, his breath forming a mist in the air, soft brown eyes crinkling into a smile.

"I beg pardon, Mrs. Riley, I hadn't expected you to attend Wednesday Evensong."

"My soul is in as much need of saving as the rest of your flock, Reverend Staines," Eleanor said. "And I have to confess curiosity. On Sunday you had alluded to a sermon about St. Nicholas, and I was anxious to hear it."

"Did it meet your expectations?"

"Your sermon surpassed my expectations, reverend," she replied, smiling.

"In what way?"

"In its brevity."

He let out a laugh. "Bravo! An honest critique is preferable to flattery."

"Oh, forgive me, reverend."

"Mr. Staines, please."

"Forgive me—*Mr. Staines*."

"There's nothing to forgive."

"There's *always* something to forgive," she said. "At least, that's what you said in your sermon last week."

"An honest critique and an accurate recollection of my sermons. The holy grail of congregants."

"Careful, Mr. Staines—I wouldn't let Mrs. Fulford hear you say that."

He rolled his eyes then gave her a very un-reverend-like wink.

"Is there something you wanted, Mr. Staines?" she asked.

"I wondered whether you were attending the children's party at the vicarage later."

"Harriet and I have been baking biscuits all day, and we've already arranged for Thomas Ham to bring them over."

"But you'll not come yourself."

"Forgive me, reverend, but no."

"Not even the prospect of seeing your beautiful landscape taking pride of place over my fireplace can tempt you?"

"Now you're flattering me," she said. "I've no objection to Harriet attending, but I dislike large parties—all those people crowded together in a room."

"Isn't that what a congregation does every Sunday? You seem at ease during the service."

"That's because a service has structure and certainty. Everyone knows what to do and say—when to speak up, and when to be silent. It's a time to reflect—not a social occasion."

"And there's me thinking you attended because of my sermons."

"I *do*," she replied. "I find them fascinating—they lack the pomposity of the sermons I was subjected to as a child."

"There's no place for pomposity in the modern age," he said. "Now I have a living of my own, I can write my own sermons in the manner I see fit."

"You couldn't before?"

"No." He smiled, his brown eyes radiating warmth. "When I

held a curacy, I was under strict instructions from Reverend Frogmore—who lived in the parish before he passed last year—not to deviate from his ideal of what a vicar should be."

"Which was?"

"A man responsible for striking fear into the hearts of the souls in his care, by warning them of fire and brimstone if they strayed from the path of righteousness."

"Heavens!" She let out a laugh. "I would hope you wouldn't place such a burden on *your* curate."

"Of course not," he said. "Far too many vicars leave their curates to undertake all the work, while they drink port and wallow in the self-righteousness. Have you never wondered why so many members of the clergy suffer from gout?"

"You don't paint a very flattering portrait of your vocation, Mr. Staines."

"Too few see it as a vocation, Mrs. Riley," he said. "Instead, they consider the clergy as a profession—a means for financial, not spiritual, enrichment."

"And yourself?"

"My father wanted me to go into the army. Every second son in our family—dating, no doubt, back to the first Earl Staines—purchased a commission in the militia. But I lack the temperament, and have no desire to distinguish myself."

"There are ways to distinguish oneself other than leading an army into battle," Eleanor said.

"How right you are," he said. "If it's not too forward of me to say it, I'm glad you are come to Sandcombe—even if it was under such tragic circumstances."

Eleanor's gut twisted in apprehension—did he know how she came to be here?

"T-tragic?" They reached the lych gate, and she leaned against it.

"Oh, forgive me!" he exclaimed. "I've no right to make reference to the late Mr. Riley, when you're only recently out of mourning."

Relief flooded through her, and she suppressed the urge to laugh.

"Of course you cannot be expected to attend parties," he said. "You must think me an awful cad for asking."

"It's not that. I—" Eleanor began, but Harriet placed a hand on her arm.

"Forgive us, reverend, but Mrs. Riley needs her rest. She finds company tiring, don't you, miss?"

The reverend tilted his head to one side and narrowed his eyes, his gaze shifting from Harriet to Eleanor. Then he nodded and smiled.

"Of course, Miss—*Mrs.* Riley," he said. "Please enjoy the rest of your evening."

"Reverend!" a sharp voice cried. "Reverend Staines!"

He winced, then turned back toward the church. "Mrs. Fulford—how may I be of assistance?"

"I wanted to speak to you about the flowers again."

He leaned toward Eleanor and winked. "Duty calls—at least duty to my patron's wife." He bowed, then returned to the church.

"I'm sure he suspects something," Eleanor said.

"You can trust him, miss," Harriet replied.

"In what way?"

"He's a good man—and he's unlikely to judge. He'd do very well for you."

Eleanor let out a laugh. "He's pleasant enough, Harriet, and I like him—after all, he was kind enough to purchase one of my paintings. But with three unmarried daughters, I doubt Mrs. Fulford would allow him to pay attention to me—a widow living on her own in a cottage on the outskirts of the village? Hardly an appropriate partner for the second son of an earl."

"You're younger than the eldest Miss Fulford," Harriet said.

"She's an *unmarried* young woman, Harriet."

"And so are you," Harriet said. "He likes you—I'm sure of it."

Harriet rattled on, extolling the virtues of the vicar, until they reached Shore Cottage.

"I think I'll retire," Eleanor said, interrupting Harriet's monologue. "I find myself a little tired. There's no need to tend to me—I can see to myself."

"Very good, miss."

Eleanor climbed the stairs to her bedchamber. After shedding her jacket and bonnet, she approached her dressing table and pulled out her sketchbook with its precious drawings. Each day since she'd arrived at Sandcombe, she'd not been able to summon the courage to look inside. But tonight…

Perhaps it was talk of another that brought him to the forefront of her mind—or perhaps it was her conscience, berating her for disloyalty against the man she loved.

She flicked through the pages, feigning nonchalance, even though she was alone in her room, until she reached one of the first portraits she'd ever drawn of him—where he looked out from the page, his beautiful eyes clear and wide, a soft smile on his full lips.

A smile for her.

She traced the outline of his face with her fingertips.

Did he think of her as she thought of him? Or had he forgotten her?

CHAPTER THIRTY-SIX

London, December 1815

MONTY HUNCHED HIS shoulders against the cold.

London, out of season, was a different world. Gone were the bright colors and vibrant chatter of the *ton*. The cold weather had driven them indoors, or to the sanctuary of their country estates.

Snowflakes swirled about him, thickening the air and almost obscuring the buildings at the far end of the street. Monty continued along the pavement, which was already covered with a thick layer of snow, bearing the occasional footprint of other fools who'd chosen to venture outside.

Then his destination came into view—a white-fronted building with steps leading to the main door, flanked by two thick columns. He approached the door and lifted the brass knocker, wincing as the cold from the metal penetrated his gloves to the skin of his fingers.

He waited, but there was no response. Then he stepped back. The windows were unlit. Most of the houses were lit from within by flickering lights visible in the windows, which resembled a row of eyes watching over the world outside.

Except this one.

Footsteps approached, and a bright accent of color emerged from the gray air as a couple approached him.

"I say—Whitcombe!" a voice cried. "What the devil are *you* doing here?"

It was Dunton, his greatcoat barely covering his porcine frame, the buttons stretched almost to breaking point, his multiple chins resting on the scarf about his neck, giving his head the appearance of a blotchy mushroom. Beside him, her hand possessively on his arm, was Lady Arabella Ponsford.

Monty inclined his head. "Dunton, Lady Arabella—a pleasure. I could ask you the same question."

"I'm escorting Lady Arabella to take a turn about the park," Dunton said.

He turned and gave her a smile, his eyes glittering with lust. She sneered but nodded, a cold smile on her lips. Monty could swear he saw her shudder.

"Is your aunt in town, Lady Arabella?" Monty asked.

"Why should she be?" she replied, a note of irritation in her voice. "I'm of age now, and can do what I please."

"No young woman may do what she pleases," Monty said.

"I beg to differ, Whitcombe," Dunton said. "This delightful creature is now mistress of her destiny."

Lady Arabella scowled, her brow furrowing into a frown, rendering her usually beautiful face quite ugly.

"I can speak for myself," she snapped.

To think—Mother wanted me to marry that creature!

Dunton glanced at the building, then let out a bark of laughter. "Of course! Have you come to satisfy yourself that they've reaped the reward of their labors?"

"They?"

"The Howards, of course!" Dunton chuckled, spraying droplets of spittle. Beside him, Lady Arabella wrinkled her nose in disgust.

"Have they left London?" Monty asked.

"Sir Leonard's given up this house," Dunton replied. "I believe he's somewhere in Cheapside—or so Lady Arabella's modiste said. I suppose it's best that he return to his kind."

"His kind?"

"Shop folk," Dunton said. "I can't abide shop folk who try to foist their hideous offspring onto the likes of us. And he's no reason to stay now both daughters have left."

"Both?"

Monty's small bud of hope disintegrated at Dunton's words.

"I think congratulations are in order," Dunton said. "What do you think, my dear?"

Lady Arabella, her eyes the color of ice, inclined her head in the manner of a queen acknowledging her subjects.

I'm too late.

Eleanor must have married Colonel Reid. And some foolish man had taken her sister on. Monty thought Juliette had managed to snare Dunton, but Dunton must have transferred his affections to Lady Arabella, with her title and significantly larger fortune.

Honestly, he didn't know which out of Juliette and Arabella was the worse prospect for a happy marriage. Not that Dunton would care—he'd resume his whoring once Arabella had given him an heir.

"Is Colonel Reid in town?" Monty asked.

"Why the deuce would you care?" Dunton scoffed.

"I'd like to pay my respects to him and his bride."

"His bride?" Confusion clouded Dunton's expression, then he threw back his head and roared with laughter, emitting another spray of spittle. "Ha! You don't know, do you?"

"Know what?" Monty asked, itching to slam his fists into that fat, fleshy face.

"Reid's returned to his regiment. The congratulations are for myself and Lady Arabella."

For a moment, Monty simply stared at them.

Then Lady Arabella frowned. "Have you forgotten your manners?"

"Forgive me, no," Monty said. "I congratulate you both. I cannot think of a couple better suited to one another."

Dunton licked his lips as he glanced at Lady Arabella, who

met Monty's gaze, her eyes narrowing, as if she caught his true meaning.

"So—Reid has gone," Monty said.

"It's no wonder, considering the scandal." Dunton shook his head in mock indignation. "That fool should never have entangled himself with the Howards—to be publicly humiliated by the younger daughter might garner pity, but to be fooled a second time by the elder is to expose oneself to ridicule."

Monty's stomach clenched. What had happened? Where was Eleanor?

"A scandal, you say?" he said, his voice rising.

"Involving both Miss Howard and her sister." He turned to Arabella. "The younger Miss Howard was your particular friend at one point, wasn't she?"

"I've told you *not* to speak of her," Arabella said sharply. "She was never a true friend—I always had reservations about her background, and her behavior proved me right."

"For heaven's sake, will one of you tell me what's happened?" Monty cried.

"I say, old boy, there's no need to speak like that," Dunton said. "I don't know rightly what happened, but a few months ago, Miss Howard was revealed to have leanings of a very...*sordid* nature."

"Revealed?"

"I believe it happened during a dinner party, where the two Howard girls entered into an altercation about a lover. Something to do with erotic drawings, or so I heard."

Monty's gut twisted. *Drawings...*

"You had a fortunate escape there, Whitcombe," Dunton continued, "or the scandal could have tainted *your* name."

"And...the lover?"

"It must be Reid," Dunton said, "given that he fled London the next morning. I should give him credit for his virility—but only a desperate man would shag a daughter of a trader, let alone two of them."

"Dunton!" Lady Arabella slapped her fiancé's arm.

He stared at the offending hand, and for a moment, Monty thought he'd forcibly remove it. Then his hoglike eyes creased with a smile of obsequiousness.

"I apologize, my dear. A man shouldn't speak of whores in front of his betrothed."

"Miss Howard is no whore," Monty said.

"So *you* weren't foolish enough to shag her, then." Dunton chuckled. "Just as well—you'd likely catch the pox, given how often she'll have spread her legs by now."

Lady Arabella gave a sharp huff, her breath misting in the air, and Dunton glanced at her, spite glittering in his expression before he smiled.

The two of them were as bad as each other—and they deserved each other. But Monty would gain no satisfaction from quizzing them. Clearly they knew very little and merely indulged in gossip born of speculation.

But he had to find Eleanor.

And if he had to turn over every house in Cheapside to do so, he'd not stop until he had.

CHAPTER THIRTY-SEVEN

E LEANOR DIPPED HER paintbrush into the jar and swirled it around, releasing a cloud of ultramarine that dissipated like wisps of smoke until it dissolved, rendering the water a pale blue color.

"Are you not cold, Mrs. Riley?"

She turned to see Reverend Staines standing over her shoulder.

"Not particularly," she replied. "I find I can get so absorbed in my work that I lose all sense of the world around me."

He glanced at the easel. "Exquisite."

"Hardly," she replied, laughing. "The proportions of the steeple are all wrong—see?"

"Why do you always do that?"

"What?"

"Talk yourself down whenever someone compliments you. Can you not accept praise with grace?"

"I'm only speaking the truth," she said. "I've made the steeple too tall, which means the angle of the roof is out of proportion."

He sighed. "Perhaps you consider yourself unworthy of kind words? I often wonder what your life was like before you came to Sandcombe to make you distrust the praise of others." He gestured to the space beside her on the bench. "May I?"

"We're in *your* garden, reverend—which happens to have the finest view of the church."

He sat beside her. "In that I agree with you. The building's at its best in the spring, when the May trees are in bloom. You must come and paint it then—that is, if you're still in Sandcombe."

"I've no intention of leaving, reverend."

He tutted. "I thought I said not to call me *reverend*. I'd prefer Mr. Staines, or"—he hesitated, and she could swear she saw a faint blush on his cheeks—"perhaps, in an informal setting such as this, I might prevail upon you to call me Andrew."

She averted her gaze at his familiarity.

"How do you manage to depict the walls?" he asked. "There must be hundreds—nay, *thousands*—of stones. Do you paint them all? I wouldn't have the patience."

"Neither would I." She laughed. "Art isn't about replicating a subject—it's about depicting what we see. Much like your sermons, a work of art exists to challenge the observer."

"In what way?"

She gestured to her canvas. "What do you see when you look at the walls of the building?"

"Stones," he said. "Hundreds of stones."

"But, if you look closer, you'll see that I've depicted only a few stones here and there. Everywhere else, I've merely given the impression of stones by blending the colors."

He leaned closer, then nodded. "Remarkable—how did I not see that before?"

"Because your eye fills in the detail. With your sermons, you select verses that mean something to you, rather than merely reciting what's in your Bible. That way, you permit your congregants to take whatever message feels right for them."

He drew in a sharp breath, then shook his head in disbelief. "You understand! In fact, I believe you may be the only soul in Sandcombe who does. It's what I believe my vocation to be—to give guidance and understanding, rather than enforcement and instruction."

Eleanor dipped her brush into the jar once more, then wiped it on a rag and closed her paintbox.

"Forgive me," he said, "I didn't mean to disturb you."

"You could never be a disturbance, Mr. Staines. Besides, I must let the canvas dry before painting the foreground."

"Which do you prefer?" he asked. "Portraits or landscapes?"

"It depends on the subject," she said. "A portrait is more challenging because the smallest flaw in proportion renders the subject unrecognizable."

"Is that why you've painted so many portraits of me?" he asked, laughing. "Even Mrs. Ham has one of your pencil drawings of me on her wall at the inn."

Dear Mrs. Ham had taken pity on Eleanor at first, purchasing her sketches for a shilling each. But now, she adorned the walls of her guest rooms with Eleanor's seascapes with the intention of attracting the interest—and custom—of travelers, from which Eleanor had managed to earn a modest, but steady, income.

"Mrs. Ham has portraits of *everyone* on her wall," Eleanor said. "There's one of her terrier beneath one of the candle sconces in the bar."

"Don't you find faces difficult to draw?"

She nodded. "The trick is to see a face as areas of light and dark, with the bone structure beneath as planes and angles. When I'm drawing a nose, for example, I see shadows and curves. I don't see a *nose*."

"Except, perhaps, in the case of Mrs. Fulford, where, I fear, one cannot help but see a nose—and little else."

Eleanor suppressed a giggle. "Honestly, reverend, I should reprimand you for such uncharitable thoughts."

"Or commend me for my honesty."

"Then I'll be honest in turn, and tell you the reason I sketch you so much," she said. "It's because you have the most interesting face in Sandcombe."

His eyes widened, and a flare of regret rippled through her at the desire in his expression.

"Ought I to be flattered?"

"Forgive me, but no," she said. "I'm afraid a flaw of mine is my inability to say the right thing without giving offense. I was merely remarking, from an artistic point of view, that you have an interesting bone structure—the way the shadows play across your cheekbones…"

He took her hand, his fingers warm to the touch.

"Heavens! You're cold," he said. "We must get you inside."

He leaned closer, and her heart somersaulted in her chest.

What have I done?

"I would hope you see me as more than a mere subject. I should like you to see me as a friend."

Panic swelled inside her, and she withdrew her hand.

Disappointment flared in his eyes, followed by resignation.

"And now it is I who must beg forgiveness," he said. "Though you are out of mourning, it's thoughtless of me to assume that you no longer grieve for your late husband. Here…" He picked up the easel. "Let's get your things inside before you catch cold. There's tea waiting in the parlor—with some of my cook's leftover Christmas cake."

"How can I refuse an offer of leftover Christmas cake?"

Eleanor followed him inside to the parlor, where tea had been set out. He escorted her to a chair, then poured the tea. When he returned with her cup, stirring the contents, she caught the faint aroma of cinnamon and honey.

Perfect.

He gave a soft smile. "Your maid told me how you like your tea. The cinnamon arrived shortly after Christmas. Have I made it right?"

She nodded, returning the smile, and his eyes sparkled with pleasure.

"I know tea is a poor substitute for the late Mr. Riley, but perhaps it will be enough to enable you to forgive my crassness of earlier."

She met his warm brown gaze, and her conscience pricked at her heart. This good, kind man did not deserve to be deceived.

"I fear I'm the one who must beg forgiveness," she said.

"What for?"

"I've not been entirely honest. I-I'm not—" She hesitated. "I mean—I'm not a widow."

"Your husband's alive?"

She looked away, her cheeks warming as she felt his gaze on her. "I am unmarried."

"I see," he said after a pause.

"B-but there *was* a man."

He drew in a sharp breath, and she fixed her gaze on the window, anticipating admonishment. The ticking of the clock on the mantelshelf filled the air, together with the steady sound of his breathing.

Then, with a rattle of crockery, he set his teacup down and sat beside her.

"There *is* a man," she said. "A man that I—"

"Don't speak of it," he said, and she flinched.

But what did she expect? Of *course* he'd judge her. Who wouldn't—particularly a vicar?

Then his warm hand took hers. She glanced up, meeting his gaze, expecting to see disgust.

But she only saw understanding.

"I had wondered if you were unmarried," he said. "Your maid often refers to you as 'miss,' and though at first I thought it a slip of the tongue—particularly if she'd served you before your marriage—you often seemed uneasy being referred to as Mrs. Riley."

"Then you're more observant than most."

"In my vocation, observation is a necessity. As is the capacity to listen without judgment."

"I fear you may condemn me for having sinned," she said.

"We're all sinners in the eyes of the Almighty," he replied softly. "It's in our nature. Every day we commit thoughtless acts that serve our own gratification at the expense of others. Who am *I* to dictate what is, and isn't, a sin? We must all look to our own hearts—and consciences. Did you love him?"

She hesitated, then nodded slowly, biting her lip to stem the tears.

"I see," he whispered.

She tried to withdraw her hand, but he caught it in both hands and held it firm.

"No. Eleanor—if you'll permit me to call you by your given name—there's no sin in having loved another. And whatever happened, I can see you suffer for it."

"H-how do you know?"

He stroked the back of her hand. "The first time I set eyes on you at church—sitting in a pew at the back, set apart from the rest of the congregation, with your maid beside you—I saw pain and weariness in your eyes. In the weeks since your arrival, that pain may have lessened, but it's still there, isn't it?"

"Perhaps."

"Then I would venture to say that, rather than having been the sinner, you were sinned against."

She reached for her teacup and took a sip.

"Did he take advantage of you?"

Her teacup rattled against the saucer as she looked up. "Did he *what*?"

"It happens more often than you might think. A young woman, blinded by love and tempted by promises, accepts a man's attentions, only to find herself heartbroken, abandoned, and ruined." He shook his head. "Some men are utter cads."

"Reverend, I—"

"No, Eleanor," he interrupted. "*He's* the sinner—and is, no doubt, indulging in sin while you live in obscurity, shouldering the burden of his whim. If there were any justice in the world, I'd—"

"*Please!*" she cried. "It wasn't like that."

"I'll wager every naïve young girl has said that after finding herself abandoned, willingly taking on the sins of a blackguard because she's foolish enough to—"

She withdrew her hand. "I'm no fool—and he didn't abandon

me! We had an agreement. W-we were always going to part. It was *my* doing. I wanted to know what it might be like—just once—to be loved. Truly loved."

"Yet he didn't love you in return."

"Perhaps he did," she whispered. "But not enough."

"But surely, when you declared your heart, he ought to have—"

"I never declared my heart," she said. "I wouldn't—I mean, that's a risk I'd *never* take."

"I understand," he said quietly. "The deepest love goes hand in hand with a fear of rejection that overcomes all hope. And you therefore take what is on offer, knowing that the pain of rejection if you admit—even to yourself—that you yearn for more would be too much to bear."

She drew in a sharp breath at his words. How could he possess such insight, almost as if he'd crawled inside her mind? Such an ability to understand her—she'd only seen it in another…

But she could no longer think of *him*.

"So, you ran from him," the reverend said.

She shook her head. "He and I parted as friends. We're still friends, I believe."

"You believe?"

She forced a smile. "I'm hardly likely to see him again. Doubtless he'll live out his life with little thought for me, and I'd rather remove myself from his path. I shall always hold him in high regard, but I would rather never see him again than endure the prospect of being merely his friend."

"Is that why you came here, changed your name, and removed yourself from London Society?"

Her stomach flipped at his words. "H-how did you know…"

"Your accent betrays you," he said, smiling. "Having two sisters who are readying themselves for their first Seasons, I can tell when a young woman has been subjected to years of elocution lessons. But running from your problems is not the solution. And running from your family…" He hesitated. "Unless they cast you out—*Sweet heaven*, Eleanor, is that why you're here?" He shook his head. "I despair of the world sometimes. A parent's duty is to love their child no matter what. Perhaps if I wrote to your family on your behalf, they might relent. I'm ashamed to say it, but we live in a world where the word of a man of the cloth may be enough to effect a reconciliation."

"I'm here by choice," Eleanor said. "My father hasn't forsaken me—he set me free. I have no wish to return to London." She smiled at the memory of the last time she saw Papa—his strong, steady arms around her, the familiar smell of him, of cigars and spices, while he bade her farewell and a prosperous, happy, and independent life. "Most fathers would have thrown their daughters out after what happened. But Papa didn't, not even when…"

"When what?"

"I promised myself I'd never speak of it again," she said. "Harriet knows, of course, for I couldn't bring her with me under false pretenses, but we agreed that neither of us would mention it. But I find myself compelled to speak of it, just once, so that you may judge me as I ought to be judged."

His eyes widened, but he remained quiet, as if he waited for her to trust him.

As another had done, that beautiful night at Rosecombe when she had given her heart and body to the man she loved.

Perhaps it *was* possible to have a friendship with a man. Here—and now—was a man who offered that friendship.

"You can trust me with the truth, Eleanor," he said, his voice catching at her name, "though I understand that your trust is not something I can ask of you. If you cannot trust me today, I shall be patient and wait until tomorrow—and all the tomorrows thereafter. Then, if you are still unable to trust me, I shall accept, with grace, my flaw in not being worthy."

He leaned back, then retrieved his teacup and took a sip. "Perhaps you might like some fruitcake after all?"

"I lay with him," she said quietly.

He said nothing, but when she looked up, his gaze was filled with understanding.

"And then I drew portraits—to remember him by…" Her cheeks warming, she looked away. "*Intimate* portraits."

He remained silent for a while. "You mean like William Etty?"

Etty—where had she heard that name?

"Etty's making something of a name for himself for depicting nudes," he continued. "Causing something of a scandal, due to the accuracy of the color tones when depicting the—ahem—flesh. Or so my father tells me. He's a patron of the Royal Academy."

"Oh." Her cheeks grew hotter until they almost burned.

"I take it you drew a rather *detailed* nude of your lover."

Shame needled at her.

"I *knew* you'd judge me," she said. "Like all the others, when my sister—" She broke off and sighed. "They weren't meant to be seen. They were a private treasure for me to keep, to remind me that, for a brief moment, someone found me desirable." She rose. "I should go."

He leaped to his feet and took her hands. "Oh, Eleanor! You think I'd judge you merely for loving another? It breaks my heart to hear that you believe yourself unlovable, and undesirable, when you are quite the opposite. But what do mean, *all the others*?"

She drew in a deep breath to steady herself, but the despair threatened to overwhelm her. "M-my sister showed them to the guests during a dinner party."

"She *what*?" he cried, tightening his grip. "Was she mistaken?"

"I'm afraid it was intentional—though I fear she wasn't in possession of her wits."

He set his mouth into a firm line. "She must have known what she was doing."

"Perhaps." Eleanor sighed. "But I fear she didn't fully understand the consequences."

"Even the dullest wit would know that such a revelation

would ruin you—and most likely ruin your family also. I cannot comprehend that a woman would do that to her own sister! Does she hate you *that* much?"

Eleanor opened her mouth to deny it, then hesitated. Perhaps Juliette did hate her—a hatred born of a failure to understand her difference. She'd been unable to disguise her resentment of Eleanor's betrothal to Montague—or her glee when it ended.

"Many things give rise to hatred, Mr. Staines," she said. "I'd ask you not to judge Juliette too harshly. I believe she suffers—and perhaps she acted because she hoped it would end her suffering. Did you not say in one of your sermons that those who commit acts of evil are merely trying to restore a perceived imbalance in the world? That it's human nature to resent the happiness of another and to destroy it if they can—even if it leads to one's own destruction?"

"That doesn't mean acts of evil should go unpunished when they lead to the suffering of others. Your sister ought to be horsewhipped."

Eleanor flinched at the anger in his voice. "Is that how you treat someone who commits a transgression?"

"That was more than a transgression, Eleanor. It was a deliberate act to destroy another. Why in the name of the Almighty would she do such a thing?"

"I've asked myself that question every day since I came here," she replied. "I can only think she did it because she failed in her own pursuit of a man."

"There it is," he said. "The folly of an unmarried woman desperate to do anything to snare a title. My elder brother has experienced such a woman—ruthless, immoral, and willing to destroy any female rival in her quest to ensnare a man so that she might plague him for the rest of his days."

"Do you have such a low opinion of my sex?"

"I do of women like your sister, who think nothing of destroying the lives of others for their own gratification." He shook his head. "Forgive me—before I was ordained, I experienced much of the desperate debutante. I can understand why you left London Society. It's somewhere I have no intention of setting foot in. I pity my poor brother, who, as the heir, is obliged to submit to the Marriage Mart. I pray he never encounters your sister."

Eleanor shrank back from the force of his anger, which was almost tangible.

Then he sighed. "It's to your credit that you defend your sister, but I'll never understand why a woman would treat another so cruelly. To have driven you from your home—she must have known what she was doing."

"What does it matter?" Eleanor said. "I'm here now, living my own life—somewhere quiet where I can do what I love."

"Paint?" he suggested, his expression softening.

"Not just that—but live on my own terms, not being dictated to."

"By a husband."

She nodded. "When a woman marries, she surrenders her freedom to her husband."

"Not *all* husbands."

"Almost all," she said. "So, Juliette didn't really do me any harm."

"But what about the man you…" He made a vague gesture in the air, his cheeks reddening. "Didn't he come to your defense? After all—he was the subject of your drawings."

"He doesn't know," she said, "and I won't tell him."

"Why not?"

"I don't want him feeling as if he needs to act out of obligation."

His chest rose and fell in a sigh. "Ah," he said. "There it is."

"There what is?"

"The consideration for another with little regard to your own gratification. The purest form of love."

Her throat constricted at the thought of…*him*. Her eyes stung with tears, and she lifted a hand to wipe them away. The reverend caught her wrist and held it in a firm but tender grip.

"You still love him, don't you?"

She longed to deny it, but her defenses crumbled at his gentle touch and tender gaze, and she bowed her head.

"I'm sorry," he whispered. Then he placed a hand on her cheek and wiped the tears away with his thumb.

Then she looked up and let out a low cry.

"Mrs. Riley?"

Harriet stood in the doorway.

He withdrew his hand and stepped back, his blush deepening.

"Begging your pardon," Harriet said. "Mrs. Palmer's expecting you—for the sitting, for her portrait?" She stepped into the parlor, and her eyes widened. "Reverend, what have you done to my mistress?" She rushed toward Eleanor. "Oh, miss! Look at you—you're trembling all over. You—" She broke off as she realized her mistake. "I-I mean, Mrs. Riley, ma'am."

"It's all right," he said. "I know."

"Y-you *know*?"

"Yes, Harriet. I commend you for taking such excellent care of your mistress after what happened."

"He knows everything, miss?"

Eleanor nodded. "You needn't worry, Harriet. Mr. Staines is a friend." She took his hand. "A *good* friend. He'll not tell a soul, will you?"

"No—Eleanor."

Harriet flinched at the familiar address. "Miss Eleanor deserves a friend after what that sister of hers did."

"And she does have a friend," he said. "Eleanor, I'll ask nothing of you other than that one day—in your own time—you might find it in yourself to trust me with *your* friendship." He glanced at the clock on the mantelshelf. "Now, don't let me detain you if Mrs. Palmer's expecting you. Do you wish to leave your easel and canvas here? I can keep it safe for when you resume your painting of the church."

"Yes, thank you," Eleanor said.

With Harriet's assistance, they gathered the rest of her materials, then he ushered her out of the vicarage, pressing a wrapped slice of cake into Harriet's hands.

"Oh, reverend—I couldn't possibly."

"Please," he said, giving Eleanor a wink. "If you don't take it, I'll be expected to eat it all myself, and though my tailor would appreciate the custom, I am not minded to purchase a new wardrobe just yet."

"Then we shall accept both the cake, and your friendship, with pleasure," Eleanor said.

Arm in arm with Harriet, she took her leave. Halfway along the road, she turned back to see him standing in the doorway, watching her.

"He loves you, miss," Harriet said. "There's none kinder than him. You could do worse."

For a moment, the image flashed before Eleanor—of a comfortable life with a kind man whose company she enjoyed, and, one day, a family of her own. The image was perfect, save for one thing.

She didn't love him.

Her heart belonged, irrevocably, to another.

CHAPTER THIRTY-EIGHT

To Monty, Bishopsgate Street looked as if it belonged to a different world, not just a different part of London. Even the people looked different—*cits* bustling along the street as if they were driven by a purpose, as opposed to the aimless wanderings of the *ton*.

Perhaps that was what the necessity of having to earn one's living did to a man.

And a woman. Here, women jostled the men on the pavement, striding out with the independence that Society ladies lacked—women who earned their own living and thought, as well as spoke, for themselves.

Women such as…

He approached the door and knocked. At that moment, a couple approached. The man glanced at Monty's carriage, taking in the Whitcombe crest. Then he turned his attention to Monty himself and stared—an open, direct gaze, filled with curiosity and a little disdain.

In Society, Monty was revered, but here, where meritocracy ranked above aristocracy, he was nothing more than an idle creature who languished on his estate while better men worked. Against the neat, plain attire of the *cit's* perfectly tailored, but simply designed, suit, Monty must seem like an over-frilled fop.

The man tipped his hat, gave Monty a nod, then strode past, his wife on his arm.

"Ahem."

A young woman in a plain gray gown stood in the doorway, a set of keys dangling from her waist.

Who in the name of the devil employed their *housekeeper* to open the front door?

"Oh," he said. "I'm at the wrong house."

"Who have you come to visit, sir?" she asked.

"Sir Leonard Howard."

"This is Sir Leonard's house. Whom shall I say wants to see him?"

"The Duke of Whitcombe."

"Very good. Come in." She ushered him inside and led him into a parlor. "Wait here. I'll see if Sir Leonard is happy to receive you."

Before Monty could respond, she exited the parlor. No curtsey.

And rather than pander to his sensibilities and tell him she'd check whether Sir Leonard was at home, she gave him the more direct narrative of whether Sir Leonard *wanted* to see him.

He didn't know whether to find her frankness insulting or refreshing. Perhaps those who worked in commerce were required to adopt a more open and honest approach to their lives—and he'd noticed such frankness in her.

My Eleanor...

Footsteps approached, and his heart rate quickened.

Then the door opened and the young woman appeared. "Sir Leonard will see you. Follow me."

Feeling as if he were a wayward schoolboy at Eton on the way to the provost's office for a birching, Monty rose and followed her up one flight of stairs and along the hallway to a heavy, oak-paneled door. She knocked and paused.

"Send him in," a voice said from the other side.

She pushed the door open, and Monty entered the room.

Unlike the parlor, which was almost stark in its simplicity, Sir Leonard's study was the peculiar contradiction of extreme order and chaos that Monty recalled from their previous meeting—row upon row of books filling one wall, and opposite, an array of brightly colored silks and jars of spices. At the far wall, behind a squat mahogany desk, silhouetted against the window, sat the figure of a man.

A chair had been placed in front of the desk, presumably for interviewees or subordinates, but Monty remained standing. In his world—in Mayfair, where everyone submitted to his rank—he'd sat without a qualm.

But he wasn't in his world.

The figure rose, and Monty caught sight of two bright eyes regarding him coldly.

"Whitcombe."

"Sir Leonard," Monty said. "I must thank you for—" He broke off as Sir Leonard raised his hand.

"I wondered how long it would take before you came sniffing round again. How did you find me?"

Yes—it was just like being in Mr. Goodall's office having been caught transgressing.

Monty glanced about the room, half expecting to see a cane ready for use. "Madame Chassineux gave me your address," he replied.

Sir Leonard let out a huff. "Under duress, no doubt, after you reminded her of your rank. I find it a great shame that anyone in business must pander to the whims of a titled gentleman who, in my experience, is less likely to settle his accounts than a merchant on time—if at all."

"I always pay my dues, Sir Leonard," Monty said.

"I doubt that."

"I do—I instruct my steward to settle—"

"I wasn't referring to *financial* matters."

Monty glanced at the chair beside the desk. "Sir Leonard, may I sit?"

"When discussing certain matters, I prefer to remain standing."

"For what purpose?"

"It ensures that a discussion remains on point, and that time is not wasted on unnecessary niceties with individuals whom I hold in little esteem."

Monty flinched. "I understand your anger, Sir Leonard, but—"

"I'm not angry, Whitcombe—just disappointed. I expected better of you—and had even come round to the notion of having a high opinion of you."

"You had?" Monty asked, a bubble of pride swelling in his soul.

"Not at first, of course."

Of course…

The bubble burst.

"At first, I thought you yet another privileged profligate. Of course, men like you patronize my business all the time, with your countless mistresses on whom you shower trinkets and new gowns at every opportunity, to gratify your sense of self-worth in having a bird of paradise on your arm."

So much for ensuring the discussion remained on point with no time wasted on unnecessary niceties.

"But then," Sir Leonard said, weariness in his voice, "I saw how my Eleanor blossomed—how she grew in confidence, accepting herself for what she was rather than berating herself for not conforming to the ideal of a young lady. Fool that I was, I gave *you* credit for that."

"I take no credit for your daughter's—"

"Do *not* speak of her!" Sir Leonard cried. "I promised that if I ever saw you again, I'd not waste my anger on you. You'd better go before I break that promise."

"I won't go until you tell me where Eleanor is."

Sir Leonard raised his arm, then struck Monty across the jaw with a punch that sent him sprawling to the floor.

Devil's toes—for a man who looked old and weary, Sir Leonard had the right hook of a prizefighter.

"How *dare* you speak her name!" Sir Leonard caught his

breath and placed his hands over his chest. "Get up and fight me like a man, at least," he hissed. "Or do you define your manhood only in terms of how many maidens you've violated?"

"I didn't come to fight, Sir Leonard."

"I won't tell you where she is."

"Shouldn't *she* be the one to decide that?"

Sir Leonard let out a bitter laugh. "Arrogant to the last! Haven't you done enough to her? Forcing her into an engagement only to be discarded at the end—but taking what you wanted anyway. Not to mention"—he wrinkled his nose—"strutting about like a prize bull, posing like a dandy for your own gratification, with no thought to the consequences for my daughter!"

"I didn't think—"

"No," Sir Leonard snarled. "You *didn't* think. Men like you never do."

"Please," Monty said, "I only want to speak to her. You cannot imagine the guilt I suffer."

"Even now you only think of *your* suffering," Sir Leonard scoffed.

"I suffer in the knowledge that I've caused her pain," Monty said. "Please, sir, believe me—the last thing I want is for her to be unhappy."

"Then you should have thought of that before you tricked my daughter into believing you loved her! I thought you realized she's unlike other young ladies—she's more easily duped by those who seek to deceive, and she suffers more than most when her trust is betrayed."

The earlier flash of weariness in Sir Leonard's eyes returned. Monty struggled to his feet and offered his hand.

"Please, sir, I only want to see if she's all right."

"What does it matter to you whether she's all right or not?"

"It matters a great deal."

"Oh, spare me!" Sir Leonard replied. "You never looked at her twice before you plotted your nefarious little scheme! Then you had the effrontery to look me in the eye while we discussed a marriage settlement—a marriage you never intended to take place. Tell me, *Your Grace*, why should I believe anything you say? And why can't you have the decency to leave my daughter alone?"

"Because I love her!" Monty cried.

Sir Leonard's eyes widened, then he swayed to one side, clutching his chest. Monty caught the older man and guided him toward the chair.

"Sir Leonard, you're not well."

The man gave a watery smile. "In that, at least you speaking the truth."

"I've not said anything that's untrue, sir," Monty said. "And I'll not shirk my responsibility for your troubles. If your business is suffering for it, I can give you—"

"Stop there," Sir Leonard said. "I've needed to retrench, but I can weather it. Your little corner of the world may look down on me, but here, I'm back among my people."

"And…Lady Howard?"

"My wife chose to return to her family until the scandal dies down. And my younger daughter…" He hesitated. "She's taken a vacation for her health. So you see, Your Grace, your scheme has scattered my family across the country."

"For that, I'm truly sorry," Monty said.

Sir Leonard smiled. "We'll survive. I can live more simply here, and my wife is where she's happiest. As for my daughters, they're resourceful. Eleanor is doing what she always wanted—in a place she used to love, filled with dreams and memories. Even my youngest child—my poor, misguided Juliette—will survive her ordeal and emerge the better for it."

"What can I do?" Monty asked.

Sir Leonard rose, the color returning to his cheeks. "You can leave."

"But Eleanor—"

"Has endured enough at your hands—and the hands of others."

"But—"

"Tell me, Whitcombe," Sir Leonard interrupted. "Who, out of all of us, deserves most to be happy and at peace?"

"Eleanor, of course."

He placed a hand on Monty's arm. "Then leave her be, Whitcombe. It broke my heart to say goodbye to Eleanor—but I let her go because I love her."

The older man's gentle plea pierced Monty's heart more deeply than his earlier words of anger—for it was motivated by love.

And while Monty may have been able to argue against anger, or vengeance, he could never argue against an honest man doing what he thought best for his beloved daughter.

Admitting defeat, Monty bowed and retreated.

If he were to find Eleanor, he'd have to search elsewhere. What had Sir Leonard said?

A place she used to love, filled with dreams and memories.

Not much to go on, but it was a start.

THE CARRIAGE DREW to a halt outside Marlow's townhouse. The building, which Monty had expected to be empty, was ablaze with light.

Marlow was at home.

Monty opened the carriage door and climbed out. Then he leaped up the steps to the front door and knocked. Moments later, a footman appeared.

"Is your master in?"

"Yes, Your Grace." The footman ushered him into a parlor. "I'll tell the master you're here."

"And your mistress?"

"Lady Marlow is resting, on account of the baby."

"Shit."

The footman arched an eyebrow in disapproval.

"Is she in the country?"

"No, sir—she returned to London for her confinement, but she's not receiving visitors."

"I particularly wish to see her on an urgent matter."

"Perhaps the master can relay a message."

"I'd rather speak to her myself."

"Very good."

The footman bowed then retreated into the corridor, closing the door behind him.

Damn—Monty had forgotten Lady Marlow's confinement. She'd looked ready to give birth any day at Rosecombe, and it was the height of incivility not to congratulate a new parent.

Though he'd not cared about such things before…

Before Eleanor.

Too restless to sit, Monty paced about the parlor, taking in the décor, which had a decidedly more feminine touch than he recalled. But the last time Monty had visited, Marlow was a bachelor. Gone were the heavy colors that absorbed the light— gone was the reek of cigars. They had been replaced by warm, welcoming colors and the gentle aroma of lavender.

Monty's gaze fell upon a picture on the wall, nestled among a series of watercolor landscapes. A simple pencil sketch, with very few lines, but the likeness was unmistakable—as was the artist.

The subject looked out from the picture, a smile of bliss on her lips. Her hands were placed on her belly, and an expression of the purest love shone from her eyes.

Monty had never seen such an expression on the prickly Lady Marlow. But perhaps that was a reflection of her opinion of him compared to her obvious love for the woman who'd drawn her likeness. Eleanor's love for Lady Marlow shone through every line, every pencil mark.

The door opened, and Marlow entered.

"Whitcombe! I didn't expect to see you. I thought you were overwintering in the country."

"And I you."

"I brought Lavinia to London for her confinement," Marlow said. "She insisted on being close to Dr. McIver."

"Couldn't you send for him from the country?" Monty asked.

"Lavinia insisted, on account of McIver's other patients. She said she'd never forgive herself if another of his patients fell ill while he was wasting time riding back and forth to Marlow Park. Always thinks of others, does my Lavinia."

He gave a sigh, a look of contentment in his eyes, which, though Monty might have ridiculed a few months ago, he now found himself envying.

"I hear congratulations are in order," Monty said. "You have a son?"

"A daughter. Lillian Mary Eleanor."

"You're not disappointed?"

Anger sparked in Marlow's eyes. "Unlike you, Whitcombe, I don't see a wife as merely a vehicle for procuring an heir."

Ouch. But when had Monty ever expressed a different view on the role of a wife?

"Is Lady Marlow at home?" he asked. "I'd like to congratulate her in person."

"I doubt she'll want to see *you.*"

"I understand she may be delicate after her confinement, but—"

Marlow snorted. "My Lavinia wouldn't let something like a confinement slow her down. I meant she'd be unwilling to see you given that you're the cause of her losing her dearest friend. She's devastated that Miss Howard has gone."

"And you think I'm not?"

"*You* ended your engagement."

"Yes, but…"

Marlow let out a laugh. "Don't say the infamous rake has lost his heart?"

"It's no laughing matter!" Monty snapped.

"That it's not," a female voice said.

Lady Marlow stood in the doorway.

"Lavinia, my love," Marlow said. "What did I tell you about the need to rest? I—"

"Spare me, Peregrine," she said, turning her unsmiling gaze on Monty. "I thought I heard *your* voice."

"Lady Marlow, you don't know how delighted I am to see you," Monty said.

"And I you," she replied.

Marlow raised his eyebrows. "Really?"

"Yes, Peregrine. I've been wanting to give him *this*."

She stepped forward, raised her hand, then slapped Monty across the face.

Devil's toes! He'd been slapped by women many times—a hazard every rake must accept—but never as forcefully. Most women slapped a man out of indignation, mainly because their ruse to get what they wanted—his hand in marriage, a trinket, or a greater bounty for their services in the bedroom—had failed. But the look in Lady Marlow's eyes spoke of rage on behalf of a beloved friend, rather than the selfish disappointment of a harpy.

"Lavinia!" Marlow cried. "I hardly think—"

Ignoring him, she slapped Monty across the other cheek. Though he anticipated the blow this time, he remained still.

"You blackguard!" she cried.

Monty nodded. "I suppose I am."

"I should hit you again."

"Please do," he said. "I rather think it's making both you and I feel a little better."

She raised her hand again. "You make no attempt to move."

"Why should I, when I'm receiving punishment for my transgression?"

"So, you admit that you ruined my friend and drove her from her home?"

"I say, my love," Marlow said, "we can hardly accuse Whitcombe here of—"

"Juliette would never have done what she did had *he*"—she jabbed a finger at Monty—"not taken advantage of Eleanor."

"Juliette Howard only has herself to blame," Marlow said.

"Oh, spare me!" Lady Marlow cried. "Why must women always bear the consequences of the actions of men? Much as I dislike Juliette, not even she deserves her fate."

"Is Juliette not with her mother?" Monty asked.

"She's in Bath," Lady Marlow said, "taking the waters for her health."

"She's unwell?"

She rolled her eyes. "Just like a man to feign ignorance of the misdeeds of his kind! She's expecting Dunton's child."

"Lavinia, darling, we don't know for certain—"

"Well, I do!" she said. "Why else would she throw herself at Dunton one moment, then hide away the next while he parades about the place with that Arabella creature declaring to the world what a slut Juliette is? The whole family's the laughing stock of the *ton*, and it's *his* fault!" She jabbed at Monty in the chest.

"Miss Juliette cannot be in Bath. Sir Leonard told me—"

"Ah—*that* explains it," Marlow said.

"Explains what?" Monty asked.

"The mark on your face. I daresay Sir Leonard's opinion of you is even lower than my wife's. You'll have a devil of a shiner tomorrow, to accompany my wife's adornment."

"I won't apologize," Lady Marlow said. "It's the least he deserves."

"In that I agree with you, ma'am," Monty said. "But I'll weather whatever is necessary to find Eleanor."

She curled her lip into a sneer. "Is that why you're here—to plague her again? You won't find her. Sir Leonard wouldn't even tell *me* where she's gone—and I'm the only one, save him, who has any regard for her."

"You're wrong," Monty said. "I love her."

"You don't know the meaning of the word."

"I know that I've not stopped thinking of her from the day we parted," Monty said. "Every waking moment I wonder if she's well—and happy—and I wish I could be with her again."

"That's not love. That's obsession and a selfish wish to enjoy the company of one of the loveliest women to walk this earth."

"In part, I agree with you," Monty said. "Eleanor *is* the loveliest woman to walk this earth. I'm not asking because I want her—I'm asking because I cannot live without her. And whatever her sister did, you cannot lay the blame at *my* feet."

"Oh, can't I?" She stepped forward, her face flushed with anger. "Don't you see the consequences of your actions? That the ripples from your false engagement spread across Society? When you, the worst rake of the *ton*, made such a public offer to Eleanor—a woman the whole of Society thought to be decidedly beneath you in looks, temperament, and station—you gave false hope to every fortune-hunting young woman hungry for a title. Even the meanest of wits would surmise that Juliette attached herself to Dunton in the hope that, with one duke marrying into the Howard family, a second could more easily be persuaded. And Dunton—foul lecher that he is—took advantage, and added Juliette to the list of maidens he deflowered."

"Lavinia!" Marlow said. "Whitcombe doesn't wish to hear—"

"Perhaps I *do*," Monty said. "Perhaps, as your good wife says, it's time I opened my eyes to the full consequences of my actions. Including that of my own heart."

He gestured to the drawing on the wall.

"Lady Marlow—I'll confess that I do think primarily of myself, and of the better man that I can be with Eleanor in my life. But on seeing this drawing... A few lines on a piece of paper have shown me that I am not the only one who suffers in her absence. I can see that you have lost a friend who loves you dearly."

"How can you see that?" she asked.

"I see it in your portrait," he said. "Every stroke of her pencil—every mark—has been delivered with love. It's a love to be envied." He swallowed, drawing in a sharp breath to temper the moisture pricking at his eyes. "I recognize, and honor, that love, for I've seen it before."

"Where?" she asked in a whisper.

He blinked, and a tear splashed onto his cheek. "In a sketch she drew of me, which she gave me leave to keep. A-and in other sketches that she kept, which…"

His cheeks burning, he averted his gaze.

"So it's true," she said. "The gossips said Juliette had displayed a sketch of Colonel Reid. But the subject was *you*, wasn't it?"

Monty nodded.

"How could you have been so foolish?"

"Because she asked me—she said she wanted something to remember me by."

Marlow let out a snort. "You certainly gave her *that*, old boy. I think—Ouch!" he let out a cry as his wife slapped his arm.

"The less you say, the better, Peregrine."

"I must defend my friend," Marlow said. "I saw a different man at Rosecombe to the one I've always known. Even I can see that he loved Eleanor."

"Then why end your engagement?" Lady Marlow asked.

"Believe me—that's a question I've asked myself every waking moment," Monty said. "Before we parted, I'd long lost any understanding of why our engagement had to come to an end, other than it's what we'd both agreed from the start."

"And your male pride dictated that you ought never to be seen to change your mind."

"My mind—and my heart—changed a long time ago, Lady Marlow," Monty said. "But I was too afraid to admit it."

"To yourself, or to my friend?" She tilted her head to one side, and the corner of her mouth lifted in a smile.

"You find my pain amusing?"

"No, Your Grace. But I marvel at how Fate conspires to ensure that the path we take comes full circle. Eleanor once told me that she loved you so deeply that she feared it. She feared both the influence it had on her every waking thought, but also that, were she to have it confirmed you thought little of her, it would destroy her."

"Then you understand my pain, Lady Marlow," Monty said.

"Tell me—is that a fitting punishment for my sins?"

"Perhaps," she said. "But it's not a punishment I'd wish on anyone."

"Then you'll help me find her?"

She shook her head. "I cannot. I spoke the truth when I said Sir Leonard wouldn't tell me where she is."

"Is there *nowhere* you can think of?" Monty asked. "Anywhere she might have visited as a child? Sir Leonard referred to somewhere she used to love, filled with dreams and memories."

Lady Marlow paused, and for a moment, Monty thought she might throw him out. Then Marlow took her hand.

"Lavinia, my love—don't you recall the pain we suffered when we were parted once? You said you could bear our being apart if you knew I was happy—but my suffering was, to you, as a knife to your heart, because you loved me."

She sighed, and her expression softened.

"Whitcombe, do you love my friend?" she asked.

"With all my heart," Monty replied.

"Do you accept that if you harm her in any way, then you should expect to lose your balls if you come within ten feet of me ever again?"

"If I harm my Eleanor, you can not only have my balls, but my head."

At length, she nodded. Then she crossed the floor to a bureau, drew out a piece of paper, and began to write.

"I'm afraid you'll have a task on your hands," she said. "Eleanor told me her family traveled extensively when she was young. Brighton, Wells—she has a beautiful sketch of the cathedral—Sandcombe, York—even as far north as Arbroath. Peregrine—can you think of anywhere else?"

"Didn't Miss Howard mention visiting France? Or Italy?"

"The family spent some time in Rome when Eleanor was much younger—before Juliette was born, I believe."

"Sounds like an impossible quest," Marlow said.

"But it must be done," Monty replied.

"Count yourself lucky Sir Leonard never took the family with him to the Far East," Lady Marlow said, continuing to write. "I believe he sailed there several times."

She continued to scribble names, then handed the paper over.

"Will you visit them all?"

"I'll begin my quest tomorrow," Monty replied.

"Then go, with my blessing."

"Thank you." Pocketing the paper, Monty bowed, took Lady Marlow's hand—the same hand that had struck him earlier—and brushed his lips against her skin.

"I shall use this wisely," he said. "And rest assured, I'll not do anything to make Eleanor unhappy."

The footman opened the doors, and Monty stepped out into the street.

"Your Grace."

Monty stopped and turned. "Yes, Lady Marlow?"

"If you find Eleanor—what if she rejects you?"

"Then," he said, "my punishment will be complete."

CHAPTER THIRTY-NINE

Sandcombe, Lincolnshire, March 1816

THE PARLOR AT the inn—the Dancing Sailor, or some such—
was quieter than he'd expected. A lone gentleman,
consuming a plate of eggs with enthusiasm, sat near the fireplace,
and a couple with a young woman were engaged in conversation
at a table by the window. The rest of the tables were unoccupied.

A plump, ruddy-faced man appeared at the doorway—the
same man who'd ushered Monty inside last night when he
climbed out of the mail coach.

"Oh, Your Grace!" he cried, "I didn't expect you to be about
at this hour after you arrived so late last night. I was going to send
my Johnny to tend to you, seeing as you have no valet."

"Thank you for your consideration, Mr. Ham, but I've become quite adept at dressing myself."

"Very good, sir. Sit ye down and I'll send Mrs. Ham over."

The innkeeper ushered Monty to a table set for one in the
corner, then exited the parlor.

"Mary—Mary! The *duke* is up!"

Monty sat and glanced around. The lone gentleman gave him
a cursory glance. But the family eyed him with interest—the man
with envy in his eyes, and his wife with curiosity. The young
woman, most likely their daughter, and barely out of the
schoolroom, blushed and lowered her gaze. Her mother took her

hand and smiled. The man looked at his wife, and the envy in his eyes disappeared as the two of them exchanged a loving glance.

They might envy Monty his title and wealth. But, in truth, they were the ones to be envied—a husband and wife indulging in a simple seaside vacation with their daughter, experiencing the pleasure of being together as a family.

The door opened, and a woman even plumper than the innkeeper appeared, with graying hair peeking out from beneath her cap, rosy cheeks, and warm brown eyes. She approached Monty's table and bobbed a curtsey.

"Begging your pardon, Your Grace, we didn't expect you up so soon. Are you happy to take your breakfast in the parlor? Or I can make up a private dining room."

"The parlor will do very well, Mrs. Ham," Monty said.

"Very good, sir. We serve very fine bacon here, if you don't mind my saying. It's from Mr. Long's farm. He has the finest herd of Curly Coats in the county."

"Curly Coats?"

"The Lincolnshire Curly Coat, Your Grace. You'll taste none finer—not even in London."

"In which case, some bacon will do very well, thank you."

She bobbed another curtsey and disappeared. Monty glanced about the parlor, noticing, for the first time, the paintings on the walls. Most were seascapes, but by the window was a painting of a church, framed by trees and shrubs, its tower reaching to the heavens, toward a clear blue sky.

When Mrs. Ham returned with a plate of bacon, Monty gestured to the paintings. "Are these images of Sandcombe?"

"That they are. They're for sale, if you take a fancy to any of them—to remind you of your stay. Are you on vacation?"

"After a fashion."

If a vacation were defined as spending time away from home being waited on by strangers and avoiding the daily responsibilities of life, then yes, Monty was on vacation. And he had been since the beginning of the year while he traveled up and down the country on his quest.

Yes—he was *on vacation*, and would remain so until he'd found her. The Lakes had proven fruitless—as had Brighton and Exeter. Wells yielded a glimmer of hope after the innkeeper confessed to having seen a woman fitting Eleanor's description, but she turned out to be a happily married mother of four in her early forties, with a broad Scottish brogue.

He was now running out of places to search. If Sandcombe proved fruitless, there was only Arbroath left.

At least in Britain.

"The parlor doesn't seem very full," he said. "Do you have any other guests?"

"We expect to be full tomorrow. Several visitors arrive tonight, including a large party from Lincoln. I can make up the private parlor if you want to dine in peace—and I'll set aside a portion of my fish pie for you."

Monty took a bite of his breakfast. "If it's as good as this bacon, you should set aside *two* portions. I suspect some of your guests have no wish to leave."

"That's much appreciated, sir," she said. "We had a young man here last December—he stayed almost a month."

"Why did he stay so long?"

Her smile disappeared. "My guests are free to come and go as they please without being gossiped about."

"Of course," Monty said. "Some of my acquaintances stayed here and spoke highly of your inn. A Miss Howard—perhaps you recall her?"

"We've had nobody by that name."

"Are you sure?"

"I recall the names of every guest who's stayed here, sir. There was a Mr. Howarth who stayed here with his sisters, on their way to a house party. Perhaps that's who you mean?"

"No—this would have been a woman. Unmarried."

"As I say," she said, a hard edge to her voice, "we respect our guests' privacy."

"Of course—an admirable quality, Mrs. Ham. I didn't mean to intend otherwise."

"Do you have much to occupy yourself with today, sir?" she asked. "My husband tells me you weren't certain how long your stay was going to be."

"I fancied an impromptu vacation by the sea," he replied. "Somewhere quieter than Southend or Cromer. I might undertake a little exploring."

"If you wish to explore on horseback, we've a mount that should be suitable," she said. "A gelding—sixteen hands, with an excellent temperament, who responds well to strangers. You only need ask and I'll have Tom saddle him up."

"That would do very well, Mrs. Ham, thank you." Monty resumed eating, and, recognizing her cue for dismissal, the woman curtseyed and exited the parlor.

Devil's toes—the last thing he wanted was to arouse suspicion. Unfortunately for him, Mrs. Ham seemed to be that rare beast—a woman averse to gossip, despite all the tales she must have picked up from travelers over the years. Perhaps he'd have more luck with the husband, who seemed ruled by his wife.

After finishing his breakfast, Monty returned to the main hallway, remembering this time to stoop on his way through the doorway. Older buildings had their charm, with their uneven floors and beams that stretched across the ceilings, but those ceilings were low enough to necessitate a man of his height having to duck to avoid smacking his forehead on a door lintel, as he'd done last night on entering his bedchamber.

He strode along the hallway, toward the doors leading outside. Several oval-framed portraits adorned the walls—likenesses of Mr. and Mrs. Ham flanked the candle sconce beside the parlor door, followed by a portrait of a fox terrier, the same yappy creature that had nipped at his ankles yesterday. He continued along the hallway, glancing at each painting, until he came upon the one at the end.

It was the likeness of a man. The subject had strong features—a high forehead, sharp cheekbones, and deep-set, wide eyes that looked out at the observer. Their clear expression showed a sharp intelligence, and the firm set to the jaw spoke of a strength of character that few men possessed.

Monty took a closer look, and caught his breath.

"Are ye all right, sir?" Mr. Ham said from behind. "It's a fine likeness, isn't it?"

"Is it an old drawing?"

"No, sir—it was drawn recently. Last month, I think."

"Was it drawn by the same hand that painted all the sea-scapes?"

"That's right, sir, though this one's not for sale."

Monty studied the portrait, taking in the pencil strokes that had been drawn with care and love.

A love he recognized.

No—it can't be…

His heart somersaulted in his chest. "Wh-who's the subject?"

"That'd be the vicar, Reverend Staines."

"The *vicar?*"

"As fine a gentleman as you're ever likely to meet. He's Earl Staines's youngest, but he lacks the reckless arrogance seen in so many young folk these days."

"A veritable paragon."

If he recognized Monty's facetious tone, Mr. Ham showed no sign. "That he is. The village is waiting to see who he'll settle down with. A vicar needs a wife, don't you agree?"

"A-and the artist?" Monty asked.

"That'd be Mrs. Riley."

"Does she live in the village?"

"On the edge—just past the church. My Mary has often said to her it's wrong for a lady to live on her own away from other folk, but Mrs. Riley seems to like it."

"And Mr. Riley?"

"He's passed—though she doesn't speak of it," the innkeeper said. "And why should she, is what I say? Killed at Waterloo, that's what old Cobbers reckons. She says Mrs. Riley's haunted by something—ye can see it in her eyes. Though we shouldn't set much store by what an old crone like Ma Cobbers has to say. Some folk hereabouts reckon she's a witch. But in one aspect, she's right. A young woman like Mrs. Riley shouldn't shut herself up in the prime of life just because her husband's passed, for all that he was a hero."

"But you don't know?"

"Lord no, sir—I wouldn't like to ask. She's not lived here long, but she's a part of the village, though some folk hereabouts say that you can never be part of the village unless you're born and bred here. But she's liked among them that know her, and she gives some of the proceeds of her painting to the poor. Which is more than Mrs. Fulford does, I can tell you. Mrs. Fulford may portray herself as a paragon of charitable work, but she sits back and lets others do the work while she takes the credit."

"Who's Mrs. Fulford?" Monty asked. Evidently in some marriages, it was the husband, and not the wife, who loved to gossip.

"That'd be the squire's wife. A little too eager to poke her nose in everybody's affairs. But I daresay her nose will be put out of joint soon, now Mrs. Riley's here."

"How so?"

"Mrs. Riley helps the vicar with the church flowers, you see. A fine job she does, much to Mrs. Fulford's dismay. Everyone in the village knows that Mrs. Fulford wants the vicar for one of her daughters. But Reverend Staines needs a good woman for a wife—not a pampered miss who thinks too much of herself. I can think of none better than Mrs. Riley."

"Jim—Jim!" a voice cried. "Are ye prattling on with the guests again?"

The innkeeper colored. "Coming, Mary, love!" he called. "Beggin' yer pardon, sir. I must get the place ready—we've a large party staying tonight. I'll have Tom saddle Copper for ye. It's a fine day for a ride on the beach, but take care of the tide—it can catch ye out if ye ride too far."

"Jim—where are ye? I need that wood chopped before noon!"

The innkeeper scuttled off, leaving Monty with the portrait—and his conscience.

He reached out and traced the outline of the subject with his fingertip.

"Who are you, Reverend Staines?"

The subject stared back at him with an air of superiority—not a superiority born of arrogance, but arising from him being the better man.

What had Eleanor said? That she always drew the subject as she saw them—not as they were.

Did that mean that this Reverend Staines was, in her eyes, the *better man?*

Then he shook his head. This was mere speculation. Mrs. Riley's similarity to Eleanor was due to wishful thinking—nothing more.

⇒⇒⇒✦⇐⇐⇐

COPPER WAS AN appropriate name. The gelding's chestnut pelt shimmered in the spring sunshine like polished metal. The animal was a fine beast. Not a thoroughbred—it had been bred for sturdiness rather than stamina—but it served as an adequate mount, to the point where it was tempting to ask Mr. Ham whether he'd consider selling the animal.

After pausing at the church with its squat tower and mottled stone walls, Monty steered his mount along the road leading out of the village until he spied a small dwelling—a white cottage with a red roof, surrounded by a garden fence. The garden was a blaze of color, and the air shimmered with the scent of the sea and a heady floral perfume.

Monty slowed his mount to a walk, then dismounted and tethered the animal to the fence. He lifted the latch on the gate and slipped through, following the gravel path to the building, where he knocked on a door surrounded by roses just coming into bloom.

There was no answer, and he knocked again.

Then he stepped back, glancing at the windows for signs of activity. But there was none.

The horse let out a snort. Seagulls squawked in the air above, their slim shapes circling toward the sky. The faint hum of bees filled the air, and he caught sight of their tiny shapes flying to and fro between the blooms in the garden.

Then he heard it—a woman's laugh.

His skin tightened in recognition, and he glanced about, but there was no sign of anyone. Then he moved along the side of the cottage until he caught sight of the figure of a woman, framed against the backdrop of the sea.

She sat at an easel, engrossed in her work, sweeping her brush over the canvas, then dipping it in a jar at her side, swirling it in the palette in her hand, before working on the canvas again.

Monty's heart swelled in his chest.

It's you… Sweet heaven above—it's really *you.*

Having endured disappointment after disappointment, week after week, he'd almost been driven mad with having his hopes raised, then crushed. Perhaps his mind was toying with him. Perhaps she was an apparition, formed out of hope—with her softly rounded curves, and the pure white skin of her neck visible as she bent her head, concentrating on her canvas.

Monty blinked and wiped his eyes. But the vision before him didn't disappear.

She was real—she was here.

And she was even more beautiful than before—perhaps because he now knew the sweet soul that resided within her delectable form. And perhaps because, having experienced the pain of having lost her, he understood the joy of having her in his arms—and in his life.

"Eleanor… My Eleanor."

Though he spoke in a whisper, she stiffened, as if his mind

had reached out to hers. She looked up, a frown creasing her forehead.

I'm here, my love.

She smiled, her face illuminating with joy, and his heart soared. An invisible thread bound them together, uniting their souls. All he need do was call her name and she'd return to him.

Then another figure came into view.

A man—evidently a gentleman, given his apparel—approached her and placed a hand on her shoulder. She tilted her head up, her smile widening, and her eyes filled with friendship, and…

…and—*dear Lord!*—love.

Monty's gut twisted. He reached for the wall to steady himself and stepped back. He collided with a flowerpot, knocking it over with a clatter.

"Damn!"

He cursed, stopping to set the pot upright. Then he glanced up and froze.

Eleanor had risen to her feet and was staring directly at him, her companion by her side.

The peaceful smile had gone, and his heart ached to see the pain in her eyes.

Then she shifted her body toward her companion. Almost imperceptibly, but Monty saw it for what it was—an instinctive gesture where she looked to another for comfort.

But the pain in her eyes could not match the pain in his heart at knowing he'd lost her.

CHAPTER FORTY

*E*LEANOR—*I'M HERE, MY love…*

The whispered voice, which so often visited her dreams, had never disturbed her waking moments before.

Eleanor glanced up from her easel. But there was nobody there. The landscape stretched before her—the softly undulating sand dunes sloping toward the shore and beyond, the headland jutting out toward the sea.

"Eleanor."

Mr. Staines—Andrew—appeared before her.

"Is anything the matter?" he asked. "You've gone dreadfully pale. Perhaps it's too cold to sit out of doors."

"I'm warm enough, thank you, Mr. Staines."

"*Andrew*, please," he said. "There's no need to observe formalities when Mrs. Fulford's not here to remonstrate the world over its lack of decorum."

"I'm warm enough—*Andrew*. But, to alleviate your concerns, we can take tea inside when Harriet returns from her walk. You said yourself on Sunday that spring's come early this year, and I can see that for myself—the blooms are visible already."

"That's because the climate here is particularly temperate."

"And in your sermon last week, you said that fresh air was beneficial to one's spiritual wellbeing, even on a frosty morning."

He laughed, his eyes twinkling in the morning light. "Do you pay attention to every sermon I write?"

"Isn't that what parishioners are supposed to do? Listen to your sermons and apply the principles of the underlying message to their lives?"

"Most parishioners believe that an hour or two spent in church each week is sufficient to absolve them of their sins. They may hear what I have to say, but they fail to *listen*."

He stood beside her and placed a light hand on her shoulder.

"Something's distressing you, and it's not the cold."

She tilted her head up and forced a smile. Andrew may not be the one she dreamed of at night, but in the months since her arrival at Sandcombe, he'd proven to be a good friend.

What more could a woman ask for in a world ruled by men where she had little choice in life?

"I'm content with my life," she said.

"That's not what I asked. You shouldn't aspire to be merely *content*. I would see you blissfully happy, if it were in my power."

A flicker of desire shone in his eyes, and Eleanor's stomach twisted. She had no desire to see their friendship marred by a declaration of love that she must inevitably reject. But how could she articulate her feelings to such a dear, kind man, whose heart she had no wish to break?

Before she could reply, she heard the sound of scraping crockery, followed by a smash.

Was someone eavesdropping? Mrs. Fulford was such a busy-body, always poking her nose in everybody's business—and she'd taken a marked dislike to Eleanor.

She rose to her feet, turned toward the noise, then froze.

Montague…

He was standing beside the cottage, a broken flowerpot at his feet. His hair had grown since she'd last seen him, framing his face in thick, dark waves. His eyes—his beautiful eyes—were as blue as they were in her dreams each night, when her body thrummed with life as she fought the urge to touch that secret place where the memory of pleasure still lingered…

Sweet Lord! Had he come to remonstrate her over the scandal?

What of Papa—had he bullied him into revealing her whereabouts?

Nausea clawed at her. Would she have to flee once more, to avoid scandal?

"Eleanor? Who is this man?" Mr. Staines asked.

"M-Montague..." she whispered.

"Montague? You know him intimately?"

She winced at the anger in his voice. "H-he's the one I..." She shook her head. "*Sweet heaven*, I'm sorry!"

The world slipped sideways, and she closed her eyes and pitched forward, chasing oblivion.

But oblivion never came. Two strong arms caught her.

"Eleanor—I'm here."

She clung to him, focusing her mind on the gentle, whispered voice. Then she opened her eyes.

The arms holding her were not those of the vicar—but a stronger, more muscular pair, bedecked with a jacket of finely spun dark blue wool. She inhaled, and the familiar aroma assaulted her senses—the heady scent of wood, spices, and man. For a heartbeat, she clung to the memory of that glorious moment when he'd opened his soul to her as she had opened her body to him.

Then the memory faded, replaced by the harsh reality of the world. She tried to break free, but he held firm.

"Let me go!" she cried.

He freed her, but rather than the relief she'd expected, she felt nothing but loss. Cold air brushed against her neck, and she shivered.

"Eleanor—we should get you inside," Mr. Staines said.

Montague's gaze darkened, and he set his mouth into a firm line.

"Eleanor?" he said. "You're *married*?"

"N-no," she said. "This is Mr.—I mean, Reverend Staines. The vicar."

Did she imagine it, or had she caught a flicker of hurt in his eyes, followed by relief? Then he blinked, and the darkness returned—the enigmatic gaze that had captivated her before he even knew her name.

"Why are you here?" she asked.

His brow furrowed. "Isn't it obvious?"

Dear Lord, she'd been right. The scandal…

"Is that *him*?" Mr. Staines asked, taking her hand. "Eleanor, you're distressed. Shall I send him away?"

Montague lowered his gaze to where Mr. Staines had caught her hand, and a flash of fury sparked in his eyes.

"Who might *you* be?" he said, curling his lip in a sneer.

"I'm Eleanor's friend," Mr. Staines replied.

"An overly *familiar* friend, by the look of it."

"N-no, Montague," she said, freeing her hand. "Andrew—Mr. Staines—is a good friend. I have precious few friends in the world, and I won't have you casting aspersions on our friendship. If you're here to admonish me, please say what you came to say, then leave."

"Admonish you? Whatever for?"

"F-for disgracing your name!" she cried. "I never meant for anyone to see those pictures—I p-promised I'd show them to no one, and I kept my word. That's why I left—I couldn't bear the thought of being talked about, of *you* being talked about."

"So you ran away," he said. "Did nobody ever tell you that running away from your troubles is never the answer?"

"Is that why you're here—to lecture me on decorum?"

He shook his head. "No, Eleanor," he said, and her heart almost cracked at the fatigue in his voice. "Why would you think I'd want to admonish you, when you have suffered at the hands of others—including myself?"

"In that, at least, we find agreement," Mr. Staines said. "Eleanor, aren't you going to introduce this man?"

She glanced from Montague's face, creased with weariness and apprehension, to Mr. Staines's, with its gentle, calming expression tinged with an undercurrent of righteousness.

"Th-this man is Montague FitzRoy," she said. "Fifth Duke of Whitcombe."

"A duke?" Mr. Staines replied. "You never told me he was a *duke!*"

"Does it matter?"

"It only matters in that it makes your sister's sin against you more heinous."

"And in that, Reverend Staines," Montague said, "you'll find *me* agreeing with *you*. But I must ask how you come to know Eleanor's history."

"Because she told me, *Your Grace*," Mr. Staines said, with a sneer in his tone. "Eleanor's past has tormented her ever since she came to Sandcombe. Would you rather she suffered in silence?"

"I'd rather she didn't suffer at all!"

"Then perhaps you should return home, and plague her no more."

"I'll leave only if Eleanor wishes it," Montague said.

"And she does wish it. She said so herself."

"She said nothing of the sort, reverend. Must I silence you?"

"Try it, sir—and see where your attempts to cow me will leave you."

Their angry voices stabbed at Eleanor's senses, and a wave of pain rippled through her head.

"Please, stop—both of you!" she cried. "The last thing I want is for you to fight."

"What do you want, Eleanor?" Montague asked.

"I-I want it all to go away." She shook her head as the world tilted out of focus. Then the aroma of spices broke through the fog and a firm hand took her wrist, slipping her bracelet off before placing it in her hands. He curled her fingers over the bracelet, and she clung to the smooth metal as the fog in her mind dissipated.

"There," he said in a gentle whisper. "Is that better?"

Her vision cleared as she looked down to see Montague's hand over hers, guiding her fingers around the edge of the bracelet. She glanced up and met his gaze—the pure blue of his eyes sparkling with warmth as they creased into a smile.

"H-how did you know?" she asked.

"Do you not recall the day after I asked you to marry me, Eleanor? I saw how your maid tended to you when you became a little overwhelmed."

"And you remembered?"

He nodded. "Why would I not? I have committed to memory every waking moment that we shared together—each precious moment of pleasure that I have relived in my dreams, and each moment when your distress has wounded my heart."

"A-and you came here to tell me that?"

"No, my darling," he whispered. "I came here to bring you home."

A ripple of fear threaded through her, and she tried to pull her hand free, but he held firm.

"Unhand her, sir," Mr. Staines said. "You may outrank me, but that doesn't give you the right to force her to bend to your will."

"Is that right, Eleanor?" Montague asked. "Am I forcing you against your will?"

"I-I can't go home," she said. "Not after what happened. My father…"

"Your father loves you, Eleanor. And he misses you."

So, that was how he'd found her. By bullying Papa—as he was bullying her.

He released his grip and raised his hands in an act of supplication.

"I'll not force you to do anything if you don't wish it, Eleanor."

"But you forced my father to tell you where I was."

He shook his head. "I tried to persuade him, but your father stood firm." The corner of his mouth lifted in a wry smile. "He gave me a shiner for my troubles."

She caught her breath at the thought of his pain, and lifted her hand to place it on his cheek, but his face was unmarked.

He placed his hand over hers. "It's faded now."

"When did you see Papa?"

"As soon as I heard you'd gone," he said. "A week after Christmas."

"That was months ago!"

"And you waited this long to come?" Mr. Staines said. "Hardly the act of a man in love."

"I didn't *wait* to do anything, you fool!" Montague said.

"Then what have you been doing?" Mr. Staines sneered. "Occupying yourself with doxies in London, no doubt. Why come here now to disturb Eleanor's peace?"

"If you must know, I've been looking all over the country," Montague said. "With the help of Lady Marlow…"

"Lavinia?" Eleanor said. "But Papa promised he'd tell nobody! Is there nobody in the world I can trust?"

"You can trust *me*," Mr. Staines said. "I won't ruin you then abandon you."

"I did no such thing!" Montague growled.

"Eleanor may have given herself to you freely, but she knew no better. *You*, on the other hand, knew exactly what you were doing. Then you abandoned her to the ridicule of others, no doubt to carry on with your profligate existence."

"Devil's toes—she *told* you?" Montague asked. "Did you hear how she screamed my name as I showed her what it was to make love?"

Mr. Staines flinched, his cheeks reddening.

"Aha—I see what's afoot, reverend," Montague said. "You want her for yourself."

Eleanor's heart sank as Mr. Staines's blush deepened.

"What I want is immaterial," he said, "but Eleanor came to Sandcombe with a broken heart and her world in turmoil. She's now at peace, and if you have not come here pure of heart, then you should leave, rather than shatter her peace again."

"You love her," Montague said.

Mr. Staines inhaled sharply. "Why would you ask such a question?"

"It wasn't a question."

"What if I *do* love her?" Mr. Staines cried. "At least I didn't take advantage of her for mere gratification. Are you here to break her heart again, because you didn't break it properly the first time?"

"No I'm not, you pompous arse!" Montague said. "I'm here because I cannot live without her!"

"If you can't live without her, why didn't you come in December when you discovered she'd gone?"

"Oh, you really are a numbskull, aren't you, reverend?" Montague replied. "Has a lifetime of pontificating and preaching addled your wits? I didn't know where she was! I tried *everything*—bribery, threats—but her father refused to say where she'd gone. So I've spent the past three months wandering up and down this godforsaken country, trying to find her!"

He wiped his brow and sighed, the anger fading from his expression, and moisture swelled in his eyes.

"Y-you've been looking for me?" Eleanor asked.

He nodded. "Lady Marlow gave me a list of all the places you visited as a child. Brighton, Wells, York… I spent a fortnight in the Lakes because she couldn't recall the name of the village where you'd stayed."

"Braithwaite," Eleanor said quietly.

"Yes, I know that *now*. The innkeeper recalled a Mr. Howard visiting with his family some ten years ago."

"You went to all that trouble—for me?"

He took her hands in his. "I'd go to the end of the world to find you." He gave a wry smile. "I almost did, but I decided to save that trip for last."

"The end of the world?"

"Lady Marlow said you'd accompanied your father to France when you were a child. She assured me you never accompanied him to the Far East, but I'd have sailed there if I had to."

"Why?"

"Do you not know, my Eleanor?" he whispered. "What else is a man in love to do when he cannot bear to be apart from the one woman who can make him whole?"

"But we agreed—"

"Speak no more of that," he said, his voice hoarse. "It pains me to recollect the arrangement I imposed on you. I was a selfish creature, thinking only of myself, and I convinced myself that you'd benefit as much from our arrangement as I. But what I didn't bargain for was how deeply I'd come to love you."

He drew her to him, and she surrendered to the need to feel his arms around her.

"Oh, my Eleanor—my darling," he said, his voice thick with emotion. "I promised to teach you the ways of the world, to elevate your position in Society. But instead, you taught me more than I could ever teach you."

"Me?"

"Yes, my dear one," he said. "You taught me to view the world with different eyes—to appreciate that there are angels who walk among us who should not be fashioned into Society's ideal, but who should be celebrated and valued exactly as they are."

Eleanor heard a footstep, and she glanced to one side to see Mr. Staines retreating, his eyes filled with sorrow.

"Are you leaving, Mr. Staines?"

He nodded, then let out a sigh. "I love you, Eleanor," he said quietly. "I'd hoped that might be enough for the both of us. But..." He hesitated, then shook his head. "I believe there's one who loves you more. And while I want nothing more than to see him turn on his tail and leave you be—what I want is immaterial compared to what would make *you* happy. I cannot compete with him."

"Are you saying that you cannot compete with a duke?" she asked.

"No," he said. "I'm saying that I cannot compete with the

man you love."

"I've never said—"

"You never *had* to say it, Eleanor. Had you said it outright, I'd have doubted your conviction, for we say what we want others to believe. It's only through what we don't say that we convey our true feelings. I've seen the longing in your eyes, and though I wished it was for me, I knew it was for another. For *him*."

Then he turned to Montague. "But let me say this, Whitcombe. You're the luckiest man on this earth to have secured her heart. I pray to the Almighty you'll take the best care of it. If you don't, I'll make a pact with the devil to hunt you down and deliver retribution, even if it condemns my soul for eternity."

Montague's lips twitched into a smile. "Your soul is safe, Mr. Staines, and though we can never be friends, I honor you for your praise and understanding of her."

Then he took Eleanor's hand and lifted it to his mouth. Her body tightened with need at the sensation of his lips against her skin.

"Eleanor, my darling," he whispered. "Would you make me the happiest of men and consent to become my wife?"

She tempered the flare of joy.

"I-I have no wish to be pitied, or wed out of a sense of obligation."

He shook his head. "My love—what will it take for me to convince you that I don't ask out of a sense of obligation? I ask because it is what *I* want. My hand is yours if you wish it. My heart, and my soul, will forever be yours."

"A-and you mean it?"

"I do." He lowered to his knees and placed his head on her stomach. "My beloved Eleanor," he said, "it pains me that you still doubt my intentions. I came here with one purpose—to make you mine. I returned to London to confess my love. I'll admit a spell of selfish joy in hearing that you'd not wed Colonel Reid— but my heart shattered when I heard about the pictures. If only I'd been there to defend you against your sister! I'd have declared to the world that you were the most delectable, beautiful, wonderful creature in the world, and that I had no shame in loving you in every manner possible."

His chest rose and fell in a sigh. "I want nothing more than to sweep you into my arms, take you back to the inn, and make love to you all afternoon. But…" He hesitated and caught his breath. "If you love another, I shan't stand in your way—not out of a wish to surrender, but out of a wish to place your happiness above my own."

"You would let me go?"

He tilted his head until their eyes met. "I want you to be free," he said. "I'll give you the freedom to do what you wish—to paint, to live your life how you see fit, in your own unique way, unbound by the constraints of Society. I can give that to you— and as my duchess, I can spend the rest of my days loving you. If you desire freedom from me, then I'll accept defeat and leave you in peace. But you shall, forever, be my model of what a good soul and a kind heart should be. I will return to Rosecombe knowing that while I cannot have my heart's desire, I can, at least, cherish the memory of having had the privilege of having you in my life, if only for a short while."

His words, and the raw, honest plea in his sapphire eyes, unlocked her heart. She blinked, and a tear splashed onto her cheek. He reached up to wipe it away.

"Shed no tears for me, my love."

"Can I not shed tears of joy?"

Her heart swelled at the raw hope in his eyes.

"Oh, Eleanor!" he cried. "Am I to be the most fortunate of men?"

"I-I wouldn't say fortunate," she said, "but…"

"And now, I must admonish you."

Her stomach curled in apprehension as he rose to his feet. He cupped her face and dipped his head until their mouths almost met.

"I would not have you believe that I am not blessed to have

secured your affections," he said. "The world may not value you, but *I* do. There are many who love you—Lady Marlow was most distraught that you'd gone—but, most of all, you must love yourself for who you are. I would have you see yourself through my eyes. And if you consent to become my wife, I shall spend the rest of my life showing you."

Her heart soared at his words—spoken with such love.

"Then," she whispered, "I consent."

For a moment, he remained still. His eyes widened, at first in disbelief—then the disbelief turned into pure, unbridled joy. He dipped his head and claimed her mouth, sliding his lips against hers in a hungry kiss. A fizz of need threaded through her as she surrendered, parting her lips in invitation. He slipped his tongue inside, a groan of need reverberating throughout his body.

He pulled her close, and she drew in a sharp breath at the wicked pulse of need deep within her center as she felt his hard length against her stomach.

Sweet heaven! Her body ignited with an instinct born of need—the need to have him inside her. He shifted against her, moving his hips, and she caught the faint, but unmistakable, scent in her nostrils.

The scent of pure male desire—that called to her on a visceral level.

"Yes," he whispered, his voice a low growl. "Oh, yes..."

"Ahem."

The voice broke the spell, and she froze, drawing in a deep breath to dissipate the fog of pure animal lust.

Mr. Staines stood at the edge of the garden, his cheeks flaming red.

"While I consider it a privilege to have witnessed the reunion of two people so obviously in love," he said, "I fear I'll have to do much to reconcile myself with the Almighty if I witness any further..."

He made a random gesture toward them, and Eleanor felt her cheeks warming.

"Mr. Staines, f-forgive me—what must you think?"

He grinned. "That the Duke of Whitcombe is one very lucky devil." He approached them and offered his hand to Montague, who stared at it. "Permit me to be the first to congratulate you on what I believe to be your *genuine* engagement. Eleanor—I wish you all the happiness in the world, for none deserve it as much as you."

Montague took the proffered hand. "In that, I agree with you, Staines. I only hope you'll forgive me in taking this glorious creature away."

"Make her happy, and you'll need no forgiveness."

The two men shook hands, and a spike of pain tempered Eleanor's joy on seeing the sorrow in the vicar's eyes. Then he gave her a bright smile, bowed, and made his way toward the gate, pausing to pat the chestnut horse on the nose before he set off along the lane and disappeared.

"Poor man," she whispered.

"I should hate him for being a rival for your affections," Montague said. "But he wished us well."

"He's a good man," she said. "But I didn't love him—and a marriage without love is not to be borne."

"A year ago I'd have disagreed with you," Montague said. "But you taught me what it was like to love—with my heart, as well as my body."

He dipped his head and captured her mouth in another kiss. The flare of need curled in her belly once more, and she drew in a sharp breath. His eyes darkened with desire, and a wicked idea formed in her mind—too wanton to voice. But hadn't Montague taught her that she had the power to secure her happiness?

"Sh-shall we retire inside?" she asked. "Harriet is not due back for some time. We'll have the cottage to ourselves."

"Why, Miss Howard, do you intend to have your wicked way with me?"

Her cheeks warmed, and she lowered her gaze. He caught her chin and tilted her head up.

"No, my love," he said. "You must never hide from me again. I want nothing more than to make love to you all day."

"Montague!"

"Oh yes," he growled. "I've missed hearing my name on your lips. I intend to make up for lost time this afternoon, and hear you cry my name as you come apart at my touch. Oh, Eleanor—you cannot even begin to imagine how much I love you. But, for the remainder of this day, I shall refrain from telling you how much."

"Oh?"

"Instead, my love, I'll show you. Thoroughly, wantonly, and completely."

He took her hand, and she led him into the cottage. Almost as soon as she closed the door, she found herself swept up into his arms.

"Montague, shouldn't we wait until we're married?"

"Woman—do you seek to prolong my torment?"

"N-no—I just thought…"

"A man in love doesn't *think*," he said. "He *does*."

"Then what are you waiting for?"

"Hmmm," he said. "I like this bold, independent Eleanor. Is she as bold in the bedchamber, I wonder?"

In answer, she gave him a saucy smile and flicked her tongue out, running it along her top lip. His eyes flared with raw, primal need, and he gave a low growl—the call of a savage beast, ready to claim his mate.

Then he carried her upstairs, where pleasure awaited.

EPILOGUE

Four months later
London, July 1816

THE WALL WAS filled with paintings—brightly colored landscapes and portraits of distinguished gentlemen bedecked in finery—and in the far corner, near the doorway, a line drawing, with a plain wooden frame.

Monty glanced at the booklet in his hands and read the inscription.

THE

EXHIBITION

OF THE

ROYAL ACADEMY,

M.DCCCXVI.

THE FORTY-EIGHTH

He approached the drawing and smiled. Elegant in its simplicity—yet that very simplicity spoke of the complexity and insight of the artist, who, through a few pencil strokes, was able to capture the essence of the subject.

The likeness was astonishing—it was as if his sister was smiling out from the picture at him. What would she think of being immortalized on the Royal Academy's walls?

Monty flicked through the booklet in his hands, stopped at

one of the pages, and ran his thumb down the list, until he found the item he sought.

Exhibit eighty-four. Young woman reclining by E.M. Howard.

Footsteps approached, and an excited voice called out.

"There he is! I *told* you he'd beat us to it! You couldn't wait to see the picture, could you, brother?"

Olivia rushed toward him, her eyes shining with excitement.

"So you found it," she said. "Doesn't it look lovely? Eleanor, come and see!"

Her companion crossed the floor at a more measured pace, the elegance of her gown not completely concealing the discomfort with which she wore it.

Monty held out his hand, and the discomfort in her eyes disappeared. She took it, and he lifted her hand to his lips.

"Why didn't you sign your real name, Eleanor?" Olivia asked.

"Because my wife didn't want to secure her place in the exhibition merely for being the Duchess of Whitcombe," Monty said. "She wanted to be judged on merit. Unlike my wayward sister, who is only too eager to describe her portrait as 'lovely.'"

Olivia blushed. "I-I didn't mean…"

"Montague, you mustn't tease your sister," Eleanor said. "You know as well as I how lovely she is. She's bound to cause a stir this Season, so you should concentrate your efforts in warding off suitors."

"At least the worst bachelors have left London," Monty said. "Mr. Moss has left England—rumor has it to evade his creditors. And, of course, Dunton is engaged to Lady Arabella Ponsford."

Eleanor stiffened, and Monty silently cursed himself. Her younger sister was still taking her *rest cure* after having endured ruination at Dunton's hands. And while he could never forgive Juliette for the damage her jealousy had caused his wife, she was, nevertheless, Eleanor's sister, and Eleanor still cared for her— wherever she may be.

Monty squeezed her hand. *Sorry,* he mouthed.

She smiled in response, and he captured her mouth in a swift kiss. Desire gleamed in her eyes, and he squeezed his thighs together to temper the flare of need in his groin. They had made love almost every night since their marriage. And several afternoons—his knees were still tender from making love to her that morning on the hearth rug, after he'd devoured her while she lay before him, open and willing, trusting him with every part of her body, as much as she trusted him with her soul each time she looked into his eyes.

She drew in a sharp breath and shifted against him. His mouth watered as he caught sight of two little peaks poking against the fabric of her gown—just begging to be feasted on.

And oh, what a feast it would be!

Then she withdrew, a faint blush on her cheeks. His Eleanor—the woman who gave herself to him with such uninhibited glory each time they made love—now blushed as coyly as a maiden on her first Season.

"Montague!" she chided. "I mustn't act like a wanton in public."

"Quite so," he said, then he lowered his voice to whisper in her ear, "But when we're alone…"

"You're insatiable!"

"Only for you—would you have me any other way?"

Her saucy smile was all the answer he needed.

"And I would not have *you* any other way," he said. "Now—I think we've earned ourselves some ices. It's such a hot day, and we're all in need of a little cooling off. Come, Olivia."

He offered his arm, and his sister took it. His heart soared to see them standing on either side of him—the two women he loved the most, whom, had he succumbed to convention, propriety, and expectation, he would never have associated himself with.

As he strolled out into the sunshine, he lifted his eyes to the heavens and uttered a silent prayer of thanks that he'd defied convention to secure a blissful union with the woman who, a year ago, was the very last woman he would have chosen—the oddity of the *ton*, who, through her unique perspective on the world, made him a happier man than he could ever have hoped to be.

Author's Note

Autism is a neurodivergent condition that affects how an individual views the world. Typically, autism will impact an individual's verbal communication and social skills. Autistic people are often considered deficient in those areas, particularly when engaging in general conversation such as "small talk," and they have a tendency to take things literally and therefore struggle with metaphors. But there are many positive traits common among autistic people, such as a strong sense of fairness, attention to detail, spotting patterns and connections, and the ability to focus on a subject of interest and recall a great deal of specific information about that subject—in Eleanor's case, the subjects she draws and paints, and the artist George Stubbs.

As well as viewing the world differently, autistic people respond to sensory stimuli differently to neurotypical people, and they often struggle to cope with an excess of stimuli. This may be manifested in the inability to hear a conversation when there's background noise, or becoming overwhelmed by lights and noise in a crowded shopping mall—or, in Eleanor's case, a crowded ballroom with an excess of chatter and bright colors. An excess of sensory stimuli can cause distress and anxiety in autistic people, leading to meltdowns or shutdowns. A meltdown may look, from the outside, as a "tantrum"—lashing out as an outward response to a distressing situation. A shutdown, on the other hand, is what Eleanor experiences, where the individual falls quiet and withdraws. A coping mechanism autistic people can adopt is a repetitive motion that can have a calming effect, known as "stimming," which may be as simple as twirling their hair, or a more complicated repeated maneuver. Eleanor uses her bracelet, twirling it in her hands, using the repetitive motion to calm herself.

A number of stereotypes exist around autistic people, but in reality, each autistic person is unique, exhibiting different characteristics, and having differing levels of support needs compared to other autistic people. The saying goes—*if you've met one autistic person, then you've met one autistic person.*

Autism has historically been more often diagnosed in boys. This may be because the condition presents differently in girls and women, but also, women often conceal their autistic traits by mimicking the behavior of those around them in order to "fit in," which is known as masking. As a consequence, many autistic girls go undiagnosed, but may, like Eleanor, be viewed as awkward, painfully shy, or prone to unexplained socially unacceptable behavior.

Eleanor wouldn't have been diagnosed with autism in the Regency era, given that autism wasn't known about until the early twentieth century. However, her unusual behavior would have placed her at risk of being misdiagnosed or even institutionalized. Aware of her difference to the rest of Society, and the risk this poses to her, she tries to blend in by masking.

Autism is one of a number of neurodivergent conditions, including ADHD and dyslexia, and each condition presents different challenges and strengths. For example, while dyslexics are more commonly known for their struggles with written communication, a common strength among dyslexics is verbal communication and the ability to see the big picture when solving problems.

This note represents my own view on neurodiversity, based on my experiences as an autistic author. Personally, I believe neurodivergence is something to be supported, understood, and celebrated, just as Montague, in the end, supports, understands, and celebrates Eleanor just as she is.

About the Author

Emily Royal grew up in Sussex, England, and has devoured romantic novels for as long as she can remember. A mathematician at heart, Emily has worked in financial services for over twenty years. She indulged in her love of writing after she moved to Scotland, where she lives with her husband, teenage daughters, and menagerie of rescue pets—including Twinkle, an attention-seeking boa constrictor.

She has a passion for both reading and writing romance with a weakness for Regency rakes, Highland heroes, and Medieval knights. *Persuasion* is one of her all-time favorite novels, which she reads several times each year, and she is fortunate enough to live within sight of a Medieval palace.

When not writing, Emily enjoys playing the piano, baking, and painting landscapes, particularly of the Highlands. One of her ambitions is to paint, as well as climb, every mountain in Scotland.

Follow Emily Royal
Newsletter Signup: subscribepage.io/RKBvRE
Facebook: facebook.com/eroyalauthor
Bookbub: bookbub.com/authors/emily-royal
Instagram: instagram.com/eroyalauthor
Amazon: amazon.com/stores/Emily-
Royal/author/B07NCBKJZ4
Website: www.emroyal.com
Goodreads:
goodreads.com/author/show/14834886.Emily_Royal
Twitter: @eroyalauthor